BANYAN MOON

THAO THAI

QUERCUS

Published by arrangement with Mariner Books,
an imprint of HarperCollins Publishers LLC.
First published in the United States in 2023 by Mariner Books
First published in Great Britain in 2023 by

QUERCUS

Quercus Editions Ltd
Carmelite House
50 Victoria Embankment
London EC4Y 0DZ

An Hachette UK company

A CIP catalogue record for this book is available
from the British Library

HB ISBN 978 1 52943 197 1
TPB ISBN 978 1 52943 198 8
EBOOK ISBN 978 1 52943 200 8

This book is a work of fiction. Names, characters,
businesses, organizations, places and events are
either the product of the author's imagination
or used fictitiously. Any resemblance to
actual persons, living or dead, events or
locales is entirely coincidental.

10 9 8 7 6 5 4 3 2 1

Typeset by Renata DiBiase

Printed and bound in Great Britain by Clays Ltd, Elcograf S.p.A

BANYAN MOON

To my daughter and my mother,
both of whom bookend every story I hope to tell

Chapter 1

1998

At first, there was no sign of the red tide, except for a tightness in their throats as they picked their way through dune grass that bristled against their legs. Three shades of brown, three sets of stalks, wild as the vegetation prowling along the coast. Ann, seven years old and dying to run down to the surf, reached down to scratch her ankle, but her mother, Hương, pulled her up, in a silent hurry, though there was no appointment to make, no work to rush to that day. A rare day of repose for the Tran women, and one that each measured with her own internal expectation, none of which overlapped. The morning was still, if portentous.

"You're so *slow*, con," Hương said. "Little lost turtle."

It was hard to tell if she was teasing. Hương's voice shouldered an edge, something related to sarcasm, though Ann will never be able to pinpoint exactly what, even years later when she is an adult.

Ann peered up at her mother until she saw the shadow of a smile. Really just a pull of Hương's lips, drawn out like a concession. Ann let herself relax when her mother took her hand, smoothing her thumb over Ann's knuckles.

As the three of them tracked through the shell-pebbled gray sand, their noses began to twitch, an unfamiliar push of sinuses against their skulls. The red tide hit them then. They coughed, then hid their coughs from each other, trying to smile against the thrash of a March wind, a product of the unseasonable cold front this time of year.

Ann's grandmother Minh, Hương's mother, led the way. Her gait was purposeful, but pinched. There was something dry and dangerous about her, like flint meeting flint. She wore wide-legged trousers in eggplant and a button-down shirt that covered her arms entirely, except for a sliver of wrist, shaded exactly like sun-warmed hay. All that morning, she couldn't shake a faint prickle of dissatisfaction, though she could not name its source. It was her way to listen for signs.

"The water looks like a sunset," Ann cried, pointing.

The red tide shook out in front of them like a scarf. Delicately, a fuchsia-mixed-with-orange bloom spread from the edge of the shoreline, into the deep blue of the Gulf of Mexico. The dance of colors was manic, hallucinatory. Each wondered, privately, what it would be like to bathe in the algae-dredged water, to feel the sunset on your limbs, washing through you. No one else was on the shoreline that day.

"Not a good day for the beach," Minh observed.

"I didn't know about the tide," Hương said, a touch of whine in her voice. "How could I have known?"

"It's okay, con," Minh told her daughter. An awkward pat on the shoulder.

Hương threw up her hands. "Should we leave, then?"

Ann scrunched her face, the beginning of her temper showing through. Most of the time, she was obedient, but when she roared, they listened. Her power was quiet and sure, as yet unclaimed but wedged deep nonetheless. It unnerved them all, to see her face darken so, especially Hương, who saw in it a shadow of warning.

Minh laughed, a sound scraped from the pit of her belly. "Okay, my lion cub. We'll stay for a little bit."

Hương laid down their makeshift blanket, an old dirty-blue bedsheet they had found in one of the many linen closets of the Banyan House. She sat sullenly, watching as Minh spread sunscreen on Ann's bony arms, up onto the ridge of her nose and in the shallow dips under her dark, watching eyes. The day had not gone the way Hương intended, starting that morning, when she woke and found Ann in Minh's room, the two of them gasping over one of the ridiculous Vietnamese folktales Minh liked to tell, the ones that made Ann squirm against reality for days afterward, unable to resettle in their life. Those stories were too scary for a young child, but Minh never listened.

"We learn nothing without our legends," she said to Hương.

Hương didn't tell her mother this, but she had wanted to be the one to wake her daughter and reveal the surprise—that the three of them were playing hooky, for the first time ever. Hương had traded shifts at the restaurant with a friend, and Minh had postponed her cleaning clients, feigning illness. Hương had even called the school and told them Ann had a dentist appointment. She didn't know what had possessed her to arrange the drive to the beach.

Perhaps it was seeing that family of three trooping into the Chinese restaurant where she worked a few days earlier. A man in Bermuda shorts, his wife in a sarong that clung tightly to her middle, and a girl around Ann's age, but tow-headed, her hair twisted in salt-crusted locks. They'd smelled of coconut and conviviality. When the father had turned to toss a fried wonton strip into the daughter's mouth, the mother had reached over and snagged it, popping it into her own mouth with a grin. The sight had hurt Hương deeply. Another reminder of the life she could not make for her child.

But the beach was free; the beach was for everyone. Hương wanted a day with her daughter, amid the languishing palms and the baking sand. A storybook day, the kind Ann used to read about in her picture books. She felt Ann was growing apart from her lately, her babyish features lengthening, the shadow of adulthood flickering across her brow. It was happening too fast.

But of course, Minh had decided to join them, and how could Hương say no, after everything her mother had done for them?

Then there was the fuss over the bathing suit. Ann wanted to wear her old orange suit, the neon one-piece with black piping, rubbed raw at the bottom from scraping herself along the concrete steps of the public pool, but Hương had gotten her a new one as a gift, pink and ruffled, fit for a princess. More expensive than she could afford, really. But Ann's brows had lowered when she held the suit. She did not consider herself a pink girl. Minh had finally stepped in, telling Hương that life was too short to fight over bathing suits. That's how it always went at the Banyan House. Minh decided what was worth caring about.

At the beach, Ann coughed, then found a stick. She wrote her name. She drew a bird in the sand. Hương noticed that it was a surprisingly good drawing for a kid—she'd captured the midmotion rise of the wings. Then Ann wrote her mother's and grandmother's names in a row. Their whole family, a chain in the sand. The wind blew over the uneven letters.

"Can I swim?" Ann asked.

Hương's breath caught. The ocean. So beautiful and unpredictable. It reminded her, in some ways, of Ann's father. In her mind, she saw the flash of an ashtray flying through the air. A muslin blanket falling too rapidly to the ground. There was no safety in the ocean, or in love. She wanted to keep her daughter on land. Plus, Ann didn't really swim. None of them did. They only waded in gingerly, hoping that gravity and common sense could keep their feet tucked into the undulating seafloor.

"No, con, the water is poisoned," Minh answered, saving Hương from having to reply.

"How do you know?" Ann asked.

"Just wait. The fish will start to wash up on the shore. Their rot will stink it up. We're lucky we got here before the tide got really bad."

"Ew," Ann squealed, delighted. "Rotting fish here, rotting fish there, rotting fish *everywhere*."

Hương hated to admit that sometimes her daughter annoyed her. There was such energy in her, and Hương was so tired.

They sat to eat bánh mì Minh had packed tight in layers of plastic cling wrap. Headcheese and pâté with sticks of carrot and daikon for the adults, and shredded chicken with sweet soy sauce for Ann. In a cleaned-out old yogurt container were thick slices of mango, dripping sweet and sticky. Ann went to feed her leftover crusts to the gulls, laughing as they tossed their heads to catch the missiles she threw at them.

Somewhere after the sandwiches, Hương's mood shifted, and she began to settle into Ann's reflected glee. She smiled at the sight of Ann prancing in the sand, her gangly body silhouetted by the hazy sun behind her. Something about that joy—unselfconscious and spontaneous—whispered a half-cogent sense of familiarity to Hương. Maybe she had once been that girl too.

"It's a nice day," Minh said, placatingly. "This was a good idea."

Hương was pleased at the compliment from her mother.

Ann tucked herself on the mat, and Hương, flushed with shyness, said, "Tell me about school, Ann."

And to Hương's surprise, Ann released a flurry of words that reminded Hương of a piñata breaking open, scattering the ground with the choicest sweets. It was nice to sit alongside her daughter, hearing her babble about school and friends, the plot of a chapter book about teenagers abandoned on an island. At the Banyan House, there were so many rooms that sometimes she felt she saw little of her daughter. They could too easily escape into their own corners. Time sifted quickly through her day. At night, before Hương knew it, Ann was asleep, and she was alone again, hearing the odd chime of the grandfather clock, staring at the ornate flowers pressed into the wallpaper. Nighttime was when she felt most alone.

Now, watching Ann, Hương was forced to admit she did not quite know her daughter. It wasn't a surprising thought, but it did trouble her. She had made a lot of mistakes in her life. "Mistakes" was an understatement. She couldn't afford to make another one.

"Come here, Ann," she said, beckoning.

She sat Ann in front of her, then splayed her legs open, making a moat around her daughter. With deft hands, she French braided Ann's long, shiny hair, looping it around and around into impossible twists. She didn't have a hair band, so she left the ends loose.

"You are a mermaid," Hương said.

"Again!" Ann demanded. She toed the sand.

So Hương took apart the braid and did it again, and again, pausing every now and then to tuck a strand behind her daughter's ear. Little Ann with the rosebud lips and long lashes, the upturned eyes that were an unexpected light brown, the color of crema on top of espresso. So gorgeous that even as a baby, strangers would gasp over her. They would tell Hương to enter her in baby beauty pageants. "For the exotic factor," they'd smile, as if bestowing a great compliment.

"You have such soft hair," Hương said.

"It's the same color as yours, Mẹ," Ann answered.

Minh, her own hair short and well threaded with iron, looked them over, gently and tenderly. For once, it was as it should have been. Hương and her daughter, wrapped up in each other, and Minh in the background, watching. Doting from a distance, as a grandmother should.

Minh broke the spell by standing and brushing the sand from her lap. "I'm going to go find a bathroom."

After the last braid, Hương let Ann's hair fall over her shoulder. There was a slight flush to Ann's cheeks. She coughed again.

Hương said, "Should we go home? The red tide is getting stronger."

"Five more minutes," Ann pleaded.

Hương sat back on the blanket and closed her eyes, listening to Ann humming a lullaby, something odd and anachronistic, the off-key notes slowly dulling against the pounding of the surf.

> *Let the birds sing, dilly, dilly*
> *And the lambs play*
> *We shall be safe, dilly, dilly*
> *Out of harm's way*

Hương was drifting into the water, at one with the algae bloom, her skin darkening to fuchsia, her hair falling in great big clumps. She was a neon whale, sluggish yet spectacular, the only one of her kind. For once, she felt calm, swept up in inevitability.

Then she opened her eyes. There was no humming. There was no Ann.

She pushed up from the blanket and began to cough hard. It felt like there were two iron rods in her nose, thrust up behind her eyes. Her throat was on fire. She called her daughter's name.

"Ann! *Ann*!"

When her feet hit the sand, she slipped a little, and reached out a hand to catch her fall. Her wrist ached. The gulls were so loud, their cries drowning out hers. She scanned the beach, but there was no one. How far could a little girl go? How long had she been sleeping?

"Come out, Ann. Right now. I will spank you!" she said. She'd never hit Ann before, but thought, wildly, that the mention of violence might pull someone closer. As if it ever could.

She looked to the red-tide-scummed ocean. No, Ann wouldn't. Ann was only ever allowed to wade in to her ankles. Hương took a breath and moved close to the water's surface, looking for a break in the waves. She took her shoes off, ready to dive in.

Once more, with despair this time: "Ann! Please."

"What's wrong now?" Minh asked, emerging onto the sand, though her quick eyes took in everything.

"Ann is lost."

"You lost her?" Minh asked. The rephrasing was not lost on Hương.

"We don't have time for this, Mẹ!"

They resumed calling Ann's name, running down to the water to scan the waves, now dark and opaque. The red tide made their throats hoarse. Hương wished she had never suggested they drive to the beach. They should have stayed in the Banyan House, cloaked in that stifling silence, but safe. At least safe.

When Hương thought her heart might combust, when she felt the hot push of tears at the edges of her eyes, when she wanted to dive into the ocean, sweep its floor with her bare hands to find her daughter, she heard a small giggle in the distance. Minh started toward the sound, but Hương was faster. She sprinted to her daughter and hauled her out from behind a thick fan of dune grass. At first, Ann was grinning, but when she saw her mother's face, her smile dropped. Her eyes widened.

"What the hell is wrong with you?" Hương demanded.

"Hương," Minh said warningly.

"Are you *stupid*, Ann? Scaring me like that?" Hương's voice was deadly and quiet; no longer panicked, but cold, colder than the sea.

Her hand tightened around Ann's arm, like one of those Velcroed bands for taking blood pressure. She didn't realize how hard she was squeezing until Ann cried out.

"That hurts," she said.

"Let go of her," Minh said. She was beside them, extricating Ann. Rubbing her arm, where Hương's grip had left red ladyfinger marks. "Are you okay, con?"

Hương laughed, humorlessly. "Is *she* okay?"

"Enough," Minh said sharply.

Ann was crying outright now against her grandmother's shoulder. Hiccupping her explanation. She'd seen the hiding place in the dune grass, and it had reminded her of a castle, where you could see everything through the gaps between the fronds, but no one could see you. A secret place. She thought she would play a trick on them. She was just about to hop out. *Surprise!* she would say.

"I'm sorry, Bà Ngoại," she sobbed. "I didn't mean to be bad."

"I know, con, I know," Minh whispered, her brusque voice softening in the way it only did for Ann. "You did scare us, though. The world isn't a safe place."

Hương breathed deeply, but the red tide got into her lungs, and she choked, pulling Ann's reproachful attention to her. She started toward her daughter, but when she saw Ann flinch, her hand dropped. She felt like crying, too.

"Let's go home," she said instead, turning away from them so they couldn't see her biting her own hand, trying not to weep in front of them. Motherhood was so lonely sometimes.

In Minh's Oldsmobile, Hương got in the back seat next to her daughter. Maybe she thought their proximity could ease the tension between them. She started to open her mouth to say that she was sorry, that her barbed words only emerged from worry, that she loved Ann more than anything, couldn't she see it?

But Ann moved far away from her, to the opposite side of the car. She pressed her face to the car window. And so Hương turned away, too, sighing into the silence. They stayed that way until the car rumbled up the drive toward the Banyan House, which would once again keep them all safely caged.

Chapter 2

Ann

Dusk has always been my favorite time of day. That in-between space where the warmth of the sun begins to give way to the squeeze of night. Stars scatter on a purple sky, reminding me of spilt sugar on a Formica counter. I think if I can fly to them, swipe one with my fingertip, it would taste cold and sweet on my tongue.

But then Noah says, with the tiniest hint of impatience in his voice, "Coming, Ann?" and I turn from the stars.

Two men in black tuxes open the double doors to the two-story B and B in the woods, with its wraparound porch and white Adirondacks out front. Before I step inside the too-warm ballroom to meet the opulence and expectations of Noah's world, I peer up at the glow of lights through the curtained windows, behind which I can see shapely shadows clad in undeniable luxury. A light breeze wafts past my legs, skin goose-pimpled underneath thin stockings that offer hardly any shelter against the late-winter weather.

"Will they be announcing us?" I whisper to Noah.

"Mr. and Mrs. Fabulous," he quips.

His arm is draped around my waist, but he's not looking down at me. Instead, I see his eyes run over the room, snagging on all the details that are slightly awry—the less-than-resplendent flower arrangements (baby's breath, by God!); the cake we had to substitute at the last minute because the genius baker Alice favored had gone on a breakup-induced bender; a server hurriedly scrubbing cocktail sauce from her starched shirt. Noah frowns.

"Do you think it looks okay?" he asks.

"It's perfect."

"The flowers are kind of droopy, aren't they? I'm pretty sure I said no carnations."

"What's a word that's better than 'perfect'? Your parents will be delighted."

Noah is the youngest of the Winthorpe clan, and he's been tasked with throwing his parents' thirtieth anniversary party. It was supposed to be a surprise, but someone—probably his brother, Mitchell—blabbed the secret at one of their Sunday brunches, so now the expectations are higher than ever. No doubt Alice wishes she had been planning the whole thing all along.

"You are better than perfect," he says to me, glancing down at last.

"Thanks. But I feel . . . off," I admit. I did not want to come tonight, that much is clear to us both, but it would have offended Noah's parents for me to beg off at such a late hour.

"That headache again?"

I nod, though it's not just the headache. Over the past few days, there's been a new alienation of my body, a sense of clumsiness, nausea. I think it's because I've been working too hard, leaning over my sketches deep into the night to meet all the many deadlines that wedge into the tiny boxes of my calendar, like rainbow Lincoln Logs, carefully color coded to announce urgency.

Or perhaps it's this very party, the stress of which has infiltrated our normally calm household. I think about how once, when I was young, another kid had spun me around the merry-go-round so hard and viciously that when I got off, I felt my brain would never settle back into my skull the same way.

Noah asks, "Can you make it for just a little bit? Then I'll call you a cab?"

As I look at his concerned face, with its even planes, sand-colored hair, and deep blue eyes, I try not to be offended that he doesn't offer to go with me. After all, it's his night.

He kisses me, lightly. "You don't look ill, though."

"I'm wearing your favorite dress."

He runs his hand over my hip, across the ocean-blue silk of my one-shouldered gown, modest yet bold. My hair is twisted into a complicated hairdo I saw online, and it doesn't suit me at all. But Noah tells me it's elegant. Usually, my hair drapes to my waist, swishing a trail in our house.

Tonight, I'm feeling detached from myself. There is a low, pressing discomfort in my stomach I can't shake, even with the antacid I popped on the way here. Nerves. Just before I left, I had retched in our toilet, but my stomach is empty. My appetite has fled.

I can't help feeling that there's something a little dreamlike about this night. But it's the kind of dream that feels just left of normal, the sort that discombobulates more than a nightmare.

Stop it, I think. *This is perfect. Noah is perfect.*

Inside, we run into Mitchell first, who gives me an assessing look, measuring me as always against his wife, Tina, who is tall and lovely and dull. She's adjusting the straps of her fire-engine-red gown. It lines up beautifully on her, but she seems uncomfortable in it. The candlelight on the tables around us sparkles, reflecting all the jewels and gold in the room. Someone in the distance laughs, a tinkling Champagne laugh that pulls everyone's eyes to her. It's such a wildly fabulous bunch of people.

"You're gorgeous, honey," Tina says, wrapping her arm around my waist.

"You too," I tell her, feeling my body instinctively draw away from hers.

"How's the drawing going?" Mitchell asks me.

He's fascinated by my illustrating career, having always wanted to be an artist himself, though I often get the impression he's laughing at me for having done something adults are categorically not supposed to do. I haven't a clue what he does for a living.

He continues, "Is it casseroles with faces this time? Dogs wearing snowsuits?"

Editorial assignments aren't always groundbreaking, but they pay well. Currently, I'm working on a spread about a French fragrance house run by a woman in her seventies. It's a late-in-life career pivot for her. I'm supposed to convey dignity and glamour.

At Mitchell's words, there's something stuck between my chest and my throat. A tiny ball of anger.

"I'm considering a new illustration. Maybe a party full of people who are too self-satisfied to relate to anyone outside of their silver-spoon circle?" I answer sweetly, causing Noah to raise his eyebrows in alarm.

"How about that," Mitchell says, his eyes glazed.

"And the girls?" I ask, chastened by his unwillingness to engage. I know it's low of me to trade barbs with him.

Mitchell pulls out his cell phone to show me a video of twins Shiloh and MacKenzie at their last recital, in sequined purple gowns with outrageously big hair bows that peek out from behind their buns like cat ears. They're on a big, spotlighted stage with a dozen other girls, sashaying to "Girls Just Want to Have Fun." At the end of the routine, they jut their hips out, such an adult gesture for such tiny bodies. I don't have to pretend to be delighted. Children are not abundant in my life, but I've always liked the thought of them—anthropologically, as a species with its own customs and rituals. Nothing more ritualistic than six-year-olds cartwheeling across a stage in smudge-proof makeup while their parents wring their hands nervously, calculating all the steps toward international stardom.

I hold the phone to Noah so he can see, but his eyes are elsewhere, scanning the servers to make sure their bow ties are just the right shade of blue, looking to confirm there is no cilantro on the canapés, because Brandon absolutely hates cilantro.

"Sweet kids," Noah says absently.

Mitchell grins. "Always too busy, our man Noah. It's okay. You're excused from perfunctory gushing. Just wait until you have your own—you'll be as boring as the rest of us."

Noah's face freezes into a grin. He reaches for a glass of Champagne. I feel something brushing against my mind at Mitchell's words, like a hot breath, and it's so close I can almost grasp it, but then Noah sweeps me away and I forget again.

We waft through the party, Noah accepting congratulations on his parents' behalf and sycophantic praise from people he grew up with. They are always so impressed by him, so excited to hear about the tenure process. Noah's publishing his first book, one that is already touted as the next exciting thing in the classics, if there is such a thing. I once peeked at the manuscript and couldn't quite understand the revelations that make Noah's breath hitch, his voice rising to match his excitement. These days, he thinks only of Spartan mating customs. I live in fear of him suggesting some kind of Peloponnesian War role-play in bed. But I trust in his greatness. It is one of the truths of our lives, the foundation of a future I can almost taste.

"Dr. Winthorpe," his family friends say, shaking their heads, so pleased. Once in a while, they turn to me, forgetful smiles plastered across their faces.

"Tran, is it?" one woman asks. I've met her half a dozen times.

"Ann," I say. My dress feels tight and I take a sip of my soda water. The bubbles break onto the underside of my nose. "Tran is my last name."

"Of course, dear. I'm getting old."

Alice and Brandon, Noah's parents, soon descend on us like lightning bugs, billion-watt smiles stretched across their faces. Brandon is remarkably good-looking for his age, his face frozen by affluence, timeless in a way that always appears cruel to me for its very unnaturalness. He leans over me, an imitation of a hug, and reaches to muss Noah's hair with the enthusiasm of a man greeting his best hound. He spills just a bit of whiskey on his son.

Brandon says, "All hail the professor. My youngest, and my brainiest—no offense to old Mitch. Noah gets his smarts from his mother. Fortunately for us all."

The room chuckles at him appreciatively, though he's said nothing funny. Noah is trying to hide how pleased his father's words make him. Brandon has always taken pride in his possessions. Once, he took me to his library to show me a mounted rhino head, a souvenir from a trip to Africa for big-game hunting. They'd spent thousands of dollars to have it shipped back in a wooden crate. The rhino was cast in bronze, its eyes black pinpricks in its skull, horn polished and formidable. Standing beneath it, Brandon looked like a conqueror, though I'm almost sure he didn't even do the shooting himself, just pointed out the rhino to a khaki-clad guide who willingly cocked his rifle.

"Dad, come on."

Noah disentangles himself from his father. Alice reaches over to wipe the whiskey off Noah's jacket with a cocktail napkin. For all their lives, she's been their family's center, their glowing little sun. Alice and her men. She has that cherished look about her. Tonight, she's wearing an unusual dress for her: pink chiffon in a swingy pattern, the color of a shell's pearlescent interior, a direct affront to the white-and-blue theme. Of course, her pale, shoulder-length blond hair is perfectly blown out. She wears youth like an accessory, something purchased with good WASP money. Her kiss on my cheek feels light, the quick flutter of a moth's wing.

"Look at them, acting like a bunch of boys," she whispers, threading her arm through mine.

She pulls me closer to the window, where the chill brushes against my bare back. In this position, Noah and his father look like a well-heeled theater troupe, performing gaiety for an open audience. I feel separate from him, and I don't like it.

But seeing that Alice expects me to reply, I say, in a poor imitation of her weary affection, "Noah does love the attention."

She doesn't like that. A small frown mars her face.

"Of course, it *is* a very exciting time for him."

"And for you," I say, trying to smile. "Congratulations on your anniversary, Alice."

"It's hard to believe. Thirty years. Just the other day, he was picking me up for our first date," she says girlishly. Charmingly. There is no shortage of charm in this family.

"To many more years to come," I say, raising my glass.

Her perfume is heavy with English rose (what makes it English versus anything else?), and something underneath, like acetone. Alice always insists on standing too close, using her physicality, limited as it is, as a form of control. I would rather not be touched, especially in such a crush of people, and especially not right now. But she presses her fingers into my arm, their little ridges indenting my skin.

"What a pretty dress, dear," she says. "Young people should wear pastels, or bold, flashy colors. In my day, we just screamed color; couldn't get enough. You're in the *flower* of your youth."

"My grandma calls me an old soul."

"Why's that?"

"Well, I suppose it's being an only child. They say we tend to observe more."

"Ah yes. Well, perhaps that's better. Women just mature so much faster, you know. Noah is still a boy. He needs someone wiser."

Alice seems like she'd want to muss his hair, too, but I can't shake the feeling that she regards me as a dowdy governess of sorts. Someone to facilitate Noah's life, unseemly as I may be.

"Well," she says, turning to me. "How have things been with you, dear?"

"Wonderful. Marvelous. We got a new espresso maker. What about you?"

I can tell it annoys Alice that I don't confide in her. Maybe she's right that I'm aloof, though I don't mean to be. I genuinely *want* to be more conversational, but she and Brandon make me turn inward, an instinct of self-protection. I'm afraid of saying the wrong thing. I didn't grow up around people like them.

Her eyes flick away from me. "Oh, you know how it is. We're going to Vermont in the fall. Is there anything we haven't seen? But I think we'll peep the leaves like the senior citizens we are," she says.

"You're hardly senior, Alice," I tell her.

"Of course we are. Ancient. And someday, we'll be grandparents again. Before long, it'll be a whole brood of Winthorpes!" Her hand on my arm withdraws. "Of course, we can wait for that."

"Oh?"

"You know, I had children when I was thirty, downright elderly in my day! Doesn't that seem like ages ago. I can still remember the way they'd wail all night. I honestly thought I was dying. That's how real the sleep deprivation is. And their tiny violence. I still have a scar on my breast from where Noah *bit* me, the ridiculous child."

"How awful."

My eyes involuntarily flicker to the front of Alice's dress. I imagine a bloodstain in the fabric, blossoming outward.

Alice turns to her husband. "It's just the price of motherhood. That, and the horrific morning sickness. Wouldn't wish that on my worst enemy. You start to feel trapped in your own body."

I watch her turning away from me, and it is then that my mind shuffles to take in her words. The knowing flutters gently inside me at first, a bird brushing against a screen window. And then, it hammers, thumping insistently, begging to be let in. I lose my breath. Vaguely, I feel my hand reaching toward someone, something solid. But there's only air.

"The price," I murmur. Alice gives me an odd look.

"Well, *ooh*-kay. I better see—" She calls, "Brandon, darling, these shoes are just killing me."

"You insisted on them," he says tolerantly.

"Well, we will *have* to cut that cake soon. I wonder if Noah used a different bakery. It's gaudy, isn't it?" she says to me, apologetically. "Let's get this show on the road."

Pulled from a circle of admirers, Brandon protests a little, but not much. Alice flutters her fingers at us. They drift away. The room spins.

Someone pours me a glass of Champagne, which I sip absentmindedly. At some point, there's a toast and everyone cheers wildly, like we're at a soccer game instead of a sedate anniversary party. Everyone is so very glad that all that money, all that time, has landed someplace tidy and safe, in the hands of these gorgeous people who will continue the legacies expected of them, including my own boyfriend, who carries the weight of his parents' trust so ably. The only unexpected thing he's done is fall in love with me.

At dinner, I'm served steak, which I ordered a long time ago, back when the RSVPs were first sent. The meat is red in the middle, juices pooling like Kool-Aid on my plate, darkening the edges of the mashed potatoes. I remember the way I'd dip my fingers into Kool-Aid powder as a kid and paint my lips until they turned a vampy crimson, the sweet grit making its way into my teeth. It took forever to wash off, but I never lost my taste for it, carrying around plastic cans like it was snuff for a tobacco addict. Later, a friend in college told me that Kool-Aid was a trash drink, and even though I hadn't exactly known what that meant, I felt ashamed anyway.

I swallow hard, then press my napkin to my lips. For some reason I think of Noah as a baby, biting his mother's breast.

Noah sees my face, and without a word, he gestures to a server and whispers something into his ear. In a flash, the server takes my plate away and brings back a neutral-looking cod fillet glistening in a butter sauce, with translucent slices of lemon placed on top.

"Thank you," I say, squeezing Noah's hand under the table. "I didn't even know they had fish on the menu."

"You like fish," he says.

"I love fish. It's the only thing I'll ever eat again."

Of course, they do not have fish on the menu, but somehow Noah makes things happen by wanting them hard enough. I should be grateful, I think, that he wants me. His smile is a little sappy, wet. The goodwill has filled him up like a hurricane glass. He's going to spill over soon.

Tina, who's seated on my other side, sees the exchange. "You don't like steak, Ann?"

"Not today," I say, trying for a smile. It falls quickly, so I shovel in a bite of cod.

"And Noah was right there to rescue you. You two are a dream couple," she says, twisting the stem of her wineglass. "Opposites attract."

"Opposites?"

"I just mean. His hair and yours. He's this serious professor with this important job and you're—well, I suppose you're both very successful. Ignore me, dear."

The butter slicks my tongue and I press my lips together so I won't say anything I'll regret.

Tina's sloppy at this point in the night, as she usually is, but also very affable. She says that they have to get home to the babysitter soon, and I get the feeling she's pounding down as much of her wine as she can before reality sets in. There's nothing I dislike about Tina, except perhaps a little viciousness that makes its way into conversation at unexpected moments. A buried rage spiking through. She gestures with her wineglass and a drop spills on her delicate, diamond-clad wrist. She licks it off like a cat.

"Back in the day," she says, "Mitch and I would have partied into the night. But now we have to leave just when things get interesting. And to do what? Pay the babysitter. Learn about whether Shiloh shat in the toilet or not. Here's my secret: I don't *care* if she did or not. We're so very boring."

"I don't think anything more interesting than this"—I gesture to the group, chewing like cows on cud—"will happen tonight."

"Well, probably not." She sighs. "But sometimes I wonder, when will we get our lives back? You just wait until it's you."

I don't know what to say to that, so I look at her until she waves a hand in front of her face, a gesture of dismissal. I'm outside their club of beleaguered parenthood, and she wonders why she's confiding in me about this.

But it's too late—the seed is planted. I can't help imagining what it would be like to open the door to a nursery, step inside to watch a sleeping child. My sleeping child. Oak-colored curls and fists that tuck against his chest. Something sweet and quiet moves through me. But where is Noah in this fantasy? I can't see him, and that thought makes me blink away the image, as if I've somehow betrayed him.

"You know we're just waiting for your engagement announcement," Tina continues. The wineglass seems like an appendage for her, so trusty and present. "Why aren't you engaged, Ann?"

My laugh sounds creaky. "Haven't been asked."

"And why not?" she demands.

I'm desperate to pivot out of this conversation.

"We haven't really talked about it. It's such a busy time for Noah."

"Oh, tell me about it. Mitchell is only half there, even when he *is*. The other day, he put a shoe in the fridge. Can you imagine? What's the point of all this work if your man is going to put a shoe in the fridge at the end of the day!"

"At least it wasn't underwear," I observe.

She gives me a surprised look and then laughs, a loud guffaw that pulls everyone's attention to her. "I would have left him for that. Well, we are just *dying* for Noah to make it official. You two are so beautiful together. It makes a person sick."

"No higher compliment."

"But of course," Tina says knowingly, conspiratorially, "there are his parents to consider. But don't worry about a thing. They're more bark than bite. Trust me, I'd know. Alice is a lioness with her boys."

"His parents? Alice?" I ask. The room tips some more.

She stares at me for a beat or two. Then, quick as anything, her eyes dart to Noah and back to me. Her face is a little ashen and she laughs self-consciously.

"Everyone has them."

"But what—"

I try to press her, but she's already turned around, talking to someone across the table about the latest thriller in their book club. They are speculating on the murder weapon with an eagerness that strikes me as indecent. The conversation puffs and moves away from me. I catch sight of Alice and Brandon across the room, sitting at the head table with their friends, their sly smiles and pleasantly smothering manner.

When I first met them, at a lovely terrace downtown for lunch, Alice and Brandon had asked questions about my degree and my job and my family. Brandon, with a heaving magnanimity, had said that I should order anything I wanted from the menu, even the lobster rolls, and had I ever eaten lobster before? He was generous, I told myself, if a little glutted on braggadocio. Alice asked for recommendations for the best places to eat in Florida, for their winter snowbirding, and when I mentioned some of the oyster shack dives I used to work in as a teenager, she blinked, repeating the words "oyster shack" as if they were in a whole other language.

She said repeatedly, "What a *cute* thing you are, Ann!" I didn't think of "cute" as a diminishment then.

But now, taking a swallow of water, I remember the way Alice's icy eyes often held mine, like she was solving a puzzle that was just beyond her. Brandon's all-too-booming laugh that covered awkward silences, even when no one had made a joke at all. Noah has always insisted that they adore me. Without clear reason to believe otherwise, I had relaxed into his assurance. Some things *could* be as easy as that, I had told myself.

I turn away from Tina, to Noah. I whisper, "Noah, do your parents have something against me?"

He looks quickly at Tina, who has her back to us, then back at me.

His eyes are stormy, in a way I rarely see. "What kind of question is that, Ann?"

"I want to know if they talk about me to you."

"You already know they love you."

"But why can't you answer?"

He folds his napkin in his lap, his hands lean and fingers long, stretched out from years of practicing piano with private teachers on the family Steinway.

In a firm, slow way that makes me crazy, he says, "This is not the time."

I leave the table for the ladies' room. The room pinches and expands, as if reflected in a fun house mirror. Suddenly, I rush to the nearest stall. I retch and retch. It feels like I'm expelling more than Champagne and cod—I'm leaving the remains of the night behind.

More than anything, I want Bà Ngoại. She wouldn't have advice; that isn't her way. But she'd know to sit next to me, holding my hands tight in her gnarled ones until her strength bled into my bones. Until I'm able to face what I know to be ahead.

I rinse my mouth and the last of my lipstick away. My reflection in the bathroom mirror is composed, if a little wan, lips leeched of color.

Some of Noah's old friends barge through the doors in a tangle of silk and microbladed brows. They simper toward me.

"Ann! It's so good to see you," says a redhead with perfect teeth and a silvery dress. She looks familiar. "I've been telling Noah we just don't see him around enough anymore."

I try to smile back. "Join the club. All he can think about is the book."

The redhead says, "It's amazing, isn't it? I don't know a thing about classics, but he makes it fascinating. You'd know more than me, of course."

One of her friends raises an eyebrow at her. "Didn't you two have lunch a few weeks ago?"

She blushes. "Oh yes, we may have."

I can't remember her name, but it discomfits me that she and Noah talk. They are the "we" in her story, and I'm somewhere outside that.

"Alexis," she supplies. She smooths a lock of hair behind her ear. "From St. Andrews. Noah and I went to school together for years."

One of her friends says, "They dated in high school—and into college. The golden couple."

Alexis is quick to add, "But that's all in the past, of course."

"Prehistoric," I say.

"It's good to see you both here. Together. I didn't know if—well, I'm glad to see you."

"Delighted," I agree.

Alexis studies me. She looks like she wants to pat my shoulder or—horrors—hug me. But instead she just nods and leaves with her friends.

Over her shoulder, she says, almost sadly, "You look beautiful, Ann."

This veiled wonderland, where nothing is what it seems and everyone is just atrociously polite. I feel that I will never be able to grasp the undercurrents beneath those pretty words. Not for the first time, I miss my grandmother's frankness; even my mother's curtness, which I understood—or at least felt prepared for. I wonder if living in Noah's world would feel like a constant battle. Me in a loincloth, a spear in my hand. Jabbing at hidden predators until I'm so tired I sink into a mud pit, asking to be left for dead.

When the women leave, I pivot and peer at myself in profile. One hand rests on my stomach; I don't remember putting it there, but the gesture is a natural one. I am certain. My grandmother's courage rises in me, like a sleeping dragon.

When I was six, my uncle Phước gave me a baby doll with tightly wound brown curls and wide hazel eyes that, for all their synthetic long lashes, looked severe and disapproving. I didn't really like dolls—they scared me—and after a day outside, I left this one in the rain. Maybe it wasn't an accident. Cậu Phước said I was ungrateful, that I'd never get another gift from him again. He told me that little girls were supposed to take care of their dolls, and what was wrong with me, I had no womanly impulses. Bà Ngoại laughed about it afterward, tossing the moldy doll right in the trash. She said it was a cheap thing, not worth another thought. But still. Are good mothers born that way? Is the DNA strand an invisible one, winding through the others?

Later, I see Alexis leaning toward Noah by the big French doors, flipping her waves over one shoulder. She looks like starlight in that dress. Soon, Noah's parents join them, and the quartet stands together under the chandelier, each tipping their heads forward to laugh at a joke Brandon has told. Alexis places one hand on Noah's arm, and he's smiling down at her, easily. It's the least distracted I've seen him all night. Alice beams. I'm watching them, and I feel something unfurl inside me, a sense of dread or knowing. It's like I'm watching another family in the making.

"Oh, don't worry about *that*," Tina says. She hiccups faintly from my shoulder, where she has appeared out of nowhere, a drunk sprite about to vanish from the fete. "Alexis and Noah go way back."

"So I hear."

"His parents are just comfortable around her, you know. She's not ambitious or anything, like you, just wants a nice life with a good husband. They thought Noah and Alexis would get married someday. Or if not her, a girl like her."

"A girl like you," I say.

She seems surprised. "Yes, I guess we all kind of grew up together. It's incestuous that way. We talk about all the same little arguments and sagas, over and over again. It's all the same. Comfortable, but not terribly interesting. Which is why we're dying for new blood like yours."

My stomach turns a little, imagining a circle of ball gown– and tux-clad cannibals staring hungrily at my flesh. I'm about to reply when Tina brandishes her phone.

"Whoops, there's the babysitter," she says. "You'd think we were *hours* late instead of just a few minutes, hardly an hour, and everyone

knows that time is just a suggestion with these parties. Teenagers these days get so panicked. Mitchell!" And she's off, carrying her sandaled heels in one hand, kissing Alice on both cheeks.

I sit on a bench outside, counting stars. I think about how I'd sneak out to lie in the grass as a kid, staring at the twinkling sky through the spindles of the banyan tree. I imagine I'm counting the cells of a child's body. How many cells need to combine before it's a real, live person? I understand, vaguely, the science of it. But how much of life is hope? Starlight turned into bones and skin, into eyelids creased in sleep, blue veins etched behind them like branches.

At a hundred, I know Noah's not coming to get me, and I make my way back inside, tucking myself into the crook of his arm.

"There you are." He smiles down at me and I know I'm forgiven.

My own smile ricks into place.

But toward the end of the night, Noah seems distant again. He slides tips into the hands of the head servers, gives a few instructions for cleanup, and leads me out to a waiting SUV. He makes idle conversation with the driver, who brandishes a caddy of water bottles and snacks at us, the consummate car host. Noah's starting to wind down, the light in his eyes fading, but he still makes time to be polite. He compliments the driver on the cleanliness of his car.

"Some party." The driver whistles, staring up at the fairy-light-strung building, the yawning pines and that faint sheen of light pollution that reminds me of illustrations of the Milky Way. "I always wonder what it'd be like to hang with those folks. Is it like *The Great Gatsby*?"

"Hardly. Maybe a paunchy version," Noah jokes.

"Still. I bet it's a time. The top-shelf booze alone."

"You didn't miss much. Fun is not one of the hallmarks of these parties. Or self-awareness," I say suddenly.

The driver laughs, but Noah gives me a leveling look, and I know I've said something wrong. It's okay, apparently, for him to joke, because it's his world, his people. I'm still an outsider, bathed in empty gratitude.

It's only after we change out of our clothes and wash our faces that Noah meets me on our bed. He folds his hands in his lap. I think there's resignation in his pose. I turn toward him, my beloved, the golden boy with the sea-blue eyes. The culmination of my wildest romantic fantasies. The old blood to my new.

"I have something to tell you," he says finally.

And then, when it all comes out—Alexis, the afternoons spent at hotels together, the pressures of his world, so gleaming bright and wondrous and full of treachery I never fully grasped—I can't help it. I throw up at his feet, right on top of his favorite black wingtips. For a second, the sight of my vomit on his shoes gives me a feeling akin to triumph. At last, I've managed to shock one of the mighty Winthorpes into silence.

Chapter 3

Minh

The stereotype is true: hospital coffee tastes like shit. It's as if some cruel bureaucrat decided that the dying need to be reminded why life on earth isn't all *that* great. I think of my favorite medical soaps, with their bustling, capable staff, but there's no resemblance between those well-lit studio halls and these dingy ones. It's not a bad hospital, and I don't begrudge anyone doing their job, but what I can't forgive is the lack of George Clooney.

I find myself longing for the taste of *good* coffee, the terrifically strong kind that hollows out your throat—even though for most of my life, I drank jasmine tea. In Việt Nam, I bought leaves from the boy who came to the door, though I knew he charged too much. But I liked him and the company, especially after Xuân died, so I continued to buy bags of leaves that molded in monsoon season. I'd throw them in the river, where they floated like puffer fish.

"Where's your family?" I asked the boy once.

He leaned on one foot, then the other, eager to continue his route. "Don't have any, Bác. They are gone, long gone."

"Ah, dead," I repeated. "I'm sorry, cháu. It's a sad thing to lose family."

He gave me a surprised look. "Not dead. They just left. Sometimes people do that."

I think of that boy now, the purposeful way he'd push his cart of random goods through the stray animals yapping by the side of the road, the rivulets of mud running down the center of the village. That wide, cocky smile. I was charmed by him, as I always was by audacious boys. When he'd left, I'd take my tea inside and work on my books, running through long columns of figures until they all made sense to me. I was a terrible student, but when it came time for me to learn how to run a business, after opening the jewelry shop, I did my best. Xuân would lean over my shoulder, pointing out my mistakes with such a sweet, hopeful air that I could forgive him for seeing my stupidity.

"You're not stupid, em," he'd say, his breath tender on my cheek. "It just takes you a while to learn. But once you get it. Watch out."

Later, I found out the boy was taken during the war amid a skirmish in the paddies, another young soldier riddled with bullet wounds. A tragedy. I wondered if his mother, somewhere far away, felt that loss.

When I began to drink coffee, much later, after we'd moved to the States and were firmly enmeshed in the Banyan House, the taste tugged at me like a memory: the fullness of it. Dirt and sweetness, a potion that sang into my veins. I couldn't get enough.

My daughter, Hương, tells me, in that shrill voice she uses when she forgets her place, that caffeine isn't good for someone my age. "Your heart, Mẹ!" She says it's because she wants me to live longer, but I've lived long enough to know that you hold on to your joys, small as they are. You wring them out like laundry, until all that's left is the residue, scenting the very last bits of your memory.

Hương is more impatient with me than usual lately, and it makes me snappish toward her, too. We're like two old tortoises, nudging our heads out of our shells for the sake of quarreling alone.

If Hương's father were alive, he would have understood how to placate her worries. They only make me feel itchy, like a coat I would rather not be forced to wear.

I wish Ann were here to drink a cup with me, though now she tells me she drinks espresso, drawing out the sinuous consonants. Even when she was a child, she snuck sips from her mother's glass, winking at me when she did. Mouth open when she realized how hot it was, pantomiming a fan with her hands. After she went to college, in the rare times she visited, we drank coffee outside under the banyan tree, sitting in silence before the full weight of the day's heat descended. We swatted mosquitoes off each other, laughing when we caught a bloody carcass in our palms.

"Bà Ngoại, this is the happiest place in the world," she'd say, in the days before she decided otherwise. "This house. With you."

The Banyan House could be ghastly at times, grime-speckled and overcrowded with other people's furniture, but I agreed with her. Love can cast a light like no other. Afternoon heat shimmered in her hair, making it wave like a crow's wing. She'd always seemed more miracle than human to me. I think of her hair now, the way it fell through my fingers as I braided it in the morning before school, how it spread on her pillow at night, a midnight fan.

That is, like so many things, a sense fast slipping from my fingers.

"Are you comfortable?" a nurse asks, ducking her head in my room, her brow furrowed in sympathy.

I want to tell her to save her sympathy for people who haven't lived. I'm not a pleasant woman to be around these days, but I just want to be left alone, and no one seems to be able to do that. In Việt Nam, I would have been relegated to some attic, waiting it out while my children spooned bone soup into my mouth. The old way. Now I'm in a place that smells like cotton balls, where women flutter around me like moths, trying to prolong the inevitable.

Death is sterile here, as clean as new laundry.

"Comfortable enough for a dying old woman," I rasp.

"You're not dying, Minh." The way she says my name sounds like the trill of a dove.

"Shows how much you know."

The nurse's downturned smile, that familiar mimic of grief, falters as she shuts the door with a decisive click. They like their dying meek, something I haven't been in decades.

They don't know exactly what I'm dying of, or they won't tell me. I fainted the other day on the way to the bathroom. I remember reaching for the counter as I fell, the cool lip of the porcelain sink bracing on my fingertips but, in the end, not enough for me to hold on to. Hương found me that day, erupted into hysterics, then hauled me here to this sanitized hell. I've broken a hip, it seems, and it hurts like a motherfucker. The slow drip of morphine helps, though the visions come faster with the drugs. They say I must be careful—my heart, my lungs, my very soul is teetering on a precipice.

"You've got to fight to get better," Hương says. She has that wild, determined look in her eye.

I love her and I'm impatient with her. It doesn't pain me to say that now. "I'll do no such thing. Go get me another pillow, con."

She scurries off, this daughter of mine, her hair bouncing as she moves, so quick and capable. Serving at others' pleasure. I have wanted so many things for her, but I'm no witch. She has to claim them for herself. Perhaps Ann is the only one of us to seize her own fate, to lead with will, rather than by another man's promise.

Once, when Ann was five or six, after watching a movie about an abducted princess who finds her prince in disguise, she wondered, "Why doesn't she just move into the castle by herself? Then she can dance with the teacups all day long."

"Maybe she wants to have company," I suggested. "Castles get lonely."

"Well, she doesn't need *him* for that," she said with a huff. So used to the company of women, in a kingdom without princes, that she never thought to question her absolute insularity. When had that changed for her? For any of us?

In the corner of the room, I see the outline of a faintly stooped man. Then it shimmers, and I think he's translucent. A shadow-being.

A trick of the light. Even in my drugged state, I know the vision is not real. But still, I wonder. Is he my father? My dead husband?

"Don't rush me," I say into the corner of the room.

The shadow glimmers.

"I'm not ready," I say.

The shadow moves a little closer and I think it sighs, perhaps in impatience, or perhaps in sadness. An old woman, clinging to the last of her life, even as all signs point to an ending. Even the spirits are bored of this story.

I'm so very tired. But for me, tired does not, will never, mean defeated.

"One more year," I bargain with the shadow. "I'll get things in order. Make sure my children will be okay. You know what that's like, right? To exist for others?"

The shadow stretches out, like a grin on a child's face, and then pops into a gust of air. Particles float in the sunlight. That feels like an agreement to me.

"Just a little more time," I say aloud, alone now. "A little more living."

I stir sugar into my coffee with a spoon, scratching the edges of the Styrofoam as I do, blooming the dark liquid into something more palatable. There are unbearable things about dying, but sometimes, the things that pull out the most longing are the quiet rituals you never thought you'd miss.

Chapter 4

Hương

I go to the beach to escape my mother. There, in the first glimmers of dawn, I'm myself again. It's Valentine's Day, which means the beach will be particularly bare, though it often is this time of year. February is chilly for us Floridians. The waves swell like cresting blue hills, though on the Gulf, hardly anyone finds them impressive enough for surfing. It's not good swimming weather, either. The snowbirds may power walk in their cardigans, the sprightlier among them jogging with huffing terriers, but they like to sleep in, congratulating themselves on the cushy life they've earned. It's just me and the water.

Except it's not. Out there, I see a speck making its way outward, then back in toward the sand. A swimmer. From this distance, he looks like a struggling mantis. I stand, ready to call for help, even though there's no one at all, but the mantis looks like he knows what he's doing after all. I sit back down, drawing the hood of my sweater over my head. The sky casts a pink wash on the sand, and beyond, there's a strip of omelet yellow near the horizon.

A stray breeze makes me think of Ann in Michigan, where she walks along the sparkling snow, her boots crunching against the ground. I've never seen snow before. Have never left Florida, though sometimes when I'm particularly low, I imagine hopping on a plane to surprise Ann. I'd bring her a jar of seashells, an offering from sea to lake. But then, in my fantasy, Ann shuts the door on me, refusing to let me into her home. This ending, I know.

I watch the swimmer for half an hour, wondering when his energy will deflate. Then, just as I stand, he emerges from the sea and shakes the water from his wet suit, like a dog after a run in the sprinklers. His shaggy hair is threaded with gray, but his body is lean and—from what I can tell—toned. He raises a hand at me.

"Thought I was alone," he calls.

"Sorry to disappoint," I answer. *I wanted to be alone, too,* I nearly say.

"Come on in next time. The water's not so bad once you get used to it," he says, with a friendliness that assures me he's not from around here. He likely comes from one of those safe Midwest neighborhoods where people bring each other muffins and water their neighbors' plants when they're vacationing.

"Can't swim," I say, surprising myself with the confession.

Mẹ never made it a priority for us to learn as children, and once I grew older, there was Ann and a million other things to think about. And, of course, my own terror at the thought of open water. Ann learned to swim, though I don't know how she did it. Another thing I forgot to teach her.

The man makes like he wants to come over to talk. He says, "No time to learn like the present."

I give him a half smile and, before he can come closer, turn on my heel and walk back to my car.

Then I drive the twenty minutes from the ocean back into the heart of the swamp, to the Banyan House where Mẹ lives. When I let myself in, I hear nothing. She's asleep, as she usually is these days. I go to the altar in the kitchen, changing out the wrinkled black grapes for new ones that I wash and place carefully next to the photo of Ba, long gone but always present in our memories. I tap off the burnt old incense and light three new sticks.

These days, when I'm around Mẹ so much, I think about Ba and the four of us back in Việt Nam. Phước doesn't remember anything about him, but I do. I remember his tobacco-stained fingers, the way he'd bound into the house, eyes searching for Mẹ before any of us. "Where's my flower?" he'd ask. He loved her more than a person should love another. There was something reckless about it.

In the mornings before school, he would tuck me into the front of his bike and take me to school that way, pinning his arms on either side so I wouldn't slip. When we hit a bump or had to swerve out of the way of a speeding moped, he'd whispered in my ear, "Don't worry, littlest. Ba's got you." They said as a baby, nothing could calm me the way his voice could. I don't remember enough. But I remember being held by my father.

Sometimes, in the trailer we lived in after moving to Florida, I would pretend he was still alive. I'd peer at the silver door so hard I could almost see it slide open, Ba's gait jaunty as he bounded inside. He'd swoop me into his arms and bury his nose in my hair. The only thing that revealed it as a dream was that he was so very young in it. Still in his midtwenties, the age when he died, frozen in terrible youth.

He was the first, and likely last, person who made me feel safe.

Now when I watch Mẹ shuttering herself from life, locking windows and doors like she's going on a long trip, I think that it would be helpful to have a father. He could tell her to rest, leading her to the sofa with his strong arms. It wouldn't just be us knocking around this big house, a puzzling pantomime of the past.

Of course, I could call my brother, Phước, but he is just so magnanimous about everything that it would irritate me more than help. And he would bring his brood, Diane and the girls, and they would start sniffing around the house, those sharp eyes accounting for every little thing that will one day be theirs.

So, alone, I tend to Mẹ. After I refresh the altar, I make her a bowl of porridge, lacing it with pork floss the way she likes. In her room, she's sitting up, looking out the window with a querulous expression.

"What's wrong?" I ask, setting the tray up in front of her. I think, *How could the world have pissed you off already?*

"Why does anything have to be wrong? I don't need this," she says, trying to push the tray away. "I'm not an invalid."

But of course, she is, and she's the only one who doesn't see it. She keeps saying that she still has time. Muttering something about a shadow man. That it's all fine because they made a deal.

Today, I can see something different in her eyes. A new kind of resignation.

"Have you heard from Ann?" I ask.

She's silent at first, then says, "You are her mother. You could call her."

She struggles with the porridge, even though I've given her such a small portion. She eats so little lately that I find myself tracking her food like I would a baby's feeding schedule.

"Here, let me," I say.

I try to help her spoon the porridge into her mouth, but she gives me such a fearsome look that I hand her the spoon and slink away.

Sometimes I wonder about the utility of caring for someone who seems so determined to leave you behind. But I know that's not the whole truth. The one who's truly gone is Ann. The last time I heard her voice, she called me wondering how to make thịt kho for dinner. I told her what cut of pork to get—you always mix the pork belly with some loin, to cut the fat—and how to make the caramel sauce.

"The sauce is going to get hot and very dark. It's going to take a lot of watching," I said.

"But how *long*?" she asked, frustrated.

"Five minutes? Ten? It depends."

"Mom. I'm trying to make a special meal for Noah. I can't mess this up."

I don't tell her that that boy Noah will not like thịt kho, that it's wasted effort on her part. Finally, I sent her a copy of a Vietnamese cookbook. Let her rage at something other than me for a change. She thinks I don't understand her.

On my own bookshelf, I keep an album of clippings I've never shared with anyone. I go to Ann's blog every Sunday and print out her newest illustration on the color printer I got for this purpose. I clip it carefully, then paste it into the book. I use my neatest hand-writing to record the date and publication. Sometimes there isn't a new illustration, and I feel an emptiness, as if I haven't been fed one of my regular meals. I leave anonymous comments under username GreatArtIsHard2Find. It's my pet deception.

Love this one! The colors are very serene, I write.

Thank you J, she writes back.

Thank YOU for sharing your art with the world! I say.

In this way, I'm her biggest fan—at least in this weird virtual world where we don't have to account for any of the past.

As I make my way through the Banyan House, I find it's even more of a mess than usual. I stumble past the piles of appliances, all still new in the box, waiting for the day Ann gets married. I want to tell Mẹ that Ann won't have any use for these odds and ends from department store sales. She'll have the best of the best; Noah's folks will ensure that. But I can't bear to shake my mother's hope that she will be the one to pro-vide for Ann. She feels guilty that there was no money when I married Vinh, that I had to start so low. Sometimes Mẹ focuses on all the wrong things.

I can't resist the urge to scrub the counters. They're just so grimy, with a scrollwork of rust-colored stains, flecked with coffee grounds and bits of dried-up scallion. After I finish, I find Mẹ, who has moved to the couch with a soap opera, an afghan spread across her lap. My once active mother sitting still in front of the television; I never thought I'd see it.

"Don't you get tired of this crap?" I ask her.

"So judgmental," she says. "Cháo was good, con. Perfect texture."

I'm surprised by the compliment, but I don't let on.

"You are a good daughter, Hương. You've been here for me. When I die," Mẹ says, "I want you to have the house."

"Mẹ," I begin, "you aren't going anywhere."

She sighs. "The shadows haven't accepted my bargain after all."

I feel my forehead crinkling. Her odd asides, that languid air. She's slipping, sure as anything, and it feels like the hardest work of my life to pull her back to us.

"Stop talking like that." My voice is sharper than I intend. "You will still rule over this old house. Ann will come home someday soon and we'll all have dinner together, like usual."

"Now, listen. It's in bad shape, I know, but there's nothing I can do about it now. It's like a naughty child, one you can't get to behave. You just have to accept its faults. You will love it for what it is, right?"

"This conversation is not lucky."

"Luck." She laughs. "I was lucky once. When I had you, and your father, and your brother. The four of us. It was the very worst of times. Wartime, when everything was scary and hard. But then I'd come home and you'd be in our room, huddled up together in one bed like twin dolls. And I saw what it could be, afterwards. We never got to the after part."

Phước would sleep with his back to me, and in the winter, I would reach out to him, to make sure he wasn't too cold. Even in his sleep, he shook me off. My angry little brother. Across the room, Mẹ and Ba slept deep, their snores slow and rumbling. We'd hear motorbikes on the street, the distant laughter from the bar, sometimes even the popping of gunshots, but when we were together, we felt safe. I barely remember this time, but I know she's right. That we were lucky, despite it all.

"Anyway, I don't want the house," I say. "I've got my condo."

She seems surprised. "Of course you do. Look at them there, in the show, fighting over this or that. They think that their rivalries are worth all that. But in the end, Hương, it's family. Family and home, two sides of one coin. You understand?"

I don't ask how long it's been since she's seen Phước, her own son. He appears when he needs something, money or validation or some home cooking to remind him that he's Vietnamese. But I know what

Mẹ means. I have her, and she has me, and in the distance, we have our Ann, the girl we share.

She looks at me intently. "Hương, there are things I never told you."

"That doesn't surprise me."

"I think perhaps you're ready."

"Hold on, Mẹ."

I take her dish to the sink and scrub and scrub. I should be opening my arms to her confessions, but I can't. It signals defeat. In my mind, I tell myself there is plenty of time to rifle through her old secrets. We'll go through them together when she's well.

When I get back to the living room, the soap opera is over and Mẹ is dozing again, one thin arm slung over her eyes like a sleep mask. I turn off the TV. Her eyes flutter open as she sees me at the door.

"Going so soon?" she asks, a light smile on her face.

"I'll be back before you know it," I tell her.

The sunshine is warm on the knob as I shut the door with a neat click. Sometimes, when it's quiet like this and the light filters through the trees in planked yellow streaks on the grass, I think I could like it here back at the Banyan House. I could like it very much, if it didn't hold the weight of so many years, so much cruelty. I feel the house sigh behind me, as if in agreement. Glad to see me leave. I drive away, thankful that it's not my burden.

Chapter 5

Ann

"Ann, I made a mistake," Noah says, his voice tremulous and uncertain. This scares me more than anything else, how he flounders in this new weakness.

He's stepped out of his shoes and stands next to me, a hand outstretched, as if he wants to shake mine. As if he's saying, "Agree to put this behind us." The thought is so absurd I want to laugh. I ignore his hand and it falls limply against his side.

He tells his sordid story about meeting Alexis—I won't forget her name again—one night after a late seminar on Homer where the kids were just so sleepy and deadlocked and *depressing* that he needed company, a friend, someone to bring humor back to the world. She'd texted him, fortuitously for them (though not for me), exactly when he was debating whether to go home or shuck himself over to Mitchell's for a beer. They met for a drink that turned into four at the local dive bar, aptly named the Library, where books were hollowed out and filled with random mementos from patrons, like ticket stubs and love notes that never found their recipients, and Ziplocs of leftover weed from a generous pot fairy. Alexis and Noah played pool among his students, Lady Gaga and Sister Hazel blaring in the background. Then there was a stray kiss by the jukebox. A stray something in her apartment.

"Just a few times," he is careful to say, over and over again, like an incantation that can make me forget the image of sweaty limbs, the memory of his quiet and capable lies.

He says they were drunk that first night, the tired excuse for so many sins, and I can see it all playing out, his gallantry turned seduction, the trope that would make me yawn if it wasn't happening to me. I picture those red curls spread across his chest, then the way she smiled at me in the bathroom at the party. Sadly, but knowingly. Noah's betrayal is one of imagination, or lack thereof.

He goes to put his shoes in the bathtub. He cleans up the mess and hands me a wet towel. I blink down at him, now kneeling next to where I sit on the bed, like a supplicant in front of a priest, waiting for absolution. Though I've just vomited, my mouth feels dry. I wish I could fill it with crushed ice.

"You are perfect," he says miserably. "It wasn't you. Couldn't be. It goes without saying that I love you. Adore you."

"Feels like it." He shoots me another surprised look. I'm never sarcastic, never impolite.

But it's not just *me* anymore. There's an us that does not include Noah—me and the Fetus. Whatever docility I had cultivated is gone. In its place, something wild, unquenchable.

I want to throw things at him and wail, waking our neighbors, shuddering the windows with my fury. Once, I saw my mother throw her fist through a window in a rage. It shattered so neatly, the delicate glass spilling like rain onto the floor of the Banyan House, the blood glowing into being like Elvish script on her knuckles. She seemed surprised at first, but then she wiped her hand on her pants and swept up the glass, like nothing had happened. Like destruction was another matter of course. Something we step past and through.

Horrifically, he continues: "The stress, Ann. Sometimes there are so many expectations on me. You have no idea. I feel like everything in my life is so perfectly balanced and if I drop one thing, just one, it'll come crashing down, it'll bury me, and us, and there will be no future.

Alexis was something outside of that. Just light and familiar and safe, you know? And she has known me for so long. My parents, too."

"Well, might as well let them fuck her, too," I say. He flinches.

I notice a tiny streak of gray growing in his hair, and I think resentfully about how beautifully he'll age. Chiseled granite and wildly eligible, well into the years when everyone will have ceased to see me or women my age as sexual objects. The injustice.

I take a shuddering breath. "And you don't want us to be together, because of . . . Alexis?"

"No, God, no. It's not her. I'd stop talking to her tomorrow if it would help anything between us. And it's not my parents, or any one thing, really. It's just that everything is messy, Ann, incredibly messy right now. Do you ever feel like you can't breathe?"

"I do now," I say.

I study the slow swoop of the ceiling fan, the way it begins to cast shadows on the wall, feeling oddly removed from it all, impatient for the scene to be over. Noah is weeping openly. He is a papier-mâché man, filled with an airy space where treasures should be hidden.

I tell him, "I'm not going to do this with you, Noah. I'm taking a break. We are."

"I don't want that," he says.

"You are not the only one who gets to want things."

"Please, Ann. Can we talk?"

"Later, Noah. I'm done with you tonight."

His face crumples at my dismissal, but I'm just so tired. I want to sleep and sleep. Noah goes to the couch with a hangdog expression. His contrition would be funny if it weren't so enraging. I think, somewhere inside, that the rage feels good. The cracking of my poise at last. After all the pieces of myself I've squashed—the uncomfortable dinners, the parties I hosted for his friends, the way I forgave his late nights and absentmindedness—have led me to nothing but more anguish. What's left of me, after he has taken it all?

I dream about fire spreading in a valley. The flames are shaped like a phoenix, skirting from tree to tree, so agile and beautiful. Red-hot sometimes, then blue at others. I burn with it, and feel only satisfaction, like something has been checked off the list.

Once, Bà Ngoại accidentally set fire to our kitchen. She had been cooking with chicken fat, and it dripped off the side of the pan. When the flame below the burner hit the dripping, it all erupted wildly, so beautifully. We stared for a moment before Mom came in and threw a dishcloth on it, then a kettle of water for good measure. We were drenched and mute.

"What the hell is wrong with you two?" she'd asked.

Then Bà Ngoại and I fell into hysterics, which only pissed Mom off. It was just a baby fire, and it was so lovely. There was no danger. Mom gave us a disgusted look and walked out of the room. She barely spoke to us that day, only to say that she was "sick of being the only sane one in this goddamn house."

We didn't have chicken for dinner. As a treat, Bà Ngoại ordered pizza, and the delivery boy grumbled at us for taking him all the way to the outskirts of the town. He said he didn't even know they delivered that far. Bà Ngoại gave him an outrageous tip and we ate the pizza in the den, paper towels on our laps to catch the grease.

In the morning, Noah is gone, though he leaves a latte on the counter for me. He has the grace to forgo the usual love note. Later, at the store around the corner, an older man with watery eyes rings up the pregnancy test. He doesn't blink, but when I exit, he calls, "Good luck!"

There are two lines. I don't need to see them; my body knows. Has known for a while now, through the exhaustion and the vertigo, the sensation of being pulled apart like taffy, to make room for another.

In the mirror by the bed, I look at myself, tracing a smooth line from under my breasts down to the apex of my thighs.

"There you are," I whisper. And what I feel is not love at first sight, that flip of the organs, but something like misplaced recognition. Like catching a glimpse of yourself in a department store window.

I call Bà Ngoại. My chief pugilist in the wings would have words about Noah and Alexis. I haven't told her much about Alice or Brandon or the discomfort I've begun to feel in this ill-fitting cashmere life, but she would know anyway. Her voice is the one I crave.

She doesn't answer. Her phone is frequently in her purse, or on mute, and she doesn't really see the necessity of it.

She may have asked, "What did you get yourself into now?" Always thinking that I'm a toddler who needs to be chastised.

And I do feel very small right about now. I can't shake the thought of red hair on linen shirts. But then that image is replaced by another one. Me, with a baby resting on my chest, swinging on a hammock on a sweaty afternoon. We sway like the branches of a sapling.

I whisper down, "I am yours now. We're in it together."

Chapter 6

Hương

My mother leaves the world in the middle of the night, when I'm in my own bed, sweating through another nightmare. They've been coming fast and hot lately, shadowy images that I usually forget when I wake. In some, I see Ann's father's face, that devilish handsomeness, the way he could lean forward and summon every part of me to attention. In others, I see my father. The men who have left us behind.

But when I wake, it's Duke, my boss, and lover (I truly hate that word, but no more than I hate the word "boyfriend"), snoring next to me. He never spends the night, but his wife and daughters are away at a dance competition in Phoenix. They stay whole weeks in hotel convention centers, the girls' makeup dripping as they try their hand at another gold medal. The clouds of tulle, the shiny tights, cold chicken wraps in cellophane bundles. I don't like having Duke in my bed as much as I thought I would. He takes up too much space.

"They'll make the world championship, for sure," he said once, as if I can even remember his kids' names. Duke seems proud when he talks about them. He likely wonders why I don't speak about Ann, but she's too sacred to entangle in Duke, a part of my life that is starting to feel increasingly tawdry. His boxers are in a pool on the floor.

The phone wakes us both, but he goes back to sleep, turning with a grunt. The days are long for him. When I raise it to my ear, I know.

The nurse is brief. "I'm sorry, Ms. Tran. Your mother is gone."

Alone, in her bed. Discovered by the night nurse I finally convinced her to hire.

I palm my phone, drop it onto the table without responding. The clatter makes Duke grumble. Inside, a hurricane begins to gather in my heart. I feel the sweep of reality, rustling around me like leaves in flight. There's nothing I can hold on to now.

The tears are raking down my cheeks. I try not to wake Duke. This isn't a time for anyone but us, me and my mother. And my daughter, whom I haven't seen in years.

I see my mother in the hospital bed after the fall, only a month ago, looking smaller than she ever had, hair spread thinly on her pillow, like clouds that couldn't quite clump together. She was pathetic. I prefer to imagine her as she was in my youth, rod-straight and full of that hard old determination. I remember how a boy once tripped me on the way to school in Việt Nam. When I told her, she chased him with a bamboo cane, her mouth determined, until she caught him. You could do things like that back then and no one would bat an eyelash, probably not even his parents, who knew he had it coming. He limped at school the next day and didn't dare look my way again. My mother, the force.

Extinguished.

I slip from the bed and put on my shoes. An owl hoots in the night, and to me, it is mournful, a dirge pulled from nature.

What comes to me now is also her gentleness, the rare cube of her affection, slipped to us when we least expected. She was always most tender when Phước and I were sick. Her cháo—the one dish she mastered—was the stuff of legend. Simmered in chicken broth, scented lightly with ginger, and dotted all over with pulled chicken and scallions. At night when I couldn't sleep from fever, she would wring out a washcloth in a bowl of ice water and press it to my forehead. I never told her the cold cloth didn't feel as good as her hands on me.

"There, con," she'd say. "Mẹ will make it better."

I think of how much the word "Mẹ" resembles "me" when written out. Two different languages, that same connectedness, stretching across the miles.

I go outside to where the racoons gather, their yellow eyes glowing under the sliver of moon. There, I call my daughter, her number memorized despite disuse. When she answers, she sounds tired.

"Mom." Her voice is flat. "What is it?"

"Ann, baby. Your grandmother."

"What?" Irritation floods her voice.

"She's gone," I try to say gently, but gentleness doesn't come easily to me anymore. I think maybe I've been too abrupt, but there's no way to couch this news. It will ravage her. "She died in her sleep."

"No," Ann says. I almost *hear* her shaking her head at me. "She's not even sick."

"She was. I'm so sorry. She's gone."

I let the silence stand, let the truth sink in, but then I hear my daughter's giant heaving cries. My heart feels as if it's getting grated, pink flesh littering the ground. Is there any pain larger than the echo of your child's heartbreak?

"No," Ann says again, her voice rattling against her tears. "You're lying."

"I'm not, con."

"She never said anything about being sick."

"She didn't want to worry you. She was convinced she'd get better."

"Bà Ngoại," she says.

Her cry is a howl, and I want to gather her up, but she's so far away. Maybe I can howl, too, and our cries will fill the sky, even so many miles apart. I wonder if it's cold where she is, if she's warm enough, if Noah can keep her safe.

"I'm sorry, Ann," I say. "I know you loved her."

"You'll never know how much," she hisses.

And her voice, laced with pain and anger and something jittery underneath, is like a whip against my face. Her grief, on top of my own, is too much. I consider hanging up the phone, running from the threat of our pain, multiplied when we are together.

Instead, I say, in a voice too faint for even my own ears, "You are not the only one who loved her."

Then, the last words I expect, muffled but unhesitating: "I'm coming home."

Chapter 7

Ann

I don't know how long I'll be gone. I don't know anything, except that Bà Ngoại is dead and no one thought to tell me she was sick. I hung up with Mom as soon as I could last night, unable to think of anything outside the dreadful numbness in my limbs. I've never gone to her for comfort. I wouldn't start now.

Noah skates around in concern, sneaking granola bars into my bag, trying to book me a hotel, even though I tell him I'll just stay at the Banyan House. He pulls me into random hugs that last longer than usual and says I shouldn't be alone. He offers to go with me. I can tell that in his mind, the breakup was just an overreaction, something we can pretend never happened.

"We're not together anymore," I remind him.

He says, "Let's just take a breather from all that."

"A break from the break?"

"You're going through something. I want to be there. Let's not make any decisions just now. Please, Ann."

Too tired to argue, I tell him that I'll call him when I land.

"Just remember. I'll be on the next plane, as soon as you tell me," he promises.

"I'll be fine."

"I just hate that we're leaving things like this."

He looks so helpless that I have to fight the urge to comfort him. I realize that Noah has been my child for a long time, the gorgeous professor who needs me so very much, to make homemade bread and attend faculty parties and placate his parents. I am a helpmeet. But what does he offer me? There's the charm and flattery and a host of generous gestures. He is kind. He is also weak. There's no incongruency in these observations, but they gut me all the same. He's polish without substance, and I've hitched my wagon to nothing but a handful of glitter. The loss of Bà Ngoại reminds me about what love can feel like: crude yet formidable. Strong.

I don't tell him about the baby. That secret is mine, and I won't share it with someone who has betrayed me. The cold metal of satisfaction coats my tongue as I lock it tight within my mouth.

As I drive away from Noah, I have an odd feeling, as if it's the last time we'll see each other. Bà Ngoại's death brings up an old part of me, one that is elemental and bone-deep, a mixture of comfort and fear and vulnerability. Noah has nothing to do with that. In fact, when our beautiful house disappears in the rearview, I feel nothing but relief. There's nothing tying me to this place, to Noah. I'm spooled backward into the past.

I realize, belatedly, that he never met Bà Ngoại or my mother, and the thought fills me with such sadness that I have to cover my mouth for fear of crying out in the middle of the airplane, rousing passengers half asleep, folded up in their seats. How could I have ever made a life with someone who didn't know my past? If not for his betrayal, perhaps I would never have questioned any of it.

At the end of my trip, when the taxi pulls up to the Banyan House, I see my mother's car out front. She's driving a silver Toyota now, new and gleaming. I pay the driver.

"Whoa," he says, leaning his head out the window. "This house is like a movie set. Horror movie."

"It's all that," I reply, staring up at the big eaves and the porch with the paint-chipped black spindles. "But trust me, there's nothing glamorous about it."

"You really got family here?" he asks.

"I did. Grew up here, too. Off and on."

He whistles. "It looks haunted. You be careful out there. Bring your ghost spray."

He's laughing out the window as he drives back down the lane, and it suddenly feels too quiet out here. Unearthly. The old wooden board I once used as a swing teeters lightly on the rope holding it to a dying oak. If I squint, I can see myself clutching the rope, bowing my head to scan for mosquitoes at dusk.

But then the Banyan House greets me with its lofty, threatening, patrician air. It's a mixture of Spanish and Colonial styles, as if the architect couldn't decide which to commit to. The columns are stately, but the faded pink exterior is even shabbier than I remember, and it was never well maintained to begin with. I can see spots of mildew creeping up the sides, and overgrown brambles patterned along the doors and windows. And out back, looming beyond the house, is that old banyan tree, huge and spindly, with branches that grow downward, sweeping the dirt like the hem of an antique gown. I resist the urge to run to the tree, seeking just one more glimpse of my grandmother sitting under it with her cup of coffee, turning her head to me.

"At long last," she'd say, that rare smile tugging up the sag in her cheeks.

Grief is a lake of perilously thin ice. You never know when you'll fall through it, or when you will fight your way back to the surface.

I drag my gaze away from the tree, back toward the house. Growing up, the house, like the surrounding acreage, was unwieldy for us. We lived like feral beings, patching things up here and there, clearing the Spanish moss when it tangled on the ground in brown-green clumps. I remember having friends over and putting the moss on my hair, chasing them around and around the yard. "I'm a witch!" I'd cry. We shrieked and kicked up the dirt, with no neighbors to reprimand us.

Once I snagged my foot on a nail come loose on the front porch, and it ripped into my skin. I bled into the cracked wood and wailed until Mom ran around the side of the house and scooped me into her arms.

"Goddamn this house," she'd said, as if it were the fault of the house and not a consequence of me running wild in a patently unsafe place.

We never did fix all the boards, though later I saw her crouched down low with a hammer, trying to find the loose nails.

Now Mom greets me at the door in jeans and one of those clingy polyester shirts printed in a mandala design, somehow making it look fashionable, though I know she's had it for years. Her hair is threaded with gray, but her face is youthful and unblemished. My friends would give anything to have skin like hers. I do, I know, and my hand reaches up to stroke my own face.

"I could have gotten you from the airport," she says.

"It's easier this way."

When I hug her, I smell her perfume, Estée Lauder Pleasures, in the silvery curved bottle she used to keep on the bathroom counter. It's a glamorous smell, one I always associated with her, even years later as I was shopping next to Alice at a fancy five-story mall in the Midwest. I'd catch a whiff and think of Mom with surprise, turning to catch a glimpse of her, no matter where I was.

I'm the first to pull away from the hug, which I don't expect. Mom has always been unaffectionate.

"You're here," she says.

"I'm here."

We stand awkwardly until Mom says, "Come in, come in."

It feels odd to be invited into a house I once roamed with abandon, my legs bruised from darting in and out of odd corners and rifling around the abandoned shed in back. But I step in, and it feels like releasing a giant breath. The smells come to me all at once.

The Banyan House is really a mansion, so it seems to sprawl, one room leading to another through a series of narrow hallways lined with battered old rugs. Each room once served a very specific purpose, but are each now filled with teetering stacks of magazines, bolts of fabric, appliances that have never been removed from their packaging. The ballroom seems to have become some discount shoe emporium. Size 6, I note, picking up a pair of tan mules. The parlor is so crowded that I can't do more than squint into the darkness inside. Cardboard boxes rise in tall columns, covering the windows.

The smell of it all stifles me—musty, but also sickly sweet, like a stale pastry left out on the counter. There's odd artwork all over, portraits of people we haven't met, landscapes we haven't seen, framed in gilded glory. There might be some valuable work in the midst of all the paintings, but I don't think so. The art collection feels like something meant to emit the impression of wealth, rather than a true curated selection. Like the Banyan House as a whole, I suppose. Sometimes it felt like a museum we happened to be caretaking, rather than a home.

Once, during a bedtime story, Bà Ngoại told me of her inheritance. She said something about a lady with white hair, long dusty afternoons in Gothic splendor. I never wanted to think about the Banyan House as it once was, belonging to those outside our family, though we used the linens and plates of the previous inhabitants. I didn't like thinking of us as renters of someone else's history. Later, every time I asked more about the Lady, she shut her lips tightly, as if regretting her story.

"Let the past lie, Ann," she said. But how could we have done that, when we were surrounded by it, choking in memories that were not ours?

Now the parlor is lined with mahogany shelves, each full of animal figurines: tigers and monkeys, an elephant or two. I don't remember these from my childhood. The wallpaper is a faded blue fleur-de-lis pattern, blooms edged in gold. It was once very striking, but now looks a bit moldy. I reach out to touch it, then draw my hand back from the damp surface. Sometimes, it's better not to investigate a rotting thing too closely.

There are mismatched rugs covering every inch of the floor, so I can't see the hardwood underneath. I flip through piles of books with totally unreadable titles about insurance and Y2K, fly-fishing, and all kinds of outdated things Bà Ngoại had shown no interest in. Like she'd collected without discernment. Collected to fill.

"Wow," I say.

"I know. It's a shock. It was always bad, as you know. But your grandmother became obsessed with *stuff* in her later years."

"She never told me."

"It embarrassed her."

I swallow my irritation. It hurts that my mother knows things about Bà Ngoại that I don't, though of course, that is the curse of leaving. You withdraw the privilege of access to the quiet, everyday details. The relationship loses its texture. And now, with Bà Ngoại's body cold in a morgue somewhere, there is no chance of reclamation. I clench my jaw so hard, I hear a popping at the back of my head.

"This is just the start of it," Mom says. I think, maybe, there's something gloating in her voice.

Edging past the piles of things, the last relics of Bà Ngoại's life, I put my bags in my old bedroom. I see Mom has placed her things in Bà Ngoại's office on an air mattress, wedged between two large filing cabinets overflowing with detritus. My chest feels heavy in here.

"You could have taken the main bedroom," I say to Mom, who watches me from a distance, as if she can't bear to get too close. "Or your old room."

"No, I have a condo. I'm just here to clean things up. It's temporary."

I nod. "For me too."

She says, "There's a lot of shit. We can purge it now, finally."

"Why didn't you do anything about it?"

Mom glares at me, then shrugs. "She got bored alone in this house. Started shopping at all these antiques stores. And the garage sales. People knew to open their cash registers when she came in. No one could stop her, and so it just . . . piled up?"

My mouth sours at the thought of cleaning Bà Ngoại's things without her. Dozens of plastic bags that would have to go, the house scoured out and sold. In the living room, I sit heavily on a recliner. The arms are worn down to a dull red, the clotted color of an old scab, and I run my hands over it, hoping to feel the last warmth from Bà Ngoại's touch.

"She would be angry that we're touching her things," I say. "You know she cared a lot about this stuff."

"It's junk."

"Not to her."

Mom snaps, "Well, she isn't really here to object, Ann."

We're silent for a second, and I shrug off my sweater. I forget that even in winter, some days can get hotter than sin in Florida, especially in the afternoons, especially in a house without air-conditioning. I turn on the ceiling fan and it deposits a fine layer of dust that makes us choke, but Mom doesn't comment. She sits looking at her hands as if they might fly away, pinning them with a frown. Her index finger is slightly shorter than the rest, the nail never growing beyond a stub. I've never asked her about it, and now she rubs it against the tip of her tongue, like a tiny violin. A part of me softens, remembering that she has lost her mother, that I am not the only one to claim Bà Ngoại.

"I'm sorry, Mom."

She makes a strangled sound and doesn't look at me.

"How did it happen?" I ask.

Mom says, "She had heart problems, it turns out—and a month before, she'd taken a fall in the bathroom. She was in the hospital for a few days, but they said they thought it'd be okay for her to go home. To rest in her own house."

"By herself?"

"I was there every day. And there was a night nurse at the end. Her body couldn't handle it, I guess. It was quick. An embolism. She died in the night."

The thought of Bà Ngoại dying alone makes me want to scream.

I ask, "And you never thought I should know that she was in the hospital?"

A flash of irritation crosses her face. "I told her this would happen. That you would blame me."

"You were the only one here."

"Yes, that's right," Mom says pointedly. Then she relents. "Your bà ngoại begged me not to tell you. She didn't want you to worry. We thought she was improving—and then it was too late. It was fast. Like I said."

"But you could have called," I insist. "You didn't have to do everything she wanted."

Mom looks tired. "Sure, you can tell yourself that. You know your bà ngoại."

We're lost without her, our faithful interpreter. Mom offers me a cup of jasmine tea, which I accept. She doesn't add sugar like Bà Ngoại does, so the tea is strong and bitter, but I don't say anything. Things are fragile enough. The china in the Banyan House, as always, is absolutely pristine, kept in a glass-front display case. It's so fine that I think I could break it by staring at it the wrong way. But after all these years, the cups and dishes remain unbroken. Sturdier than they look.

I go to Bà Ngoại's room, where I can still smell the scent of her, that familiar mix of herbs and musk. In her bedroom, unlike the rest of the house, there is order. The walls are striped, coral and ivory, and there's a king-size four-poster bed, with a dent only on the right side of the mattress. It feels empty, as if she gave up in the middle of furnishing it. This has always been too big a house for one person, but Bà Ngoại was proud that it was ours. She wanted a place for me to come home to, when my mother's house might be unwelcoming.

"Besides, where else would I go?" Bà Ngoại had asked.

"You could join one of those assisted living communities. You'd make friends."

"And get STDs?" she said, indignant. "You know those places are no better than spring break in Cancun. Can you imagine? No, thank you, con. I'll stay right here."

"Who'll take care of you?"

"You could move back," she joked. "No, con, I'm kidding. I have your mother. She's really good to me, you know."

"Okay."

"She is."

"I believe you."

"It's time you forgave her for whatever you're holding tight to that chest of yours. She wasn't always the best mom, I'll give you that. But she did her best."

"*You* did your best. Now I just want to make sure you're safe."

"Stop bothering me with this. I'm fine. You're fine. You stay in that beautiful house up there. I'm hardy like a cockroach."

I carefully place the tea on the nightstand and plop down on the bed. If I strain my ears, I can hear the echo of her voice, that deep, tobacco-laced cackle, even though she'd never had a cigarette in her life. I pluck a few stray gray hairs from Bà Ngoại's pillow, pulling them taut with my fingers. Somewhere outside the window, there's a trumpeting from a sandhill crane, the throaty warble I remember so well from my childhood.

Every breath I take feels like a rebirth into a world without *her*. A pain that renews itself. A suture that won't close.

My mother's in the doorway, leaning against the jamb.

"This house is always the same," I say to her. "It's too much."

"A museum to you," she says. "Or a shrine."

She points to the wall above Bà Ngoại's dresser, where she keeps framed photos of me as a child, a copy of my diploma. There's even a photo of me and Noah, though I don't remember sending it to her. In it, we're at a friend's wedding at a vineyard on the West Coast. He's wearing a light gray suit, his pale pink pocket square matching my dress, a flowing number that stops at my knees. We're smiling and tilted toward each other, like we're taking a homecoming photo.

"You were her third child and her greatest love," Mom says. "Maybe her only real love."

The bitterness in her voice hurts. "She was mine. What do we do now?"

"The funeral is this weekend. Her lawyer wants to speak to us afterwards. And your cậu Phước. There are affairs to settle."

In the corner of the room, a shadow is cast through the yellow Roman shades. I see a flicker, and it looks like a person turning to me. Lifting a finger to her lips. After I squint, the shadow is still again. I close my eyes, feeling that now familiar turn in my stomach.

"Are you okay?" Mom asks.

I nod and press my lips tightly together. For Bà Ngoại, I won't break apart.

Noah texts me: *Have you landed?*

I feel anything but landed; I feel adrift, as if I'm floating in the air somewhere above all this. I ignore his text. It's easy to do when I'm back at the Banyan House, almost as if the new life were falling off me like a robe, and all that's left is the nakedness of my youngest self.

"I'll leave you alone, then," Mom begins. "I can make us some lunch, if you want."

"Just stay for a bit, Mom," I say, eyes closing again. "Please."

Timidly, she approaches Bà Ngoại's bed, then sits next to me. Her breathing is low but steady. With my eyes closed, I can imagine that her body is Bà Ngoại's, small and wiry, capable of so much. The quiet strength of it. I think of the revolting mundanity of life: all the breathing, the consuming and excretion, the panting desperation of it all. And in the Banyan House, we have formed our own ouroboros, snakes swallowing each other until we forget which body is ours, which soul belongs here, and which is meant to have departed.

Mom and I don't speak at all, having run out of things to say a long time ago.

Chapter 8

Hương

While Ann sleeps, I drive to the water. My mind is restless lately, and I feel as if my body can't stop moving. The roads are silent and dark, but I can see the moon begin to fade into the sky. Once I'm away from the Banyan House, I can breathe again.

Grieving my mother is complicated. And with Ann here, my emotions overlap in ways I can't control. Gladness at seeing her face again. Sorrow for what we are experiencing, separately. And anger, always anger. At my mother for leaving? At myself for never being enough? When I try to follow the string of one emotion to its genesis, I find another one tied right next to it, inseparable and unable to be parsed. I'm tangled.

This morning on the beach, the swimmer is out again, and I find myself moving closer to the water to see him. His movements are rhythmic, laced with intention. I wonder what it would be like to move through the world with such purpose. I only ever had one purpose: an intact family. A mother and a father for my beautiful child. With that dream long gone, I still flounder to find another.

A wave brushes against my feet, icy cold. How can he bear it? A translucent crab scuttles out of his hole and up onto the sand. Then, reconsidering, he dives back down, into the safety of home.

Ever since Ann's arrival, I find myself studying her secretly. She looks different, older and heavier in spirit, though I would sooner rip off a fingernail than tell that to her face. She would take that as another reason why I don't love her. Lack of love has nothing to do with our unease around each other, but she won't believe it.

We never told my mother why it got so bad, but I remember it well. Years ago, when Ann was in high school, she was a flippant kid with such an overabundance of energy that being around her made me tired. And she thought she knew every damn thing. That superiority, so haughty, so self-evident. I hated that I felt like I had to lock the door to my room to get away from my child, but the world back then felt like it was wrapped in gauze. I could only partially see Ann, and myself. I know now I was likely depressed, but back then, I didn't think I had time for depression. It was something that happened to other people.

One night during a terrible lightning storm, Gary, my then husband and Ann's stepfather, stopped her as she was trying to leave the house. He screamed at her not to get in the car, his eyes darting out the window at the sheets of rain, voice panicked. He tried to pry the keys from her hands, but she snatched her arm away. She went to the door.

"It's too dangerous," he said. "Sit your ass down, Ann."

I could tell that he wasn't really concerned about her safety; he just didn't want her driving the new car. Over the years of our marriage, Gary had become clearer to me. Yet he was my husband, and don't husbands and wives have a responsibility to cleave to each other's vices, to excuse the things we're most ashamed of in our partner? His rage frightened me, and I didn't want it showered on Ann.

"Don't go, Ann," I said. "Just wait until tomorrow."

"I go out in hurricanes, Mom. Hurricane parties? They're a thing."

"It's not a good idea, con. Please. Stay for me."

She laughed at us and went out anyway to meet her friends. The car streaked down the street, way too fast, especially in the rain. I clutched the side of the curtain, squinting to catch a glimpse of her. I wanted to run out, haul her back inside, but she was bigger than me, an adult.

The shame of motherhood is that your instincts never leave, even as everyone decides they aren't needed anymore.

"You see?" Gary said, his face purple with anger. "Your daughter does this every time. And you just sit back. She's your goddamn princess. Spoiled as rotten milk."

"I know," I said soothingly, because what else could I say? "I'll talk to her tomorrow."

"All you do is *talk to her*," Gary said, slamming the door to our bedroom.

He wanted me to lock her out that night, but I didn't. Couldn't, as mad as I was. I waited up, staring at the jagged rips of lightning in the sky. Praying, though I had no religious loyalty to speak of. I would have prayed to the devil himself to get my child home safe. The hours ticked by. Soon, it was midnight, an hour past her curfew. I felt something shatter in my bones, a deep knowing. Then a phone call.

That night, Ann got into a car accident. She said it was just a fender bender, but I could only think of how close she'd come to another fate. In my mind, I saw her body starfished in the road, those precious golden limbs smeared with blood. The unseeing in her eyes. The thought of it turned me into an animal. When Gary said he would not come to the hospital, I knew I could never love him again.

I raced to the hospital so fast that I felt the car trembling, trying to match my urgency. I ran a stoplight. I nearly crashed into a parked Jeep. All the while thinking, *what if, what if, what if.* The nurses gaped at my wild expression, my flailing arms, but they took mercy and brought me to Ann.

And there she was, placidly sitting up in bed with a bowl of blue Jell-O—I remember the Smurf shade, so comical in the midst of my panic—and drawing on some scrap paper with her good hand. Her other wrist was in a cast; a sprain, they told me. Only a few weeks with the cast, which, against all odds, had already been signed, probably by her friends, who got off without a scratch. She laughed at some joke on the television, and it was then that my fear transformed into anger.

My entire neck heated up, like someone had run a lit match around my head.

"Ann. What the hell happened?"

Her face shuttered from me. "Don't freak out. I'm fine."

"I told you. I begged you to stay home," I began.

"It could have been a lot worse," Ann told me. Her eyes were fixed on the television screen. When had she become so disrespectful?

"Look at me."

"Mom, you really need to calm down," she said. "You're embarrassing yourself."

And maybe it was that deep superiority that loosened my temper. I didn't even know what I was saying, only that the words wouldn't stop coming, louder and faster with every breath. An unstoppable flood.

"Embarrassment? You know nothing about what it's like to feel shame until you have a child that defies you. You stupid fucking girl."

The nurses began to check in on us, their foreheads creased with disapproval. I shooed them out. This was our business.

"Look at you," I spat. "Wasting your damn life, even with all you have, all we have given you."

She shrank back, looking so small on the pillow, like my baby who'd fallen into the rosebush all those years ago, riddled with scrapes from thorns and wailing that roses shouldn't poke because they are too beautiful to hurt you.

I should have apologized then, but my words were crystallized. I could only stare at her. The moment of silence stretched on.

"Do you hear the way you're talking to me?" she asked. Her voice was quiet.

She was right, but I'd gone too far to step back. I could only dig in deeper.

"It's a curse to have an ungrateful child."

"Like me?"

"Like you."

Then Ann's face took on a determination that shocked me even more than my own outburst. She looked like her father, the brows thick, her nostrils flared. I stepped back from her.

"Don't pretend that any of this anger is for me. It's about that car. It's about how you look in front of Gary," she said, her voice ringing and clear. "No wonder my father left. How could he stand to be with someone as clingy and pathetic as you?"

"Stop it, Ann."

"You are nothing but your husband's *dog*. Do you think he'll stay if you lick at his feet long enough? But here's a secret: You'll never be able to keep anyone, because you have no love to give. Only hate."

"Shut up," I whispered, shielding myself from her.

"But no one hates you as much as you hate yourself."

The truth in her words made my throat spike, brought tears to my eyes. Then it angered me, that she saw so clearly what I tried to hide for all my life.

Without thinking, I slapped her across the face. It wasn't the kind of slap you feel obligated to give, so your kid feels the bite of discipline before they get in any deeper. It was the slap of a million small annoyances piled up, disagreements and misunderstandings fermented over the years, a slap that rang through the room and out through the corridor. It was vengeance.

For a brief second, I felt the elation of justice, delivered after many years of brittleness between us, even as she lay there with her sprained wrist. Did it matter that I regretted it immediately afterward? That I tried to gather her in my arms to apologize? She shook me off.

"Don't touch me," she hissed.

"Con," I pleaded.

The doctor, a younger woman in her midthirties, poked her head in, studying our faces. "Everything okay?"

Ann looked small but fierce in the bed, like a queen, one hand raised to her reddened cheek. She looked out the window, at the moon's silvered light on the Gulf. My distant daughter.

"It's fine," she said at last. "My mother is just leaving."

The doctor stared at me with reproachful eyes. I turned on my heel and left.

Later that day, when I was at work, Ann moved her things back to the Banyan House. We'd moved out when I married Gary, when Ann was ten, though she still kept her room there, like a backup plan in case the marriage didn't work. It hurt me, her lack of belief in my ability to make a home for her. But maybe she was right.

I called to beg her to return, but she never came back, saying she was done with me and Gary. We fixed the car, though Gary and I never fixed what was between us. In time, we separated, then divorced quietly. His rage never surfaced again, and I was grateful for that. Later, he remarried and had kids of his own. I wondered if he had mellowed with them, in a way that he never could with Ann. If he could finally understand the endless equivocating every parent had to do. Sometimes I'd see him at the grocery store, kids piled up in his shopping cart smacking each other with bags of marshmallows, shouting loud enough to rouse the dead, but he didn't so much as raise his voice at them. We pretended not to know one another. He and his family moved away years ago.

After that day at the hospital, Ann wouldn't give me more than a cursory word when my mother forced her to call me. We saw each other sometimes, over holidays and whenever I popped over to the Banyan House, hungry for news of her last years at high school, her plans for college. But things could never be repaired. I tried to apologize, but the words were pale and sapped of meaning, never a real indication of my sorriness.

Sometimes fear works like that; it twists us and makes us monstrous. I would have torn her flesh apart to keep her safe. And it felt impossible to say that to her.

"Come back home," I begged. "Your room is here."

"My room is at the Banyan House," she said, her voice so lofty, I shuddered from its distance.

In her eyes, I'd chosen Gary over her. She thought I'd always chosen the men I was dating over her, though she never knew the truth of it. I was straining so hard to build what I thought she deserved, that fairy-tale life, where a mom and a dad are sitting together at dinner, eyes dancing over the table as they smile at their child. That was what she deserved. And in the end, we never even got a moment of that together.

Now Ann is back in Florida, under the same roof as me at long last, and I should be overjoyed, but I'm also weighed down by the loss of my mother, the woman who raised us both. Ann isn't the same. Neither am I. These new versions of ourselves will have to meet again.

At the ocean's edge, the swimmer is reaching for his towel a few feet away from me. We're closer now and I can see the lines in his face. He looks like he's in his thirties, somewhere between Ann and me in age. He sheds his wet suit like a snake, winding his long limbs from the rubbery fabric. Again, that friendly, blinding smile.

"Ready to swim together?" he calls.

I press my lips, trying not to smile at this stranger. The rising sun is behind him, and there's something about his tall form that feels a little prophetic. Jesus walking on the water.

"Still don't know how," I say.

He stretches his arms wide, dramatically, with the palms facing toward the sky, as if to ask, *What are you waiting for?*

I straighten my legs so they are in the waves and mime a little kick.

He laughs. "See? You're a natural."

Later that day, I sign up for a swim class at the local Y, one for adults like me who skipped this essential part of their upbringing. If I am going to survive a world without my mother, I have to learn a new way to move through it.

Chapter 9

Minh

On the day they create my altar, the sky weeps in needlelike threads of rain, drenching the wetlands even more, so they seem to glisten from within. The birds flee to the branches of cypress trees miles down the road, their cries drowned out by the sound of the storm dimpling the swamp water. Outside by the front steps of the Banyan House, I see the creep of a mud turtle with a long yellow scar running along its shell. For every inch he gains, he slides backward into the muck. I wish I could tell my children to watch out for the floods, and the cottonmouths that come out after storms, their coiled bodies angry and waiting. How the cleansing of this impossible land has always come with a price. I wish I could tell them many things. But my shadow bargain remained unhonored, and I am here and not here, at once.

Ann stands on the rotting porch, barefoot, staring into the storm as if she can end its onslaught through will alone. Maybe she can. She glances down at her phone, then, with a graceful pull of her arm, like a bowstring stretched taut, throws it into the rain, where it sinks slowly into the earth.

"Good fucking riddance," she says.

She sits on the rocker and pushes herself with the tips of her toes. Rain sluices through the rails of the rotting old porch and wets her feet.

She whispers, "Why would you leave me now? I don't know where to go from here."

I want to tell her just how much I understand. The aloneness of bearing a child no one wants but you. It's a brutal kind of sorrow that will never leave your soul. I wish I could have saved Ann from it, or at least given her an incantation to dull the pain. Yet even if I wanted to pierce the thick curtain between us, I do not have the strength. My corporeality has fled. Her face crumples into my silence. I can feel nothing, and everything.

"Ann! It's time," Hương calls.

Ann crams the heels of her hands against her eyes, stopping the flow of tears before her mother can see. She goes back in, her feet dampened.

Inside the Banyan House, the altar is their first task together, before even the purging of the house. I taught them well in that, at least, though I suspect neither of them truly believes in the old ways. I have always believed in the power of our ancestors' souls—their cravings, griefs, and boundless love still indenting reality from beyond the grave. When I was alive, Xuân's altar was placed on a high shelf in the kitchen, nearly out of our eyeline, but always laden with fruit and fresh incense. I could look up at him while I was cooking.

It touches me that they would think to do this, despite their skepticism. My cynical girls.

Now Hương transforms a credenza into an altar in the living room. It's wider and more lavish than I thought she'd reserve for me, but then I see that she wants to combine my altar with Xuân's, to allow us to find each other after death. It's a lovely thought. But in this place, between heaven and earth, I don't see any traces of my husband. I'm tied to the Banyan House, even in death. I only have the living for company.

I feel their grief singing through the walls of the house, and I want to let them rest their heads on my chest, taking their pain as my own.

Ann spreads out a piece of white Chantilly lace from the Lady's linen closet. Maybe it was meant to be sewn into a dress once, or a veil.

She'd kept her secrets well, doling out just enough to form the edges of a person. Her artifacts confound us, but we can't escape them, so we lean into them, taking them for our own.

"Let's use this," Ann says. "It looks expensive. Bà Ngoại would have liked it."

"But we have always used red cloth, Ann. It's traditional."

Ann's chin juts. "Bà Ngoại always said we have to make our own traditions. Remember? The old ways, mixed with the new."

In Ann's level gaze, I see some new determination. Perhaps it is the little one growing inside her, giving her this courage at long last, after years of hovering on the edges of her own life. Supporting Noah, and all those around him, none of them with an ounce of the stardust inside her. Ordinary folks. Not like my Ann.

"And doesn't white represent grief anyway?" Ann continues.

I can tell Hương wants to argue—her eye is on a piece of red silk we bought from Đà Lạt months before our journey to America—but she nods, giving in. They place white roses from the market on the altar, then a large brass bowl full of sand to hold the incense. They count out twelve candles.

Hương finds an old photo of me from Việt Nam, taken at the fancy studio in town with Xuân, where I am sitting in a hard-backed chair, my hair wound in a low bun at my nape. I'm wearing a brown áo dài. This was before Phước was born, and there's still a swell of girlhood in my cheeks. I am clearheaded and beautiful, though there is something coarse about my beauty. Later, after our success with the store, my edges would smooth out into something like refinement. But in this photo, I have a shred of the country wildness left in me.

"That one?" Ann is skeptical. "But it doesn't look like the bà ngoại we knew."

"Maybe not. It's customary to use photos of the deceased in their youth. So they can remain healthy in the afterlife."

"I hate that you said 'the deceased.'"

"Well, call her whatever you want, Ann. It's all the same, isn't it?"

Finally, Ann concedes. The photo gets framed, then placed in the altar behind the flowers and fruit. They move Xuân's portrait and candles over to this altar, and the sight of his portrait next to mine satisfies me. I see Hương lifting a finger to trace his face. Is she looking for a hint of herself in him? My soul weeps to think I cannot give her this small gift. In truth, I never could.

Ann washes a bunch of grapes and carefully dries each one before putting them in a bowl next to a green palm of unripe bananas. After they yellow, my girls will unpeel each and consume them, taking my luck into their bodies. Leftovers from the ancestors; waste nothing.

Finally, Ann adds a cup of coffee to the altar, in one of those unbreakable china cups from the Lady.

"But Ann," Hương begins, "we should present wine. Or beer, even. It's traditional."

"She didn't drink wine."

"I know. But she would want to have the proper respect in the afterlife."

"There's nothing disrespectful about coffee."

"Are we going to argue over every single thing on this altar?" Hương runs a hand through her hair. Her gold bracelet twinkles in the light.

Ann doesn't respond, only touches the handle of the cup, as if to pick it up and bring it to her own lips. Her eyes are lowered, and I know she's thinking of the afternoons spent under the banyan tree. Breathing in the briny green scent of the wetlands. Hương sighs.

Together, they agree to skip the Buddha statue, not that we ever had one. Our family has never believed in a monolithic god, though we have our own pantheon of guardians, among whom I now stand.

"You light the incense, Mom," Ann says, generously.

I can't smell it, but I know it must fill the room with a deep musk scent, the smoke tendrils curling slowly away from the altar like overflowing waves. I imagine the grit of the incense rubbing against their fingers. Hương holds three sticks of incense against her forehead and bows three times before placing them back in the brass holder. Then she gets on her knees and presses her head to the ground, cushioning her forehead with open palms. Once, twice.

After a second, Ann follows her movements. Then they are both kneeling and staring up at my photo and Xuân's with their hands pressed together in front of their hearts. Twin pillars of beauty, of grief. There will be a funeral soon, a smallish, petty affair that would earn no jealousy from anyone, but this is our true farewell. Complicated. Loving. Somehow, still unfinished.

From where I stand, beyond and above and within—everywhere at once, as I said—I blow a kiss to them. My kiss ripples down to the altar, where it quenches the lazy swirls of smoke so that the incense tips sputter from lava red to a crisped gray.

Hương doesn't notice, but Ann starts at the sight of the incense blowing out. She peers at the altar so intently, I wonder if she can feel my breath. If I am not as dead as I thought. But then she shakes her head. She helps her mother stand, and in her tenderness, I see something of the girl she left behind, and the mother she will someday be.

Chapter 10

Ann

Over the next few days, we fill countless huge garbage bags for the thrift stores. Some are so heavy I can't lift them myself, or I know I shouldn't. Mom hires a boy looking for work and he whistles when he throws the biggest ones in the bed of his truck.

When my back is turned, Mom adds more to the donation pile. She's not sentimental about things the way Bà Ngoại and I are. Were. And maybe she's right. The dead don't take these things with them, and I don't need them in my house in Michigan. It sounds strange to call it my house now. I remember the vaulted ceilings, the sparkling lake, the beautiful cocktail dresses Noah bought me that hung on velvet hangers in a neat row. Would Alice have thrown another party by now? To celebrate spring, or a new charitable cause, or just a regular old Friday night being so filthy rich and beautiful? Would Noah be meeting Mitch and Tina for cocktails, the giant round ice cubes bouncing around their glasses, their talk overflowing about the newest TV drama, the latest think piece from their favorite journal? Would he have called Alexis for comfort? I stop the thought in its tracks, sending it scuttling out of my brain like an overeager mutt.

None of them exist in the Banyan House. Each breath of air I take—sometimes bright and fresh, other times moldy and choked—takes me farther away from them all.

Away from my old life, I see that there wasn't much I actually contributed to that wonderfully intact circle that Noah had built around himself. I was a well-meaning ghost, sweeping up messes and adding ornamentation. I could have gone on endlessly, I think, if it weren't for Bà Ngoại's death.

After I retrieve my phone from the wet ground where I'd hurled it and dunk it in a bowl of rice to dry out, I see a series of texts from Noah. *I love you*, he says again and again, though in different iterations, sometimes with poetry and sometimes with an inside joke. The words are beginning to lose meaning here.

What I know is that love is a thousand tiny, useless things saved in a parlor. Stacks of cooking magazines bookmarked with things Bà Ngoại wished she had made for us. Clothes folded like dumplings with the tags still on, waiting to be worn. Photos upon photos of us all: me in my homecoming gown, Mom standing next to the famous rose gardens, Phước and Diane and their daughters, smiling with the ocean in the background.

I tell Noah that I'm safe in the Banyan House, and then I let my phone battery run down to zero. It's not a decision, I know this. But I want to live in this suspended space for a little longer. After what he has done, I am owed this time to myself.

When we sort the kitchen cabinets, Bà Ngoại's stained Tupperware is the first thing to go in the trash, along with old takeout utensils and moth-eaten towels. We get rid of bags of rice speckled with black mites, and rows and rows of plastic-wrapped water crackers saved from cafés where they were served alongside bowls of soup. Brown sugar turned to bricks, unrevivable even with wet toast. Bottles of fish sauce, soy sauce, and sesame oil, crusted around the openings.

"There is so much," I say.

Mom's hair is wrapped in an old kerchief. It makes her look young and flippant in a way I never see from her. She wipes the sweat from her brow with the back of a hand.

"It's a relief for me. To clean all this finally."

"How'd it get this bad?" I try to strip the accusation from my voice.

Mom shrugs. "She was in her own time loop. She wanted everything to be kept this way in case we ever came back."

"That's tragic."

"Or hopeful." Sometimes I think Mom understands Bà Ngoại better than she lets on.

When I get to the old drawings I made, Mom stills my hand.

She holds up a drawing of a dalmatian I did in grade school. "You were always a good artist."

"It eventually paid the bills," I say, remembering how Bà Ngoại scrimped to buy me fine art supplies. She laid the charcoals and acrylic paints neatly on my bed, turning away when I tried to thank her, pretending she had no idea what I was talking about. Like the supplies were a gift from the Banyan House, the source of all our luck.

Mom gathers the stack of papers and clips them with a clothespin.

"I want these," she says, her eyes impossible to read.

"It's just junk, Mom," I say.

"Still." She puts the drawings in her purse. "Missed years. Your bà ngoại always got the best of you. Even after you were an adult; she hoarded the memories. I got nothing."

"Whose fault was that?" I ask, sharpness creeping into my voice.

"Why does it have to be blame for you all the time, Ann?" she asks. "Can't you just accept that some bad things happened?"

"Some things are preventable, Mom. We have to take responsibility for the past."

"Those are the words of someone who hasn't had enough past to account for yet. You just wait until you are a mother."

Can she know? Is pregnancy something a mother can scent out, the way she could tell when I had my first kiss, running in flushed from the backyard with Wes, my old childhood friend? But she's not looking at me anymore. Her eyes are trained somewhere above me, at a water spot near the ceiling. I think it looks like a jellyfish with creeping tentacles.

We're quiet for a while as we sort through more things. I find a little wooden jewelry box at the bottom of one of Bà Ngoại's drawers. I pull out a deep green jade bracelet, polished beautifully and smooth as a river. It doesn't seem like the sort of thing she would wear—she liked flash and bold jewelry—but it's beautiful. A perfect circle. I slide it over my wrist and it feels cold, clacking gently as I rest my hand on a drawer.

"You take it," Mom says. "It looks good on you."

"Bà Ngoại always had good taste," I say.

"She owned a jewelry store. In Việt Nam."

"I didn't know that."

"There's a lot you don't know."

Mom drives us to a secondhand store that opened a couple of years ago to give away another load. Nothing much has changed in town. I see the Dairy Queen where I did homework, sneaking bites from Wes's Blizzards. The movie theater with its worn marquee, only showing one or two movies at a time, and never anything I wanted to see. Even so, I went anyway, because what else were we going to do in this crummy town? Crystal and I would sneak in between showings, our purses bulging with candy from the drugstore, eyes widely innocent when the ushers' flashlights streaked across our faces, confusedly noting girls they didn't remember letting in.

Mom points out the elementary school, with its bright blue trim and high wire fencing, the encouraging aphorisms on its sign out front: "The Most Valuable Gift Is a Friend."

"They added a new wing a couple years ago. Expanded the library, too."

"Huh."

"And after you left, they fired Principal Taft. He was having an affair with the art teacher."

"Ms. Dupont?"

Mom snorts. "Her real name was Sherry Dudley. They stayed together for a while, then Taft decided to become a boat captain. Giving tours in the swamplands."

The old church has been torn down and replaced by a drive-through car wash, all bold lettering and black-clad ninjas, their unlikely mascots. Car ninjas. The last time I went to the church was for a friend's First Communion. It reminded me of an old schoolhouse I toured in one of those replica colonial villages. Everything smelled like pine and prayer. Holy places shouldn't be replaced by car washes, but that's how it goes sometimes. The faithful falling in line with progress, with cold necessity. And who doesn't need a car wash?

I consider taking Bà Ngoại's Oldsmobile there. It's clanky, but the key still turns in the engine, and it deserves new life, too, I guess.

We wait for the huge garage doors to open. There's a sign in the back that reads "Treasures by the Sea."

"Cheeseball," I say.

Mom agrees and pops the trunk.

A man in a faded black tee comes out to help us unload. At first, with his hand raised to his forehead to guard against the sun, I don't see it. His hair is longer and tucked behind his ears, there are more tattoos, and he's got a bit of stubble now. But that strong, wiry frame and those green eyes are still the same. Intense, shining with attention. So handsome, the women in the store turn to look at him, eyebrows lightly raised. His gait is slow and steady, a mix of confidence and something liquid, caramel.

"Oh my God," I say. "Wes Asher?"

The last time I saw him, we'd shared one drunken night, making out outside a bar after Thanksgiving. He'd pushed me into an alley and we'd kissed and kissed, giggling, full of too-sweet cocktails (Orange Bombs, the signature drink of Joyland, the country bar we all found our way back to), delighted at having discovered each other again.

Still, when he asked me to come back to his apartment that night, I refused. There was something dangerous about him that I did not want to take on. And the weight of history. I refused that, too. I met Noah soon after, and Wes shuffled back into my memories, where he belonged.

He's still tall, two heads above me. His arms shine with sweat and ropy veins. I see a little rubber duck tattoo near his elbow, out of place among the vined roses and music lyrics running up his sleeve. His smile is radiant and crooked and feels like sinking backward in time.

He shoves a lock of hair off his head. "Ann? Oh, lord. Haven't seen you in years."

"I know," I say, guilty.

I remember how he used to call, write letters sometimes. I was a piss-poor correspondent, or maybe I wanted to distance myself from it all. Banyan House and Florida and lazy afternoons after school, limbs tangled, hands batting at the flies.

"It's really good to see you," he says. Or I do. Our words are canceling each other out, full of excitement and awkwardness.

He begins unloading the car with me. It's odd seeing him handling Bà Ngoại's junk, but also reassuring. If anyone were to take care of her things, it would be Wes.

"What brings you back here?" he asks. A woman beckons for his attention, hovering over a wicker rocking chair, but he doesn't notice, just stares at me as if I'm the only person around. I don't want to get into it here, with Mom waiting in the front seat.

"Just visiting," I say.

"How about that," he says. His eyes are inscrutable, but I know he's thinking, *Why, after all this time?* "Need a tour guide?"

I laugh, and his face falls lightly. "I think I can find my way around still. You work here?"

He gestures expansively at the warehouse behind him, the storefront attached to it. "I own the place. I repair furniture, give things new life. Sell other things."

"Wow, look at that. This is cool, Wes."

"Maybe, yeah. I keep thinking I might sell the store. Getting kind of bored of the retail life."

The sun beats down as he unloads the rest of our things, then brings me in for a hug. I want to relax into him. I cling for a second too long, anxious for his warmth. Something cracks in my chest, the feeling of his uncomplicated kindness breaking through the ice.

"What do you want for all this, Annie?" he asks, gesturing at our bags.

I'm surprised. "Oh, nothing at all. I wasn't selling it. I just didn't want to keep it myself. You take it. Make beautiful things out of it. Or whatever."

"You sure?"

"Not worth it to me."

"Fair enough. Let me buy you a coffee for your trouble."

His smile is a spotlight cast on me. I want to bask in it a little longer.

But I say, "No thanks. Mom is in the car. We've gotta get going. It was nice to see you."

"You look good, Annie," he says. He leans down to give a wave to Mom, waiting in the driver's seat with a tight smile. "Call me some-time? If you want?"

I know I won't want to, but I'm grateful for the offer. Sometimes over the years I'd flip through the old high school yearbook and see his photo, that grin of his peeking through, like a surprise gift left on my doorstep. I'd wonder what he was up to, but was too lazy to actually put work into seeking him out. Too many years had passed for a casual catch-up call.

In the rearview mirror, I can see he still has one arm raised, a cow-boy goodbye.

Back at home, Mom starts to scrub the mildewed powder room downstairs, while I tackle Bà Ngoại's bathroom. Her medications are on the counter and I sweep them into the trash, where they clatter. They are a reminder of how she could not be saved.

There's some hair clogging up the tub drain. I put on yellow gloves and pull it out, one glob at a time, until I'm left with a rat's nest speck-led with old soap residue. Leaning toward the toilet, I throw up. My third time since I've been back. I wonder how long it'll be before I show.

Noah calls, and this time, I answer.

"Are you . . . okay?" His voice sounds far away.

"Yes, just dandy."

"Ann, come on. It's me."

I'm quiet, wondering what that means anymore. He sighs.

"Do you need me to come?"

"No, we've got it. The funeral's this weekend, then the trip to the lawyers. Should be quick to wrap up. The house should be cleared out next week and good to go. We've sold a lot of the furniture."

"That's good," he says. "And what else is going on?"

"I ran into an old friend from high school. That never happens to me."

"Happens to me all the time," he says. I hear a smile in his voice.

"That's because we live in your hometown."

"Right. I miss you."

"Yeah," I say, my tone wooden. "It's kind of nice being here."

I feel a surge of craving for limes dipped in salt. It's so intense that I'm fighting the urge to hang up the phone, drive straight to the store, pile an armful in my shopping bag.

"And where does that leave us?" he asks.

"We're on a break, Noah. Remember?"

"I don't want that."

He can't see me, but I puff up my cheeks. I've spent the past few days sorting through my dead grandmother's things, and Noah has slipped from my mind, like a marble I don't remember liking all that much. Out of my pocket, rolling on the ground for someone else to pick up. A week ago, the thought of Noah dating someone else, bringing her to our house and introducing her to his parents, would have felt like the end of the world. I would have sobbed for days. Now I'm a shade from indifferent. Relieved, even. Does this make me utterly heartless? It's just that my grief is laser-focused right now. Everything else feels secondary.

I tell him, "I don't have time to think about us right now. There's so much going on."

"Can we talk about it later?" Noah pleads.

I agree, to get him off the phone, then go down the stairs, past the altar with its flickering shadows, the incense that inexplicably burns out too soon. This house is getting to me, like it always has. Weird, musty. Unknowable.

In the kitchen, Mom is slicing oranges. She hands me a plate with a little pile of salt for dipping.

"I was just thinking I wanted fruit and salt," I tell her. "Limes, actually."

She says, "I craved limes when I was pregnant with you. Could have eaten a whole dozen without blinking. Would have given me endless diarrhea if your bà ngoại had let me."

The oranges are sweet, coarse pebbles of salt cutting through that drippy tropical flavor, making my tongue curl in on itself. I hum in satisfaction. *More,* my body seems to say, *more.* Mom slices another orange, and another. We could have gone on the whole afternoon in the kitchen, with her slicing and me eating, the sun setting on my gluttony. I'm sticky with juice, happy to be taken care of. She hands me a wet paper towel for my fingers.

"How's Noah?" she asks, not even pretending she wasn't eavesdropping. The Banyan House has always had poor insulation. You can hear a sigh from the opposite corner of the house.

"How's your married boyfriend?" I ask.

I heard Bà Ngoại talking about the dentist once, and it gives me a ripple of satisfaction when Mom is taken aback. I'm being cruel, but habits don't die easily here. I'm sixteen again, staring my mother down when she comes to the door, demanding I come back to her and Gary's house. Bà Ngoại standing between us, trying to placate, as she always did.

"Fine, you don't want to talk about it," Mom snaps. "You've got a viper's tongue, Ann."

"Sorry. Can we just not talk about Noah?"

"What *do* you want to talk about?"

"Something that doesn't depress me?"

She doesn't reply, just sits down next to me, looking expectant. I don't know what she wants, but I'm not capable of giving it to her. Not now. I can't want to confide in her while Bà Ngoại is dead, waiting for her burial. It feels like a betrayal. So I continue to eat, each drop of citrus pooling on my tongue, another excuse to stay silent.

Chapter 11

Minh, 1965

The young always think they're the first to experience anything—love, heartbreak, fear. I see it in the way Ann holds herself at that kitchen table, discarded orange rinds around her. I see it in how Hương sets her jaw, like she's preparing a speech for Congress. They are each mired in their individual pain. They can't break free. It is everything to them, this darling pain; they cradle it close like children. But it doesn't belong to just them, and they forget that every time.

Later, while my girls' slow breaths commune with the night wind, their own dreams carrying them away, I travel back in time, which feels like watching a movie where the film has been left in the sun for too long. The edges are scratched and the colors are faded in some spots, blown out to white in others. Some faces are sharp and others so pale and forgettable, I think of marble, lined faintly and elegantly, but indistinguishable from the next slab.

My secrets, however, they poke through the cartography of my past, spiky as tacks. I remember them all.

The first: I conceived Hương in the middle of the hottest summer I can remember. I was seventeen, though I looked younger than the other girls, my breasts budding where they should have been in full bloom, nowhere near ready for childbearing. The plain-faced girl down the street, six months younger than me, had married already and recently given birth to a red-faced baby boy. She was fat and nubile, a suckling pig, and her husband, two decades older than her, had plucked her right up. Everyone acted like it was an achievement, swarming her bedside with fruit and hand-sewn wool hats for the baby, even though it was the heart of monsoon season and we were all rolling up the hems of our pants, shoving our shirtsleeves up to catch a whiff of breeze on bare skin. My friends envied the girl for her luck—a husband with a thriving farm, and a baby besides. But I didn't want any of it. I clung to my youth, knowing what motherhood meant after watching my own mother sink into her seat at the end of the day, too exhausted to even eat the meal she made us.

We were ten years into what we'd later call the American War. A country divided, with brutality on both sides, though the story we told ourselves was that we were the civilized ones in the South. We repeated stories of VC crimes—rapes and burnings of whole villages, children run through by scythes, or worse—and fed ourselves on the promise of independence. It's the only way to sustain zeal amid the horrors; you tell yourself that it's all for a higher cause.

When I was fifteen, two years before that fateful summer of Hương's conception, I heard the news of Thích Quảng Đức burning himself in the streets of Sài Gòn as a protest of Diệm's injustice against the Buddhists. There were no Catholics in our town, and we sympathized with the monks, revered as conduits to the holy unknown. I had nightmares of Đức's lovely golden robes bursting into fire. The smell of flesh as it swept the streets teeming with the monuments of colonial Indochina.

Once when I woke crying, my mother leaned over to stroke my forehead.

"How can men be so terrible?" I asked her, as quietly as I could so I wouldn't wake the rest of them.

"It's not just men. We are all capable of terrible and great things, Minh." She meant it as a kind of comfort, though to me, it showed only more of the cruelty of the world.

My family had no relationships in the North, but our next-door neighbors had two grown sons who had moved up near Hà Nội, and every time news came, their faces drained, pale as silkworms. Hoping and fearing, and ashamed of their torn allegiances. Sometimes, other townspeople spat at their feet, especially when news came of boys from the South who'd fallen.

"Việt Cộng trash," they muttered. "We should open your guts in the streets."

We are all capable of terrible things.

I hadn't mustered many political allegiances or impressions, but even I knew that we would continue to suffer this bloody war before we could find peace. I could hardly imagine a world without war—war with the French, the Japanese, our own brothers in the North—and the prospect of peace felt like something that happened in other places, other countries. But though my heart still seized with fear every day, in a million ways, the familiarity of it became another ritual of life. We swept the floors. We prayed to our ancestors. We laughed into the face of the fear. Later, when I watched the American documentaries, I thought: *Yes, and?* They fail to capture the life amid the death. For them, the Vietnamese are shorthand for a whole generation's worth of resentment, more symbol than people. I suppose the reverse is true: to us children, the GIs signaled vigor and exoticism, a kind of cornfed hardiness that we could not conceive without peering into their sunburnt faces.

The bombs had started in the North that year, and we felt the reverberations in the South. No one knew if or when the Americans would turn on us, despite their reassurances to the contrary. We were a small nation, unimportant except for this war, this never-ending war that lined everyone's pockets but ours. But it wasn't just this war. Our country had risen from numerous claims of sovereignty by other nations, their eyes cast on our rich lands, our proximity to the water. The labor of our people. Our children hungered for safety, for rice, while the generals commanded from afar. Full of words for the nation and nothing else. I had learned early on the emptiness of men's words, though it was a lesson I would have to keep relearning all my life.

The spring before, American troops had entered Đà Nẵng, their youthful bodies resplendent in the sand, smiles lighting up their faces, even while staring down war on another continent. I always thought there was something disastrously hopeful about men going to fight. They immolate themselves with principle, as if they have a choice but to fight. The stories they tell themselves of bygone gallantry; a chance to reclaim the honor that muted itself in times of peace. I imagine them looking up past the coastline, into the vastness of possibility.

Once, when I was young, my parents took me and my brothers to the beaches of Đà Nẵng. The air felt cool and light and we bathed in our underwear, modesty put aside for an afternoon in the sun. We had the beach to ourselves. This was the time before all the surfers came, gaping at the cheap real estate, shoveling fifty-cent bowls of phở into their mouths. In the distance, my family and I could see the holy mountains covered in forest, stone, and grass together. Later, much later, I watched a TV special of a famous chef parading around Đà Nẵng. They filmed a giant golden bridge with two hands holding it up, a tourist destination, a place to marvel at and take photos of. But what they didn't understand was that Đà Nẵng before the war, before the Americans, the five-star resorts and sushi restaurants, was its own marvel, a place just for us, even common people without that much to claim.

Within all this turmoil, womanhood arrived for me, though I felt dragged to it. One moment, I was a child. The next, I wasn't.

One day, in the summer I turned seventeen, my parents sent me down to the market to buy a cup of rice for the family. The coins felt heavy with promise in my palm. They made me reckless. I imagined myself a fine lady, a purse swinging behind me as I chose what to buy. My more worldly friends described French wives they'd seen over the years, resting on wide balconies with their clear skin and tidy curled updos, icy drinks on frail little tables beside them. I couldn't imagine such sophistication, but I pretended anyway that I knew something of it. What I mean is that I was still a girl.

On the dirt path, I ran into a classmate of mine, the handsome and notorious Bình. He was throwing a coconut back and forth between his hands, looking bored, though his eyes widened at the sight of me. Maybe it was my pretend-lady pose or the way I had parted my hair that day, allowing it to swing behind me outside my braids. My áo dài tightened at my waist and I saw him glance at my body. Boys had looked at me before, of course, before my mother shooed them away, but none were so bold as Bình that day in the market. I tried to hide how much his gaze thrilled me.

"Want to play ball?" he asked, knowing I would refuse.

I shook my head. I was on a mission and felt important saying so. "I have to go to the market for dinner."

"Such a proper little lady," he teased.

I held my head high and lifted my áo dài from the dust. My pants hem grazed the road. It was hot, and I wished I had chosen something silky and easy, rather than this heavy brown fabric. Bình followed me, tossing his coconut the whole way, his dark eyes observant like a jungle cat.

"You're always so quiet in school," he said musingly. "We thought you were too good to talk to us."

"There's nothing to say."

He laughed. "I disagree. There's always something to say."

"Maybe for those who like to hear themselves speak."

"You're a funny little mouse. You make me want to scoop you into my pocket."

"Go away," I gritted. We were close to the market and, bluff called, I was afraid of what the neighbors would say. My parents would never let me out of the house again.

"Little Mouse, that's what I'll call you," he continued.

His smile was wide and guileless, brilliant as the sun. I could see the glint of silver from a filling in his teeth. I wanted to lean toward him, even though I knew I shouldn't. I could tell he liked how I was rebuffing him. Later, I learned some men thrive on that. They see a challenge rather than a true refusal. Those are the men to watch out for, because their rapture is tied in with rebuff.

"Even little mice bite, you know," I retorted.

He laughed again, this time, genuine and surprised. "I guess so. Look at those sharp teeth! Here, let's be friends, em."

"I have enough friends," I said, palming the coins in my pocket.

"You don't have *me*," he replied.

I chuckled then at his boldness, which made him stop and look again at me.

He said, "Listen to that laugh. I could chase it into the fray of battle."

"Don't be ridiculous."

"Come on, I know a shop that serves ice cream. Have you ever had ice cream?"

I hadn't and he knew it. I looked up at the sun; they weren't expecting me until closer to dinnertime. I couldn't help myself with Bình; he was so gracious and fun. Light, in this age of unending heaviness. I'd had so little fun in my life and the promise was intoxicating, like a first sip of beer, bubbly and fresh and a little bittersweet, like leaving childhood behind.

Before long, Bình and I were seated on low chairs at a café, scooping cold ice cream into our mouths. He had a little white smear on the side of his lip, which made me want to reach up and wipe it away. Later in America, when I'd hear the urban legends of little kids stolen in ice cream trucks, it would, inexplicably, remind me of this first taste, half a world away.

He reached for my hand. I tried to remove it, but it stayed firm, as if tied to his. "You're sweeter than I thought a girl could be. You surprise me, really. Will you meet me again?"

I should have said no; it wasn't time for me to marry—not that he was interested in that—and I knew my parents would have questions about this handsome boy. I had questions, too. He was so loud and jocular, so different from the other boys I knew. There was an unquenchable light in him that the war hadn't managed to dim.

I thought of the coins in my pocket, the paltry cup of rice it would bring, and the dirty laundry waiting at home for me, the attic room where we all crowded at night, breathing in the scents of too many bodies in one space. There was too little sunshine. Who could blame me for snatching this bit for myself?

When I nodded, he straightened in triumph.

That summer, Bình and I met in pockets of hidden time we found for ourselves. Sometimes, we walked by the river. Other times, he treated me to a cup of soy milk, or a bowl of noodles from a stand. I never knew where his money came from, but he spent it easily, as if he knew it could be replaced. We talked about everything, from the war and the American soldiers slowly spilling out from our shores, like a swarm of sand mites, to all the places we wanted to see. He was still a student, so he was spared from going to serve for the moment.

"I'd go to Hà Nội if I could," he declared.

I was shocked. "You can't. The Việt Cộng."

"Oh, it's not so bad, Little Mouse. Sometimes you swallow some things that you don't agree with for a taste of something new. You know. It's a big city. A real city."

"Promise me you won't go there."

He laughed at my urgency. "Okay, fine. We'll just go to America, then, after the war. There are big cities there, too, right?"

He slid a bit of a sesame ball into my mouth and I tasted the oil on his fingers. That bite was so sweet and harmless that I didn't argue when he broke off another piece and lifted it into my mouth, brushing the edge of my lips as he did.

In the shadowed paths by the river, we often held hands, his sweaty in mine. Once he even leaned over for a kiss. I didn't know what to do with my mouth, but I must have done it right, because he looked at me eagerly, as if I were a bowl of chè to be devoured.

"Will you meet me tonight?" he asked. "By the forest? I want to be alone with you."

I began to shake my head, but he stopped me. He pulled a photograph out of his pocket.

Shyly, he said, "I had this taken in the city. It's very expensive but I want you to have it, Little Mouse. Just you, no other girl. Because you and I are true. You know the meaning of true?"

I nodded. He smiled gently when I took the photograph.

His expression in the image was solemn, but his pointed eyebrows were playful. As if he were tricking us all. I had never owned a photo before, and had never had occasion to take any of myself. I held it to my chest, tears swelling in my eyes for the purity of his gift. What a beloved girl I must be, to receive a gift like this. I wished there was something to give him in return. I said so aloud.

"Little Mouse," he said, his lips quivering so slightly.

There was a sinking in my stomach, a kind of pleasurable anticipation. I knew I should say no. Girls who said yes did not find good husbands, did not go to heaven and enjoy the company of the gods or partake in the everlasting banquet. But I wanted to know what it felt like to behave like a boy for once, not like a girl, to abandon my responsibilities for a gasp of pleasure.

When I snuck out a few nights later, I was afraid every moment that someone would awaken and hear my soft footsteps, but they slept like the dead. Life was hard then, and you clung to sleep like it could save you. Bình was waiting where he said, under a dark net of trees. When I came to him, he grabbed at me quickly, sensing my indecision, the urge to retreat. He kissed me until I melted into him. So many kisses my mouth felt bruised. I thought of stars, and purple grapes, the expensive, cold sweetness of getting what you finally wanted. When he eased his hands into the pants of my pajamas, his rough palm meeting the softness of my lower belly, I accidentally bit his tongue in shock. I tasted the blood. No one had ever touched me like that.

"Please, Little Mouse, please," he whispered.

I felt waves of unknowing, then bliss, separated from my own body, lulled by the sound of his voice, the sensation of his probing fingers. Before I knew it, he had slid me onto the ground, and himself on top of me. His breath panted against my neck; one, two, three. My pain was acute. I gripped the earth with my nails. We were done before I understood what had happened.

"Little Mouse, I think I love you," he said softly.

He traced my jawline with his kisses, and I knew I would let him do it again and again, as many times as it took to keep him mine.

That summer, we met several more nights under a moon that seemed alternately so bright, then dim, as if gradually turning its light from us. Each coupling became faster and more frantic. Bình pulled his pants on quickly afterward, sometimes forgetting to help me up from the dirt, where I brushed myself clean. I snuck back into my house, past my sleeping siblings and snoring parents, smiling into my pillow, even as I knew I'd yawn in exhaustion the next day. I liked his scent on me. Throughout those lazy months, my mother gave me sharp looks, opening her lips as if to speak. But she never said anything. With all those mouths to feed and a war going on in our backyard, there was no time to wonder where her daughter had found herself.

Bình's sweet nothings were rare after those first few times. But those nights carried me through the busy days, when I'd volunteer to run errands, hoping to catch a glimpse of him in the streets. He was often by his bicycle, arm resting on the handlebars, or at a café with his friends. He'd wink when he saw me—even once brazenly blowing a kiss my way. But when the chill of autumn began to ease over us, sightings of Bình became rarer, too. He didn't seek me out anymore; the mouse had to become the hunter. And he was wily, disappearing into buildings when I approached, shooting me apologetic smiles as he turned to his friends. Suspicion fell like lead in my stomach.

I began to see him with a girl from the village with immaculately curled hair and glittering jewelry that she flashed in the streets. What could I do with all my resentment? He'd never given me any promises or intentions. Only a single pallid declaration of love, pulled from the heat of our first coupling. That kind of love is as good as a lie. It's meant to cleanse the lovemaking, give it a sheen of respectability. Separating it from mere fucking. I was just the stupid country girl who had opened my legs without asking for more. The other girl would never have done that. She was smart and savvy. She could wait for the real prize.

Soon, Bình's parents announced that he was engaged to the bejeweled girl. My friends sighed, imagining themselves married to such a fine man.

"She'll live like a princess," one friend said. "She'll never have to work another day in her life."

I looked down at my feet.

"She's not even that pretty," they said to me sympathetically.

"I don't care. Why would I?" I'd asked.

"No one said you would, Minh," they said placatingly.

I hadn't told anyone what had happened between Bình and me, but they guessed that I was infatuated, though no one could have possibly known we had shared so many nights, so many forgotten intimacies. They did not suspect someone like me could have lured someone like him. Less so that I would have given in, dismissed our parents' stern teachings for a whisper of pleasure under a waning moon.

"Bình," I said once as he passed. He pretended not to hear, and his name died on my tongue.

Sometimes I imagined cursing him, with impotency or, worse, ugliness, but I knew it did no good. The gods don't listen to sinful girls.

Bình and his girl were married that year. They moved into her parents' house, a gated monstrosity with huge windows and a pointed red roof. I never thought I'd see him alone again, as we had been, and made a kind of fretful peace with that. He had never been mine, anyway. Meanwhile, I missed one cycle, then another. Even so ignorant, I knew what that meant. I had destroyed my own life for a lick of ice cream, a chance to stand in the sun with a handsome, fickle boy. This indiscretion was my legacy, though I turned from it for years, refusing to let truth complicate the destiny I wanted for myself.

Chapter 12

Hương

Mẹ's funeral is a small affair with few of the traditional gestures she would have liked. No one wails. Everyone wears black instead of white. The grief is sedate. If Mẹ had died in Việt Nam, the guests would have paraded through the streets, pounding their chests, our family wearing white headbands and clutching our sorrow like shields. But for me—and Ann—grief is intensely private. Not meant to be experienced as a collective, but as a singular and piercing pain that strikes fast, like a snakebite.

Even still, I feel like apologizing for the civility of her funeral. A woman like her should have commanded more fanfare.

Phước brings his daughters, Meg and Scarlet, and I can tell they're antagonizing Ann, who somehow manages to look cold and polite at the same time. Meg places a hand with rhinestoned neon-yellow nails on Ann's forearm and leans too close, lips curving in a malicious smile. Ann looks down at Meg's hand in distaste until the girl pulls it away. I'm proud of how she carries herself, even though I've felt the bite of her coldness myself, know that it can sting worse than the bitterest wind.

The others mill around us, old acquaintances, people in town who knew Mẹ. They poke at the food, surveying the house with bald curiosity. Sometimes they pull at my shirtsleeve, tsking sympathetically.

They tell me stories I already know about my mother. I can't wait for this to be over.

I could have asked Duke to come, but it didn't seem right to have him here, among my mother's oldest friends and our family. After Mẹ died, we faded from one another's lives. I saw him often at work and he grinned without intention, the way he did with all the other women at the office, and that was fine. I was relieved not to have to discuss it further. Once, his wife and daughters stopped by to pick him up on the way to their family vacation. They wore matching sun hats, and I could tell even the littlest one had polished her toes like rainbow jelly beans. "Daddy! I have a shell bag with *my name on it*!" I had forgotten her name again and felt a shredding guilt inside me, so I turned from them, going into an empty exam room to polish tools that didn't need polishing.

At the funeral, Ann looks lovely, in a black sheath dress that lies stylishly against her. To the outside world, she looks just as she always has. Elegant. Svelte. But to me, she has a new softness about her, apparent in the slight rounding of her hips, the dreamy look that often passes like fog in her expression. How could she have thought she could hide it from me? I have seen pregnant women before, and I know the signs. The long afternoon naps. The vomiting. She thinks I don't hear, but the walls are thin at the Banyan House. Throughout the day, she retches in a nearby toilet, then appears again, wan and sweaty. I want to help, but when I go to her, she turns her back to me.

Finally, when I can't stand it anymore, I grab her arm in the hallway, where she can't avoid me. "Ann, I know about the baby. Please, talk to me."

"Not now," she says tiredly. "After the funeral. Please."

It won't be long before she shows. I wonder how much more time will pass before she acknowledges this baby. Ann, who has always done everything in perfect order, her eye trained toward a future that gleamed as surely as a trophy. But with Noah and her career and that beautiful home in the Midwest, this baby can only be a blessing. I want that joy for her. That stability I never had. Yet I also wonder about the many paths to joy. Hers, I fear, will wind more than others.

Once, I tried leaving a bag of ginger candy on her pillow. The next day, I found it in the trash, not a single candy unwrapped. The stubborn girl.

After the funeral, Phước sets a tray of subs from Publix on the long folding table, each glistening with herbed oil. It's the only thing he contributed, even after the hours of cooking that Ann and I did, but he still lords it over us. The generous brother, who somehow only managed to visit our mother once in the hospital while she was sick. I try to tell myself that not everyone loves the same, but that reasoning doesn't stick.

"I hate hospitals," he'd said.

"No one *likes* them," I replied.

"Get off my back, chị."

He waxed pontific about all his duties as a businessman and how I just couldn't understand because I was *only* a dentist's assistant. His Rolex always flashes as he talks, silvery and beautiful, his prized possession.

Scarlet and Meg, his daughters, are both nurses, and have that capable yet intimidating air I've always associated with the profession. I saw my high school bullies transform into magnanimous, perm-fluffed angels once they became nurses, but secretly, I thought maybe they still lorded over their patients, laughing about the awkward ones in the break room. I'm not a generous person, perhaps. Scarlet and Meg have both gotten nose jobs since we last saw them, and their faces are frozen in formidable expressions, from an excess of Botox, maybe. Beautiful girls, both, though that beauty has already begun to wear thin, like makeup that slicks off in the glaring sunlight. Both have perfected that air of busy nonchalance that Phước gathers around himself.

As I move plates into the dishwasher, Phước's wife, Diane, finds me. Her honey-blond hair is swept into a bun, though her bangs still stick straight out, irrepressible. Today, her eyeshadow is brilliant blue, and her expression reminds me of a pigeon that's just been kicked—startled yet also somehow resigned to its fate. I've known her for decades, and her presence still baffles me.

"How ya holding up, hon?" she asks.

Diane is from north Georgia, near Stone Mountain, and she uses little endearments like seasoning. I don't really like being anyone's "hon," but she's my brother's wife. And he could have done worse. She's not helping with the dishes, but I don't expect her to.

"We're all sad," I say. "It came too soon."

"Yeah, of course, and Minh was so young—well, youngish. You know, Phước"— she says his name with a drawl that I've never gotten used to—"is such a sensitive man that he cried when he heard about Minh? Actual tears, Hương. He didn't eat anything for days. Not even my famous cobbler. Such a good son. They don't make 'em like him anymore."

"Is that so."

"Oh, you bet. I should know, too. My own brothers are trash. And Scarlet and Meg are heartbroken. My sensitive little daisies. They left their jobs to come all the way here, isn't that something?"

"What a gift."

"You're probably glad to have Ann back after all these years. We never see her around anymore."

"She's been here all week," I say, pride touching my voice. "She's been a big help."

"Yes." Diane sighs, her elbows leaning on the island's wooden countertop. "I can see how overwhelming this house is. How hard to take care of. I just imagine the dusting alone. Well, I feel for you."

She ends with a breathy little laugh.

I wait. Diane always has a point, even if it takes her half her life to get there. She's visibly uncomfortable with my silence and begins to pick a nearby napkin into shreds. The detritus looks like a pile of shorn feathers.

"I just mean," she continues, "I can't imagine one person living here by themselves. All that land out back, too. What a *chore*, darlin'."

"My mother managed."

"Well, did she? The place isn't what it used to be. No offense."

Diane never saw the house in its heyday, even, but the Banyan House was never grand. It gave the impression of grandeur from the outside, but nothing about its crowded, faded interior would make anyone envious. With my nail, I scrape a bit of chili sauce off the counter, where it has fallen and stained.

Diane continues, "You know, Phước and I were thinking of upgrading to a bigger place. Scarlet and Meg might even move back home. Of course, with real estate prices, it seems tricky. And this house could be gorgeous with the right touches, you know. As pretty as a B and B in a magazine. Picture it, on the cover of *Garden & Gun*."

The pieces snap together. I stare at Diane until she looks away. I could singe her with my glare if I tried hard enough. All that would be left would be her pearls, clacking on the floor.

"You two have done a lot of planning, haven't you," I say. I hear the acid in my voice, but don't try to contain it.

"Phước talks about it all the time," she says dully, almost apologetically.

He bounds into the kitchen at that moment, rolling up his sleeves to ferret around in the fridge until he finds a bowl of noodles. It annoys me that he makes himself so at home, even though this is his mother's house, too. I study his broad back, already sweaty in the middle, and I think of the boy he was, frail and uncertain. As much my boy as Mẹ's. It's my mental trick—I create these reminders as a way to summon the old love again. It's a horrible thing to dislike your blood sibling.

"What am I talking about now?" he asks, around a mouthful of noodles, slurping loudly. "These could use salt, chị."

He reminds me of a goat when he eats, but Diane looks at him so adoringly, I think, *There really is someone for everyone.*

"You're looking for a bigger house," I repeat.

"Ah yes. Chị, you know how high property taxes are, think of it!

We were hoping to take this house off your hands ... you know Mom would have split it between the two of us, and we would use it so much more. And you have your *own* condo."

"You have your own house," I return. "You never visited."

"Well, I have a family, you know," he says calmly. "Plus, we need the room."

"I don't?"

"Ann is never going to live here and you know it. She'll marry that fancy professor and never come back. Banyan House should go to me. Us."

My mother is hardly in the ground. My daughter is pregnant, though she won't tell me anything about her plans. Yet she is family, of course she is, along with the life inside her, if she decides to keep it. She grew up in the Banyan House, ate at that big oak table until the day I married Gary, planted flowers that never budded, drew on the walls as a toddler, much to my ire. The imprints of her childhood are deep in the grooves of the Banyan House. This house is *hers*, too. At the moment, I am unable to summon an ounce of sibling love for my brother.

"You are a *donkey's asshole*," I grit.

In the wake of his open mouth, his mounting rage—the one trait we do seem to share—I grab a plate of scallion-speckled bánh hỏi and leave him to Diane, who pats his hand as if she's consoling a child.

"Hon," she whines plaintively, "it's not the time. Let it go."

Ann is sitting by herself in the backyard on a canopied swing that my mother bought on a whim at a garage sale and made the homeowner deliver at no extra charge. She was always so proud of the deal, gloating that her nose for a bargain never left her, even if no one in America believed in haggling. It's rusted at the screws and makes small squeaking sounds as it moves. Ann's studying her phone, but tucks it under her thigh when she sees me. I venture to sit next to her.

"Have some noodles," I say.

She puts a square in her mouth. "Mmm. Good."

"Important calls?"

"Never," she says.

"Work?"

She shrugs. I know Ann hasn't drawn at all since she's been back. As a child, she was never without a pencil in her hand, or a brush, filling up sketchbooks and old reams of printer paper I gathered from the dentist's office for her. I'd leave supplies on her bed, silent offerings she never acknowledged. Back then, she drew the house and its weird porcelain dolls, who had lived there long before us. Jungle cats and alligators with gaping maws. The distant outline of airboats in the wetlands. Once, she said she wanted to illustrate a natural guide to the Everglades. This was when she was ten, before she made it her life's goal to leave us behind.

"You could set up a studio in one of the rooms," I say. "Where the light is good."

"*You* want me to set up a studio?"

I don't blame her for her incredulity. When she said she'd be getting a degree in illustration, I scoffed harder than anyone. It was no way to make a living. I wanted to see her in a job where she never had to struggle. I thought of my own days at the restaurant, flitting past the groping hands of men, the sizzle of the woks in the kitchen. To me, being an artist meant living a night life at a restaurant or bar to make ends meet. I was wrong, but I don't think she's ever forgiven me for instilling the doubt within her.

"This is just temporary," she reminds me, "playing house here with you. I'll go home soon."

I'm surprised by how much those words sting. "Okay. I'm just saying."

We rock for a little longer. The branches of the banyan tree in front of us are noodly, white-fleshed in the glow of afternoon sun. Beyond them, the cypress trees are dense, clustered together as if avoiding the banyan tree, that giant tentacled bully. A hornet lands on a pink thistle nearby and we watch it loop away from us.

"It's so hot out here," Ann says, fanning herself. "Florida. Global warming. Hell on a platter."

She moves her phone to the other side of her. After all these years, she's so protective of her privacy. I think about the time I ransacked her room, looking for any information on the new boyfriends she was dating—a condom or an illicit note, I'm not sure what. When she found me, she just looked disdainful. I was holding a shoebox full of notes from her friends, folded into origami hearts, each one as innocent and silly as the next. I was looking for smut and was vaguely disappointed, I admit, that I didn't find any.

"It's hot in there, too," I joke. "You were surrounded on all sides by those ridiculous girls."

She cracks a smile. "Scarlet and Meg are something else. They kept talking to me about how they were going to open up a *bistro*; an upscale Vietnamese French fusion place. Nursing's boring, I guess. Fusion. Not the worst idea, imperialist politics aside."

"They're like their dad. Always looking for bigger and better."

"Aren't we all."

"Have you talked to your uncle?"

"He hasn't found me yet. Though Diane did. Look at this." She juts her cheek out toward me, where I can see the faint outline of a pink lipstick stain. "I scrubbed and scrubbed."

"You'll have to move quicker next time."

I'm surprised when she starts to laugh, but the sound is so lovely that I have to close my eyes, basking in it as I would in a warm bath.

The lightning bugs begin to emerge. They dip in and out of the banyan tree, their green lights flashing for just a second. The tree looks like it's lit from within, sparkling, even. Ann jiggles her foot and a lightning bug darts away. When she stops laughing, her expression tugs downward.

"I hate that she was alone when it happened," Ann says. "I can't stop thinking about it."

"Me too. She made me go home early that night, said she deserved some peace after so many years of raising us all."

"I guess she did. You think Bà Ngoại died peacefully?" Ann asks.

"I do," I tell my daughter, though I don't know anything for certain.

Maybe I'm reassuring us both. "She lived a big life. Saw more than most people have. She would have been content with everything she accomplished."

"Really?" Ann is skeptical. "She always seemed so . . . traditional. Like she only wanted a safe life."

"Your bà ngoại had her secrets. Her life didn't start with you, you know."

I think about how my mother once bundled me and Phước up in our winter warmest, scarves and gloves and coats that cost a fortune, all to get us on the plane to America. We never knew why we had to leave so quickly, with scarcely time to say goodbye to our friends and teachers. I remember how, on arriving in Florida, we had silently accepted cardboard boxes full of clothes and canned goods from the Baptist church ladies who clucked their tongues at the mosquito bites on our legs, the unwashed garments that hung from our thin bodies. The parking lot was full of refugees like us, each looking sadder and more displaced than the last.

"Say thank you," Mẹ reminded us, her lips barely moving, her face ashen from the journey.

When Phước tried to whine, she pinched him on the arm and he bit off his cry with a hiccup.

We were gangly brown kids who fit every vision of at-home missionary work those church ladies ever had. They pressed Bibles into our hands, which we took without comment. Later, we'd use them as coasters, placing cups of ice water on them until ivory circles melted into the covers.

"Thank God y'all are here now," those ladies said, each bland expression covered in pity. That pity was almost erotic to them, though I couldn't have named that back then. The exquisite pleasure of schadenfreude.

"Yes, thank you, yes," Mẹ said, nodding her head, using the only English words she knew.

Every morning in those early years, the three of us ate Spam sandwiches with a side of canned green beans and big glasses of whole milk, because Mẹ thought it was good for us. She said, "You get big and strong, my little soldiers." The milk of the heaven-bound, so white and cold. Mom poured it into our mouths until we were sick from all the sodium and lactose. We went to school uncomfortable, but knowing we should be grateful anyway. To the church ladies, to America for accepting us, the people our own country didn't want. I usually vomited up all the milk at school in the bathroom and tried to clean it up as best I could. I heard the girls whispering.

"Is she bulimic?" The word was new to me, of course.

"No way. I thought them people were all *starving* or something, that's what my mama said."

"Sure looks like a skinny mantis."

"But brown. Not green."

Phước later admitted he'd been sick at school, too. Neither of us drink milk now. That memory makes me feel a little softer toward my brother, the two of us trying so hard yet never quite finding our way.

So in my estimation, Mẹ lived a life that could only be counted as brave. Who could blame her for wanting some safety, after those years of war and uncertainty? But how could I say that to my daughter, the child we all protected like she was a glass figurine? Her privilege was cultivated; we were all complicit in wrapping her in tissue, shielding her from the outside.

"I guess I always knew she had secrets," Ann says. "You both are good at hiding things."

You too, con, I want to tell her.

"We don't really know what's inside another person's heart," I say instead.

"Probably for the best."

We stay out there, swaying gently, until someone calls for me in the house. I get up, reluctant to leave Ann, but to my surprise, she follows me. Her eyes are downcast, but I can see the fading damp spot on her dress where tears have fallen.

Chapter 13

Ann

Mom, Phước, Diane, and I cram into the lawyer's office, with Phước and Diane sitting in the plush chairs in front of the desk, and Mom and I leaning against the ledge near the shelves. Scarlet and Meg are back at their hotel, likely working on their suntans by the pool.

"They were just *overwhelmed* with grief," Diane says, her eyes misty.

"Hope they can find the strength to carry on," I say, blinking wide eyes at Phước's glare.

The lawyer, Mr. Vincenzo, is apologetic that there isn't more seating. He says the conference room is undergoing renovations. I'm not sure why I'm there, except that Mom asked me to come. The coffee is outrageously bad, thin and a little rancid, but I'm desperate to drink it. I haven't slept well in ages. I can't seem to get comfortable in my old bed, lumpy and mildewed as it is.

"Well, let's get down to it," Phước says. Whenever he uses American idioms, he claps his hands together, like a tic to cover up how uncomfortable they are for him, a kind of costumery he's trying on. He's flush with impatience.

Diane examines the hem of her flowered dress. Her heels click on the ground as she rearranges herself. She's dolled up like they're going to church, and maybe after this they are. I know she's converted Phước to Christianity, which is its own kind of hilarity, imagining

Phước jittering his legs in a pew, tallying up the cost of all the hand-carved Christs and stained-glass windows. But living here, where churchgoing equals decency, Phước plays along. Always the survivalist, my uncle.

"Right." Mr. Vincenzo clears his throat. His speckled beard has a Santa Clausian feel to it, wiry and neatly pointed, like the end of a heart. "I need to start by saying that your mother wrote this will when she was of completely sound mind and has committed to it entirely. My role is to make sure everything is carried out."

"Of course," Phước says. "We know how this works."

He's literally sitting on the edge of his chair. His desperation makes me uncomfortable, and I counteract it by closing my eyes, imagining myself anywhere else but here. There's a sheen of unreality to the day. Reading Bà Ngoại's will. Navigating this life without her. I feel like standing up and politely leaving the room. "I'd rather not," I'd say.

Mr. Vincenzo goes on.

"To you, Phước and Diane, your mother bequeaths the contents of her savings. After funeral costs, you're left with a very tidy sum. And your daughters will receive her investments, which are considerable."

My mind hums with the word: *bequeath*. It's so elegant. A gift, buoyed by the dignity of the law.

"Really?" Phước asks. His eyes bug. "Investments?"

"Her advisor was a shark. And she spent very little these last few years."

Mr. Vincenzo pushes two pieces of paper toward Phước, who shares them with Diane. They look pleased. I never put much thought into Bà Ngoại's finances, only that she reassured me she was just fine, I never needed to send money her way. It's hard to imagine my grandmother at a bank or making choices with her savings. But of course she did. She was savvy. It does her no justice to think of her as incapable in any aspect of her life.

The lawyer continues, "To you, Hương, your mother has bequeathed her Oldsmobile."

Phước grins into his fist; the car is a piece of shit, more an object of sentimentality than one of usefulness. Mom takes the news stoically, as if she needed another clunker sitting in her driveway beside her new Toyota. But I actually like the Oldsmobile. Bà Ngoại used to take me to school in it, and it was in such bad condition that the top of the car was falling apart, the cloth scraping the crown of her head as she drove. We used thumbtacks to attach it back in place. The car is in no better condition now, but I think of the soaring songs we'd play, the way we'd rap the top of the car with our knuckles through the open windows. It felt like we were flying down the coast, away from everything that tied us down. I wonder if Mom would sell it to me.

"And for you, Ann, your grandmother wanted you to have her jewelry. Here's the safe combination." At this, Phước looks like he's about to protest, but then he droops when the lawyer says, "As I mentioned, this is fully binding."

"And what about the house?" Diane asks softly. Her bangs wave slightly, ridiculously.

"Oh yes. Well, this is a bit peculiar. The house is split," Mr. Vincenzo begins.

"Oh, we expected that. My sister and I have a plan," Phước says with a blustering little smile. Mom won't meet his eye. Instead, she's holding her hands tight in her lap, worrying the edge of her mouth with her front teeth. Without thinking about it, I reach over to take one of her hands.

"Well," Mr. Vincenzo says, discomfited, "It's split in half between Hương and Ann, actually. They are joint owners of the home and its land."

I drop Mom's hand, and it lands with a soft sound on her thigh. For a moment everyone is silent. Then Phước erupts, his eyes bulging, his fist banging on the desk while Diane fruitlessly grabs his arm, tries to get him to still. When he stands, it's at a slight angle, as if he'll topple over on the lawyer if pushed with a featherlight touch.

"The fuck they are," he says.

"Hon," she pleads.

"Goddammit, I *knew* something like this would happen," Phước says. "She's always liked Hương best, and Ann, even though she isn't even her child. Did my mother ever give Scarlet or Meg a bit of attention? My poor children."

Mr. Vincenzo, with a crackle in his officious manner, says, "They do receive Minh's investments. If they choose, they can cash those in for quite a bit."

Phước ignores him and turns to my mother and me. "How did you do it? How did you wedge yourself in?"

"Shut up, Phước," Mom says. She's calm, preternaturally so.

"I think we should take a beat," Diane says.

Mr. Vincenzo stands, as if to usher us all out. "Excellent idea. Well then, if that's all."

"This isn't *legal*," Phước fumes. "I'm going to go see a lawyer about this. A real one."

Mr. Vincenzo nods. "You're welcome to contest it. But mostly, it would mean a loss of time and money for you, Mr. Tran."

"My mother couldn't have meant this."

"We talked about it at length, and I assure you, she did. Her reasons were her own. Good day, all."

Dismissed, we find ourselves deposited in the book-lined waiting room. Mr. Vincenzo seems to find this bit of his job tawdry, and I have to agree. Humming softly, I look through his law books, not a single one of them interesting. There's a little sketch of a farmhouse in the waiting room, and it's very pretty, detailed. I think of *Anne of Green Gables* when I see it, and wish I could escape to Prince Edward Island, or anywhere else, away from this room where my aunt and uncle are staring at us as if we've committed the biggest of betrayals.

Phước glares for a few moments longer, then turns to leave, pulling Diane along with him.

"This isn't the last of it," he throws over his shoulder.

Diane waves faintly, forgetting already that she's supposed to be mad at us. "Stay out of the rain, y'all."

It's not raining, but by the time we get to the car, big drops do indeed begin to fall. Diane is flighty, but she's rarely wrong about the weather.

At home, Mom dangles Bà Ngoại's Oldsmobile keys in front of me. "Do you want a crappy old car?"

I huff a laugh, the tension of the lawyer's office steaming out of me. I take the keys and settle into the driver's seat, which smells faintly of fast food and car freshener. There's a paper straw wrapper in the center console, coiled up like a weather-beaten worm. The radio is set to the local news station. Mom gets in the passenger seat.

With nowhere to go, we drive to the beach. We don't discuss this as our destination, but the call of the surf pulls us closer, past the old sandwich shop that made mayonnaise-clumped tuna subs, the beach hut that sold expired sunscreen, and the weird little New Age boutique where I worked my first job, asking the owner on my first day what a "yoni" was and blushing red-hot through the explanation. The sameness is a comfort.

"Your brother is horrible," I say to Mom.

"I know. A real shithead, isn't he? He wasn't always, though."

"As long as I've been alive."

"That's right," she agrees.

"Did you know? That she was going to give us the house?"

She sighs. "I guess she did say something to me about it. I didn't really think she would. I don't know what I thought."

"You okay, Mom?" I ask.

"No," she answers. "I'm supposed to say I'm fine. To be the strength for you, but I don't have it in me today."

The wind is salty that day, and I can taste the aftermath of the storm. I feel wild. Like I could fly.

"It's okay, Mom. You don't have to be anything but who you are."

"Bà Ngoại was the string tying us all together. Mẹ and Phước. Mẹ and you. I feel like I'm unraveling without her."

"We both are."

That acknowledgment seems to comfort us, the naming of the grief. We park, then sit on the beach, our feet pressed into the damp sand. The waning day is starting to cool, and I wish I had a sweater. The water feels restless, as if sounding answers to questions we never asked, each wave lapping over the next, a series of clamorous interruptions. Once I thought it would be nice to be absorbed by a big family like the Winthorpes. Kids scrambling over laps, trailing their shoelaces in wide loops. Adults throwing back cocktails while they gossip lightly about the neighbors. But rather, my fate seems to be an attenuation of family. One less grandmother. One less lover.

"Ann, tell me about the baby," Mom says.

Here, outside the Banyan House and all the history holding us back, I describe the small fluttering of hope I feel, along with the dread of raising a child on my own. The loss of my life with Noah, the tidiness of it all. I tell her about his infidelity, his family's crushing gaslighting.

"Those absolute fuckers," she says fiercely.

"You always liked him, Mom."

"I never met him. I just liked that he was able to give you this life that . . . well, a different life. You seemed happy. Were you?"

"I was really good at pretending I was. And some of the happiness was real. Not enough, apparently, but some."

"Women have stayed for less."

There's a catch in her voice and I think she'll say more, but when she doesn't continue, I say, "I haven't told him about the baby. Because now it's just pathetic. A ploy or a trap."

"Do *you* think the child is a trap? Not for him. Who the hell cares about him. But for you."

I don't have an answer. I *want* the baby. But that desire doesn't make me any less afraid. Is that how all mothers feel? If this were a sitcom, I'd ask Mom that question and let her comfort me. The waves absorb the sounds of our voices, washing them away and around us. I'd been afraid Mom would find a way to scold me, even though I'm past scolding age, but she takes the news calmly. No mention of wedlock or sin, though that was never really her way. Maybe it's good timing, strangely, the grief of Bà Ngoại dulling her more primal instincts toward anger. Or maybe I have again underestimated her capacity for empathy.

She glances down at my stomach, still the same, and I have this sense that she would like to touch it. But I don't offer. If anything, I angle my body away from her. This baby is mine, all mine. I don't realize I said it aloud until Mom speaks.

"Of course it's yours, con, who else's would it be?" she says.

"Sorry, I didn't mean that. It's just been a day. A series of days."

"What will you do, Ann?"

"I never really thought there was a decision. I just know that my body screams yes. My heart, too."

"Will you stay?"

"The million-dollar question."

Though the Banyan House is legally mine, too, I think of how easily it would be to just leave it with her. I know she would take care of it; sell it or live in it, whatever. And I could go back to Noah. He'd apologize and dote on me, feeding me ice cream while speculating on names for the baby. We'd likely get married. Alice and Brandon wouldn't be able to argue against the rightness of our marriage if there was a Winthorpe heir on the line. It would be so easy.

And yet the thought of drifting back to the old life makes my stomach feel taut. It's as if I've walked into a gorgeous new house, looked it over, and stepped off the threshold, thinking politely yet firmly, *No, thank you. I'll wait for better. I'll wait for truer.*

But Noah is not the only choice. I could pack up and go somewhere new. I feel the edge of excitement at the thought. A small acceleration of my heartbeat. There are beaches in California, too; strangers, among whom I could start a new life. The sequoias and deep canyons of the West could call to me. I could work anywhere and be anyone. I don't have to be the woman Noah cheated on, or the grieving grandchild caged in a crumbling house. The past doesn't have to mean anything for me and my baby.

I tell her, "I'm thinking of moving away. I don't know where."

"Alone?" Mom is aghast.

"People do it all the time. I can, too."

"But the baby. You would raise it without a father?"

"You managed. So did Bà Ngoại."

"Neither by choice," she says.

"So maybe I'll do things differently."

Mom is quiet, and I trace the sun's slow dip. We hear the gulls' cries drown in the crash of the surf. By the water, a family poses in their blue jeans and white shirts, the unofficial uniform of family portraits, a photographer in black trailing them. The purple sky is shot with gold, framing a glowing sun.

The sun makes me think of the yolk of balut, creamy and primal. Bà Ngoại knew the fertilized duck embryo terrified me, with its thicket of wet fur and the tiny fragile beak. So after she'd cracked the blue-white shells, she would scoop the embryo out and eat it herself, turning her back to me so I wouldn't see. She'd leave only the rich yolk behind on a plate for me. Sanitized of context, though still streaked with brown veins that I tried to ignore. She had taken my fears and left behind a gift of comfort.

On the beach, the family's silhouettes become molded together until they are one shapeless blob rather than a series of individual shadows. Somewhere down the way, someone laughs loudly. The sand blows onto our feet.

"Whatever you decide, we need to make sure the baby will be healthy. So take your time. Go wherever you need to. I won't stop you," Mom says.

"You won't?"

She sighs. "You're an adult, Ann. But you haven't done this before. Just for now, let me help. Let me be your mother."

"I might not stay for long," I say. She hears the warning: *Don't get too attached. Don't hope for what I can't give.*

"Understood," she says, brushing her lap of sand. She stretches her hand toward me and I take it. Her grip is surprisingly firm. "We have a lot to do."

"Like what?"

She cocks her head, as if in disbelief that I would not remember this basic teaching. "We're going to the temple. We have to get your baby blessed."

Chapter 14

Minh, 1965

The fall after my summer indiscretion, after my own body's terrible betrayal, we learned about a young Quaker in America who had set himself on fire in protest of the war. He had been holding his eleven-month-old infant in his arms. My mother covered her ears when she heard. She shouted at my father to keep his horrible news to himself. We all sobered at the thought of the child, Emily Morrison, going up in flames. But later, we learned she was spared at the last moment. Alive, if traumatized, like us all.

"Emily," my father said, sounding out the syllables on his tongue. "Em. Lee." Phonetically spoken in Vietnamese, the words mean "bad child."

"What did I say?" my mother screamed. She refused to talk about the deaths in the village, even as the boys began to leave for war. Sometimes, I found her crouched in the shade in our backyard, weeping silently.

Through her, I understood that another mother's horror could touch us in the darkest of places, even a world away. I did not yet feel tied to that great tribe of mothers; to me, my indiscretion shut me off from the tender feelings of joy, of hope. I could only survive.

That was around the time when I began to notice Xuân. He was one of my brother Thien's many friends, and the least memorable of the bunch. There were always boys running around our house, inside and out, causing me more trouble, more cooking and cleaning and shushing. For all our lack of money, our parents never begrudged friends in the house. They were sociable people and liked the cry of boys, their loud clamor. Now more than ever, when they began disappearing to the jungles, bravely outfitted to fight a war they barely understood, my mother seemed to open her arms wider, as if she could save them all by loving them harder.

At first, Xuân was like another brother to me, long legged and annoying as the rest. He'd lean over the pot as I steamed the fish, reaching in for a hunk of white flesh with his dirty fingers.

"Out," I'd say, snapping my tongs at him. Sometimes throwing a heel of ginger at his laughing, retreating form.

"You're so vicious, em. Luckily, you make the most delicious food," he said, even though I was a terrible cook. "One day you are going to be a good wife."

I shooed him away. "Don't worry about my future. Worry about yourself, boy."

He grinned, his silliness so unprotected that I had to hide my own answering smile, until we heard Thien call, "Xuân! Leave my sister alone. Let's go fish."

Xuân followed him around like a puppy, eager and sometimes a little cowed by Thien's authority. The rest of the boys liked to wrestle in the dirt, hitting each other where it hurt when the adults weren't looking. They weren't troublemakers, but there was violence in them that they needed to get out. It sank into their skin like dust. But Xuân never hit anyone, standing to the side with a lopsided smile as his friends beat each other to a pulp. Something about that unwillingness to engage in the fighting—even the pretend kind—made me feel safe. I saw in him the things other girls overlooked.

His face was pockmarked lightly with a childhood illness, and he had a shock of dark brown hair that glinted with red highlights in the sun. He wasn't terribly ambitious or charming, but he was steady.

Maybe it was that knowledge that made me change my mind about him. I could see the goodness, shining like a streak of light in his eyes. Maybe it could be as easy as that.

When I sought him out, he gently turned to me, like blossoms toward the sun. We talked shyly at first, then with increasing intimacy. We spoke about his parents' worries for his younger sister, a sickly child prone to seizures. I divulged my dreams of far-off travel. Of opening a business in town.

"You'll go anywhere you want. You just have good fortune, I can tell," he said.

It pleased me to be spoken about so flatteringly. "Oh, you are a psychic now, anh?"

"A face like that is destined for much more than this village of ours."

Once I stopped thinking of him as an annoying older brother, I trusted him like a friend. We knew each other's secret hurts by that time, almost all of them, and we reveled in this new sensation of adulthood. Of being together. Everyone in the house saw it happening and gently let us alone, even Thien, who was at first put off that his friend was now angling after his sister.

"He's not even that handsome," Thien said over dinner. "Not that you're a catch either, Minh."

My mother pinched the skin of his wrist with her chopsticks until he yelped. "There are better things than handsome. We know his family. He grew up with Minh. He'll keep her safe during these unsafe times."

After that, Thien didn't say anything else, and I found myself relying more on Xuân than I ever thought I would. One day, standing by the river where I first met Bình, I told him about the pregnancy, then starting to shape itself inside me. At first, Xuân didn't believe it, but when I repeated myself, my head hung in shame, he cradled his face in his hands. I didn't think he'd look at me again. I worried he would tell my parents. They would send me to the nuns. I would never see my baby.

Then he said, "We can solve this together, em."

When I looked up at him, I saw only shining hope.

He asked my brother if he could ask me to marry him, then received the same blessing from my parents. They were at first reluctant to lose me, their only girl, the helper in the household of four children, but I was almost done with secondary school and we had all felt this coming, like distant drumbeats. It was my time. Our engagement was quick, at Xuân's insistence. Our parents grumbled about the rush, but they relented. Within a month, we were married in my parents' house, under the shade of the trees. No one thought to wonder at mischief; I had been a shy girl all my life, and Xuân was as solid as an old mountain.

There was a slow fall of rain the day we married. He was earnest as he approached me in a newly purchased suit the color of a river stone. His eyes took in my silk áo dài, overlaid with a jacket of white lace, and they were adoring, not a hint of admonishment in their depths. This was a man wholly incapable of cruelty. He was only foolish enough to love a woman who didn't yet love him in return. I tried not to think of Bình as Xuân planted a chaste kiss on my lips in front of our families. Our hands were sweaty during the reception, but I often caught him looking for me, awe in his expression.

On our wedding night, he was gentle, stroking softly around my rounding stomach. He looked to me for permission, though he was my husband, and any other man would have taken what he wanted without asking. Did he fool himself into thinking he was the father? Was I worth the delusion? When he entered me, I felt no pain, and he saw no blood, but we never mentioned my past transgressions, not then and not at any time during our marriage. We were joined; we were a new family. We ached for it, so it happened. Forgiveness our baptism. That's how dreams sometimes work.

When he rolled over afterward, I saw the mole on his back, and thought how familiar it would become over the course of our marriage. The years of staring at one man's mole. I loved what Xuân had done for me. I also hated myself for taking advantage of such goodness, and truthfully, I hated him a little for allowing me to. Our marriage started on complicated terms, is what I mean to say.

Months later, Hương was born. She was small enough that we could pretend she was premature. Each tiny toe was curled inward, almost amphibian in their bland, shiny smoothness. Her eyes were large and seeking. She latched onto my breast immediately and suckled so hard that I gasped from the pain. I named her for the scent of flowers, for that arching sweetness under the trees, fragrant and young and stupid. It was the closest I got to acknowledging Bình as her father.

Xuân and I didn't have much to our name, but we were comfortable, living with his parents in their three-story house. One story for each offshoot of the clan. His sister liked the company of another young woman, and we would sit together on chairs near the altar, breathing in the incense as we read together. The top floor was ours, and though it got hot up there, I tried to make it nice by sewing curtains out of voile and pillowcases out of fabric his parents gave us. For all the outward prettiness of our new home, it wasn't easy. Hương's newborn wails shook the house at all hours. I imagined my in-laws clutching their hands to their ears, but like their son, they were flawlessly kind. They never said a word of reproach, though I knew young couples who'd gotten kicked out of their ancestral homes for lesser disturbances. Xuân's mother often came up to hold Hương, gently bouncing her on her knee.

"What's the matter, little one, my angel, my precious?" she would murmur.

"Nothing at all," I'd say, frustrated.

"Don't you worry. She'll find her way. Such a fighter, this one. She'll be a general in the army before long."

"No," I said angrily. "She won't bloom in war. She will live a perfectly ordinary life."

Xuân's mother nodded. "A mother's wish."

I thought again of the Quaker and his immolation. Some walk toward the fire; others, like me, skirt far away.

Hương seemed discomfited in her own body from the start, as if she were ready to waddle away from our grasp. She was never content, even after she'd glutted herself during a feeding or had a long night's rest. I wondered, sometimes, if she understood how deeply flawed I was as a mother. If she was hoping to find someone else to carry her to safety. To me, there has always been something unearthly about babies. They exist on the very fringe of the sublime. I trust their wisdom more than I do that of grown men. Yet it felt difficult to love my daughter in the way she needed.

During Hương's third month, she settled down, resigned to the new world in which she'd found herself. She never quite lost the sullen look, but she wasn't screaming anymore, at least. Xuân tucked a blanket around her proudly.

"What a beauty she is," he said.

"She is that," I replied, a little bitter still from the sleepless nights, all that horrible crying.

"And so are you, em."

He crept into bed beside me and gently lifted my shirt. Everything about my husband was gentle, even his lovemaking, a far cry from the sharp pain and rearing passion I had experienced under the trees with Bình. But our pleasure still came, easy and unrushed. I know I was luckier than most. I sighed under his hands, wrapped my legs around his body.

"My flower," he whispered in my ears. "My great love."

Xuân never indicated that Hương was anything but his; if anyone wondered at the timeline, they kept it to themselves. His name protected me from any gossip. But still, I wanted Xuân to have a child of his own. I thought that would be the last thread to tie us together.

"I'd like a boy," he answered when I brought it up. "Or another girl. It doesn't matter, if it's ours."

"Ours," I repeated, feeling a scabbed-over part of me start to reopen.

"Just like Hương," he said quickly, kissing me on the bare shoulder.

We waited for the child, another link, but every month, the blood ran from me.

One day, I went to the market for winter melon, Xuân's favorite. Hương was strapped on my hip, and together we were one, darting carefully past the crowds of people, skipping across muddy yellow pools. For once, she didn't cry, though she grunted fitfully. Later, we'd discover she had colic, but there was nothing much we could do for her.

The market was cool that day from a sudden rain, and everything felt fresh and green. I sprung for a bit of pork, hoping to fill out the dinner soup. Pork was rare and precious, and in America in my later years, I'd marvel at the different cuts at the grocery store: ground pork, loin, ribs, belly, whole pink rectangles of luxury. The refrigerated, spotlighted rows went on and on, and everyone leaned forward, grabbed what they needed, not one bit grateful for the bounty they had.

At the market, there was only one vendor who sold meat, and she was stingy. We all suspected she weighted the scales in her own favor. I had to haggle for five minutes, with increasing loudness, and even then, I had only a couple of ounces in my plastic satchel when I left. Enough for flavoring, but not for satisfaction.

Across the way, at a stall that sold drinks and salty snacks, I saw Bình sitting with some friends in front of beers. They were playing cards, loudly pushing each other when someone lost a hand. Bình's face was beet red and gleaming, but still, that smile caught the light, his white teeth winking. I caught his eye and for a second, I thought he'd turn away. But then he looked at Hương. His mouth slackened. Even inebriated, he may have done the calculations. I thought he'd get up and come to us. Maybe I hoped for it. What would he have said? Would anything have been enough to make up for his betrayal?

"Old man," one of his friends said, "stop looking at pretty mamas. Focus on your hand."

"He forgets he's married," another man said, clapping Bình on the shoulder.

"No, he definitely doesn't forget, but he hopes his mistresses will," someone guffawed.

Bình cleared his throat and took another swig of his beer. He turned to his cards and punched his friends lightly. He never looked back at us. Like that, the moment passed. We were strangers again, former classmates who could barely remember each other's names.

I looked down at a squirming Hương and said, "Let's get home to your father."

That night, after I served the melon soup that Xuân raved about, I put the baby down to sleep and took my husband to bed, this time with purpose. We moved together in the night, muffling our moans so his family couldn't hear, again and again, unable to resist pulling each other closer for one more embrace. It was the most passionate we'd been with each other, and we woke shyly in each other's arms.

Two months later, to Xuân's great joy, I found out that I was pregnant with our son, Phước, named for "luck." Now that I am dead, I can say it was not so much a conception of love as desperation. Wanting to create an undeniable foundation that no one could take away from our family. Before Phước's arrival, Xuân spent hours sitting on the doorstep, whittling a little boat out of wood for his new son, then carefully painting the sails blue. He painted one for Hương, too, but she lost it within days, crying as it sailed away down the stream.

"I'll make you another," Xuân promised, though time got away from him, and he never did.

After Phước was born, I watched Xuân bend his head over his son, admiring the same reddish-brown glints in the baby's hair. He handed the baby the blue boat, which he couldn't pick up, of course, but flailed toward anyway.

"Our boy looks just like you, anh," I said.

"Little man. And my gorgeous girls. How did I get so lucky?"

I was the lucky one. I pledged right then and there that I would change our fortune. My children would never want for anything, and my husband would be proud that he'd married me. I'd never be a burden to these treasures that the gods had entrusted to me.

Chapter 15

A n n

In the midst of scouring and purging the house, I find the albums.

Bà Ngoại doesn't have many photos from Việt Nam, but there is one photo of her and Ông Ngoại, before he died. Even in this small glimpse, I see that they are an unlikely match. Where she was fresh in dewy beauty, he seemed to exude a certain coarseness, uncomfortable in front of the camera. He wasn't handsome or stately, but I think I would have liked him.

Bà Ngoại never remarried, but she also didn't like to talk about Ông Ngoại.

When I had asked as a child, she rebuked me. "Hush, child. The dead don't like to stir."

Mom tells me her father was a kind man, from the limited memories she has of him, but that he was never the driver of the family fortune. Bà Ngoại was the one who had saved their pennies to open the little jewelry shop. She worked there tirelessly, day and night, her kids playing on the mat next to her as she talked to customers, able to coax a purchase out of everyone who walked through the doors. Ông Ngoại was helpful, hanging signs and taking over for her so she could cook dinner, but he was just as content sitting on the front porch reading the newspaper. He had none of her ambition, but took her goals as his own out of love and loyalty.

I think of Noah and how driven he is, the opposite of my ông ngoại. He continues to call. Sometimes I answer and we talk lightly of other things. He asks when I'm coming home—just to talk, he insists—though every time, there is a little less conviction. Less entitlement in his right to know the answer.

I know it's time to tell him about the baby, but still, I don't. I can't, until I know what to do. I'm afraid that if I tell Noah, he'll swoop in and claim the baby for himself. He's a current. He pulls and pulls, until my feet lift from the ground, and I have no choice but to follow. It gives me no pleasure to think of myself that way. But that's how it's always been.

When I first met Noah at the University of Michigan, I was a college junior. He was, in a predictable turn of events, my handsome, bespectacled TA. By then, I knew I would be an artist—or at least get really poor in the pursuit—but I couldn't fill my schedule with only studio classes, so I enrolled in an Intro to Classics course that my roommate assured me would be an easy A, since the professor was more prone to napping than lecturing. I noticed Noah immediately, as all the girls did. He stood to the side, a serious look on his face, that handsome sandy hair always perfectly arranged, the loafers shined to a gleam. I wondered what it would be like to see a man like him in a mess. All my life, I'd only been with messy men. Other artists, musicians, boys who preferred to get drunk on Pabst in a friend's den than go to a museum with me. But I was ready for something new when I met Noah. A real love story.

Once, when I turned in a paper, Noah grazed my hand with his. He smiled. "All okay with the assignment?"

"Peachy." I beamed.

More often than not, my eyes stayed on my notes, throughout which I had doodled all sorts of things I missed from home. Bà Ngoại's spring rolls, nearly bursting from the rice paper, dense with filling. An egret stalking across a parking lot. The shadowy exterior of the Banyan House. For someone so determined to flee their home, my longing often escaped through my drawings. Once, during an assignment for a studio class, I built a three-story dollhouse with miniatures, each grimed over purposefully with paint, the rooms haunted with objects and dirty clothing.

"This is Southern Gothic," my teachers praised. "The detail here."

I didn't tell anyone that it was a real house, and we were a real family that lived there. Let them think that the macabre lived in my art alone.

One day, I caught Noah's eye during a lecture on the Roman gods. The professor was speaking about bacchanal rituals. In a perfectly dry tone, he discussed orgies as if he were describing root canals. Noah yawned, but tried to hide it.

"Flesh met flesh, in a slapping symphony of hedonism. It was highly exciting," the professor said, his voice so flat and sleepy that I burst out laughing.

"Ms. Tran?" the professor asked, turning to me with owl eyes suddenly become alert and a little irritated. "Is everything all right?"

"Oh. Yes. I was just . . . overly excited," I said.

Noah choked into his hand. When the professor wasn't looking, he winked my way. Afterward, he stopped me on the pretense of talking to me about my paper on Roman amphorae. We met for a drink. Then another. And on the day of our last classics quiz—I got a B+—we went back to his apartment, where he lived alone, not with roommates like everyone else I knew. The furniture was tasteful, and the art lovely, if predictable. He later told me Alice had picked it out. She liked an outdoor art fest, that one. We drank a whole bottle of wine, plus a couple of cocktails. He reached out to tuck my hair behind my ear and leaned close, so I could smell the Luxardo cherries on his breath.

"I think kissing you would taste like panna cotta," he said, a little drunkenly.

"Like what?"

I vaguely remembered what panna cotta was. Wes once took me to a candlelit Italian restaurant before our senior prom. We never went to such places and didn't know how to pronounce most of the dishes, and when the panna cotta got delivered, on its little plate with its perfect milky exterior, we spooned crescent-shaped white moons into each other's mouths, tasting the cool cream as it slithered on our tongues.

"This shit is good," Wes had said.

"Rich shit," I laughed back.

Despite myself, I was impressed that Noah could, even after all those drinks, reference panna cotta. It felt like an oddly urbane kind of compliment. The people I grew up with, Wes and Crystal and the rest, would have scorned such a compliment. We would have called it bougie. But I liked it from Noah.

"And maybe a swipe of strawberry ganache," he said, crooking a small part of his mouth.

He kissed me. I was a goner.

After that night, we were inseparable. Our friends began to refer to us as "A & N," not bothering to say our full names. At his place, my toothbrush moved in first, then a pair of silky pajamas, and before long, I had let my lease run out. After I graduated and he got a position at a liberal arts university nearby, he bought a lake house for us—with help from that old trust fund. Our lives slid together like tectonic plates, ever so infinitesimally, until we couldn't picture them apart.

In the years after college, with Noah's encouragement, I became an illustrator. First a few odd jobs here and there as I worked office jobs, then a full-on career in freelance illustration. Bà Ngoại had been befuddled: "You really make a living this way, con?" Mom, less tactful: "What a *waste* of an education, Ann." But I was surprised to find how much I loved my job, the mad dash of it, the unexpected storytelling and lightning-quick deadlines. I also liked proving Mom wrong.

Everyone said to Noah and me, "What a happy couple."

I believed it most of all.

Now, in Bà Ngoại's house, I study the photo of her and Ông Ngoại. I don't know if their marriage was a passionate one, or if it was sedate and quiet. Mom couldn't give me any answers, and there was a deep canyon, a lifetime, between us all.

Chapter 16

Hương

Spring has arrived on the Gulf Coast, but in any other part of the country, some might call it summer, with its days edging toward triple digits. Snowbirds have gone back to their big old houses up north, carrying with them overpriced seashell trinkets for their grandchildren and artisanal berry-flavored vinegars that will remind them of the shore. They leave middling tips for their housecleaners and the unwanted detritus of their prolonged vacations, wide-brimmed hats with polka-dotted ribbons and boat shoes that will crust with salt and mold over before winter. The restaurants and tourist traps sit abandoned before the next flux of migrants, spring breakers with oversize beach bags and bustling entitlement. For just a few weeks, the coast belongs to the locals again.

Though the mornings are still cool, by afternoon heat pulses across my skin, through the layers of clothing I wear. At five A.M., before work and before Ann wakes, I drive to the Y. I put on a rubber swim cap and slip into the water, where I, along with four other adult swimmers, learn the mechanics of swimming while trying fervently not to fall asleep in the icy water. We practice angling our bodies, stroking with proper form. Our teacher, Beth, a younger woman with thick waterproof mascara and a nest of pine needle hair, shows us how to place our faces in the water. Like a kiss, she says.

"Don't panic," she says gently when I flail, her hand bracing my shoulder. "Trust that you'll get air when you break the surface."

I splutter. "I can't do it. I'm afraid I'll drown."

She studies me, then pats my shoulder again. "You won't learn to swim without some risk, Hương. Try it again."

In the lanes next to the beginners, there are the habitual early-morning swimmers. Businessmen getting exercise before their first meetings; moms squeezing in a few minutes before the school rush. I admire the way they slice their arms through the water, how they are so sure, so graceful. I want that for myself.

That day, I manage to hold my face underwater for ten seconds, then twenty. When I open my eyes, I see my own feet, planted firmly on the concrete floor of the pool, wavy from the reflections and water distortion. The chlorine burns my eyeballs. I choke my way to the surface, where air rushes into my lungs, even as the water tingles up my nose.

"Thatagirl," Beth says.

I drive home with the windows down, my wet hair trailing out the window. I haven't done any more than a toddler could, but I'm proud. If only Mẹ could see me now.

At home, I shower quickly, then put on a cornflower-blue sundress. For years, I never cared what I wore, but lately, I find myself paying new attention to my clothes. My muscles are sore, but when I look in the mirror, I see myself growing lean from Beth's lessons. She says it'll only be a matter of time before I can swim in open water. The thought of the unquenchable waves around me, that wild unknown, makes my stomach roil. But underneath the nerves, I'm determined to prove myself.

Downstairs, Ann is sipping her coffee, wearing one of Mẹ's robes. She gestures to the pot.

"Made plenty."

"Thank you, con."

By now, we've been staying in the Banyan House for a month. Between us, we don't talk about returning to our respective homes, the condo in that high-rise with a gym on the first floor, the lake house in Michigan. Here, we are timeless, and without agenda. Around us, the quiet pall of loss. And something more. A timid hope peeking out, like the first cracks in an eggshell.

Ann's morning sickness seems to have passed, though I don't stop making her bowls of cháo that she slides around with a spoon. Sometimes, she disappears into her room, and I wonder what she's doing in there. Drawing or calling friends. Or resting. She needs rest now.

She peers at my outfit. "You look nice. I like that color on you. Where have you been?"

"Running errands. But you need to get dressed. We're going to the temple today."

Ann groans. "Not that superstition. You never believed in any of it."

She's not entirely wrong. We do not follow most of the older Buddhist traditions. Certainly, there was never any fasting in our home, and I could count the times we tithed the monks on my hands.

But still, I can't shake the sense that this is what Mẹ would have wanted. Vinh and I never did it for Ann, and sometimes I think what could have happened if we had only done things the proper way.

I say, "Well, it can't hurt. If you don't believe, then it's just a trip with your mother. How bad can it be?"

She sips her coffee without answering, but in an hour, she's downstairs, wearing a skirt and a button-down shirt. Her hair, which has become unruly from lack of brushing, is now smooth. She looks at me pointedly, as if to say, *Happy?* And I find that I am, for the first time in a long while.

On the way to the temple, an hour away, we pass beneath an avenue of oak trees, tossing pollen into the air in yellow sprays. The humidity is the lowest it'll be all year, and instead of feeling like we are breathing through a layer of batting, the air is light, buoyant, like one of the squirrels jumping from tree to tree.

Ann puts her hand out the passenger window and flutters it in the wind. We're taking the Toyota today, and Ann studies the trinkets hanging from my window.

"What's that one mean?" she asks, pointing to a jade pendant with a red tassel dangling from the bottom.

"Your grandmother gave it to me. It's a phoenix, for prosperity."

"Not rebirth?"

"No. That's the Western phoenix. The Vietnamese phoenix is immortal, truly immortal. And jade—well, that was her favorite. She called jade 'green gold.' Said that unlike gold, it rarely breaks. I think she liked the strength of it."

"She would." Ann smiles to herself, and there's something private and sad about it. A moment not meant for me. Then she says aloud, "I wonder if she felt scared as a single mom."

"My mother? I can't see her living with any fear. She had all the courage in the world. I was the scared one."

"Yet you were a single mom, too. There's nothing cowardly about that."

I'm surprised. "I guess not."

"You never talk about my father."

The world wobbles, but I hold on tight to the steering wheel. The air smells clean, and yet it still bristles with something earthy underneath, a musk of soil. And darker things, perhaps.

Ann presses on. "Was he ever going to stay? Did you want him to?"

Vinh. She knows him by another name—a ghost name that could shut down her questions, and my own guilt. What would she say if she knew that the reason she has no father is because of me? But this is a burden no daughter should bear.

I clear my throat and press my lips together. I imagine a latch closing over the old pain. If I don't talk about it, if I don't think about it, I will be safe. Ann will be safe.

Instead of answering, I sweep my hand out toward the horizon. "Look at how beautiful it is today. We should only talk about lucky things right now, before the baby's blessing. I remember your cousins' blessings. I accompanied Diane to the temple both times, and she was so *scared*, like those old monks were secret sorcerers or something."

"Are you mad about Phước?" Ann asks.

I think of my brother's calls, alternately cajoling and angry, his seething need at the surface of every call. *I don't want to get lawyers involved, chị.* The unveiled threat from a very litigious small man. He's never had a wish denied, particularly by our mother, who treated him like the frail baby he used to be. She was never like that with me; rather, she gave me the truths she thought I needed to hear, even before I was ready. How love's shape changes with its recipient.

"I'm not surprised by him," I say.

"You didn't answer my question. Again."

"Okay, yes." I sigh. "I'm mad, often, and sad. He's discontent. Nothing will ever be enough."

"He's nothing like you," she says.

I disagree, but I don't tell her that. Discontent is our family's curse. It is also, perhaps, the thing that let us survive in unfamiliar places.

Soon, we're at the temple in the woods. It's built in the traditional pagoda style, with a sharply pointed roof that curves out at the corners like a hat. The trim is a faded marigold. Outside, there's a large pavilion shaded by a white-columned arch, surrounded by a bower of red amaryllis with lemony darts in the heart of each flower. I can smell the incense as we walk up the steps, then deposit our shoes at the entrance. The air inside is cool, and the floors gleam from the quiet industry of the monks.

We each take a stick of incense and pay our tribute to the golden Buddha on the large center shrine, though he is not our destination. A monk gives me a nod when I put a $20 bill on the brass plate.

Then we go out to the pavilion, where the lesser gods live.

"Which one is she?" Ann asks.

We find Quan Âm, the goddess of mothers and children, by a fountain. Unlike the gaudy Buddha, Quan Âm is rendered in white stone that has been carefully scrubbed, so her tranquil expression still gleams in perfect clarity. Her eyes are closed.

When Ann was young, Mẹ often told her Quan Âm's story: how she braved the fires of hell to rescue her father and sisters from eternal damnation. Ann was fascinated by the goddess, both warrior and mercy-giver. Martyr and hero. Usually, couples longing for babies would visit her statue, in hopes that an offering would improve their fertility. In this case, Ann's fertility isn't in question. Yet we still need the grace of the gods.

"Tell her what you want," I say to Ann. "Ask humbly."

She gives me a sidelong look, repeating, "You don't even believe in this stuff."

Throughout most of my life, I have felt abandoned by all gods. But maybe things will be different for Ann. For my grandchild. I don't answer, just sink to the ground in front of Quan Âm and pray silently. Ann sighs and kneels next to me, joining her palms and lifting her hands to her forehead as we taught her.

Let my grandchild know love. Give my daughter peace. For her, only light. Let the darkness end with me.

When I open my eyes, my cheeks are wet, and I furtively wipe them before Ann can see. I watch her expression squinch and flatten as she prays. When she opens her eyes and stands, I've moved to the bench behind her. I want to ask her what she prayed for, but I know that prayers are like wishes: they are private, and best honored in silence.

"Like you said—can't hurt," she says with a small smile.

"Thank you for doing this. We should go to the doctor soon," I say to her.

She looks out at the garden, where bees have begun to swirl around the flowers, lazily dipping into their pollen-heavy centers, then flitting out again, their black-marble bodies bobbing close to us. To my surprise, she answers. "I know."

"But?"

"I thought I would forgive Noah by now. If it was just the cheating—"

"What else is it?"

She just shakes her head. "I know you liked him."

"I never met him, con. But he is the father of your child, and I want to see you both taken care of."

She snorts.

I ask, "Have you told him about the baby?"

That old firmness seizes her features. "I will."

I think of when I first told her father. How the velvet night had seemed to shroud my words, so that I wasn't sure if he heard. I had clutched the sheets with one hand and rested the other on his back, feeling weak from all the tremulous wanting inside me, shivering like a thousand cold birds. How Vinh had turned to the window, playing with the shutters in that nervous way of his. "We can't afford a child." I remember thinking at the time, *We can't afford not to have one.*

Ann goes on: "I was sure I'd be back in Michigan now, and that the Banyan House would be yours to just . . . do with what you will."

"I think I'm going to stay," I say, surprising myself when I utter those words out loud.

I haven't been back to the condo since the night I got the phone call, except to get clothes and toiletries. I've hardly talked to Duke outside work. I'm sure his wife is happy to have him back, no matter what he tells me of their arrangement.

I go on: "I'm going to fix the place up a little. I have some savings. I'll sell the condo, too."

"Why would you do that?"

"Investment," I say. It's shorthand for "I don't know, but I'll figure it out, and anyway it's the last thing I have of my mother's and I don't want to give it away just yet."

"Oh. That makes sense. Maybe Phước will buy it from you after you fix it up," she says.

A shadow of a smile crosses her wan face.

When my eyes land on the Quan Âm statue, I think about how she had to journey to the circles of hell, fighting the demons tearing at

the silk on her back, walking on hot coals with her bare feet. All that
before she could ascend to the heavens, immortality her final reward.
In the cloud castle of the gods, her scars would have healed, the smoke
cleared from her lungs with her new immortal body. But what about
the scars in her soul? Did it always have to be so hard for women to
find their way? If Quan Âm had had a companion, if she hadn't been
so solitary on her journey, could she have been spared some pain?

I take a breath. "If Noah doesn't—or you don't—well. Couldn't
you stay here? With me?"

She blinks slowly, then turns to me, staring intently as if readjusting to my image. "I don't know."

"You can think about it."

"Everything feels half written," she says. "Like a storybook with invisible ink. It disappears before I figure out what I want the future to
look like."

"Not all stories have to be neat. Some can be messy and unfinished, and we can let other people pick the line up for us. Let's just
try, Ann."

I suddenly feel desperate to make her stay. This is our second
chance. Mẹ would have wanted this, I'm sure of it. Her machinations
still clicking along after death. Ann nods, listening without commit-
ting to anything as I talk about converting the room down the hall
from the main bedroom into a nursery. I could sew pillows for the
baby. We could paint the room together. There's something like déjà
vu in this conversation. My mother had pleaded with me the same way
when Ann was born. When it was clear that we had nowhere else to go.

"And I would be always on hand to help," I say.

I can hear my voice rising in excitement as I talk, with that tone
that Mẹ always described as annoying, too pleading. And I suppose I
am pleading. What's so terrible about that? I want my daughter to stay
with me.

Her bow lips curve into a smile, and I see hope sizzle into being. It cuts straight to my heart. In another life, it would have been me and her father, building the scaffolding for her new life together.

I feel like telling Ann, though I don't, "You're mine again. I will not let you leave this time."

A set of siblings spills into the pavilion in their best clothes, eager to get away from the slow chanting, the quiet sacredness of the temple. An older woman trails behind them, reaching into her bag for a piece of hard candy that she slides into her mouth. She slips sunglasses over her face. Indomitable in her focus on the children, though silent, not engaging in the conversation. The smaller sibling, a boy with a dark bowl cut wearing a giant plastic watch on one hand, throws a pine cone in the air. The wind catches it and bounces it near Ann's ankle.

"You total dummy," his sister says. She's in a red dress with a ruffle that swishes around her as she hops from one pavestone to the next.

"Sorry, ma'am," the boy calls to Ann.

She turns to him with a grin. "'S all right. As long as you never call me 'ma'am' again."

As he nears, I can see the red blush in his cheeks.

With a graceful wind of her arm, Ann tosses the pine cone back to him and he tries to catch it before fumbling and dropping it to the ground with a shrug.

"You want to play?" he asks.

"She does *not* want to play with you, Sammy," his sister says. She crooks her finger at him impatiently.

Ann says, "Maybe some other time. Thanks for asking."

When he runs away, he flicks some pebbles up behind him. Their grandmother gives us an assessing look, but ultimately lowers her sunglasses and finds a bench near them. The children develop a complicated game with the rocks on the ground and a stick apiece, near the foot of the Quan Âm statue. I'm surprised that the older lady didn't jerk them back, as Mẹ might have with me and Phước, but she allows them to play.

After a bit, the boy looks up at Ann with a shy smile. He brings over an amaryllis flower and places it in her hands, as if she is a goddess herself, ready for an offering. When she places it behind her ear, the petals lie like a swatch of velvet against her dark hair.

"Is this okay?" she asks the boy.

He giggles and runs away again.

I think there's something so heartbreakingly beautiful about boys—their softness, their vulnerability, before the world tells them that they must be something else. What could the men who hurt us have been, had they been loved enough?

"Ready to go?" I ask Ann.

"A few more minutes," she tells me, her eyes sweeping back to the siblings, though she tries to pretend otherwise. "There's no rush."

Chapter 17

Minh, 1969

We named Phước out of hope, and for a time, our boy brought all the luck of the world into our little family. The business thrived. My children flourished wildly like the flat, spiky bushes of coriander in our garden. And for my husband, I felt the kind of slow contentment that spreads with time and familiarity. Days passed in joy so complete that I felt the need to prostrate myself at the temple in front of the gods. No amount of thanks could be enough for the gifts of my life.

"So religious in your old age, em," Xuân teased.

But I was never religious, exactly, only fearful. I knew too well the cost of contentment.

And when an invisible hand put the stopper on our beautiful, precious luck, the end came fast.

By then, we'd moved into our own house, closer to the jewelry shop, and the two of us worked together with precision, as if we were rowing a boat. We took turns with the children and our growing shop, our other child. It should have been an awful time to open a new store, but even with the ravages of war, jewels were still needed, as important as food and shelter in those days. Jewelry was dignity; it showed others that even if you were half starved, covered in filth, you had hope, you were worthy. Did I feel guilty selling a thin golden bracelet to a woman who could not manage to scrape together three full meals for her children? Of course. But I had my own children to think about, and a future to plan for. And Xuân was known for his steep, stealthy discounts, the ones he thought I didn't know about. Those discounts bought loyalty, which in return brought us repeat business. Word of mouth. I couldn't begrudge my husband for the very goodness that had convinced me to marry him.

That year, the bombs stopped, and Hồ Chí Minh suffered a series of heart problems that made us all wonder how long this would last without him, this scaffolding of violence. But still, I felt the uncertainty of war, and I knew the only thing that could keep us safe was gold, and lots of it. I sewed it into our clothes, knowing that we could be evacuated at any moment, forced to go into the swamps while our village was riddled with bullets.

Every day, more people visited the shop, even out-of-towners gawking at the sparkle of our wares, unlike anything they had seen. I took pride in sourcing the finest designs from Sài Gòn. Every bride came to us, every new mother with eyes gleaming with hope for her little one. With each passing day, the shop became more successful, in a way none of our family could have predicted.

"What luck those children have brought you!" Xuân's and my parents said.

We lavished our fortune on our families, funding our siblings' weddings, setting aside savings for cousins who had to get surgeries. Where we rose, so did our families. It gave me pleasure to give. And for my husband, it was as natural as breathing.

"We must toast my resourceful wife," Xuân would declare, shoving the credit onto anyone but himself. "Find yourself someone with her brains, and you'll never have to work again."

Thien laughed. "Not such a bad bargain after all, marrying my mousy sister."

I slapped his arm. Xuân beamed at us. After all those years in and out of our house as a child, he was finally family. He exuded such contentment that I couldn't help but nestle into it.

I knew that the luck we summoned was not in the children, or in my salesmanship, but in Xuân. His steadiness became our foundation, allowing us to take risks. In the mornings, I plaited my hair and wore my best dress—no one wants to see a vendor in rags. While I put lipstick on, I let the children play on the ground next to me, Hương quietly observant while Phước kicked and screamed. No toy was enough for him. He never had colic like his sister, but his tantrums shook the neighborhood. "Naughty boy," they called him, sometimes with affection, and sometimes with annoyance. But they tolerated us, if only for my well-loved husband.

When Xuân came down with a fever in the fall, just weeks before Hồ Chí Minh died at last, I sent the children to my parents, out of fear that they would catch Xuân's sickness. For myself, I was unafraid. I owed this man of mine everything, and I would not leave his side. I mopped his forehead and gently rubbed his arms, which shivered like we weren't at the tail end of the hot season in Việt Nam. I piled the blankets on, felt the shallow breath beneath them. I wanted to lay my body on top of his, to loan him my warmth. The doctors were solemn. One rested his hand on my shoulder when he was leaving, his eyes so deeply sad as he said, "You remind me of my own daughter." That's when I knew.

"Anh," I said to Xuân, trying to spoon-feed some of his favorite pineapple fish soup into his mouth. "Please. It's sweet, the way you like it."

He tried to smile, but the broth dribbled down his mouth, pooling in his neck folds, which emerged even though he was losing weight by the hour. I wiped him up. The country doctors couldn't pinpoint his illness, using words like "infection" and "summer sickness." I wanted to spirit him away to Sài Gòn, or a city with better doctors, but he wouldn't have made the trip. Sometimes he coughed so hard, he turned purple, and I wrung my hands. My anger turned to the gods. Once, I flung a teakettle at our shrine to the ancestors and gaped at my own blasphemy. All my kneeling, all the gold coins I had pushed into the hands of the monks, had not been enough to keep my hard-won family intact. I could have killed a person with my bare hands, if there had been anyone to blame.

"Minh," he called to me, weakly. "Peace, please, em."

In the evenings, while he rested, I went to see the children. Phước didn't pay me any mind, more caught up in chasing the stray dogs or eating whatever treat his grandmother had made for him, but Hương stared at me with reproachful eyes.

"Stop leaving us," she said.

I was exhausted from caring for Xuân, and I hadn't had a decent meal in weeks, not that I was ever hungry. Her words pierced me.

I stooped in front of her. "I have to take care of Ba, you understand? He needs me."

"No. Stay."

"I can't be in two places at once, con," I said, turning my palms toward the sky.

Hương was little more than a toddler at the time, with wide eyes and a thicket of black-banged hair that edged around her round cheeks. She was so beautiful that her grandparents often professed worries that she would be kidnapped by jealous demons. We laughed at their superstition, but it was easy to see how captivating our daughter was. To my pride, she protected her baby brother with a fierceness she had rarely shown anything else, aside from her own comfort.

She turned away from me. "You're a bad mother."

"Don't say that to Mẹ," I hissed.

As if knowing the impact of her words, she began to chant, "Bad mother, bad mother, bad mother."

"Stop," I gritted out.

"Hate you," she said.

Maybe it was her nonchalance that did it. Those words out of her small mouth unbottled all my anxiety and sadness from the past weeks. I thought of my dying husband, the shop whose fate remained unknown without him, our family cast outside the loving shade of his protection. And here, my daughter, with her knowing expression. Seeing right through the love and into the uncertainty brewing inside me. I didn't think of her then as a three-year-old acting out her sadness. I felt she was a malevolent force sent to drive me mad. I slapped her.

When my hand hit her face, she crumpled. Her eyes narrowed. But she didn't say a word.

"I'm sorry, baby," I cried, leaning down. "Please forgive Mẹ. Please, my Hương."

She turned from me and wouldn't speak to me for days afterward, not even when I brought her tart sữa chua, or a teddy bear with a red bow around his neck. I learned that day that while my youngest raged like a storm, my eldest could hold a grudge for all her days. I think if I were to haunt her now, she'd find a way to bring up the slap again. And maybe she's right. What kind of mother hits her daughter in anger?

A week after the slap, Xuân finally died, holding my hand as his light in our lives was snuffed. In my mind, I thought of the two events together, the slap and the death, like his passing was a punishment for my poor approximation of motherhood. Before he took his last breath, he let out one terrifying, rasping cough, then said something so softly that I had to bend to hear him.

"Anh, I'm here," I said. "You don't have to speak. There's plenty of time."

"No time," he gasped.

The tears welled in my eyes. "Please try to rest."

"Protect our babies. *Live.*"

"I can't do this without you, Xuân."

He sighed, like the rustle of a dry leaf, and said, "You can do anything, em. Always have."

While I wept, he watched me with a patient, endless pool of love in his eyes. He said, finally, "My Minh. Even if you never loved me, I am yours forever."

When he was gone, I was inconsolable. The nurses and neighbors could not drag me from his bedside. I didn't go to my children for days, barely even thought of them. They were safe at my parents', but what about me? I was adrift in an unfriendly, reckless world. Grief sank me so low that I thought about drowning myself in the river, my body bloated in longing for Xuân. I wondered if the world would be better off without me, if my children would grow up without my bitterness coating their memories.

Losing Xuân ravaged my mind and soul, but even more than that, in his last words I understood that he had never felt as loved as he should have. That curse, I knew, would continue to leave its mark on our family.

But I remembered what else he said: Protect our babies. Even until the last moment, refusing to acknowledge that Hương belonged to anyone else but him. It was for him that I rose from the bed. For him that I choked down a spoonful of bamboo soup, the only food I'd eaten for days. I went to get my children and bring them home. By then, someone else had told them the news and they looked to me with wild, terrified eyes, feeling the loss of their father, the only safety we had known.

I wasn't enough, but even so, I vowed to survive to the last for my children. It was the only thing I could do for Xuân.

Chapter 18

Ann

The afternoons are now thick with the smells of blooming purple azaleas and starry milkweed. Bees crouch over the flowers, vampiric and protective, tibias crusted with pollen. I stand in the sunshine, breathing it in. Blood rushes to my extremities, swelling my fingertips and ankles ever so slightly. No one would see the change in me. But I feel it. The floral scent, the salt, the acute aliveness of my own body. There has been a shift, whispering hotly inside me, and I think it is my own instinct for survival.

In the doorway of Treasures by the Sea, I tell myself I'm there to shop for baby things—the baby finally a reality now that Mom has made the doctor's appointment. There's a ding on my phone, a notification of another message, probably from an editor who is "just gently circling back" about a project I owe her. Circling back—the phrase reminds me of the way I've looped through time, dragging the present along with me to the past, rather than the other way around, as if the magnetic draw is backward, rather than forward.

I still haven't begun illustrating again, though I got Wi-Fi installed at the Banyan House, just in case I decide to pop back into my old life. It takes no small amount of money to run the wires there, but it connects me to the outside world, something I know I need.

"I can help pay for it," Mom says.

I don't tell her, but I have plenty of savings. Noah insisted on paying for everything in our relationship—or sending the bills to Brandon and Alice, likely—and I never spent much on myself. My bank account bulged, as a reminder of how little I needed to work. In my old life, I was a well-groomed house cat. But I want to be something feral and self-sufficient, like those panthers in the Everglades with their silky bodies, jumping from branch to branch.

My email, which I'd avoided checking since my return to the Banyan House, is a swarm of unread notes about missed deadlines and networking events. Young and Under-Whatever cocktail hours at the lodge, where everyone would fall all over themselves to prove that they were the best, the brightest. In the beginning, my Michigan friends, most of whom are Noah's friends, sent loads of flowers down to Florida. Now they reach out with seeking tentacles. "So, Ann, when *are* you coming home?" They treat me gingerly, wondering at my mental state, unable to fathom why I would need so much time away from Noah. There's an invitation in there somewhere for a bachelorette party in the fall. As if I can think that far. In the fall, well. I will have a permanent plus-one.

Noah emails jokes he thinks I'll like, articles that are frothy and timely, full of wit. Sometimes he sends chapters of his book. I don't read them, and there is a relief in finally admitting that I do not give a flying shit about the vicissitudes of dead Greeks.

The art directors have begun calling, once they realize the emails are falling into an unanswered void. My least favorite, Marlee, works at a big beauty publication, the kind that splashes glossy photos all over their homepage so you never know where to click to find the articles. She operates like a tightly wound wire; any missed deadline spirals her anxiety outward, whipping around us like Medusa's snakes. I once admired how orderly and efficient she was. Now the thought of such singlemindedness overwhelms me.

"I'm not ready yet, Marlee," I told her when she last called.

"But we can't possibly have you out roaming about without any clue of when you're coming back. I keep making excuses, but if you can't work, well, Ann . . ."

I heard her tapping her nails against her desk and pictured her frowning down at her computer, statuesque and frightening in her capability. Wondering why she took a chance on me. Yet for all my gratitude, I have no interest in working for brands anymore. Creative briefs feel as if they've been written in another language (everything is *diverse, aspirational,* and *relatable* all at once). Deadlines are laughable and overly optimistic. Ann of four months ago would have cringed to see me so adrift. She would have told me, in no uncertain terms, to get it together.

"I'm very sorry," I said. "I just can't."

She paused. "What is going on with you, darling? Is it Noah? Have you fought?"

"My grandmother died," I reiterated.

"Well, sure, yes. That *is* very sad. But wasn't she quite old?"

When I didn't respond, Marlee agreed to leave it alone, though she was miffy. "But I can only give you so much leniency, Ann. Bereavement is a bitch, I know. But fair is fair."

"Fair. Right," I said hollowly before I ended the call.

Fair is not your world turning upside down, your favorite person dying and leaving a rotting wreckage of a home, your boyfriend and his gorgeous ex taking up permanent residence in the story of your relationship, your insides expanding and growing to welcome a life that you weren't prepared for. But still, I think of a bumper sticker reading "Bereavement is a bitch," and I think maybe that sums it up pretty well.

At the secondhand store, I thumb through old VHS tapes, the spines crackling in hard and hazardous thorns of plastic that poke at my fingers. I see *The Parent Trap* and other movies I've forgotten about over the years, where mischievous kids somehow find their way into a happy ending. They're always unguarded in those movies, Dad or Mom gone off on vacation, on a date. The assumption being that nothing bad can happen to kids when their parents are around. The opposite being true.

In the corner of the store, the baby section looks sadly disorganized. I've gotten past the worst of the nausea, and now I'm hungry all the time. Mom and I make gigantic meals, rarely talking through them, but eating as if there are eight of us instead of two. We have a routine now, mostly bookended by sleep and her work schedule. I know she wakes early, but she never tells me where she goes in the mornings, and I don't ask, affording her privacy. While she's gone, I go through the house, selling things off, organizing paperwork into boxy file folders with neat tabs that promise to bring order, wiping down anything I can reach. I expect to find more clues about Bà Ngoại, any hint of her life before me and my mother, but she's as discreet in death as she was in life.

I reach for a book with tiny, toddler-size teeth marks in the corner. It should disgust me, but instead, I feel touched by the imprint. History exists in nicks and scratches, scar tissue that pinks and puckers.

Wes makes his way over to me, wiping his brow. Again, I notice the ease with which he moves through the world. *Swims* through it. I remember how he took me to the creek in the summers, moving his arms over mine to show me how to stroke, how to use the movement of the water to help my own.

His grin is open and friendly, but there's a roughness beneath his voice, like stubble. "Ann. I wondered if I'd see you again. Hoped, even."

"And here I am. Summoned like a genie from a bottle."

"Just my luck." He slings one sweaty arm around my shoulder. "How're things, Annie girl?"

"Surviving."

"Not thriving?"

One of his coworkers edges over to us, but he pivots his back toward her and she leaves, frowning. There's an air of possessiveness in her glare toward me, and I wonder if this new Wes gets around. Not that the old one didn't. In high school, he tried to hide the hookups from me, though I'd hear the girls giggling about visitations in their backyard hammocks, rough hands behind a gas station. Those overheard conversations always clotted over my affection for him, and it would take me days sometimes to reclaim it, days he spent confused, following me around with wide and reproachful eyes. We always had a complicated friendship.

"You okay?" he asks now, peering down.

My hand flutters to my stomach, then away. No one would notice unless they knew. "Bà Ngoại died. I didn't tell you before. Wasn't ready to talk about it."

His jaw slackens. "Not Bà Ngoại. Shit. I'm so sorry. God. I wish I would have known."

"You would have wanted to go to the funeral," I say, realizing suddenly.

His eyes glint with a bit of anger. "Yeah. I would have, Ann."

"I'm sorry. I just wasn't in my right mind," I say, and watch his eyes soften. "It was a sucker punch. I didn't get to say goodbye—to tell her any of the things you tell people you love before they die."

"She knew. You were everything to her. She cheered the loudest at our high school graduation, even though she was the tiniest lady. Tough, except when it came to you. And she was so proud that afterward she went around carrying your graduation cap in her hand like it was a cat or something, stroking it. I don't think anyone's ever been that proud of me in my life."

I can't believe he remembers that. I saw her from the stage that day, sobbing and smiling at the same time, as she whooped in uncharacteristic glee. It was rare to see her lose control, but that day, she did, a little. For me.

"She liked you," I say.

"Liar." His eyes crinkle. "She hated every single one of us. Never thought anyone was good enough for you. But she was the dragon guarding you—we had to get past her for a shot at your friendship. It was worth it."

"That's not how I remember things," I say.

He shrugs. "Doesn't really matter, I guess, whether she liked me or not. I liked her. She wasn't someone you forgot easily. Never did see her much after you left, though. Would have liked to."

Wes's fingers grip the sides of his apron. His eyes are like little camp-fires, drawing me closer. I remember the frenzy of our last kiss, and it makes me tilt my head toward him. The desire feels hot and wicked. But not unwelcome.

Another memory rises, the last time I saw him at the Banyan House. We said goodbye and I tried so hard not to cry, not to be a cliché of a high school romance, but he saw the streaking tears anyway. He swiped one of them with his thumb, then placed it on his heart, like a promise. Then he was gone, down the long driveway, back into town and away from me. That last gesture, so odd, so intimate, became one I returned to in times of homesickness. The way a tear, a love, seeps from one body into another.

"Do you want to get a coffee, Wes?" I ask.

He doesn't even have to think. "I can leave in ten minutes. No coffee—I have a better idea."

I watch his retreating back, the broad shoulders and loping gait that used to charm the panties off the other girls. A part of me wonders if I'm betraying Noah, but then I shove that thought down.

I feel very little loyalty these days, except to this bean-size fetus who's so helpless inside me. And "loyalty" is a strange word to de-scribe what I feel for it, too. I'm welded to a primitive instinct to pro-tect, which is as much a gesture of self-preservation as maternal love, I suspect. I'm so insignificantly pregnant that if I lost the baby, not a single person who hasn't been told would know or grieve. Something about that fills my heart with such sadness that I pick up a board book about a blue truck from the bargain bin and buy it from the cashier, who flips it into a bag with the grace of muscle memory.

"Good one," she says. "My baby brother can't get enough of that truck. You new around here?"

Her nametag says "Hannah," and she has a creamy complexion colored by two angry red splotches. Her eyebrows are bushy, but ungroomed. She's very pretty in a coltish way, though there's a world-weariness to her already.

"No. I'm old. Very old," I say, trying to smile.

She snorts and pushes the bag across the counter to me. "Trust me, you aren't the only one coming around to see him."

I wait for Wes out front. When he approaches me, he swishes his apron off in a gaudy, theatrical way that makes me laugh. He's handsome, but a totally different kind of handsome from Noah. Whereas Noah seemed to waft security and good health around him, Wes feels a little tragic, like he's been left behind by the world. He's got this tortured musician vibe that I know women must love. Cars pass us without curiosity, on their way home from work or to dinner. I offer to drive in the Oldsmobile and he hops in the passenger side, tossing his vest in my back seat. He raises his hand to graze the thumbtacks keeping the fabric pinned to the roof.

"I remember this," he says. "I could replace it for you. Hell, we could overhaul this whole clunker."

Now I understand why Bà Ngoại kept my room the way it was after I left. It feels unfair to change what belonged to the ones who left, especially when they can't protest.

"Where to?" I ask.

I once knew how to navigate all the little hidden corners of this town, like tracing veins in my arms, Crystal or Wes in the seat beside me. Going to the mall, down to the public garden. Even to the Shell gas station sometimes, Crystal palming her fake ID and batting those thick spider lashes at the open-mouthed attendants who couldn't tear their eyes from her. When I think of her, I smell the syrup of malt liquor, like fruit punch mixed with rubbing alcohol.

Wes grins. "Dollar Movie Rental?"

After school, we'd go to the movie rental to get foreign films to take back to his basement. Kurosawa and Bergman, anything in black-and-white, with subtitles that ran across the bottom of the screen. We thought those films made us seem urbane, though the dead-eyed clerk who scanned the VHS tapes never blinked at our choices. Back at Wes's place, on that old gingham-print couch smelling of cigarette smoke, we'd do anything but watch the movie. We kissed hotly through *La Dolce Vita*. He first unhooked my bra during *Andrei Rublev*; I unzipped his jeans during the chess game in *The Seventh Seal*. Once or twice, we'd gotten further, until we heard someone shuffling upstairs. Then we'd pull our hands and mouths from each other and giggle ourselves into decorum.

Despite all the other girls, I let it happen. I told myself that if I knew what he was from the start, I couldn't get hurt. There were times when I probably could have called him my boyfriend, if I had pushed it. But I never did. He didn't seem like the type of man who could ever shine his light on only one person. And I knew I was leaving: bound for college as far away as I could get from this festering little town. Wes would never think of following.

So he remained a friend. A friend who had explored all the intimate parts of me, long before I could properly identify them on a diagram. There's a comfort in that, a certain innocence. My body, before its naming, before the rest of the world discovered it. Because Wes was never the rest of the world. He grew from the same dirt as me.

I flush, thinking of how I still haven't seen the ending to *Andrei Rublev*, yet remember the exact minute mark when I experienced my first orgasm.

"I have an idea," he says, the skin around his eyes creasing. "Have you been to the arcade lately?"

"Of course I haven't," I say.

"Gun it."

Ranger's Quest is the same: sticky and lit by neon, flashing bulbs that make me just a little nauseous. There are always kids spilling out the front, smelling like the remains of fizzy soda and butter-drenched popcorn. Sometimes an older man, looking sad with a cup of tokens.

The sign is always broken, so it reads "anger's Quest" out front. There are about a dozen ashtrays strewn on twin benches outside the place.

Inside, Wes takes charge, buying us $20 worth of tokens that are slightly blackened at the edges. I try not to think about all the hands that have touched these tokens. All the stickiness and ash clinging to them.

I don't remember ever coming here with Wes, but he insists we did. He says he won me a plastic slap bracelet once. He promises he'll win me another, that devilish smile quirking up the side of his face. We toss the tokens into every machine, feeling profligate, then end up flush with tickets. He buys me a tiny stuffed unicorn that I'll later throw in my back seat. The guy behind the counter tells us, "Haven't had slap bracelets in a decade. No one wants them anymore. Now everyone wants fidget-whatevers."

After the games, we eat giant slices of oily pizza while watching kids argue in front of a *Mario Kart* game. I try not to blot the pepperoni slices with a napkin, a habit I picked up from Noah. If I were with him, we'd be eating something thin and crispy, weighed down with burrata and fresh arugula. That's not what I'm craving.

"Hits the spot, right?" Wes says, rhetorically.

"Not bad. This is not where I thought we'd go tonight," I say.

"But wasn't it fun?"

"More than I thought it would be," I admit. "Been a while since I had fun like this. Like a kid."

"Serious big-city girl finds her hometown roots?" He grins.

I throw a napkin at him. "Okay. That's the one and only reference you get to make to that cliché. Surely there's other things to mock about me."

"You? Never." And he's solemn when he says it.

A woman is staring at us intently from across the way. She has a young girl with her, about six or seven, who is fixated on a racing game to the left of the woman. The woman is frightfully thin, clutching the largest soda I have ever seen. Her top is the color of rust. Her brows are plucked into razored, high crooks above her face, giving her a slightly wounded expression.

"Is that Crystal King?" I ask, indicating with my chin just slightly. Wes shifts.

"Ah. Yeah, that's her. She's married to someone from high school. Forget his name. That's her kid. Sweet little thing. Likes to come into the shop for doll clothes."

"I should say hi. Maybe."

He studies me. "You two stopped talking during senior year, right? We thought you'd be ride or die until the end."

"Hmm." I make a noncommittal sound.

"Then you come back in the fall and you wouldn't be caught dead next to each other. You were opposites, though, so maybe it wasn't supposed to last. You outgrew us all in the end."

"I didn't. Things happen sometimes. Friends are complicated."

"I know you're probably judging her by her looks." He sounds defensive as he says it. "But she's a good person."

"That so?"

"I mean. She's always volunteering at the church. Donating things to the store. I heard she fosters dogs. I think she's just one of those people. Kinder than she looks."

"I remember," I say. I get flashes of her old brand of fierce sweetness—the way she'd come to my door with a bag of my favorite pickle-flavored chips and a stupid tabloid that we'd pore over, or how she'd squeeze past Bà Ngoại to haul me out of bed so we could joyride down to the mall together. She stuck up for me when the other girls in high school sniped at me. Once, she got in a fistfight with some girl who had spread rumors about my dad because she had a thing for Wes.

Crystal tears her eyes away from us and picks her child up easily, positioning her on a gaunt hip. They leave before I have to decide one way or the other. I'm a little ashamed of the relief coursing through me. Coward.

"Maybe I'll look her up sometime," I say.

"No, you definitely won't," he says. His calm is delicious and perfectly knowing.

Reaching over, he grabs a piece of leftover crust from my plate and takes a big bite, his chewing dramatic and toothy. That ease crumbles another wall in me and I find myself leaning forward to catch his words.

"I really am sorry about your grandmother. My dad died last year, and it was tough. More than that. It was kinda like having surgery, while you're awake, right? A part of you gets cut out, and everyone gets to watch, and you're never really alone? When something like that happens, you should be able to go on a retreat."

"Or a solo quest," I say, warming to the idea. "You could just whisk yourself off into a yurt and grieve. Then when you come out, everyone will stop giving you those pitying faces or saying those awful things."

"Like how everything happens for a reason." Wes makes a face.

"Exactly. I'm sorry about your dad."

"He was an asshole, which kind of makes it worse. Then I felt guilty for the relief. Remember how I used to make you leave every time he came home? I was afraid he'd start yelling at us. Or worse, I don't know. I just wanted to keep you away from that part of my life."

"I guessed it," I say, thinking of his father, with his mean little face, the squinched walk, like he was reluctant to be moving. "Your poor mom."

"She's remarried now, to a good guy. They moved to Ohio, where everyone looks really healthy and corn-fed. Sometimes I hop up there to visit. They're fixing up an old cabin, and it's a lot of work for the two of them. Luckily, I can make myself useful. Dad would have never seen that coming."

"You're a good guy, Wes," I tell him, hugging my unicorn.

"Not really. But I always seem to want to make you think so. Stupid, right?"

The neon lights cross his eyes, and he looks like an enticing mistake. I don't think of Noah, or any of the many reasons not to. I just take the front of his shirt in my hands, and I pull.

Later, after we crash into his house, our clothes flying on top of all his furniture, after he locates a condom and we have hurried sex on top of his bed, I'm lying beneath him, staring up at the popcorn ceiling, the shadowed edges like goose bumps on skin. I feel like a wineglass, poured out onto the pavement. Empty, yet deliciously tingly, waiting for what comes next.

Once, I was a girl who had a boyfriend, faithful and kind, and now I'm a girl trying to revive a memory with a boy I knew in high school. That old Ann, the one who threw dinner parties and made farro salads, is not this Ann, reeking of cigarettes and cotton candy and frantic sex. Wearing a flashing sign of sorrow. *Bereavement is a bitch.* Or *anger's Quest.*

"I should get home," I say to Wes, untangling myself from him. He smells like sweet grass and stale beer, a summer evening gone too long. He reaches for me.

"Let me drive you home, Annie."

"Then how will *you* get home? We took the Oldsmobile."

"That thing is still a piece of shit," he says, "but it's a good car. Worth fixing up. I can help you, if you want."

Noah would have bought me a new one without blinking, something that's already gleaming and quiet, a whirring panther of a car that would have looked so sleek next to his Lexus. Back home, I think of my hybrid, hunkered down uselessly in our garage, waiting for me. I bet Noah has started the engine every few days, driven it around the block to keep it running. Conscientious to the last.

Wes is a fixer, always has been. His toolbox, navy blue and paint splattered, rests in the corner of the room. No monograms, no fancy edging. Incongruously, I see an open package of Band-Aids on his nightstand. I wonder where he cut himself, but he's leaning on one elbow, looking so entirely whole. I touch the rubber duck tattoo on his arm.

"I'll name him Lucas," I say. "Quack."

"A good name for a duck."

"What's it mean?"

He brushes the hair from my face and stares so intently into my eyes that I almost shrink back. I'm not used to being studied, seen in this way. He shoves me gently out of bed. "Don't be a stranger, Annie. It's nice having you home. Like old times."

"I'll call you," I promise.

Even as I smile down at his beautiful sad face, putting on my clothes, I know better. Wes and Noah are two sides of a similar dream; ways to ease the loneliness, to escape all the unknowing.

"Like you'll call Crystal," he says, turning over in the bed, one arm across his forehead. He doesn't sound angry, but neither does he seem teasing, exactly.

I pause at the doorway, gazing back at him, that lanky form thrown over his bed. The boy who took my tear as his own. My quicksilver thread back to all the older versions of me. Fleetingly, I feel an urge to rediscover him, to turn him in my fingers like those smooth little co-quina shells on the beach, thumbing the interior to see if my flesh will fit. But instead, I leave.

When I close his door behind me, I hear the low drone of a passenger plane flying to the nearby airport, trailing lights across the sky. It's a clear, fresh night, one where the salt of the sea finds its way to even the innermost corners of our town. I think of the rocker on the porch of the Banyan House and the citronella candles we placed out there to ward off the mosquitoes. I think of Bà Ngoại and her folktales, her face weathered and eerie in the flickering porch light, the water bugs flitting on the steps, dancing to their own weird silent song. The way night welcomes the old phantoms, opens the imagination. A cracked door. I spent my whole life running, but now I'm seized with a new, reckless desire to explore the hidden spaces I thought I knew so well.

Chapter 19

Minh, 1973

The air was thick with fear. At the beginning of the year, our white allies left us behind, and we found ourselves alone, flinching as we faced the encroaching soldiers of the North. We passed around stories about the rapes, three generations or more at a time; children left to run through grenade fields for sport while soldiers bet on who would blow up first; our sacred temples running with blood and refuse. Beautiful things, spoiled again. Spoiled forever. The smart ones, the ones with money and power, quietly packed their bags. A former classmate of mine traveled with her family of six to Dallas, Texas, a place with two hissing endings. They joked about rangers and cowboy hats, and promised to send back candy bars, but we'd had enough of those, left behind by American soldiers with their big boots and bigger appetites.

My dreams shifted overseas. Where I had once longed for a family, held tight and safe in our town, surrounded by my parents and brothers, I now would have traded anything to go to America. Xuân was gone. Our parents had died in quick succession. They were very old. Thien's appendix had burst and then he died while his children were still in diapers. His wife remarried quickly. My other brothers were dead or had moved to one of the large port cities, with nothing tying them back to our village. I was not sorry to see them leave; I only wished I could, too.

I was rich at that point, by our town's standards, and my children were well cared for, and often at the top of their classes at school. The gold sewn into our garments hung heavy, almost too heavy to conceal. I hired a girl to watch the children while I was at the shop, and they grew fat and round, their yogurt-white skin well scrubbed, feet clad in expensive plastic shoes. They never knew hunger. I should have been satisfied.

After my husband's death, once I had decided to live, I did it with a determination that shocked everyone. For all my faults, I had a golden hand that only seemed to glow more brightly each year. It was like a magnet for money and investments. (This would remain true until my death.) Men envied this in me, tried to marry me or burn my fortune with their angry words. I laughed about the rumors that spread—that I was a witch, that I had opened my legs to the devil in exchange for filthy lucre. Old-timey superstition. But it smarted; you never want your people talking behind your back. Xuân would not have let anyone speak of me that way. A woman alone is a lightning rod for gossip.

After Xuân passed, I found a knife among his things. He used to keep it under our bed for defense, though thank the gods he had never needed to use it. It was an old fisherman's knife given to him by his grandfather, with a wooden handle and a curved edge. Small but sharp, made to fit in your hand, made for precise incisions through the scales. The world was beginning to fissure, revealing the threat of men. I strapped the knife to me, under my clothes. It helped me pretend that my husband's protection still hovered around me.

Despite the malice of some, in my later years, I proved to have a way with men. No longer the little mouse, but someone more sophisticated, innocence dampened by loss, and confident through my wealth. I took on lovers discreetly, often widowers who had known pleasure in the brothels but longed for something more sincere. I could not offer anyone love, but I learned to give my body without shame.

One man in particular, a widower with a paunch and an oily smile, began to haunt the shop. He had power, this one, and influence that seeped from his skin. He wore it like a slippery cloak. During the week, he leaned on my glass counters with a sly air, his pressed T-shirts sodden with sweat, heat making his face swell. His parents were government officials, and they had that glutted look. They knew where to steer their ships, and even when the wind inevitably swayed against them, they would still swim in the right direction, toward calmer waters. I was a survivor, too, so I could not begrudge his family its foresight.

He wasn't bad-looking, but he felt greasy to me, like something I should wash off my skin. Still, he liked me, for reasons he never professed. Maybe because I was independent, far from my prime. I wouldn't demand anything of him, not like the virginal schoolgirls who expected marriage and gaudy gifts for a flash of ankle. Those young women looked at me like a leper. Some wondered why I hadn't remarried. Maybe I should have, but the truth was that I hadn't found anyone I trusted as much as Xuân. Love was one thing. But trust was the sterling key, the only thing that could have opened the doors to my heart. And it eluded me for the rest of my life.

This widower was named Việt, though the years have muddled my memory. He could have been named anything.

"Chị Minh," he said, his voice proprietary as he strode through the shop, "my parents would like to have you and your children over for dinner."

I know I should have been pleased. He didn't extend invitations to just anyone, and I was, after all, just a village girl who had happened into some fortune—at least, that's how he saw me. Perhaps that's why he wanted me. He felt there was something he just couldn't understand about my life. Men like him want to take a thing apart, examine all the gears until they are satisfied they know exactly how it works, the mystery gone, the object broken.

"Whatever for, anh?" I asked.

I was polishing jade bracelets. Their deep green like the bottom of a pool, a color that felt taken from a painting. He picked up one of the bracelets, the most expensive for its deep hue and flawless cut. It glinted as he slid it onto my wrist.

"I'll take this one," he said, clasping his hand around my wrist. It was uncertain whether he meant me or the bracelet.

It took a few months, but I gave in, because while I knew the power of my beauty and relative youth, I also knew it was a fleeting thing. I never went to dinner with his family, though, and I never let my children meet him. There are dangers we risk for ourselves, but never for our loved ones.

Việt and I met in hotel rooms in a neighboring city, far away from prying eyes. I demanded discretion. The price of a night in one of those rooms was more than the cost of a month of food for a family of six. But we were the fortunate ones. We didn't have to count đồng.

Before I left for the night, I would lean over to kiss my children on their foreheads, cool from the night air. I draped their beds with mosquito netting—the finest weave for my little ones—and nodded to the nursemaid, an elderly woman who wanted nothing more than a little coin and peace from her daughters-in-law, who had overtaken her own home. She didn't care enough to disapprove of my overnight visits, as long as she was paid on time. Once, she confessed that she was saving for her own house in Bạc Liêu, dreaming as so many of us older women do, of a home of her own.

Việt idled the motor on his bike a few streets down from my house and let me on the back. I wrapped my arms around his waist, tucking my thumbs into his belt loops. He liked that. I could tell by the way he stroked my thighs, curled around his body. His back was broad, and in the night, leaning my face on its warmth, I could pretend he was someone else. When we got to the hotel, we said that we were husband and wife, though no one cared either way. We were strangers with money, which covers a multitude of sins.

"One key is fine," he said to the hotel clerk.

They gave each other a jocular nod. By then, I'd transitioned to Western clothes, and I knew I looked every bit a woman of the world, in acid-washed jeans and a thick sweater, too hot for our climate but stylish nonetheless, and more important, expensive. Việt liked my fine clothes and often told me so, marveling as he ran his hands over the luxurious fabrics, under my shirt and into the waistband of my jeans.

The hotel room floor was tiled and speckled with bits of gray. I'd watch the speckles until my eyes hurt and they began to move together, ants in a swarm. Việt wanted me to wash before he took me to bed. The towels were new and scratchy, and they smelled pleasant, like a freshly worked field. I thought then of how I would scrub my brothers' washcloths in that stilt house in the wetlands, never getting the stains off because the water too was muddy, unless we boiled it for a long time like we did for our tea. Thinking of them, and the loss of family, I felt melancholy. It seemed I was destined to outlast those I loved.

In those hotel rooms, I tried not to think of my children, tried to find my own pleasure where I could. After all, I chose this, no one forced me. I could have said no to Việt. And he never offered anything more than those nights. We were clear on what we meant to each other.

He liked to watch our bodies in the mirror as he ran his hands across my torso, under my breasts, which remained pert, even after two children. I could see by the spreading smile, the wolfishness in his eye, that he had learned this trick elsewhere, from a paid woman or one of the French movies that scandalized everyone. He liked being thought of as a provocateur.

I was careful, because I didn't want another child, but I let him try all sorts of things that would have made me blush in broad daylight. I got pleasure from him, too, gasping into his shoulder in a way that made him jolt even harder against me, his hands grabbing my buttocks roughly as he finished. Those moments made him almost tender afterward, stroking my hair as he reached for his cigarettes.

"You are some kind of woman, Minh," he said. "They say widows are the fiercest in bed."

"They do?"

He blew a ring of smoke my way. "Well, I do."

I didn't say anything in return, but sometimes I put my hand on his chest, winding my fingers through his sparse chest hairs, and he seemed satisfied. It's easy to mimic affection, especially after sex. That's when we are all at our most gullible.

We waited a bit until our pulses regulated, and sometimes, we did it again, because after all, he had paid for the room for the night. But soon, he would slide his pants back on, and we'd be back on the motorbike, sputtering home. If anyone saw us driving slowly through town, our bodies smelling of each other and the rawness of the hotel room, they never said anything. I would slide off his bike and go into my house, quiet as a mouse, never looking back. I'd dismiss the nurse-maid to her room, then wash myself, again scraping a cloth between my legs. Cleaning, always cleaning, the men out from under me.

Sometimes I slid into bed next to my children, longing for the comfort of their father next to us, the certainty of our family, now a hazy dream. Even as I didn't want another man, I wanted the wholeness of that old formula. Mother, and father, and children. All pegs lined up.

That spring, there was a series of secret bombings across the border in Cambodia. I heard the news about a group of kids shot in America for protesting. I gasped, thinking of those young bodies, the mothers who would never stop longing. And slowly but surely, the Việt Cộng came for the businesses around me. Quietly, owners were relieved of their shops. They handed over wads of money in exchange for their lives. A business tax, they called it. The wealthy slowly disappeared, some to Europe, if they were lucky; others across the border to China or Cambodia. And rarely, across the world to that golden land, America. I could smell the ash on the air, that acrid scent of a fire whispering into form.

Việt and I went to the hotel one night in June. The cicadas were in swarm then, their rubbing, anxious sounds setting my nerves rattling. I made Việt close all the windows, and with the night air cut off, the room felt close. Instead of washing as I normally did, I stood in front of the bed. He seemed confused, half drunk from his evening social activities with friends, and already unbuttoning his shirt. He frowned.

"My love," he said. "What's wrong?"

I said, "I've never asked you for anything before."

He nodded. This much was true. Việt liked me because I asked for nothing. He could pretend, then, that we owed each other nothing. I knew he had other lovers, the silly girls I saw in the marketplace, the ones angling for a fancy meal, a bit of silk that they could spin into a new dress. Sometimes they went into the shop, just to see me, to test the competition. But they didn't threaten me; they didn't have anything I wanted.

"I need to leave Việt Nam," I continued. "My children, too."

He bit his lip. I knew he had influence; his family did. He could arrange a boat, a flight. He could change my life. Việt was not a bad man. He was often indifferent and callous, but not out of malice. He had been pampered all his life, first by his parents, then by women, and always by a society that valued his maleness, his inherent privilege. But in me, I often wondered if he saw something else. A defiance, an insistence on equality.

"Why are you worried, em? We don't need the Americans. One Southerner is worth a thousand Northern scum. Mark my words. There's victory ahead for us."

I lifted my chin. "You're delusional if you think that."

"Sweet one, I don't want to argue."

"I want you to get me and my children to America."

"I can't do that, Minh," he said. His eyes darted away from my face, unable to face his own lie.

"You can," I said firmly. I straddled him. I tipped my breasts forward so my nipples teased his mouth. My other hand found the ridge of his hardness. I'd never done such a thing, and his eyes widened. He reached for my cheek, and instead of letting him touch me, I took his finger into my mouth and sucked. The fire began to burn in his eyes. I smelled the smoke that was to come.

"My parents would not like it," he said, his voice gasping. I moved on him, my hands now sliding under his shirt.

"I would like it," I said.

"But I'd never see you again."

"No." I ran my tongue against the perimeter of his lips, lining them with my own saliva, my own desire. "But you'd have me now. All of me. Any which way."

I wanted so much in that moment, none of which had anything to do with him. He tightened his grasp on my waist, pushing me deeper onto his lap.

Sometimes, I think back on that night and my own power, which had been dormant for so long. I know some would judge, or think I was using Việt unfairly. But what does fair matter when it comes to survival? I ran my lips up to his ear, flicking my tongue around its lobe. When he groaned, I knew he would give me anything.

Within a month, my children and I had packed a metal trunk for America, gold still sewn into our clothes, Xuân's knife buried in a pile of towels. Phước insisted on bringing the boat his father had carved for him, though I said we'd buy new toys in America. He cried until I threw it in there at the last minute, within the folds of my wedding dress and other sentimental items I couldn't bear to part with.

Việt didn't see us off. After that night at the hotel, I never ran into him again, though the tickets and papers arrived as they were supposed to. Maybe he was embarrassed that he'd given in. Or maybe he was mortified by what we'd shared in the hotel room. I only felt gratitude, and a muffled affection. He was never a bad person.

At the airport, I swirled the jade bracelet he had given me around my wrist. It was hard and cool, a shackle that released only years later, when I learned of his death in a flood and, finally, slipped it off. He did eventually marry one of those schoolgirls, though they did not have children. They said he opened a hotel of his own, and I sometimes wondered if it was modeled after the one we'd frequented. Mostly, I was relieved he didn't die sooner; that he'd lived more than any of us were promised.

Do I think of him? I didn't when I was alive. And now, in my memories, he strikes me more as an idea—an avenue for flight—than a flesh-and-blood man. But if I met him in the mist, my lips salty with the taste of those nights in that red-curtained hotel, I would recognize him. And I would thank him, for seeing me even so briefly, and for letting me go.

Chapter 20

Hương, 1990

I have tried to let go of my past, but when I swim, it comes back to me, lubricated by the water and the rare moments of calm I feel while pushing my body to its limits. In the pool, I am driven to go harder and faster. Beth tells me to slow down. Despite my first gasps of hesitation, she says she's never seen anyone take to water faster. "You shark," she says, her voice a mixture of admiration and concern. But when I reach the end of the pool, I take a breath and dive back in. I think, *If I'm not careful, I could drown in my own memories.*

The ones that surface surprise me.

The first time I met Ann's father. That expression about stealing someone's heart? I felt that with him. After we met, my heart was never mine again.

Apart from his handsome face, Vinh had a sense of unshakable confidence, and beneath that, a mystery that, if I lingered on it too long, felt alarming. As if warning me that he did, after all, have things to hide.

We met in a bookstore on the community college campus in the halcyon days of summer. I was ringing up a flurry of students, gathering their textbooks into outrageously expensive stacks, my back sweaty and straining toward the tiny fan on the counter, blowing sweet cool air my way every few seconds. It was a day like any other day, though I have rewritten it to be pregnant with some sense of twitching excitement.

Then Vinh was standing in front of me with his pile of books, a faint smile dancing on his face. I shook my hair away from my eyes and smiled back. I rang him up and slid his books in a ghostly white plastic bag. Without a word, he wrote his number on the receipt and shoved it back across the counter to me. I noticed how he crossed his sevens in the middle, the way my mother did.

I asked, "What if you have to return your textbooks? I'll have your receipt."

"But I will know to find the beautiful bookshop girl," he said.

The bloom in my chest was hot and sudden. After years of living with my mother, her prudishness and stingy love caging me tight, I longed desperately for something free, something that felt attached to me and no one else.

"What if I leave?" I asked. "I might not work here forever."

The line behind Vinh was impatient, resentful mutiny coloring their conversations. One girl in a neon-pink blazer tapped her watch when she caught my eye. But I didn't care. This man was the kind that made you forget everyone else.

"You won't leave," he said, in Vietnamese this time, so no one else could understand. "Not until I come back. You're mine, after all."

His confidence was startling, but intoxicating. I threw my head back and laughed. Yet far from dissuading him, this seemed to make him even more eager.

He did come back, again and again, until I agreed to go on a date with him, until we married, until our lives scalloped into one another's. But even through our happiest times, he was always a man with his eyes on the horizon. I was the one who had to wait for him to return, and he did, until he didn't.

After our wedding, it was supposed to be a surprise when Vinh borrowed a lakeside cabin for our honeymoon. But as it would end up, I had to go with him to get the key, and he was already disgruntled that his plan—flourishing the key before me as we pulled up to the remote cabin—had already been derailed, like so many of his grand designs. I sat in the passenger seat, watching my husband transform into a different man.

His friend, a man in a faded blue shirt with a buzz cut, swung the key toward Vinh, easily looping it through the air as Vinh struggled to catch it. Vinh's tight smile tugged as he rubbed his thumb over the key fob. His friend had given him the key with a sense of tolerant magnanimity, as if the loan of the cabin was more than a favor. As if it were an invisible debt. I wondered what this brief luxury had cost my new husband.

"Thanks, man," Vinh said.

"Let it be your love nest this weekend." The friend winked at me through the window. "No one needs sleep on their honeymoon, am I right?"

I turned away. I wasn't a prude, but I hated lewdness. It was an intrusion into a sacred space, into my inner dignity. I could hear them laughing together as I rolled my window up. Men joking about very funny things.

We drove four hours to get to the cottage, and since we only had the weekend, we were quick about it, speeding through open farmland to get there as fast as we could. There were neat rows of crops, like a million perfect braids, and thick clumps of trees. We passed squat houses, barns that crumbled into the earth, and cows with great sagging bodies that watched us with eyes visored by their own flesh. When I said, "We're flying, anh," Vinh grinned at me from the side of his mouth. He squeezed my knee. Along the way, we ran over a skunk, and the smell filled the car, acrid and a little herbal, like pot.

"Motherfucker," he said. He pounded the dashboard.

"Đồ chó," I whispered.

"What?" He narrowed his eyes at me and I shrank into the seat, playing with the hem of my dress.

"You know. Just . . . the Vietnamese curse. 'Son of a bitch.'"

"I knew that."

In town, we picked up groceries: some fresh eggs furred over with chicken feathers, a loaf of white bread, four sausages tied up together in a bunch, mottled meat straining obscenely against its casings. I added a pint of ice cream to the cart, then put it back, remembering that Vinh was lactose-intolerant. He grabbed a few six-packs, even though I didn't drink much, had never gotten used to the taste of beer, which held all the crudeness of a burp with none of the satisfaction.

The people in the store were hostile, their eyes darting away as soon as we looked at them, then scraping up and down our backs when we turned away. We were strangers, and Asian ones at that. This wasn't a place that tolerated change to its routine. It had that foamy, vague quality like soap at the bottom of a sink: so white, so ephemeral. At the last minute, Vinh grabbed some bait, a tangle of worms in a tin can.

"You fish?" I asked, surprised.

We had known each other hardly longer than six months before we married, and these little facts came hard and fast, like minnows biting your heels. I tried not to feel betrayed by them. It's impossible to ever fully know someone.

"Yeah, now and then," he said, annoyed.

The cashier glanced between us, a smirk playing on his face. I don't know why he was amused. There was a joke that we'd never be let in on.

"You people know your way home?" he asked.

With a different intonation, in a different place, he could have seemed helpful, an old country clerk helping the newlyweds out. Here there was a vague threat in his words, a boiling violence that made me look away as quickly as I could. Behind us, a woman in a windbreaker holding a basket coughed, and with each phlegmy expulsion, I could feel my shoulders tense up.

The clerk said, "Maybe you're lost."

We didn't answer him. Vinh grabbed the groceries and thrust the can of worms at me. I didn't want to hold them, but I did, resting the cold metal between my legs in the car. I imagined them writhing against the metal, their glutinous bodies mashed and inseparable. We stayed silent on the road.

"Anh," I said gently, "don't let yourself be bothered. They're trash. Probably never left their town."

"I know," he replied, stonily. "Don't you think I know."

He stared straight ahead until we pulled into a winding drive.

From the outside, the lake house looked nice enough: pale blue siding edged with trim little windows, like the kind a child would draw on a sketch of a house. There was a wraparound porch with wood-flaked rails and columns that flared at the top. The lake, in the distance, was quiet and still, dark, shadowed by mangroves.

"How wonderful!" I cried. I clapped my hands with more energy than was warranted, hoping to squeeze some of the bad humor from Vinh.

Inside, the house was nothing like we imagined. The blankets were mothy, and the heat broken. It was chilly. I saw mouse turds loose on the ground, scattered like bread crumbs. Vinh banged his leg against a low side table.

"This piece of shit," he muttered.

His bad mood was starting to infect me, too, and I avoided him to let him cool down. Vinh's anger was new. I didn't know how to tame it. Over the six months we'd dated, he had revealed many parts of himself: the scholar, the ambitious idea man, the sweet romantic. He brought me carnations tied in twine, and once, a bunch of rambutans because I had mentioned how much I loved them. He tore off the spiky exterior, then fed the white flesh to me, sensuously, generously. The vaguely floral scent of the rambutans reminded me of perfume. We collected the pits in a Coke can, saying that we'd plant them in our garden one day.

"I'll grow my wife the biggest rambutan garden that ever existed," he declared, sweeping his arms so wide and so goofily that I giggled.

Of all the selves I knew of Vinh, I hadn't met this new one that emerged at the lake house. He simmered.

I swept the place clean, then found some rags to scrub down surfaces. At least the oven worked. Once the cleaning was done, having taken two hours of our scant, precious weekend together, I put on a new dress, a yellow one I'd sewn for the honeymoon with pearl buttons down the front. Vinh liked me in yellow. Said it made me look like a beam of sunshine. I found him on the dock of the cottage, staring out at the water.

"I think it's wonderful," I lied.

"Some people have so fucking much, you know?" he said. His voice wasn't angry now, just very tired. I wrapped my arm around his waist, and after a moment, he turned to look at me.

"But no one has me, except you," I said.

His smile was timid, then true. He kissed me, winding one finger around a lock of my hair. We had been chaste up until our wedding day. Six months of sweet kisses, not even a back-seat grope. He was a gentleman, but like any man, he was eager. So was I, for that matter. I'd never wanted anyone as much as I wanted him.

Across the way, on another dock, we saw two figures, a man and a woman in twin folding chairs. They were smoking and had their sunglasses pulled low on their faces, even though the day was cloudy and brittle. The man wore a Panama hat and held a fishing pole loosely in one hand, recreationally, like he didn't care whether he caught anything. The words "man of leisure" came to me. The woman stood and put one hand on her waist. Even from a distance, I could tell that she had a fantastic figure. She wore high-waisted white jeans and a polo shirt. Her hair, yellow-gold, feathered around her face. She was what you would call a knockout. I startled a little when she waved at us.

"Hey, y'all!" she called.

"Hi," Vinh said cautiously.

"We're comin' over," she yelled. "No need to shout across the way like a bunch of savages."

Vinh and I shrugged. These lake people were forward, but we didn't mind, exactly, even though we weren't at the house to make friends. In minutes, they'd bounded up to us. The woman's gait was quick, like a rabbit's, while her husband idled behind her, rocking back and forth on his heels. She lifted her sunglasses and I saw how her light brown eyes sparkled, ringed with lines of thick lashes that often fell onto her cheeks, as if they couldn't help but be drawn to the peach flush of her skin.

"You all new here?" she asked, that slight drawl like a wood curl, tawny and wispy all at once.

"Just arrived," Vinh said. "My wife and I are on our honeymoon."

She shimmied, then nodded. "Why, isn't that sweet! Newlyweds. Rob and I have been married for five years now, and I can't even *remember* the last time we took a trip. We just live here at this little house all year long, and he fishes, and I putter about my days. Dreadfully dull."

I thought of my job at the restaurant, the way the sweat tickled the base of my spine during the long days, how wasteful it felt to sweep perfectly good food in the trash. Then the calluses on the bottom of my feet, the ones I'd file until they were smooth again, if only for a day at a time, opening up again in painful blisters the next shift. The bookstore, which I'd loved for its quiet and the hearty gusts of air-conditioning that rained on my shoulders, had not paid enough. To afford a house of our own, I went to work at the restaurant, hoping the tips would better supplement Vinh's income from his job at the garage. I would take this woman's version of dreadfully dull.

Rob spoke for the first time, flicking his cigarette into the lake with seasoned grace. "Ashlynn forgets that some people would kill for a house like ours."

There was aggression in his manner, though it was deliberate and even lazy. Like a coiled tiger. He was a territorial man, I could tell, around his wife and his house, all his possessions.

I stepped closer to Vinh, but he was smiling at Ashlynn, oblivious to me. Vinh was a charming man, drawn to vibrant people. The first to volunteer to buy a round of drinks, even if it was with the last of his paycheck. The first to get onstage at karaoke. The last to go home if even a hint of fun lingered in the air. I wasn't surprised that Ashlynn had caught his eye. When she played with the collar of her shirt, I could see that it was unbuttoned fully, and the vee sloped down to the slit between her tanned breasts.

Ashlynn and Rob dawdled on the dock with us for an hour that night, chatting about nothing at all until we got too cold and went into the cottage. I was embarrassed about the dirt and took care to say it wasn't ours, it was just a loaner.

"We just moved into an apartment. It's not a palace, but it's nicer than *this*," I rambled.

That made Vinh's eyes darken. I guess I was showboating a little, but I was also shaming him. I wasn't accustomed to company.

"You should have seen our place before we got to scrubbing, darlin'," Ashlynn said easily, her long legs crossed at the ankles as she sat on the couch.

"You mean, before the cleaning lady got to it," Rob said.

She stuck out a dainty pink tongue at him and he smiled for the first time since we'd met.

I was fascinated by her. She was so beautiful, yet earnest. I wondered why no one had ever told her that people like her didn't have to try so hard. And Rob, certainly, didn't try at all. He rubbed tiny circles in her shoulder with one finger, the movement so unexpectedly erotic that I felt myself heating up at it. Ashamed, I looked away. Once in a while, he leveled me with an assessing look. Not so much interested as appraising. Wondering what value a person like me could have for him.

We shared our six-packs, which they drank quickly, throwing their beers back like water while I sipped mine. Vinh imitated them. His laugh got louder, freer. His face redder.

"Maybe we'll come back to the lake someday. Get our own house right alongside y'all," he said loudly, raising his bottle in a toast.

I knew we wouldn't, not ever, and I felt awkward listening to him pretend to be someone else. I cleared the bottles away and stood in the kitchen, relieved to be on my own. The moon on the water was a rippling thing, broken into little slivers. It looked like a leaderless school of fish, gathering, uncertain where to go next.

Quick as anything, I felt something brush against my buttocks. When I turned, I saw Rob, his eyes half lidded. A lassoing kind of smile on his lips. I backed up, but he only laughed lightly.

"Just telling you we're leaving," he said.

I nodded. Pressed myself back against the sink. He grinned again, secretively, as if he knew something. And maybe he did. I didn't feel as disgusted by him as I should have.

He reached out a hand and rubbed a half circle in my arm with his thumb, just as he had to Ashlynn. "Don't be a stranger while you're here."

That night, after Rob and Ashlynn had left, Vinh and I fell into the bedroom. It was our first time being together in this way, having opted to remain apart until marriage—my concession to Mẹ's frantic need to protect my virginity. Vinh and I didn't have trouble connecting in bed. Even after his many beers, he was eager. Feeling Rob's half circle in my arm like a brand, I surged to meet my husband, my passion surprising and a little shameful. Our bodies were like eels, slick and willing, knotted against the old and likely unwashed sheets of the bed. I wished, as he entered me, as he grunted and grabbed at my hair, as my body convulsed under him, rocking in waves of pleasure, that I could be sure I was really making love to him, rather than the version of him that I'd seen that night.

The next day, I woke slowly, curling my toes back and forth, as if rediscovering my body. Vinh wasn't in bed. I put on a sweater and cleaned out the coffee maker, crusted over with dregs of a long-forgotten pot of coffee. Spooned black grounds into a makeshift paper towel filter. Outside on the dock, I could see my husband with his fishing pole, the can of bait next to him. I took coffee to him.

"Anh." I kissed his cheek. "I missed you when I woke up."

His eyes barely lifting from the water. "I want to catch fish for our dinner."

"That sounds nice," I said. The coffee was very weak. I would have to get used to making it. Most of my life, Mẹ and I drank jasmine tea, steeped exactly four minutes in scalding water. Then we used the tea bags again and again, until all that was left was hot water, tinted faintly by the bag.

"Maybe I'll take a fish over to Rob and Ashlynn," he said. He laughed, but it was unnatural. There was a steely determination in his expression. "We could have dinner with them."

"We spent all last night with them," I said. "We don't even know them. They're strangers."

"So?"

"It's our honeymoon."

He pressed his lips together. I could see he didn't like that I was nagging him. I felt like a bore. Placatingly, I put my hand on his back. I slid it under his sweater, grazing the warmth of his skin, a reminder of what we shared last night. He shrugged me away.

That day, I watched him on the dock from the kitchen window, his feet dangling in the water, that fishing pole between his hands like an extension of his body. I brought him breakfast out there, then lunch, a Spam sandwich coated in a thin layer of mayonnaise. I sat with him while he ate, then went back into the house.

At some point, Ashlynn stopped over to our deck in a tight red sweater and acid-washed jeans. From a distance, I could see her throwing her head back in laughter, resting her hand on Vinh's shoulder. He could be very funny, I knew. He gazed at her, and though I couldn't see his expression, I imagined the way his pupils would dilate, staring at her hair feathered around her face like a halo.

When she left, he turned back to the lake. I thought I could see the smile lingering on his lips. Soon after, he came in briefly, throwing me onto the bed with such force that I made myself giggle to take the edge off it, telling myself it was a joke, that we were playacting. He tore my shirt accidentally, but seemed pleased when he threw it over his shoulder. He bit my lip, his teeth pulling until a droplet of blood landed on my tongue.

"Stay," I said, afterward.

He tugged his sweater back on and gave me a little wave as he headed out to the dock with his pole.

When he finally returned to the cottage with two fish in tow, I was happy for him. I'd spent the day reading the same magazine over and over again, an old celebrity rag I'd found in the bathroom. Half the celebrities were now has-beens or dead, and it felt eerie reading about them in the prime of their lives. I could have joined Vinh on the dock, but it was cold, and I didn't think he wanted my company anyway.

He set the cooler on the kitchen counter with a loud bang. I liked seeing him so jovial. The crappies he'd caught were small and speckled, their bodies slightly bloated. They didn't seem all that healthy, but I guessed they were dead, so that was to be expected. I thought I'd fry them with lots of salt and pepper rubbed into diamond grooves I'd cut into their bodies. We would make rice and greens. The thought of sitting down to a dinner my husband had caught pleased me. I wasn't annoyed at him anymore.

"Let me just run one of these over to Ashlynn and Rob," he said. He washed his hands and took the cooler with him.

I descaled and cleaned the fish he had left behind, the smaller of the two, removing its guts in a big handful. They glistened purple and red, turning my stomach a little. I hated cleaning fish, and back at the Banyan House, that was Mẹ's job. She took a particular gusto in digging through their bellies, perhaps imagining her past enemies as she eviscerated the catfish on the big round cutting board, cut like a tree trunk.

I threw the guts in the trash. Called Mẹ, even though it was long distance. Fought my mounting disappointment at my husband's absence.

Soon, the door banged open, and Vinh walked in, setting the cooler by the sink. He grabbed himself a beer, the last of the six-packs.

"Didn't they want the fish?" I asked. I didn't mean my voice to be mocking, but I supposed it might have been. Impatience sometimes made me testy.

"No," he said curtly. "They were hosting a dinner party or something. They didn't come to the door."

I imagined Vinh in the glow of Ashlynn and Rob's porch light, his fist raised to the door. The way he shifted onto one foot and the other, our old Styrofoam cooler at his feet. How he'd listened to their laughter, so near and yet so distant, and waited hopefully, foolishly. Maybe he wanted to be invited in. It made my heart ache for him, even as the shadow of superiority colored my impression of my husband. The man who wanted. The man who could not be enough, even for himself.

"Well, maybe we'll just stick to ourselves for the rest of the trip," I said. "Like we should have from the beginning."

"What does that mean?" he grumbled.

I continued to cut perpendicular lines in the fish, taking care not to look him in the eye.

"It's just that it's our honeymoon."

"So you keep saying."

"I think they're odd," I said. "Rob touched my arm the other day. And Ashlynn is a flirt."

Vinh tapped his beer bottle against the counter. "She's not. You're jealous."

"I'm not," I said indignantly, though afterward, I thought he was likely right.

"They're just friendly."

"Friendly is not grabbing my butt when my husband is in the next room."

He laughed, meanly. "I don't think that happened, em."

I flushed. "Why would I lie?"

"Rob and Ashlynn are very happy together. I mean. Married men don't do that."

"So you wouldn't, if you were alone with her?" I asked. I thought of her narrow waist, her breasts straining in the tight sweaters. My husband was a man, and not just any man. He had an eye for beauty. Still, I should have let it go. "You're not so good at hiding your thoughts, anh."

He slammed his bottle so hard against the sink that it shattered. I was confused at his expression, so cold and lofty. This was perhaps the moment I could have changed things. One of many moments. But I only stared at him.

"Never talk to me like that again," he said.

Though a snaking fear had begun to wind in me, I lifted my chin. "I wasn't raised to obey men. Especially men who throw tantrums."

When he raised his arm, the bottle still clutched in it like a bouquet, I flinched. My knife slipped against the cutting board, right into the meat of my index finger. Then there was blood, so much of it. It flowed onto the counter, into the grooves of the fish, like a kind of chili sauce, thick and red. I grabbed my finger. I'd cut the tip off.

Frantically, I wrapped my finger in a dishcloth, applying pressure. We were too far from a hospital. The cut hurt so much that tears flowed down my face. I couldn't help it. I'd never lost a part of myself before.

Vinh was silent, fascinated, watching me with preternatural calm. He didn't move to help me. I told myself it was shock, but it was strange nevertheless, like being behind glass while a scientist observed. I didn't like being so separate from him. After a minute, a truly endless minute, he came over to help me bandage my finger. He didn't soothe me, but he did lead me to the sofa.

"You should be more careful," he said, almost casually.

I knew he wasn't the one to lift the blade and cut my finger—I had done it, indisputably—but it troubled me to hear him say that. As if he had nothing to do with me. I thought I was going crazy.

"I'm going to take a shower," he said. I heard him moving around the kitchen, then the bathroom. The pipes began to clank somewhere behind me when the water turned on.

"Thank you," I whispered, dazed.

When I got up from the couch, the shards of glass were gone from the sink. The fish with its blood-laced grooves had been disposed of. Oddly, he'd wrapped the tip of my finger, the discarded bit of flesh that had caused me so much pain, in a paper towel and left it on the windowsill. It sickened me to see it. We ate eggs on toast that night. We didn't make love.

Though I felt exhausted, I couldn't sleep as Vinh snored quietly next to me. I thought about the rhythms of marriage, the way our shared memories undulate through our consciousness, pressing against us at different times. How many years would we have together? Fifty? Sixty? What would we remember from this honeymoon? The crappie that took a day to catch, the finger that I so carelessly severed? Ashlynn's tan breasts or Rob's floating cigarette, a little nicotine yacht on the dark water?

I found myself in the kitchen in the dark, reaching for the chopped bit of my finger. My hand felt ungainly, still bound in a towel, tied tightly to stop the bleeding. The fingertip was round at the end, with a little white crescent of my nail still attached. A surprisingly clean cut. I took the fingertip out to the front yard, beneath the wraparound porch with its picturesque little spindles. The lightbulb on the porch flickered on, its motion detector apparently the only thing in the cottage that still worked. With my free hand, I dug a hole in the ground. I placed the fingertip in there, then carefully covered it with dirt.

Why did I do it? I didn't want to see it anymore, and throwing it away felt sacrilegious. It was my body, after all. I wasn't in my right mind, still aching and tired. I went back into the house, changed my makeshift bandage, and tried to sleep.

That night, under the spreading water mark on the ceiling, I dreamed that my fingertip rooted into the earth, like a seed. A flesh-tree began to grow from it, appendages lifting from the ground, knuckles bulbous and wrinkled. No leaves feathered around my finger-tree, only bits of nails, stuck horizontally into the flesh like mushrooms jutting from a log. It was bare and tall, crawling toward the sky, using the clouds and the horizon as its trellis. A golden crow landed on the highest branch, watching me with narrowed eyes. Seeing right through me.

When I woke, I thought maybe I had dreamed the whole night. But the crappie guts stank up the cottage, and my finger, now clotted over, was an eighth of an inch shorter than it had been. We packed up that day and went home early.

Vinh handed me the key to the cottage. In the car, as I watched the blue of the lake slide away, the imprint of Ashlynn and Rob still deep grooved in our quavering young marriage, I held the key in my palm until it turned hot, like a brand.

Chapter 21

Ann

Noah sounds breathless when he answers the phone. It's not kind of me, but I feel a tiny, grim satisfaction that he rushed for my call. Him chasing me for once. When I glance at my watch and mark the time—2:17 on a Thursday—I remember, in the part of my mind that used to center my days around his teaching schedule, that he has a grad seminar in ten minutes. I picture him standing amid students in the classics building. He's probably inching past them, sweaters rubbing against each other in those tight hallways. Those old universities seem steeped in their own sweat, the radiators humming all day, dangerously hot to the touch.

"Christ, Ann. It's been forever. I was worried—more than worried. Are you okay?"

"Yes, I'm fine. More than fine."

He turns sarcastic. "Oh, that's a relief. Because I wouldn't really know, would I."

"You're mad."

"Confused. Are we together? Are we not together? What do I tell my parents?"

The age-old question.

"Well, I don't have answers. I'm sorry about that," I say, and I really am.

I can hear him expelling a breath. "I know you're dealing with a lot. Your grandmother."

"Your infidelity."

"Yes. Yes, that's fair. I'm so sorry, Ann. How many times can I say it? I wish I'd been at the funeral. I could have been there for you."

"She left me the Banyan House. Well, me and my mother. It's a shit show."

"How's *that* going to work?"

I shrug, then realize he can't see it. "I have to tell you something, Noah."

Two twenty-four now. Maybe it's unkind to do it this way. But I don't want to hold this in anymore. I tell him about the pregnancy. I tell him I'm going to keep the baby. That I have a doctor's appointment. There's silence. A rasp of breath.

"And, well, I think I might stay here in Florida for it all," I say. "At least until the baby's born. Then—I don't know."

"You don't know," he repeats.

"But I'll figure it out," I tell him, a flash of steel in my voice.

"Jesus. Ann. I don't know what to say. This is a lot. Why would you tell me over the phone?"

"You needed to know. I'm still not ready to see you."

"This isn't in the plan."

More than anyone else, I know the plan, as if it had sprung fully formed from my brain. It's always been there, easy as a script, with everyone's role neatly highlighted in yellow. Noah would get tenure. We would get married and buy a big house, but not gargantuan, next to his parents'. In time, we'd have a child, when he was ready to take that step. Or never. We didn't talk about children, only his career and his books. Travel and adventure and ballets that ended in late dinners talking with very smart people.

Now I feel so absurdly far from the life we led that I wonder if I haven't dreamed it all up. The big vaulted ceilings with the barnwood beams, so *cool* and ill-fitting in that modern home. Would Alice and

Brandon be glad that we've split? Maybe they've set him up with someone new, a lawyer or a doctor who actually likes hosting parties and
spending money on custom dresses. Maybe Alexis will move in. The
thought doesn't pain me as much as I thought it would.

I tell Noah, "Maybe your plan was never mine."

"Ann, I don't know what that means. But I have to go."

"Noah." I say his name without knowing how to follow it.

"I'll talk to you later."

And the phone is silent again.

The doctor says the baby is almost the size of a kumquat this week.
When I tell Mom, she surprises me with a palmful of kumquats from
the Asian market, each orange oval the size of a quail egg, shiny with
citrus oils. It's a shocking gesture of tenderness.

"Citrus is good for the baby," she tells me.

"Is that true?" I ask.

She shrugs. We're outside and the sun is high. It beats onto the
house, turning the creamy peach shades even deeper, like sherbet. This
sugary house, molded over, dappled with rot.

Mom eats everything on the kumquat, even the peels, the orange
staining her hands. She rubs the leaves between her fingers, releasing
the aching verdant scent. I cut mine open with a small paring knife,
then suck out the pulp. The sour-bitter-sweet taste sits somewhere in
my skull, straining against the roof of my mouth. A sigh of satisfaction releases from me.

"I heard you on the phone with Noah."

"Why are you listening?"

"The walls are thin," she says, but she's not apologetic. And I'm not
really that mad. We've shared so much these past few weeks that it's a
relief not to have to hide anything from her. I don't want to confess
anything new.

The plastic chairs groan as we settle into them, a plate of kumquats
between us. The plate is fine, an ivory color with a blue floral motif

ringing a monogrammed *A*. The curlicue of the *A* is lifted like a dancer's hand, flung into the sky at the end of a performance. Of course, it
isn't Bà Ngoại's. Maybe she bought it at an estate sale. Judging from
her home, many estate sales nestled inside it, like pink-cheeked matry-
oshka dolls. I use some kumquat juice to trace the monogram. A for
Ann. A for adored, A for abandoned. But that's not accurate, I know.
In Noah's story, I've abandoned him, and he's the poor suffering professor, mourning the loss of his great love.

"I told him about the baby. He said it wasn't in the plan."

"Well, Ann?"

"I know. I need a plan. You keep telling me. I thought about leaving
Florida, I did. I think about it still. But I want you here when I have the
baby. You're my only family."

She takes my hand. "It's been the three of us for so long. We never
needed a man before, right?"

"You seemed to," I say, unable to stop myself.

"I made mistakes. You know this."

I think maybe she'll talk about my father now, but she doesn't. She
never does. What do I know of him? She said his name was Duy, a
short little syllable like all our names, and that he has been gone for a
long time. Not a photo to be found. Abandoner of families. He's more
mist than memory to us now. Mom said he went back to Việt Nam, in
search of the hazy golden life before the war, one he never got to experience as a child, but I wonder. I looked him up many times, and there's
no father to be found matching that name, but I also know that people
can disappear sometimes.

I throw my sucked-out peel into the woods, where it lands with a
quiet thump. Already, flies swarm to it, their dances profoundly coor-
dinated, swooping with such polite grace that it reminds me of one of
those medieval court dances, where the men and women lightly touch
palms before backing away. The audacity of human contact.

Mom shakes her head at the kumquat carcasses, thinking of all that lost nutrition. The banyan tree winds around the peels, absorbing them back into the earth. If I squint, I can almost see its branches rippling against the ground, a flurry of helpful fingers.

"I first met Noah's parents at a country club," I say. "I picked out this dress that was so white, you would have thought it was sewn from a cloud. I guess I wanted them to think I was pure or something. But still, when they looked at me, they saw dirt. You know that look someone gives you, like they're smelling something off? It was like I couldn't get clean enough for them."

Mom waits. She squints, but her expression is neutral. I don't know if I've ever talked about Noah's parents in front of her with this level of detail. He's always seemed separate from my life here in the Banyan House.

"His mom loved gushing about how *exotic* I was, like I was a fruit she found in the market," I continue. "Something her friends hadn't tasted. She seemed proud of Noah for having expanded their palates with me, or something. I was consumed by them."

Mom picks at the threads on the ripped knee of her jeans. Her fingernails are long, but carefully ovaled at the ends. She's never polished them, and I can see the striations along the length of each nail. But with a shock I see new wrinkles in her hands. Swollen joints, the shadow of an age spot. My mother, though not old, is older than I have been acknowledging. There's a hunch of her shoulders that was not always there.

Then she says, "They're like that. White people." She seems lost in a memory, her eyes hazy and unfocused.

"That's a generalization," I say. "Noah wasn't like that."

But I think of how he would let my hair run through his fingers like a stream. He'd bring it to his nose and sniff my perfume, the move strangely erotic, a fixation I didn't begrudge at the time. He told me I was as precious as a doll. As fragrant as a flower. Do you talk about people you love like that? I don't know. We all fetishize parts of one another. Didn't I do the same with him? That golden, rich-boy exterior that made me feel so safe, so cared for—I wasn't any better.

"This house is a mess, Mom," I say finally. "We should sell it. We could use the money."

She stops picking at her clothes for a second and looks at me with such bald surprise that I feel ashamed. She protests, "It's our inheritance."

"I know, but did Bà Ngoại want us to live like this?"

"We'll fix it up, Ann. It could be beautiful."

I sigh, imagining the money that we'd sink into the house. The foundation alone would take a fortune to fix, not to mention all the many updates to the broken tiles, the waterlogged facade. It's a big house on a bigger plot of land. We'd be crazy to keep it.

"We could have a nursery for Kumquat," Mom says. "Imagine. The windows; we'd sew curtains."

She's told this story before, this beautiful fairy tale about the baby and the two of us. How we'd raise my child to love the land and the sea. The salty bite of the wetlands, and the run of Popsicle juice down his arms on a sweltering day. She repeats this story so often, I can see the pudgy legs running through the grass, reaching down to grab a fallen palmetto fan in his fists. Squealing as his toes touch the surf for the first time.

"I bought a board book for Kumquat," I tell her.

If she's pleased, she doesn't show it. I'm not sure she's even heard me, so lost is she in the house she's building in her mind. The sky darkens, a sudden storm on the horizon. I can't imagine a nursery for the baby, not really. To me, it's not a kumquat or a being quite yet. It's a weight, a pearl that turns in my flesh.

Chapter 22

Minh, 1974

When I watch my daughter and my granddaughter telling themselves stories, I think about the ones that have crossed my lips over the years. Each so familiar, I didn't have to think before pulling them out, laying them down in slow succession, dominoes that line up, then fall into my children's ears.

I wonder how much they remember of those early years in America. Some memories are best left hidden. When Hương and Phước were little, scarcely more than wide-eyed babies, in the one-bedroom trailer, I'd tell them stories nearly every night. I did it to drown out the drunken fights of the neighbors, the flapping of screen doors that never latched shut, the sound of a baby wailing in the distance. For us, stories were their own kind of protection and escape.

Once, our landlord came to our trailer in the middle of the night, high off whatever he'd been snorting, thudding at our thin metal door with increasing urgency. Knowing, perhaps, that his violence would find release in a woman and her young children. I imagined an ogre at a castle threshold, terrible violence gathering at the edges of his mouth. With Hương's help, I pushed a table against the door.

I tried to make a game of it with the children. "Here, see, we're going to be sneaky soldiers."

Hương said encouragingly, "Do you hear that bad old dragon, Phước? Stay quiet. He'll run away."

But Phước stood his ground, yelling, "Go 'way, bitch, go 'way!"

I didn't know that he was cursing then, or where he'd learned it, but his fierce protectiveness made me proud, despite my fear. It was as if his father were peering up through his eyes again. I went for Xuân's knife, but that night, I didn't need it.

"Come here, con," I said. Phước collapsed against me, sobbing.

The landlord banged for twenty minutes, yelling profanities that felt like the buzz of crickets: insistent but meaningless. His fury often came without warning, whether we paid the bills or not, whether I smiled demurely or scowled at his roving eyes. For him and so many men, violence was a birthright.

I pulled my children to me and sang in their ears until he left, hoping that my hum would flood his rage out and away from us. Phước shrugged me off and went to his bed, where he sat upright, stiff and unseeing, fists digging into his mattress. I saw his wooden boat next to him, the last relic from our old life. I never knew what my son was thinking, or whether he sought comfort in our presence. He shut down so quickly, and without warning.

"Fuck," the landlord groaned at last, his fists tired, his mission unclear perhaps even to him. I thought I heard the shadow of shame in his voice, but it's hard to tell the difference. Shame and entitlement can tangle together until they're impossible to pull apart. Then he was gone.

"My brave children," I said, jittery in my relief.

I pulled Hương into the heat of my armpit. I gestured to my son, but he turned away.

"Tell us about Chú Cuội and the tiger cub," Hương whispered. Her skinny legs wound around the body pillow I had made for her, and her fingers tapped at the fabric, as if in rhythm with my words.

If we lived in fear, we didn't linger in it. We found ways to escape.

"The man in the moon," I began. Her wide eyes lit my heart up, like an ember pricking the driest part of a haystack. Outside the trailer, we could see the crescent moon. Chú Cuội was riding a chariot across the sky, traveling away from his lunar home that night. Soon, the moon would wax again, welcoming him home.

I traced the downy cup of Hương's ear with my thumb. It was easier to be tender with her in America, but the days were longer, and full of hard work. The gold wouldn't get us far, though I knew we breathed easier than other refugee families, their hungry, vacant eyes scanning us at the grocery store, looking for kinship. The Baptist ladies helped me find work, cleaning their houses. I did a good job, so much that they marveled when they came home, clapping their hands like children. "The windows are *shining*," they'd gush. They were tickled to have a cleaning lady, this once unattainable mark of the gentry. They sent me home with leftover cookies they bought from the bakeries, hand-me-down clothing. They liked me, this pretty woman who scrubbed their toilets, reminding me of how very important they were, how charitably they helped the brown immigrants of war.

"Don't skip *anything*," Hương said, nestling down into her blankets.

In just a few years, she'd start to withdraw from me, but now, for tonight, she was mine still, my girl to protect, to love. I began the story.

Once upon a time, a woodcutter named Chú Cuội lived in a poor village at the base of a great range of mountains. The woodcutter ate slugs he dug from the ground, frying them over an open flame to disguise his misfortune, so he could pretend he was eating chicken or the more luxurious beef. He had no family, only a one-room hut with a dirt floor that barely kept the rain away during monsoon season, and a hammock where he lay at night, constantly swinging to ward off the damselflies that landed on his prone body, their slender forms reminding him of gashes in wood. The forest was lush and forbidding.

The sweeping mountains seemed to frown down upon the village and its misfortunes, and Chú Cuội along with it.

One day, Chú Cuội brought his load of freshly cut lumber into the village. The fog was heavy and he stumbled into an untrod opening in the woods. There he saw three tiger cubs abandoned in the shadow of a great banyan tree. The roots of the tree streamed down like the wrinkles on an old witch's face, and seemed to cradle the cubs. The tigers were almost tame, mewing for their mother. Chú Cuội was not a cruel man, but he had known extreme deprivation. It makes a man desperate.

He thought these cubs would fetch a sum in the market, either as a wealthy family's new, idiosyncratic pet, or as the extravagant centerpiece in some feast Chú Cuội would never attend. It didn't matter. Money was what kept the world chugging along, and who was he to turn away from such luck?

He picked up the largest cub, who stared at him with blank, golden eyes that looked like speckled marbles. Neither of the other cubs protested as Chú Cuội held their brother by the scruff of the neck. He hesitated. In that space of uncertainty, a giant roar sounded. The mother tiger was back, and her paws clamored against the earth, warning rumbles in the bush. In a panic, Chú Cuội climbed the banyan tree, scaling its gnarled, ropey branches until he got to the top, still holding the cub. Then his foot missed its mark, a groove that suddenly went smooth under him. He clung to the branch to gather his balance, but dropped the cub, who sailed down many feet and hit the forest floor below with a shocking thud. Though Chú Cuội had meant to sell the cub after all, his heart broke into fragments at the sight of the tiger's broken little body.

Chú Cuội expected the tiger mother to rage until the leaves shivered, but she only gave her cub a lick, then went over to the base of the banyan tree. She bit into a smooth leaf with her teeth and calmly placed it atop her cub's head. The mother and her living cubs stood vigil next to the fallen cub.

Chú Cuội's eyes widened as, minutes later, the biggest cub slowly got up, shaking the leaf off his head. His mother gave him another lick, a little admonishing this time, and led her babies back into the jungle. They hardly gave Chú Cuội another glance.

Curious, he scrambled down from the tree and gathered a big handful of leaves, folding them into his pocket like bills. He went back into the village with his bundle of wood. Along the way, he saw an old man by the side of the road, clutching his leg.

"Chú," the man said, his voice raspy, "I've sprained my ankle. Can you help me to the doctor?"

Chú Cuội felt sympathy for this man, clearly suffering and abandoned. He made a decision then to embrace his future, to open himself up to wonder. Silently, he took out one of the banyan leaves and wrapped it around the man's leg, tearing the leaf to release the moisture inside. He ripped a brown strip of cloth from his culottes and used it to tie the leaf around the man's ankle.

"What is this?" the man asked, his face awash first in shock, then in awe. Within minutes, he flexed his foot. He got up, leaning on Chú Cuội's shoulder.

"How do you feel, Bác?" Chú Cuội asked. He stared at the ankle, disbelieving, even though he had known what would happen.

"Chú, this is a miracle!" the man exclaimed. The makeshift bandage fell off his ankle, forgotten and unnecessary.

The old man walked with Chú Cuội to the village, where he talked to anyone who would listen about the new town healer, the woodcutter who had suddenly become god-blessed. The town, so steeped in misfortune, hungered for miracles.

They clamored at the woodcutter, reaching out to touch his arm, the hem of his shirt, as if greatness could be spread by touch. Chú Cuội let them. He ran his fingers over the smooth leaves in his pocket and stayed silent. Best not to reveal all one's secrets.

Months later, news came to Chú Cuội of a wealthy man in the neighboring village whose beautiful daughter had fallen sick. She was the man's only child, and his greatest treasure. He spread the word that he'd heap riches upon any doctor who could cure her. Chú Cuội walked to the village and presented his case to the wealthy man, who was skeptical at first, then began to show interest when Chú Cuội talked about all the people he had healed. Lepers, women in the heated throes of childbirth, men who had lost their sight, children whose faces were blue as death. The sheen of immortality, fearsome and hugely magnetic, surrounded Chú Cuội's exploits. They believed anything of him.

"I have heard of you," the wealthy man said finally. "The gods give you power. They say it comes from the mountains."

"The mountains are great," Chú Cuội said. He ducked his head, trying for modesty, but everyone had heard of him; modesty was immodest, with such notoriety.

The man led Chú Cuội to a large room with polished floors and a tapestry of parading elephants on the wall. The cabinets were made of hardwood, finely carved and rich in hue. In the cushioned bed lay the most stunning woman Chú Cuội had ever seen. Hằng Nga, the wealthy man's daughter, had long hair, the light brown of a straw roof, ends curling like fiddleheads. At the sound of voices, her eyes fluttered open, then closed again. Though her lips were dry, they were full and pink. Chú Cuội felt the inevitability of love, the brush of fate.

He took three leaves from his pocket and boiled them into a tea that he strained and poured into a porcelain cup. He

lifted the drink to the girl's lips, letting the pale green droplets
ease into her mouth. He stayed by her bedside that night.

Once or twice, she opened her eyes and smiled at him,
her cheeks dimpling. She reached for his hand and didn't
let go. Sometime in the night, they whispered their names
to one another with the sacredness of a vow. Chú Cuội was
desperately entranced. He felt that she had healed him, and
said as much in whispering tones. By the slight lift of her
mouth, he could tell she heard him, and she was pleased.

In the morning, when Hằng Nga woke, she asked for her
father. He wept at the sight of his daughter, sitting up with the
health-bloom back in her cheeks, the morning light casting a
glow around her. She'd returned from the dead.

"Ba, I will marry Chú Cuội," she said to him, her voice
clear and deliberate. "I'll marry him today."

Chú Cuội could hardly believe that she wanted him, but
he understood that this was her way of repaying him for her
life. She idolized him for what she thought he was, not who
he actually was, but back then, Chú Cuội didn't know the
difference. He didn't understand that even the holiest of gifts
could be taken away. Hằng Nga's father only hesitated a second
before he agreed. He gave Chú Cuội mounds of riches, more
than one person could ever spend in a lifetime, and offered
to build the newlyweds a grand house. Chú Cuội agreed, but
only if it were at the foot of the forest, by the banyan tree that
had once changed his fortune.

But to Hằng Nga's father, he said, "So your daughter can
see the mountains."

Hằng Nga smiled, and that was that.

Chú Cuội and Hằng Nga lived in their new house
for nearly a decade, shaded by the giant banyan tree that
sometimes felt like a grandfatherly presence. Watching,
bloated with wisdom. Hằng Nga bore Chú Cuội children

whose feet kicked energetically when they were born, so full
of life and spirit that they made everyone around them smile.
It was a family blooming in fortune. They were beloved, an
example to all. Chú Cuội continued to heal those who came to
him. They kissed his hands and his feet sometimes. He didn't
often take payment, because he didn't need it, but they heaped
worship on him, which was all he'd ever really wanted.

One day, Chú Cuội traveled to a faraway village to heal
its leader, who had come down with a mysterious fever that
robbed him of any mobility in his limbs. It would be days
before Chú Cuội returned.

He kissed his wife. "Darling, I need you to protect the tree.
It's the source of my healing. Please, enjoy yourself and care for
our children, but stay away from the tree."

Hằng Nga nodded solemnly, but her heart was newly
restless. By then, her children were older, accustomed to
running off with friends, coming back as the chill of the night
overtook them, hungry and oblivious. And Chú Cuội was
so often away and distracted. She missed the earnest young
man who had made love to her each night, cradling her like
the miracle of life she was. After her husband left, Hằng Nga
wandered the grounds of their home. It was an impressive
house, but it was gloomy. The forest cast its shade like a
coverlet, and she rarely saw the sun.

One afternoon, she found a little blue flower growing
in the corner of the yard, and became inspired. She'd plant
flowers around the house to surprise Chú Cuội when he
returned. He'd remember the beauty of their home then, and
he wouldn't go away so often.

Perversely, she wanted to plant her flowers by the banyan
tree, as if challenging its power. Besides, it was the only spot
where the light hit, casting wells of sunlight around the
branches. Chú Cuội worshipped that tree, though no one

knew why. Hằng Nga hated to admit it, but the tree annoyed her. Maybe she was even jealous of it. It wasn't beautiful. It reminded her of a mantis, gray-brown legs piercing the earth. Hằng Nga was a woman of richness, of sumptuous beauty, and the banyan affronted her aesthetic sense. Blue flowers would revive this monstrosity, give it some elegance.

With her spade, she carefully dug around the tree. She didn't intend to anger her husband, only to indulge this small defiance.

Then, somewhere, she heard the cry of her youngest baby waking from his nap. She started, and her spade slipped and dug into the root of the banyan. The tree seemed to pulse and shudder, the branches straining from the ground. One by one, the branches rose from the earth, delicately, fingers lifting cards from a deck. They whipped around her.

Chú Cuội happened to be walking home from his trip when he heard his wife's scream. He ran. He got there in time to see the giant banyan tree rising from the ground, the last root severed, hanging just a couple of feet off the ground. In his mind's eye, he saw his fortune vanishing: his large home crumbling like the mud huts his children built and dried out in the sun, his wife in the arms of another man, his children gazing at him blankly, seeing the bedraggled woodcutter he once was rather than the successful healer he had become. This life, so dear and so precious, was slipping from him.

Without thinking, he grasped the roots of the tree, as if to pull it back to the ground. But it was large, it was strong and determined and furious. It rose to the sky, and with it, Chú Cuội. His feet dangled helplessly in the wind.

"Anh Cuội!" Hằng Nga cried. Her pale face was streaked with tears, like the imprint of a banyan smacked across her cheeks. "Anh! Don't leave me."

Chú Cuội never looked back. The last his wife saw, he was

hanging on to the tree, his fingers curled into the grooves of
the branches, staring into its leaves with an adoration that felt
like religion. Hằng Nga watched the love of her life, the man
who had saved her, the famous god-blessed healer, rise until he
was nothing but a shadow on the moon. He never returned. In
time, no one remembered him, not even his children. It was as
if he had never existed.

A year later, Hằng Nga, still very beautiful, if a little
world-saddened, remarried again, and her memory of Chú
Cuội faded, too.

In the last weeks of her life, decades later, she would find
her eyes drawn to the moon, watching as it waxed and waned
each passing day. Her grown children wondered what she
saw there, having long forgotten their father, thinking their
stepfather was the only man who had held them.

On her deathbed, she stared up at the milky-white glow of
the moon, reverently and in wonder, like a memory resurfaced.
Her last words were "Mặt trăng," whispered so low that no one
else heard. *Moon.*

When I finished the story, Phước shifted in his bed. I thought I
heard him sigh. Or perhaps it was a sob. My children knew something
of fathers who'd gone.

"Why didn't Chú Cuội stay with his wife?" Hương asked, her voice
lugubrious.

I considered this but had no answer. "Maybe the banyan was his
true love."

"That's silly. A tree can't be someone's love. And Hằng Nga shouldn't
have planted those flowers," Hương said, a little petulantly.

"Should we fault her for wanting to make her home more beautiful? For listening to her own self over half explanations from a man
with secrets?"

I could have said more about curiosity and obedience, and the way that a life could rift without caution. I wasn't on Hằng Nga's side. But I wasn't naive enough to believe that we ever fully control our own fates.

By then, Hương's eyes were drooping and her mouth hung open a little. The night was quiet again, except for the distant hum of cars, the even more distant sound of crashing waves. Across the room, Phước was still, but I could tell he was awake. He turned to the window.

Hương mumbled in her sleep. "Silly," she said. Her worldview so deliberate and firm, even then. The "shoulds" were her internal compass, even against any beating desire that escaped.

In the plush night, my anger reemerged. It wasn't natural to live with this kind of fear. We had fled to the States for safety; not for more brutality. I told myself I would pull my children out of that trailer one day. We'd get a place where the silence hung like drapery, velvety and obscene, a gift to ourselves. A healing house, far away from others, big and sprawling and shaded by great trees that afforded their own protection. We would never have to lean on our stories to save us. We'd never need saving at all. Our roots would lift from the earth and carry us someplace where the dread would not pull us down.

Chapter 23

Ann

I'm in my old drawing perch in the backyard, on the swinging bench Bà Ngoại bought, the one that squeaks horrifically every time I move against it. I stare out onto the banyan tree, which has historically been conducive to inspiration or, at the very least, meditation, but today I can't draw a single stroke worth keeping. The cuticles around my fingernails are stained with charcoal, balled-up paper strewn on the ground beside me like white flower buds. Above me, the late-afternoon sun warms my head. The heat summons my thoughts upward, straining against my skull.

Earlier, Noah called. We talked again about Kumquat and the future, which for us has split into a couple of fractured mirrors. We are no longer seeing the same reflection. He talked about private pre-school waiting lists and Stokke high chairs—they transition with the baby, he insisted—and how we could take vacations on Lake Michigan during the summer. I told him about the way manatees will sometimes brush against swimmers, those gentle monsters with their scarred, slow-moving bodies.

"Manatees, Ann?" he asked, bewildered.

"Mermaids," I said dreamily, and his sigh was rough, displeased.

Noah said he'd come to the Banyan House, if I insisted on staying, and I agreed, though in vague terms. I told him to wait until summer classes were over, in that brief gasp before the fall semester. The baby isn't going anywhere, and neither am I. At that, he heaved another giant sigh.

"I just don't feel like I know you anymore," he said sadly.

I smiled a little then, thinking, *That makes two of us.*

I still think about what we'll do after Kumquat is born. I imagine packing him into one of those giant VW buses and soaring away on the open roads. The shadows of mountains behind us. Red-clay earth and tumbleweeds. And me, swinging my baby high into that cloudless blue sky. We can go anywhere. We can be anyone. The freedom I feel at the thought is like a whoosh of air after a dive into a cold stream.

And yet. Sometimes I picture the nights, the two of us alone by a campfire. Do I really want to limit our world to just us? Maybe I would like to find my way to freedom, without the loneliness.

Mom approaches the bench, home early from work. She does what they call a 4/10 during the warmer months. Longer hours in exchange for half days on Fridays to enjoy the sunshine. She sits next to me and gently takes the sketchbook and charcoal, handing over a cheese-and-jam sandwich wrapped in a paper towel. When I clutch at the soft bread, my fingers press smudges into it.

"Thanks," I say between bites. "I forgot to eat this morning."

She frowns. "You should take better care of yourself. It's not just you to think about anymore."

We sway on the bench. Nearby, a crow settles on a rock, then splays his dark tail feathers, like a brush in water. Mom picks up one of the crumpled balls of sketch paper and smooths it onto her lap. A pair of bright eyes peek out from it.

"You're drawing her," Mom marvels. "I can see it. That little chicken pox scar on her left eye. Her cheekbones."

"It's not really working. I can't capture her."

"Why don't you draw from a photo? We have tons."

I can see her getting excited at the thought of a project, unearthing the heavy old photo albums with their plastic sheeting, the faux leather covers edged in gold. But Bà Ngoại isn't there, either. Her soul eludes me.

"Photos are so"—I gesture with my fingertips—"lifeless."

"Well," Mom answers, with that maddening serenity she uses toward me sometimes, a shade too close to smugness for my taste.

And just like that, I'm angry at her again. I wipe the crumbs from my lap, shaking them onto the grass so vigorously that some fly back in my face. Somewhere nearby, a woodpecker starts up.

I say, "It's stupid anyway. It's not like— Well, she's not going to see it or anything."

"You were always fatalistic about your art, Ann. Do you remember? Everything had to be perfect. Sometimes I'd find you scribbling away late at night, huddled in your closet with a flashlight. So many drawings in the trash can. That was before recycling, and I felt sometimes like we were killing whole trees for your art."

"The trees are safe now," I answer.

In my best moments, I was lost to the world while illustrating. My eyes and my hands, the only things that mattered. The act of creation, re-forming what was into something new. There is hubris in daring to create, and then daring to think you're great. These days, my illustrations can't fool even me into thinking they have any bit of originality about them.

"I don't think I even like illustrating anymore." I sigh. "Or painting or anything. I don't *like* anything."

Mom takes my nub of charcoal and adds a nose to the wrinkled sketch. It's way out of proportion, cartoonish in a bad way, but it makes me smile. I've never seen her draw before. Then she adds a pair of plush, vampy lips, like the ones from the *Rocky Horror Picture Show* poster. She's truly awful.

"You're being defeatist, Ann," she says.

"Yeah, well. It's another layer in my Sad Single Mother Portrait— my lack of vocation, among other deficiencies."

"There is nothing deficient about being a single mother," she says severely, and I hang my head, because she's right, of course. "You need some perspective, con. Maybe you just need a new project."

"Like what?"

She raises an eyebrow. "How should I know, Ann? You're the artist. Drive yourself into town. Get out in the world. You're rotting away here like a tree stump. You smell like one, too."

An hour later, after I shower and fill up the Oldsmobile with gas, I walk into the craft store in town, hoping a change in medium might help inspire me. I'd seen Wes loping toward a coffee shop down the street and slipped into an alley to avoid him, feeling absolutely ridiculous, like I'm in high school again. He texted once or twice, light little messages that I replied to with cheerful emojis but no words, wanting to leave our one-night stand as I found it: distracting, but ultimately meaningless. I was glad when he got the hint and stopped texting.

At the store, the gouache tubes are lined up neatly in a display that stretches nearly the length of the aisle. A hell of a lot bigger than when I was last here, a decade or so ago, fishing for enough money for just that right shade of cerulean. I run my hands over each tube, the vermilions and burnt umbers, cadmium reds and goldenrods. Once, I liked the watercolors, their ethereal transparency, their fluidity, like a stream slow-flowing over the page. Now I paint with gouache, watercolor's sturdier cousin. Its opacity a statement in itself. I select a shade of brown that's so deep, it may as well be black. I think of Bà Ngoại's eyes, that impenetrability. The well of secrets.

"Still painting?"

When I look over my shoulder to locate the source of that throaty, vaguely predatory voice, I see Crystal King standing by the paintbrushes, holding a shopping basket, the metal handle dimpling her forearm. Her plucked brows give her a kind of ferocity and vulnerability all at once, as if she's given up an essential part of herself in the pursuit of beauty. She wears her hair in a high, messy bun, and I can see streaks of black underneath the blond.

"Trying," I reply.

"Nice to see some things stay the same. Hi, Ann."

"Hi, Crys. It's good to see you."

Her thickly lined mauve lips, a lush contrast to those sparse brows, quirk a little. The color of her lip liner is a shade or two darker than her lipstick, so there's something a little eerie to her expression. "Okay, yeah. We going to play this, girl? You're the polite make-good who acts like she's so happy to run into her old friends?"

"What if I am?" But even I know I'm lying. She could always see through me.

"But, like, we weren't friends in the end. Definitely aren't now."

I carefully place the tube of paint I was considering into my own shopping basket and turn to Crystal. "And whose damn fault is that?"

A bit of edge creeps into my voice, and Crystal's eyes widen. Her smile is slow, but when it shines full from her face, her eyes light, too, as if catching on fire.

She says, "There's that old asshole I used to love."

"Takes one to know one, Crystal King."

She pauses, then throws her head back and laughs, and the fluorescent lights gleam against her throat. "Come get a coffee with me. My kid's with her dad. My husband. P. J. Peterson, remember him? I'm Crystal Peterson now. When you said King, I had to take a breath. I've been married for years. Took me a sec to find my way to Peej, though. Some frogs, like they say."

"I don't know."

"It'll be twenty minutes of your life," she insists.

We buy our supplies—me with my one tube of paint and Crystal with a bunch of craft supplies for her daughter—and head to a bakery around the corner where the coffee is so bad, you want to puke from it, but the scones are so sweet and buttery that you suck it up and ignore the coffee.

"They make this shit with sewage, I swear," she says, frowning down at her Styrofoam cup.

Crystal doesn't order a pastry, but I get two for myself, blueberry and vanilla-cinnamon swirl. This time of the afternoon, there's a lovely pink light in the bakery, reflected off the creamy walls. No one is here but us and an old jukebox in the corner I'm sure has never once been used. I notice the flyers drooping off the big bulletin board, advertising dog sitters and babysitters and house sitters. Does anyone do anything in this town but care for other people's things? The vinyl seat is sticky under my thighs.

"So," I begin. "You have a husband, and a kid."

"I know. Imagine it. Me and P. J.? God, if high school me could have seen it."

I remember that one time another kid, Nate Wilkes, slugged P. J. Peterson in the face in the middle of pre-algebra. No one knew why, but we thought it was over a girl. Good-looking P. J., who always seemed to attract trouble. Strange imagining him with Crystal, tough back then, clad in all that pleather and the shoes with the silver spikes running along the back, like the bristly quills of a hedgehog.

"Opposites attract?" I say. In a flash, I remember Tina saying that to me at Alice and Brandon's anniversary party. A lifetime ago.

"Maybe. But it's more like: when you leave high school, you stop trying so hard and resisting people who aren't like you. You find out the people you *think* you should like are the ones to avoid. I was going to the community college and so was Peej, and then one day we were both at the vending machine at the same time. My quarters got stuck and he slammed the machine with his palm until the Funyuns shook free. Classic love story, you know?"

"I think that's nice. He always seemed like a good guy."

She agrees. "Great dad, too, though the asshole can't discipline a kid to save his life. I've got to be the bad guy all the time. The other day, I found him sneaking up the stairs with this tiny bowl of chocolate ice cream. With sprinkles! 'Midnight snack,' he said, like a chump. Dads are softies."

I try to shake the vague fog of sadness beginning to gather inside me.

"And you're well?" I ask, trying for casualness as I take in her slim wrists, the fidgety way her eyes never seem to land in one place for too long.

"You mean the fact that I look like a skeleton? It's fine. I'm fine. Or I will be. We've got a plan. They diagnosed me with severe celiac. I'm treatable and not contagious."

"I didn't think you were."

"Sure, Annie."

I blink a couple of times. "Well, *I'm* pregnant. Four months now. That's not contagious, either, as far as I know."

Crystal leans back to look at me, then takes a swig of her coffee before answering. "Yeah, I can see it now. Congratulations? Or not? I can't tell how you feel about it."

"You're not the only one. Oh, and my grandmother died."

That one, Crystal takes with less levity. She looks down, and I see how huge her eyes really are, enormous green pools hidden by deep half-moon lids. The first day she talked to me, back in middle school in the girls' room, I remember thinking how princesslike she looked, with her long golden hair and those eyes that she was lining so precisely with a navy-blue pencil. But if a princess could be punk.

"Wanna try?" she'd asked, gesturing toward me with the pencil.

I didn't, but I took it anyway, scribbling a messy line that made her sigh, then blot it off with a wet paper towel and redraw it for me.

"Keep that hand steady, girl," she said, and I nodded like I understood.

We were late to class, but by then, we'd decided to be friends.

I felt lucky she was paying attention to me, though later, I understood that she didn't have many friends, either. That we found each other through loneliness more than anything else. Like Wes, she was for a time a fixture at the Banyan House. Now a part of me looked forward to receiving her memories, hungry for any mention of Bà Ngoại from someone who knew her. Missing someone could make you ravenous for any mention of that person.

But resting her narrow hands on the little café table with a sigh,

Crystal says, "Dude, I'm sorry for your loss, really. No one loved a person more than you loved your grandmother. Trust me, I know."

"Is there a 'but' in there?" I ask incredulously.

"*But* if you're looking for a dirge for Minh, you're not getting it from me."

I blink at her. Then my anger makes me shoot up, knocking into the table so hard that the coffee cups wobble. Crystal catches them before they spill, reflexes honed from chasing after a clumsy child, perhaps. She is staring at me with something like wonder in her eyes.

"What the hell, Crystal," I hiss. "What am I supposed to say to that?"

"You could ask why," she says mildly, not getting up.

But I just shove off, leaving her behind me with that bemused expression. Whatever she has to say, I don't want to hear it. Mom is right—I need a new project, one that doesn't require me looking back at the past.

Chapter 24

Hương, 1990

Now that I've begun thinking of Vinh, allowing him back into my mind, I can't stop sifting through memories.

The past reminds me of a fun house full of mirrors. If I turn the right way, I can see the reflection of a younger version of me, one who believed in the wholeness of love, with her sweetly tied aprons, her modest shopping bags. One standing unknowingly on the precipice of her future. The things I could tell her. The warnings I would give.

A year into my marriage, I came across my husband's locked trunk. My curiosity seized me. Perhaps something more. Premonition. The belief that the trunk and I were meant to be. And, underneath it all, a feeling of betrayal, keen but unmoored.

I thought of handsome men who seduced women away from their homes, making wild promises that lit like fireflies in the night, then winked out in the cold light of morning. Looking at the trunk, I tasted a secret. I'd only been married a short time, and I knew there were things left to discover, even in my tiny apartment, even in my circumscribed life. Because, of all mysteries, my husband was the greatest.

It troubled me to think there was anything unknown between Vinh and me. To me, fidelity meant an unbroken familiarity, like what Mẹ and Ba had, before he died. She never married again, and to me, her widow's grief, the one that held her heart so rigid, was bolstered by an inner loyalty. Love before all else.

I fingered the cold metal of the trunk, and the small dip meant for an even smaller key. It tugged at my memory, reminded me of a steamer trunk from the turn of the century, lost and now found in an overflowing closet in our apartment.

I searched for a key but came up empty.

I tried to let it go. Puttered in the kitchen. Made Vinh's favorite banana tapioca pudding, so glutinous that my spoon got stuck in the bowl. I washed my hair for my shift at the restaurant that night, even though all the food smells eventually coated it, like chili oil on noodles. My hair was beautiful once, long and flowing down my back, but after the honeymoon, I'd cut and permed it, tiring of the tangled mass at the end of the night. Vinh had cupped the ends of my shorn hair, weighing it in his palm.

"Rapunzel loses her hair." He sighed.

"But not her prince, I hope?"

"Never," he'd said, planting a distracted kiss on my lips.

The afternoon I found the trunk, he came home in a temper. He worked at an auto shop, but he often studied in the back lounge after hours, even when everyone else had taken off, their fingers loosely hooking six-packs as they walked to their cars. His boss let him lock up, and maybe it was that trust that made his coworkers hate him. Vinh didn't care. Only dove deeper and deeper into his books, driven by ambition. One day, he would become a teacher of philosophy. He would swim in ideas all day long. It was his dearest wish, though sometimes he acted as if it were a shameful one, pulled from a stolen wealth of treasures.

In another life, I could see him in a temple by a window, a stack of books in front of him, mountain ridges rising in the distance. He needed calm and leisure to be happy. When he pressed his hands to my skin, he'd leave navy-gray stains from his pens, tender as bruises.

But here, in this life, he was very tired and, worse than that, very small. I met him at the door and planted a kiss on his cheek. He didn't quite rub it off, but he did not return it, either.

"What's wrong, anh?"

He shot me a look that shredded the words on my lips. "Who says anything is wrong?"

Even in discontent, his beauty overwhelmed me: straight nose, intense eyes. An iron jaw that squared and sharpened in all the right places. I'd spent nights running my finger over that jaw, thinking there was something like calligraphy in it. Purposeful and frank.

He took off his shoes and socks, then sat at our linoleum table in the kitchen. We ate an early dinner in silence. I watched the way he held a chicken thigh, digging his oil-edged nails into the flesh. He had sharp canines that slightly overlapped his other teeth. I hadn't noticed before.

At last, after he turned the TV on, after he propped his feet on the ottoman and his ego quieted, I said, "Anh. I found a trunk in your closet."

"What were you doing there?" he asked, not paying attention yet. Increasingly, his attention felt like a wild hare, unpredictable and fleeting.

"I've been cleaning. Making room," I told him.

My heart was full of empty spaces, and the dreams of what would one day fill them. I had an inkling. Is that what women said? They knew before they knew. I thought a child would make Vinh happy, at last give him the peace he craved.

Without looking my way, he laughed at a show about cops who chase robbers, the cleanliness of the narrative a balm to us. Good guys grab the bad guys. The mean streets are safe, all of us rejoicing in thwarted ruination. Normally, I'd sit next to him, sewing or folding laundry. Trying to keep quiet. He was used to my presence when it was quiet.

"Look how fast he ran," Vinh said. He scratched a spot on his elbow. I could tell that schadenfreude put him in a good mood.

"The trunk was locked, anh," I told him. "I wanted to know what was in it."

"What are you talking about?"

He gave me such an incredulous look that I reared back. I wasn't making things up.

I could hear my voice going shrill. "Don't lie to me."

"There is no trunk. If there is, it's not mine."

"There is. I'll show you. It's not mine, so it must be yours."

"You're crazy."

"And you're a liar."

A shadow passed over his face. The handsome man at leisure transformed into something bullish. His eyebrows gathered.

"You need to fucking drop it," he snarled.

I should have let it go then, gone back to watching the show with him. Gotten him another beer. Sometimes, I wondered what would have happened if I'd never talked about the trunk again.

"We're married," I said, my voice firmer than I felt. "It's all *our* business now. No secrets between us, remember? You promised me."

At first, he paused, and I thought maybe it was the first sign of softening.

But then he rose up, arms perched on either side of the recliner as if he were coiling up to spring. "Ah, that's your fairy tale, isn't it, em? You think we are *one*? Two threads twined together?"

Sometimes his words were beautiful enough to make me pause, turning them over like seashells. Yet now there was a looseness to his tongue that worried me—but not enough. I hadn't yet learned.

"That's what you promised," I repeated, my chin lifted. "You said you would give me a better life. What belongs to you belongs to me."

He laughed then, a high, strangled sound.

"This is yours?" He picked up the remote control.

Before I could reply, try to retreat, the remote crashed against the wall behind me, near my head. The plastic shattered, flicking against my arm. I ducked when the lamp came, such a large object to gain so much speed. Then a phone book, its pages flapping like wings. Soaring, the color of a boiled egg yolk.

"You want that too?" he called. "More, wife, more? That's all you want from me, isn't it. I'll give you everything, my darling. My princess."

The metal ashtray tore my lip and I felt at last the blood I had known was coming. I nudged at the cut with my tongue, like a talisman. *Duck,* I heard a voice whisper, somewhere in my mind, my mother's or my own, or a voice more ancestral than both. *Run.*

But I didn't listen. Out of love, or paralysis, or some combination of the two, I stayed.

He continued to throw the contents of our tiny living room at me. The objects came and came, until everything was broken around us. An earthquake had ripped our home apart. The wreckage was vast and unbelievable, as if it were happening to someone else.

Breathlessly, I touched my lip. He settled back in the armchair. The remote was broken, but the television played on. The criminal, whose crime had already been forgotten, was in the back of a cruiser, shrugging, as if in disbelief. *How did I end up here?* Later, Vinh would go to the store and get a universal remote control for us. I would sweep up the objects, repair what could be fixed. Throw the phone book away because we never used it anyway. We went on.

But that night, I began to see the darkness stretching out inside my husband. I touched my belly and listened for the sound of contrition.

It came like a chant: "I'm sorry, I'm sorry, I'm sorry."

Only after he turned to stare at me, his eyes cold and a little derisive, did I realize I was the one who had apologized. That was when I first saw how useless, how ephemeral love could be, how it gutters in the wind, a flame without body.

Chapter 25

A n n

Days later, I pick up the phone. Maybe it's the well of anger that Crystal stirred in me, or maybe it's boredom, but I decide to call Wes.

"What's happening, Annie?" His voice is easy and forgiving, as if I haven't ignored him for weeks.

"Want to go on an adventure?" The old magic words.

There's a silence, and I think maybe Wes will hang up on me. But then the warmth of his voice travels down the line, and I can feel the pool of rage cooling a bit. I almost see the smile on that rakish face.

"Ever been on an untested boat before?" he asks.

He's grinning when he stands on the porch of the Banyan House, head cocked, challenging me in the old way. We drive down the road, Alison Krauss in the background, each mile slow and pendulous. He takes us to a dock where the gnats swarm in great clouds, sticking to our skin already in the heat. His boat is a shoddy thing, hardly seaworthy, but he's proud. The boards are sanded down, smooth as glass, and it pleases me to think of him leaning against the boat, his sweat baptizing each piece of wood. It's painted white, unnamed.

"Maybe I'll name it after you," he says lightly. "*Ann's Adventure. Ann's Apology.*"

"*Ann's Awful Alliteration.*"

"No imagination," he says, leveling a mock frown at me. "You call yourself an artist."

The day is lovely and warm, but not too hot, and I can see the way the waves are beginning to break on the river. A huge wood stork flies overhead, its wings edged in thick black stripes. The insects hiss and pop among the trees. Beneath us, sky is echoed in the water, rimmed in duckweed clumped like tadpole eggs. Wes wears a pair of jeans, frayed at the hem, and a black shirt with a band name I don't recognize.

"You build boats," I say, a bit of awe in my voice.

"Just this one," he corrects, reaching toward me.

He helps me in and begins to row. I admire the capable lines of his arms, the way his tattoos seem to move back and forth across them. We talk and talk. Being with him is too heady to resist, like the first glug of alcohol stolen from your parents' liquor cabinet when you're sixteen. Like rug burns after rushed sex, and the itch of salt on your ankles as you drive home from the beach, shoulders crab-shell red, soul yawning wide-open.

"She's a beaut," I say in my best captain's voice.

"We could spring a leak," he returns. "I make no guarantees."

I'm not worried. Wes touches that old part of me that still feels a little careless. My hair is unkept, braided messily, and I'm wearing athletic shorts from my closet, the kind I used to wear when he'd whoop through the house looking for me on weekends, hauling me to our adventures, even when I would've rather been home reading. With Wes, I'm not polished Ann, the one who can name the department chair's favorite canapé, the one who has a charge account at the haute boutique in town. I'm some other Ann, one the world mostly forgot. Or maybe the one it never knew.

The air has that cool, briny quality you get when you're near water, and I want to drink it in. I see some movement and shadows near the banks.

"Are there alligators in here?" I ask. "Or crocodiles?"

"Maybe both. This is the only place in the world where they can exist together, you know."

"Goody," I say, dryly.

"Scaredy-cat. They won't bother us," he says.

"How can you be sure?" I shudder. I'm not easily spooked, but alligators are ancient; they are smart and spiky and unpredictable.

"They're lazy this time of year," Wes says. "They won't come close. And whatever happens, I'll protect you, Ann."

While he rows, I push my hand into the water, letting the waves filter though my fingers. The water feels cool and murky, a warm amber tone like tea or old piss. I wonder what it would taste like—like soil, a bit acidic, hard to choke down. I try not to think of all the unnamed creatures living underneath, just below the surface. How the swamps become dumping grounds for bodies, the site of undiscovered atrocities. Murders and rapes and inconveniently pregnant women, erased under the curved cages of the mangroves, which were themselves so like banyan trees. But today, the sunshine is bright, and there are no floating limbs or crashed airplane parts, just a slow, bobbing cadence to the day. Nothing is ever really still on the water.

"How's the house behaving?" Wes asks.

"It's a mess," I say. "The work is endless. I'm going through the doll collection now. You've never seen something as creepy as a wall of dolls staring at you. Who'd want them now? Do you?"

He fakes a shiver. "No thanks. I draw the line at dolls."

"It'd be fine if it was just dolls. But there are also old license plates, bolts of fabric, buckets, magazines . . ."

"Your grandmother was a hoarder?"

Even in memory, I'm loyal. "A collector."

Wes understands collecting. "You can bring her things my way anytime. Anyone who lives in a place as long as she did is bound to collect things."

"Anything but the dolls?"

"That's right."

I take out my pocket sketchbook. Lately, I feel the desire to create pressing against me, a breathy kind of touch. But I haven't gotten further on Bà Ngoại's portrait. The recycling bin is full of papers streaked with charcoal. A glimpse of her wry smile, iron-and-onyx hair. Just bits and pieces, and never the whole.

I draw banyan trees these days, their tangled branches sweeping the ground, those grooves in their massive trunks so like the features of an elderly woman. At night, I squint at the tree from inside the house, a window between us, and I can almost see the branches blur and shake, as if trying to muster the energy to lift themselves off the ground, the way they did in that old folktale Bà Ngoại used to tell.

"Cool drawings, Annie," Wes says. "I like how they look alive."

"Well, they are. Do you know that banyan trees are called strangler figs?" I ask. "They're called that because they smother other trees. And they don't just grow up, they grow around. They *walk*."

"That's gruesome," Wes says. "Homicidal, sentient trees."

Idly, I appreciate him: the dark hair, faintly spiked at the ends, as if he dipped his head in hair wax, and the deep tan of his skin. He's a man who's in touch with the earth, spends hours outside without sunscreen.

"They aren't even native to Florida," I say. "Thomas Edison brought them over from India."

"Thomas Edison lived in Florida?"

"Those old white guys owned everything back then."

"And now. How old is your tree?" Wes asks.

My tree. I smile a little thinking of it. It truly is mine. I get a flash of the future: Kumquat running toward it on his brown legs. Could it be his tree, too? With every day, my heart nestles a little more into this place.

"Two hundred years? Three hundred? Barely younger than this country."

"Can you imagine what was happening when the seed first dropped in the dirt? The land must have been so wild."

For a second, I can see the Florida of the early 1900s, like a sick theme park where big-toothed men pat their jacket pockets while their wives titter under parasols. Kids on columned front porches, throwing balls back and forth while grandmas never leave their rocking chairs. The showmanship of it all. I was at such a hotel once, themed for the Southern heyday with a lobby so big, you could lose a child inside it. The chandeliers dripping with crystals, Christmas trees (twenty in one lobby) decked out with more lights than a small city. Employees wearing matching uniforms and white aprons. So pristine it hurt your teeth. Hearkening back to a different Florida, the kind where a woman like me could never have owned a place like the Banyan House.

"Anyway, it's illegal to plant a banyan tree now. They're an invasive species," I say.

"Aren't we all. This land was never really ours, you ever think of that? And now we go around with our little deeds like they mean anything. It's all stolen land."

"But nevertheless, I own a house. Legally, if not spiritually."

"A mansion," Wes corrects me. "A monstrosity, even. I always loved it, though. Some of my best memories were there."

I turn so I'm facing him. "It's nice enough, if you don't mind weird rat piles and centuries of dirt."

"I never noticed any of that. I just remember the swing and the front porch. That time you snuck a joint into the house but never smoked it because we were so scared of Bà Ngoại. Then you got so freaked out that you made me hide it in my glove compartment. She was such a damn terror."

"It's easy to imagine she's still there, cutting oranges in the kitchen or out back with her chili plants. Like, if I put her death out of my mind, I think she's just in another room. About to walk in."

He takes my hand and strokes my fingertips, feeling around my nails, then up and down the knuckles, like he's exploring new terrain. I know he's back there with me, in that dining room with the serpent wallpaper.

"Do you remember when she dared me to eat ten of her chilies in one sitting?" he asked. "She said I could take you out past curfew if I did. My mouth burned like a motherfucker. Old battle-ax."

"You did it, though."

"Not all heroes wear capes, Annie."

"I ran into Crystal King at the art store. She said something weird about Bà Ngoại. Something cruel. Who talks trash about a person right after her funeral?"

It's been four months, but to me, they are just days. Wes doesn't really answer, avoids my gaze almost, but when he looks at me, his eyes are big and sad.

"It'll probably always feel to you like she just died, Annie."

I kiss him then, not because he's said anything brilliant or interesting, but because he's just Wes. He makes me want to lie down in his arms, to rest for hours, days. He's a lazy afternoon, a hammock swaying in the sunshine. He returns the kiss, hands winding into my hair, tongue skimming against mine.

I pull away first. "You should know I'm pregnant. Four months, give or take."

Wes seems nonplussed, though he hides it well. "Oh." If I were naked, he would be able to see my rounding stomach, but my clothes hide the evidence. When we first slept together, there was barely a curve. It was easy to write off as pizza bloat. A lot changes in a few weeks.

"But the dad isn't involved," I tell him. "Or, I mean. Who knows."

Noah and I have tapered off on our conversations. He asks to ship my boxes, so I will have everything I need, and I agree to let him. There's not much there that's truly mine, but the gesture felt sad anyway. Final.

"What an asshole," Wes says, his voice loaded in anger.

"No, it's not like that."

I tell him about Noah and the anniversary party, about Alexis and Kumquat, who is more of a reality with every passing day. I don't confess that I hardly know how I'll take care of Kumquat, that my sense of motherhood feels very distant, like a promotion I'm not ready for.

"Like I said," Wes puts in. "Asshole."

"He did an asshole thing, but he's just a person who doesn't know what he wants. You know? I was that person. Still am, maybe. It's gotten easier to forgive him now that we're apart. Distance makes the heart grow . . . forgiving? It's simpler, anyway, not to hate my child's father."

Wes is quiet, listening. We're in the center of the river now, and I have this wild image of jumping over the side of the boat, finding the bottom where the lady of the lake rests, a gleaming, unrusted sword in her hand. I'd brandish it around me, banishing all dark things, all doubt.

His face squinches in the way that it does when he's really considering something.

"I have a kid, too," he tells me, folding the oars neatly in front of him. "Elijah." He draws the syllables out, like a song. "He had these wild curls at birth. Made him look like a baby lion with a mane. Prettiest damn baby that ever breathed. His mother, Fiona, met her new husband and moved to California with him when he was two."

Fiona. Not someone who went to school with us.

"Elijah is a lovely name."

"I can still remember his first steps. He tripped and landed flat on his face and Fiona screamed at me for not catching him. He was so fast. But he just giggled. Undaunted, you know?"

"And they left?"

"It feels like they were there one moment, then they weren't. I had a disappearing family."

"That sounds alarming." *And,* I think privately, *a little suspect.* But then, maybe Noah would say that to his friends. That I had disappeared with his son in tow. Didn't I, though? Truth is like an onion; I have to peel it apart, questioning everything I remember, examining my own culpability. Each layer reveals a new sting.

Wes nods. "It was sudden, but maybe not as surprising as I'm making it out to be. Fiona and I didn't get along much after we married. Oil and water. Once she ran over my dirt bike after a fight. I threw away her favorite cast-iron pan. Had to listen to her complaining about how she'd seasoned it for years or something. I don't know. We were young. She was right to find someone else. I just wish she hadn't gone so far away."

"That doesn't seem fair to you."

"What's fair?" He shrugs. "Elijah was sunshine, our bright baby, but he grew up with the bickering. I didn't want that, you know, for his first words to be full of all this blame. I could have been a better father, too. I just had so many dreams, and sometimes it's hard to have dreams with a family. I made mistakes."

He doesn't elaborate, and I think about the mistakes I have yet to make with Kumquat. The ones my own mother made with me. It feels like staring into an oncoming pair of headlights, knowing that you will crash, but unable to prevent it from happening.

"How often do you see him?" I ask.

He looks away. "Fiona writes me sometimes. She sends photos of Elijah. At the playground, wearing a rainbow tutu. He's seven. I wouldn't have cared if he wanted to wear a tutu."

"No," I tell him soothingly.

His voice is dreamy when he says, "I wonder if they're surrounded by avocado trees. If they make it to the ocean. Elijah's toes digging into the sand. Running away from crabs."

"You could visit? And see?"

"I will someday," he says, without conviction. "His mom says they'll come back to visit this winter, but I don't think it'll happen. I miss him so much. Like tapeworms eating my insides."

"The rubber duck?" I trace its outline on his arm and there's a flinch, something almost like anger. I draw my hand back from the darkness in Wes's expression, and I think maybe he won't tell me after all. "Sorry."

"No, I'm sorry," he says. "It's a sore subject, you know? Elijah went everywhere with that thing. He'd stick the bill into his mouth and gum at it, like it was a teething ring. It was always wet. His mom would sneak to his crib after he was asleep, grab the duck, and run it through the dishwasher every night. We had to buy backups because he kept leaving them in sandboxes and at restaurants. I still have a bag of them in my closet. He's probably not even into rubber ducks anymore."

The image of a plastic bag full of rubber ducks makes me so very sad, but Wes seems lost in his own thoughts now, and I don't push him. He gave me a fact for mine. I'm pregnant. He lost a son. The sun clouds over and the waves slosh quietly around us.

"You'll be a wonderful mother, Annie," he says, looking right at me, into me. "In fact, I can't imagine anyone who would be more tender with a child."

Those words, the ones I've been eager to hear—never knew how much—they release something inside me, like a key I found under my tongue the whole time. For the first time, I do actually feel like a mother.

Chapter 26

Hương

It's deep summer now, and the sky blazes across the horizon earlier than ever, so that when I come to the beach in the mornings, everything's already brilliant, as if the world has been eagerly awake for hours. The pier crowds with fishermen wearing mesh-paneled hats to shield their necks. Young boys follow their dads, squeaking in delight when they're allowed to pull the squirming bait out of the coolers.

Beth graduated me from adult swim classes, not with a certificate or ribbon, but with a brusque clap on the shoulder.

"Go on, girl. You're ready for the ocean."

"It's too soon," I tell her.

She snorts. "Never seen anyone take so quickly to water. Go make up for those lost years. I know you're hungry for it."

And she's right. After weeks of swimming at the Y, I crave more. I'm drawn to the ocean for all its moods, its tempestuousness and danger. Its openness. I want to conquer it. The thought surprises me—me, who never wanted anything but to *be*. I'd always, on some level, thought conquering was meant for men, those whose testosterone ricocheted off their cells, aiming for release. But now I think of nothing but clapping my arms through the waves, kicking myself off, away from shore.

On the sand, I pull off my cover-up and wade into the water. It's wonderfully cold, an antidote to the heat that begins to crisp my skin. I tell myself I will swim parallel to the sand, never out too far from land. A beginner's journey.

One stroke, two. Ten, twenty. I'm fighting the water more than I would in the pool, moving against the tide, and though my arms are on fire, I keep going. When I stop, it's only been fifteen minutes, but it feels like something. The old, gaping fear subsides just a little, tamed. I find my way back to my beach towel, picking up shells along the way. I think I'd like to collect a jar of coquina shells for Ann's baby.

While I'm sliding my cover-up back on, a shadow falls near me. It's the swimmer from those early mornings, lean as ever, with a smile so wide it cracks his face into wrinkles that make him look older than he is. Today, he isn't wearing a wet suit, just a pair of shorts that hang low on his waist. He looks bone-dry, though the sand crusts his feet, contrasting against his tanned skin like a pair of white socks.

"Hey, stranger," he says. "Saw you out there. So you *can* swim."

I find myself smiling. Another charmer, as if the world isn't sick with them. "Decided to learn."

He crooks his head. "Wow, really? That's cool. I don't feel like a lot of people bother to learn new physical skills when they're—"

"Older?" I ask dryly.

He flushes a little. "More settled?"

I huff a laugh and stand with my things. "I'm hardly that. But I am older than you, you were right about that."

He sticks out a hand. "I'm Cliff."

"Hi, Cliff." I don't give him my name and he doesn't ask for it. But when our hands touch, his is rough and gritty and warm. I can feel the upraised veins running from his knuckles.

"Want to swim together next time? Good to have a buddy. Maybe you can actually swim with the tide, too." He winks.

"Maybe," I say.

I'm noncommittal, but that doesn't dampen his energy. He pulls a slip of paper from the pocket of his cargo shorts. "Here's my number. In case you change your mind."

I get away without saying anything, but when I look back, he's still grinning at me, one hand shading his face. There's no chance it was a romantic overture. He's at least a decade younger than me. And I'm not thinking of men, anyway. At least, not any new ones. The old ones in my life take up too much space already. But even so, I fold his number tightly and drop it into the glove compartment of the Toyota.

While I'm at the beach, Phước calls twice. I ignore him. Then he texts, ominously, *I'm coming over.* A sinking feeling settles in my stomach.

I don't know how this happened, but my brother inherited an unpredictability that wasn't his. As a baby, Phước would nestle into the crook of my arm, mewling when I tried to put him down.

"He's more yours than mine," Mẹ would say, proudly, if a little hurt.

Then, when we moved to the States, while she was off cobbling together jobs as a dishwasher, tailor, laundress, and cleaning lady, Phước and I were often alone. I never remembered exactly what Mẹ was doing, what job had called her away, but I remembered that my brother was my boy to guard. Made him a bowl of cereal in the morning, bologna sandwiches in the afternoon. If Mẹ didn't make it home before nightfall, I gave him a bath and put him to bed, his body flailing back and forth as he tried to find the best position for sleep.

In the afternoons, when he wouldn't nap, I would pluck him up with one arm and carry him around the perimeter of the trailer, wearing the dirt thin as he purred, finally at rest. More tiger cub than boy. People looked at us curiously, a little girl and her littler brother, striding endless loops in the heat.

But somewhere along the way, a changeling was placed in his stead, and he became a raging, dissatisfied thing, always hungry to be more than he was, though he presented a sweet face to the world. Everyone thought he was the well-behaved one.

One thing my mother never knew, or maybe never understood: Phước was obsessed with fire. He didn't just like it, I suspected—he was infatuated by it. Romanced by the smoke, the leaping flames, like it was a starlet, one you couldn't believe had materialized before you. Once, I found him outside burning little holes into the pavement with his glasses. His tongue stuck out of the side of his lips, intent and awed.

"Chị, see!" he cried. "It burns so deep. To the core of the earth!"

"Stupid boy, no! You will burn your own skin and then who's to blame?"

I hauled him into the trailer and told Mẹ.

"Is he hurt?" she asked.

"He was *burning* things," I cried. "He could have started a fire."

She gave him a smack on the rear, which he accepted with a scowl, not daring to talk back. He was churlish toward us for a time. Later, I'd smell smoke around our trailer like a phantom, but I could never tell where it was coming from. Then I'd see Phước coming through the doors with a sly smile. I'd find matches strewn in the trash can, but he only shrugged when I presented him with them, fanning the black-tipped sticks in my hand.

"You should stop snooping in the trash, chị," he said. "Only beggars do that."

After we moved to the Banyan House, when he was a teenager, he took up smoking. I would find ashes around the front stoop, though Mẹ tried to ignore them, as if they had fallen from the sky, another symptom of the unpredictable Florida weather. He liked to smoke around the banyan tree, though it scared me half to death, the thought of the fire on all that dry grass. In his obsession, I had also found mine, a fear of disaster I always imagined impending.

"Why can't you talk to him?" I asked my mother. "He's your son, not mine."

Mẹ said, "Leave him alone, Hương. Not everything is your battle to fight."

At school, I'd see him with his friends around the side of the building, arms wrapped around themselves, cheap cigarettes dangling from bitten-down fingernails. Such a heartbreaking detail, a crack in the pretense. Boys, after all.

"You are soooo cool," I'd say as I passed, trying to shame him, though I don't know why I cared.

He just laughed, elbowing his friends, like I wasn't a person he knew, a person he had shared a room with for most of his life. With the passing years, his body lengthened, his soul fled from us, to secret parts he never shared. He went to community college, where he met Diane, and then he started a life that was coated in such decency it made me feel slightly shamed by my own. Even when I married Vinh, we did not aspire in the same way Phước did.

Phước got so close sometimes. I'd see it in the way he wore polo shirts, collar popped like a miniature set of wings, the top two buttons undone. Aviators and leather belts, a nice American sedan. That damn Rolex that he moved up and down his wrist so lovingly, like a superhero's cuff. "Almost ten thousand dollars, chị," he'd once said, rolling his eyes like he couldn't believe his own extravagance, but I knew he was proud of himself. That he'd made it. But for all his money and things, he always had that ravenous air, like he just couldn't get enough.

I know why he covets the Banyan House. It represents all that's unfair in his world, all the ways he's overlooked. Such eagerness as his comes with its own sense of entitlement.

Sometimes Phước considers himself the elder in our family, perhaps because he has achieved more, has won respect from people we did not grow up with, those who have never even driven past a trailer park, much less dug in the dirt, nails red-gray from all that dust. Never tossed a slug from hand to hand like some twisted game of hot potato.

These days, I do not want to see my own brother. That thought fills me with shame.

Soon after I arrive home, while Ann is away with that boy Wes, Phước arrives at the Banyan House, speeding up the drive in his Mercedes. Though he lived here for nearly a decade before going to college, he was always embarrassed of it. He always said it could be so much more, if only Mẹ would agree to a gut renovation. She laughed and told him she was too old to undertake such change. To him, the house is not a shrine or a love story, but a stand-in for something bigger.

"You can't smoke inside," I say, meeting him on the porch.

He sinks heavily into a rocking chair. Today, his pants are so white I fear he'll dirty them—everything in the house is caked with decades of grime—but he doesn't seem to notice. In a smooth movement, he removes his sunglasses. Taps the face of his watch, as if reminding me how precious his time is. I sit next to him, though I don't face him but instead look out at the acreage, a yellowing green. The saw palmettos need to be trimmed. They remind me of little dinosaurs, the Dilopho-saurus scampering in the muck of Jurassic Park.

"Took me forever to get here," he says, lighting up.

"Does Diane mind that you smoke?" I wonder.

He laughs and speaks slowly, like I'm a simpleton. "She's not *here*, chị."

"But you are. What do you want?"

When I'm around him, I can almost smell the old sweat-dirt-powder combination of his skin. The way family seems to scent each other out. But he's also covered in so much expensive cologne that it ceases to smell expensive, only smothering. I would hate to be caught in an elevator with him. Even now, the air feels tight and small.

"Don't you miss being back in town?" he asks. "In all the action?"

"What action? There are three stoplights."

"But your friends are there, your work."

"I'm fine. The condo is sublet. We like it here," I say.

He changes tactics. "And Ann? Is she just *living* here now? Doesn't she have some professor boyfriend in Michigan or something?"

His eyes squint at me. Ann is a puzzle to him, and she's a puzzle to me, too, but I'm almost proud that he can't grasp her, even if that means she's beyond me as well.

"She seems to be staying for a while," I say, not able to hide the pleasure in my voice.

"She went away to get that art degree so she could wind up back here? What's a girl like her doing in the middle of nowhere?"

"What do any of us do, Phước?" In another life, maybe I would have confided in my brother. Explained Ann's dilemma, how it has devastated me, her fall, but also uplifted us. Given us a reason to be together.

"So cryptic. Like Mẹ," he sneers. "This is what happens to women living alone. You're all growing strange, speaking in riddles. Soon your hair will get witchy."

I'm almost proud then. I think I've grown inward since Mẹ died, but I've also expanded myself. I'm stronger, in body, in spirit. That's part of her legacy.

"You're very concerned with us," I observe.

His manner changes. I see the mask slip on again, and it's almost funny, the way his eyebrows release and angle upward, a picture of innocence, solicitous and endlessly kind.

"Look," he says, spreading his hands. The palms are meaty, pulped flesh straining through the skin like ground pork. "I want to tell you this: you don't have to do anything you don't want to. You probably feel like you should keep the Banyan House, for Mẹ. But Diane and me, the kids, we can fix up this house and rent it out, or live in it ourselves. We have options."

"But it's not yours," I say.

It's true that there's no part of Banyan House that belongs to Phước, and it saddens me, as if he's been cut out of our essential legacy. But he was never here for it. The raging, hot aftermath of Ann's birth, Vinh slamming his fist through the window. The fever dreams and torrential rain. My life, and Ann's, beaded through every bit of the house, our hair woven into the plumbing, our skin cells shed into the floors. Inseparable. If the house were a living thing, it would have rejected Phước, for his cool practicality, his disregard for what Mẹ would have wanted.

Phước is frustrated with me now. I can tell from the way he drums his nails (long but manicured) on the arm of his chair. I count the beats. Five, six.

"Where do you get your nails done?" I can't help asking.

"Don't be a bitch. How are you even going to pay for it?" he asks.

"We'll manage," I say. "Phước, you will not be getting this house. So perhaps you should just find a way to contain your disappointment."

When he's displeased, his face begins to purple. If he were an infant, I'd be rushing to him, trying to soothe him out of his tantrum. But he's nearly in his fifties, he has grown children. I stifle the impulse, the big sister impulse, and let him swell with anger. If he pops, he pops.

"This is ridiculous," he splutters. "You know she was my mother, too."

"You got all her money."

"It's hardly enough."

"What will ever be enough for you, brother?"

"This is fucking useless, Hương. It's like talking to Mẹ again. Crazy women."

With a huff, he gets up from the seat. There's a streak of dirt on his pants, but of course, I can't tell him that right now.

Now he's walking away from the house. As he goes, he flicks his cigarette into the grass. I can see the pinprick of light from the dying ashes, and I rush over to stamp it out with my feet.

He stops to look at me and laughs a little. "Scaredy-cat."

I feel a chill, nonsensical in the heat, shuddering away from that power he still has over me. My little brother, a storm on the verge of sweeping. Ruthless. If I could rewind to those early days, would I have held him longer? Walked farther? In my mind, we could have walked the dirt until it collapsed, formed a pit for us, far away from human spite and the wanting hunger that has swallowed him. The cigarette, flattened under my feet, looks like a sawdust bouquet, wrapped in withering white tissue.

Chapter 27

Ann

In my dream, I'm back in the big old bed with Bà Ngoại, our sour morning breaths mingling as we sweat our way into the day. Around us are the eyes of a thousand dolls, dresses smudged with dirt. Laughing. I smell fish guts, though there is nothing in the bed, just Bà Ngoại and me.

I say, "Something is rotten here."

"It's time to get up, Ann," she says in my ear, so urgently that I sit up. I'm wearing the blue gown from the anniversary party.

"We can't stay," she says.

"Why not?"

"It's dangerous here, con, you've always known that."

"Then why did you leave me this house?"

Then she looks over at me, but her face is not hers. It's the face of a crocodile, jagged smile stretched over a face.

"You are not her. Who are you?" I whisper.

She begins to answer, but instead of words, there falls from her gaping mouth a primal groan that shakes the whole house.

Then, without warning, a flood of gold-green water pushes down the door to the room, filling it up so fast that we hardly have time to blink before we are underwater, flailing. The walls around us disappear. We are in the fetid depths of the Everglades now, sunk beneath the eyes of prehistoric birds perched on the mangroves, watching and waiting. I turn to Bà Ngoại, but her body has transformed fully into crocodile form, and she's moving toward me, so fast, with that rippling spiked tail, teeth flashing, and I know it's a nightmare.

When I wake, my body seems to pulsate with heat. The ceiling fans blow slow, lazy gusts down to me, compacting the air into bales of heat.

The doorbell is ringing fast and repeatedly. Eleven A.M., another restless night giving way to midday torpor. Though the nightmare fades fast, I cannot shake the feeling that there was more I was meant to hear. Mom is at work, and I should be working, too, but I can't quite get there yet. The emails go unanswered, the Wi-Fi unused, except to track the progress of Kumquat's growth. When I slip downstairs past Bà Ngoại's altar, the dream still pushing against me, I avoid the eyes in her photograph.

Crystal King stands on the front porch with her sunglasses dangling from her hand. Today, she's in a sundress that droops on her. She's not wearing her layers of makeup, and she looks young, younger even than when I knew her, when we were all trying to appear so much more sophisticated than we really were. I open the door but I don't say anything, still trying to shake off my sleep.

"Well, you look like shit sprinkles on top of a shit sundae," she says.

I find my tongue. "This is what you drove all the way out here to say, Crystal? If so, I'm going to shut this door right now."

She holds out a hand. There are tiny little rhinestones on each painted nail. "Sorry, sorry. P. J.'s always saying I need to learn to shut up. Can I come in?"

I let her into the house and watch her take it in. Of course, she's been here before, but there's so much to remember. I've had to rediscover all the weird rooms, the corners that somehow seem to shift every time I notice them. She whistles through her teeth.

"Wow," she says. "I always forget how gigantic this place is. And you're living here now?"

"Yep. Just me and Mom."

"Forever-ever?" she asks in that way we used to.

"Trying to figure that out."

"I never thought I'd see the day. All you wanted to do was get the hell out. Ironic, huh."

She stops near the altar and I think she'll say something about Bà Ngoại that will make me kick her out, but instead she remarks, "That your grandpa? Don't remember that photo. He looks nothing like the type of man I thought Minh would be with."

"I know," I admit. "Looks nothing like my mom, either. It was a joke Bà Ngoại would tell. Something about an immaculate conception. She always made fun of the Christian missionaries running around Việt Nam, brainwashing them."

Too late, I notice a golden cross around Crystal's neck. She laughs. "That's okay, I'm not one of those devout freaks. I've got some pride left."

I take her into the kitchen and put on a pot of coffee. "You want a cup?"

"I could use five."

It's odd seeing her in the kitchen again, though she doesn't look uncomfortable. She's leaning on the heel of her hand, elbow on the table, playing with the old cow saltshaker that's been here for ages. The one that, I'm pretty sure, is empty of salt. Once the coffee is burbling, and the cream and sugar are on the table, there's nothing left for me to do but sit down across from her.

"You look good, Crys," I say.

And without the makeup, with the natural light of morning on her and a kind of peace wrapping her bony shoulders, she does look good.

"No one calls me Crys anymore. And I take back what I said," she tells me, leaning a little. "You don't look like shit. You look good, too. Or, well, you look different than I expected."

"What'd you expect?"

"I don't know. Like a Chanel blazer or like those fancy shoes with the red soles?" She laughs, self-consciously, but I do have a Chanel blazer, and it's in one of the many boxes Noah sent, now piled in a spare room. "You just never came back after college and we all thought. Well, we said you believed you were above us."

"It's not a crime to move out of your hometown, Crys."

"It's not a crime to stay, either," she retorts.

I gesture around me, implying, *Well, I know that.*

She says, "Look. I want to apologize for what I said about Minh at the bakery. It wasn't called for; my mama would have slapped me for talking ill of the dead like that. It just came out. And like I said, I know how much you loved her. I'm sorry."

I pour two cups for us and watch as Crystal adds cream but no sugar to hers. She licks her lips and I see the faint wrinkles starting to feather from her mouth. My anger starts to inch forward again.

I tell her, "That's all well and fine, Crystal, but I want to know *why* you hated her. No one hated her."

"Agree to disagree."

It's hard to stop myself from throwing the saltshaker at her head, but I do. "Is that why you stopped being my friend? Because of my grandmother?"

She puts down her cup. "God, you really don't know anything, Annie. Especially for someone who's supposed to be so smart."

"Enough of that down-home shtick, Crys. Just say what you want to say."

"You sure you want to hear it?"

I just cross my arms.

She sighs again and then takes me back to the summer between junior and senior year, right before it all went to shit between us. For a time, Crystal was the only person I let stay overnight at the Banyan House. After meeting in the bathroom in middle school, we became the kind of obsessive friends that teenagers can be, living and dying by each other's opinions. Not that Crystal offered any. She didn't judge me, so it didn't matter if she sometimes saw a lizard scampering in the bathroom, its orange dewlap expanding like a balloon, or if she came across a pot of thịt kho, pungent and simmering for days on the stove without refrigeration. Hardly a wrinkle of her nose. Her house wasn't a fantasy, either, so she took us for what we were. I was grateful for that.

One night when she was staying over, it got so raging hot that Crystal convinced me to go swimming with her down by the creek, a ways behind the banyan tree.

"It's seriously just in your backyard," she'd said. "We'll be back in an hour, tops. I just want to get cool. And listen, you've gotta be the only house in Florida without air-conditioning. Even my shitty duplex has it."

"Okay, but you have to be quiet."

"As a mouse," she said, raising a finger to her lips.

Then we were off, scampering down the stairs, out the door in our bare feet. Footsteps fleet, arms pumping at our sides, taking us faster and faster away from the house. The night air hugged us, palmettos swaying like feathered dancers. I heard the hollow sounds of owls in the trees and saw bright pinpricks in the bushes, eyes of opossum or raccoons, but we never stopped running. Once we were on the bank of the creek, Crystal hooted, then flung her tank top in the air. The moonlight glinted off her breasts, and I averted my eyes, feeling like a prude. Her shorts were off and she was in the water. I got in to midcalf, then stood looking out at her, the mermaid curls of her bleached hair floating away from her head.

"Goddamn, girl, if you don't get in right now," she shouted, pulling her arm back to push a crest of water my way.

"Okay, cool it."

I took off my shirt, too, and I was in next to her, the bathwater-warm creek now up to my shoulders, where I sank. Crystal floated and I thought she looked so beautiful there, shameless and serene, that I heaved myself onto my back, too, and we were two twigs in the water, making our way wherever the current would take us. The moon was so bright that it dulled the shine of the stars. My eyes prickled at the light. We talked into the night. She told me about her mom's cancer, newly emergent but aggressive, and about the boy she'd just started dating, some skater who liked to get rough in bed, using as their safe word "Bad Religion."

"You're better than that," I said.

"What if I like it?" She winked toward me.

"Well, that's another story then."

And we laughed until suddenly she got very solemn and said, "I feel like we won't have moments like this again."

"You're a sap."

"I'm serious. All you do is talk about leaving this place. Your big life in college. The new friends you're going to make."

"So? What's so bad about that?"

"*So,* you frigid brat, you never think about the people you're leaving behind. Me and Wes, your folks, even. That shit doesn't feel good to hear."

I turned my mind toward all the times my excitement over my impending escape bubbled over with my friends, never thinking of how Crystal would receive the words. She and Wes had no plans to leave; they liked the beach life, and their families were firmly rooted here. But I knew I wanted something different. At least to *see* what else was out there.

"I'm sorry. I didn't think of it like that."

"You never do. But I forgive you if you promise to be my friend forever-ever."

"Until the end of high school, at least," I joked, wiggling my toes on the surface of the water.

She got off her back and dunked me underwater and when I came up sputtering, she said sternly, "I'm not kidding, Annie."

"I'll be your friend forever, you giant asshole," I said, choking but sincere.

It felt like a contract, and we were both a little shy afterward, having suffered the first of what they call vulnerability hangovers. When we finally got out of the water, Crystal dug out a cigarette she'd been hiding in her shorts pocket. She lit up, then puffed into the air. When she offered it to me, I took it. We smoked for a while. But when I glanced at the watch lying in my pile of clothes, it was 4 A.M., much longer than an hour since we'd left.

"Shit," I said. "Crys, get your clothes on right this fucking minute."

She hopped awkwardly on one leg, trying to pull her shorts on. She stubbed out the cigarette on a nearby stump, then left it in the bank. "Coming, coming. You need to relax, girl. Who hasn't done a little skinny-dipping at night?"

"My grandmother," I gritted out.

When we got back to the Banyan House, Bà Ngoại was pacing on the porch, hands curled into fists at her sides. I heard Crystal curse under her breath. They had never gotten along, exactly, though I didn't know why, only that Bà Ngoại got more silent and foreboding whenever Crystal was near. It was unfamiliar to me, her unfriendliness. I ignored it, mostly, because it made me uncomfortable to think that anyone could dislike Crystal, and vice versa.

Bà Ngoại didn't say a word when she saw us there with our dripping hair, our clothes still damp and the smell of cigarette smoke surrounding us. But as we began a very slow ascent up the steps, she stopped Crystal with a hand on her arm.

"Ow," Crystal said.

"I'm driving you home," Bà Ngoại told her.

"But," I protested, "it's the middle of the night. Can't we just talk about it tomorrow?"

She didn't look at me when she said, "Go to bed, Ann."

Crystal said, in a small voice, "It's okay, Annie. I'll call you later."

Then she never did. I called her house the next day, and I showed up on her doorstep, but she was never available, never home. I thought maybe she found me babyish, with my overprotective grandmother and my weird house. She got some new friends that I'd see at the mall, whispering in front of the cell phone kiosks, sometimes slumped outside in a cloud of smoke. She and that skater boy got hot and heavy and were often inseparable, gliding down the hallway with their hands in each other's back pockets, refusing to make eye contact with me. Whenever she laughed with her friends, I wondered if she was mocking me. It made me angry, so I made myself forget about her, too. When someone spread a rumor about her hooking up with the married chemistry teacher, I didn't say a thing in her defense, even though I knew Crystal would never.

"I remember that summer just as well as you do," I say now. The coffee has gotten cold with her story and she's checking her cell phone. "So you stopped being my friend because you were embarrassed. Like I thought."

Crystal puts her phone down gently and I see her home screen, a snap of what I assume must be her daughter and P. J. at Disney World, both of them wearing giant mouse ears. The little girl has a scowl on her face and I'm reminded of a younger Crystal, so edged in defiance.

She blows a breath out the side of her mouth. "No, stupid, I did not stop being your friend because I was embarrassed."

"Why, then?"

"I stopped being your friend because Minh basically told me to. The things she said to me on that car ride home. She said if I kept being friends with you, I'd bring you down to my level, keep you from going to college. She made me feel like trash."

"She didn't say any of that."

"She did. She told me I was never allowed to set foot in the Banyan House again—irony of all ironies, I showed up anyway, though I definitely had to think about it this time around—and that if she saw me talking with you, she'd tell my parents what a dirtbag I was. You know my mom was sick that summer. I didn't want them to worry about me, on top of everything else. Your grandmother was damn scary, Ann."

My voice is low. "That sounds nothing like her."

"Well, no, not toward you. To you, she was your sweet protective guardian angel. She would have let you walk all over her corpse. But anyone else she thought was a threat? Watch out. And you know what that terrifying old coot did? When she got to my parents' house, she rang the doorbell over and over again until they came to the door. Then she handed me over like she was a police officer who caught me hitchhiking or something. Didn't say a word; just turned and drove off. Can you imagine?"

"I can't."

I remember, though, some of the things that Bà Ngoại muttered when Crystal wasn't around. How she was too bold, too reckless. She never thought about the future, only what felt good in the now. Once, she asked me why Crystal and I were even friends. When I answered that Crystal had an insatiable love for life that I wanted, Bà Ngoại only looked at me blankly. She said, "Girls like that end up fighting their way through the world. You were not made for fighting, Ann."

"Look," Crystal says kindly, putting her phone back in her pocket. "I'm not saying this to make your life harder. Or to make you sad. I'm just saying this so you know. Not a single person is perfect. Not me, not you, and certainly not your grandmother."

"I know that."

"Do you? I wonder. Sure, mourn her. She had some really great qualities. I bet you felt invincible when you had someone like her in your corner. But don't be blind about it, just because she's gone. That kind of grief can get you stuck."

I fight against a sense of hatred toward Crystal. Something in me feels shattered and broken. I walk her to the door, but before she steps past the threshold, she turns around and hugs me with surprising tightness. I would have thought her arms would be frail, but they are vise-like around me. I feel like I'm encircled by branches.

"Annie, just do what you want for once," she says near my ear. "And for heaven's sake, call me now. The dragon is gone. We can be friends again."

And when she's gone, back in her Mustang, driving hard and fast down the road, I sit in front of the altar for a long time, memorizing Bà Ngoại's portrait, then adding on new layers. The woman who called a sixteen-year-old girl trash, the one who handed her off to her parents in the middle of the night without explanation. To me, her eyes look sad now in the portrait. If I squint, it almost looks like she's on the verge of weeping.

Later that afternoon, I'm in the doctor's office staring at an envelope. My ob-gyn, Dr. Stacey Montrose, is a plain and capable woman with large hands and glittering diamond earrings that I find very distracting. She does not care how I fare emotionally, what my nursery preparations are, whether I have names picked out. But she does know medicine, and she understands the value of a good contingency plan.

"Open it when you're ready," Dr. Montrose says. Her eyes, a little foxy, try to pin me. I'm a question to her, probably, a woman who attends every appointment on her own, willfully silent most of the time.

"Do many people open it in the office?"

She shrugs. "Half and half. Most of the men want it to be a surprise."

"Why's that?" I ask.

"I think it's because women are already dealing with this great big unknown—childbirth and all the stuff that goes along with it—so we want to eliminate the unexpected. Men, well."

"It's different," I finish. She nods as she shuts the door behind her.

I say aloud, "Should we find out, baby?"

At night, I'd put a hand on either side of my round belly, as if I were covering the baby's ears. It felt like an embrace just for us. Kumquat kicked me one morning, just a light flutter that held as much heft as the batting of an eyelash, and I gasped. I was clearing out Bà Ngoại's study, shredding paper, and that little flutter stunned me so much that I dropped a stack of old bills. I should have felt sad that Noah wasn't there to experience it, but I was just thankful that I hadn't missed it myself. A different woman would have been marking these little things in a squishy softbound book with pages lined in pastel blue. I couldn't fathom that. Still, it meant something to me.

At the doctor's office, the baby kicks again, and I take that as a yes.

When I open the envelope, the sonogram has a smidge circled on it—a tiny pimple. All-caps words in white typewriter print: "IT'S A BOY"

I find the lack of punctuation interesting; neither exclamation nor statement. A thought that wafts into the ether. I pat my stomach.

"You're a boy, Kumquat," I say. "It is known."

I've been half-convinced he was a girl, because we have always been a household of women, and the trajectory of our bloodline seemed clear up until now. But this is not an unwelcome surprise. I know I'll call Noah soon and tell him. Maybe I'll even tell Wes, though we have no promises or expectation between us.

I feel somber yet celebratory. If I were near a lake, I'd wade right in, letting the water baptize us. We'd thrash in the joy of our knowing.

Instead, I walk out of the clinic and stare up at the sky, which has just started to pink over. The colors of the sunset are so pretty. I think about the old candy necklaces I'd wear around my neck as a kid, the way the pale colors would butt against one another, not so much an elegant fade as wedges of color. Baby teeth on a string.

"I haven't forgiven you," I whisper into the air. "But now I have a son. And I miss you, so there's that."

The breeze picks up.

"Any more secrets you want to share?" I ask. "Now or never."

I wonder if there's an invisible string somewhere that can carry my message to Bà Ngoại, like a phone wire between the living, the dead, and the little fluttering being in between. Kumquat, our conduit. Maybe from the heavens, Bà Ngoại could lean down, blow all that misguided goodwill into the wind, where it would find its way to me, to my womb and to my baby boy. I almost feel her breath in the sunshine, and in it is the shudder of relief and love, both so wrapped up that I think there should be another word for the feeling entirely.

Chapter 28

Hương, 1991

For many mothers, childbirth is a happy time; I hope this is the case for Ann. But for me, it was fraught with a thousand barbs. I'm ashamed to say it's a time I'd rather forget. But the memory is always hovering somewhere above me, ready to descend when I least expect it.

After Ann was born, Vinh wanted to give her an American name.

"No one will wonder then where she belongs," he said.

I looked at her little face, screwed up like a dried plum, birdlike cries shaking her body. Her hair was the color of mine—blue-black, glossy, and destined to hang in long, thick curtains around her oval face. Sharp, pointed brows landed on her face like a wing on the milky horizon. Her eyes lifted at the corners with the monolid they called "almond-shaped." There was no doubt where she belonged, but I couldn't tell Vinh that. He wanted us to be more, more. Cleaner, whiter versions of who we were.

Mẹ had lifted herself up from the wreckage of poverty. Invested her savings and settled into the big house by the swamplands, the provenance of its ownership a mystery to everyone but her. She'd stopped cleaning houses, only taking on a few jobs that she liked. Sometimes she worked a shift or two at a bakery a friend owned. It was a life of leisure, or close to it. I didn't tell Vinh, but she often slipped me bulging envelopes of cash. At first, she said it was for our newlywed life. Then she told me it was for Ann's future. I hid them in the mattress, as if they contained stolen goods. Once, she offered to let us move into the Banyan House, but Vinh wouldn't hear of it.

"There are plenty of rooms," I said, hesitantly. I didn't want to move back to the Banyan House, either—had fought against it—but now, with a baby to raise, I found myself wanting some space for us all. Distance, I thought, might save us.

"Moving in with your mother, like tramps, like losers," he said.

"No, anh," I told him. "They do it all the time in Việt Nam. That's what Mẹ remembers. It's normal for her generation. It's odd for us *not* to."

"One day we'll have a house even bigger than that one."

Vinh was born in America, and he didn't understand things about our homeland that I did. His parents had passed when he was a teenager, and he had lived with an aunt and uncle for whom cruelty was second nature. He once mentioned that the uncle used to take him out back and beat him for the smallest offenses—forgetting to rewind the VHS before they returned it to the video store, accidentally shoving his younger cousin on the way out the door. He had to press his hands against the siding, never making a noise when the fists—and worse—landed on him. He showed me the thick scar on his back, a dent from a belt buckle. When I tried to touch it, sympathetically, tenderly, he shrugged me off. He did not like speaking about his childhood.

In that sad household, no one talked about Việt Nam; they were just trying to get by. Looking forward, never back. They all changed their names to American ones, Chuck and Deena, and never put up ancestral altars. They called Vinh "Vincent," and when they moved, the Christmas cards were addressed to Vincent Nguyễn, a man I didn't know.

So I forgave him when he dismissed Mẹ's offer. After years of being nothing more than an add-on to a family, he wanted something for his own. I did, too. I'd waited for this.

"Ann," I suggested. "Let's name her Ann."

The name of a childhood friend, one whose tangled dirty-blond hair had stuck to her face when sweaty. In seventh grade, she got in a terrible car accident that took away the use of her right arm, her dominant one. She had lovely handwriting, hearts over the i's and curly round flourishes on the descenders. After the accident, she once threw a stapler across the room with her left arm in anger, cracking the classroom window. Her parents decided to homeschool her, and I never saw her again. Funny that I'd think of her in that moment, looking at my unwritten baby. But Ann she was. I liked that it sounded like Vinh and Minh, the rough ending like an intake of breath.

He was thoughtful. "I like it. She's a perfect American girl. Watch and see, she will be president someday."

"As long as she's kind and tender," I said, adding silently, *as long as she isn't like us*.

I took my baby to my breast, where she latched on with a sigh, her face relaxing. I'd thought I understood some measure of love, but this felt more desperate. I was wild with love, like I could scratch the face off anyone who looked at my child the wrong way. Vinh may have seen that in my expression. He was mildly disgusted by the whole birth, the fluids and smells, my moaning. A part of him likely thought it'd happen with a small, sweet heave, like an egg plopping quietly into a pile of straw.

He stepped forward, as if to take Ann from me, but then, seeing the flash in my eyes, retreated.

"I'll be back later," he mumbled.

But he never returned. I tried calling the garage, then his friends' houses, but they laughed and said things like, "Ah, escaping already. Smart man." Sometimes, a feminine titter in the background. I imagined them all mocking me.

One friend said to me, "Maybe he isn't sure it's his."

I heard a voice in the background that sounded like my husband's. I demanded, "Put him on the phone right now."

Silence. Then the dial tone. A day went by, then two, without signs of Vinh.

It angered me so much that when it came time to fill out the birth certificate, I left the field for "father" blank. The nurse looked at me in concern, but I turned away from her and back toward my lovely sleeping baby, swaddled in her clear bassinet next to me. She moved her mouth in her sleep.

"Are you sure?" the nurse asked. Her shoes were bright white. I remember seeing them clad in blue paper booties during the birth.

"She's sure," Mẹ said from where she sat, in an uncomfortable chair in the corner.

"You can change it later," the nurse said. She shut the door just a little too loudly behind her.

Then Mẹ turned to me. "Move in with me, Hương. I can protect you both."

"I don't need protection," I said. "I have Vinh."

"You didn't even want to name him as the father."

I glared at her, knowing she was right. After those whirlwind first months of courtship, I never *had* Vinh. He could not be possessed or even held.

When Ann cried, sensing the discord in the room, Mẹ was the one who lifted her and placed her in my arms, nudging her face toward my breast. "Find your mother, little Ann."

It was she who took me home from the hospital, straight to her house. For weeks, I stayed at the Banyan House, that crumbling mansion, wet and mildewy, but still more comfortable than our apartment with its odds and ends, its unreliable appliances and the low bass of our neighbors' music. At least at the Banyan House, I would have my mother. She shut the windows tight.

"To keep out the demons," she said, a little abashedly, knowing how ridiculous her superstition sounded.

"Mẹ, not that old-country stuff," I groaned. Ann was starting to fuss.

"I'm an old-country woman, con," Mẹ said. "Here, hand her to me."

Like in Việt Nam, Mẹ insisted I stay in the main bedroom with a pot of hot water nearby to cleanse the room of all the toxins, to keep mother and child pure. The steam rose thick from the boiling water at my bedside, a sauna. My skin stuck to the sheets, and the baby stuck to me. Outside, the sun rose to punishing heights, then fell from the sky sometime after, but Ann and I existed outside of time, two moons orbiting each other. I would have bitten off my own arm for a snatch of cool breeze. We stayed in that room for two weeks. I only sat up to eat a bowl of hot bone broth or use the restroom down the hall. I had fever dreams that made me shiver when I woke. Crying softly so as not to wake Mẹ down the hall.

I dreamed of Vinh in a canoe, rowing far away from us. He waved jauntily over his shoulder, as if he were going on any old trip. I saw that flash of a smile, the one that could make me bend toward him, basking in the light of his approval.

"I'll be back soon, em," he promised.

I felt something coming. A shadow in the water. When I opened my mouth to warn him, mosquitoes flew in, their mass so tightly compacted that it felt like I was swallowing an indigestible hunk of gristle.

His canoe capsized, as it so often did in my dreams, and the river seemed to open its maw for him. I retched out the insects and what was left, I was surprised to find, was great relief.

While I was pregnant, Vinh only hit me on the face. I think he believed that it would harm the baby if my body was damaged. I felt grateful for that small courtesy. So my arms and my stomach were safe. But my face—who cared about that? After each argument, he was impassive. He went to work. Sometimes he'd bring home dinner, a bucket of greasy chicken or sandwiches from the sub shop in town.

"So you don't have to cook," he'd say, lifting his hand to my face.

"Thank you," I found myself saying, cringing as I felt the bruise throb under his thumb.

I often wondered if I had made it all up, but then I'd catch my face in the mirror, tracing the purpling bloom, like an iris drooping in the rain. I wore a lot of makeup when I was out or working odd shifts at the Chinese buffet for a little extra cash, but every once in a while, I'd catch a coworker studying me, a mixture of disdain and pity on their face. I thought of excuses—falling down the stairs or walking into a glass door, so clumsy—but they never asked. The restaurant was dreadful, slick with oil and pumping with dissatisfaction from customers, and we all kept to ourselves. We couldn't take on one another's burdens, could only watch them from afar, keeping our hearts sternly walled off. I avoided Mẹ until the bruises were completely gone, my skin once again glowing with health. She would have killed him for hurting me.

Vinh visited Ann and me once while we were recovering from the birth at the Banyan House. He sat in a wicker chair in the bedroom—the sauna—where Ann and I were locked, Mẹ hovering outside the door, ready to swoop in. He sniffed.

"It smells," he said, slightly accusatory.

I shrugged helplessly. "I know. We can't open the windows."

"Why not?"

"Demons."

"Your mother is a crazy old witch," he said.

I heard a huff outside in the hall, then the sound of banging doors. He used to like my mother, or at least grudgingly respect her, but recently, he found her to be meddlesome. He didn't want her to be as big a part of our lives, but it was natural that she was there, I told him. Mothers are like that. I wondered if he couldn't understand because he'd never liked his own family. When the aunt and uncle moved to California, he'd spat after them as they left.

"We'll be able to go home soon, anh," I said reassuringly.

He never apologized for not returning to the hospital. Perhaps he was unable to. But I nursed my resentment as I nursed our baby, both growing stronger each day, until their firm grasps could squeeze the blood out of a beating organ.

"You should brush your hair," he said.

I imagined him in another life running a comb through my locks, gently snagging at the tangles. I had a vague recollection of my own father doing that for my mother at night by candlelight. I didn't think of my father often anymore, but when I did, it was with a sense of hollowness, an instinct to fill what I'd lost.

"Do you want to hold the baby?" I asked.

To my surprise, he took Ann from my arms, gently, as if she were a treasure. He mouthed her name. She blinked at him, working her lips.

"My beauty," he said.

For just a second, in that tight and humid room, I could see him there, so clearly, the boy I met in the bookstore. Wonder and bald delight, underneath all the things that had piled on him over the years. I betrayed myself by loving him still.

I said to him, a plea sticking to my voice, "She could be our new start."

Then, the moment broke. Vinh handed Ann back to me.

"I have to go to work," he said.

"It's Saturday," I tried to protest. "Mẹ is making lunch—catfish, your favorite. Stay, anh. Just for an hour."

He didn't answer, though he took one last glance at us in bed, as if weighing his options. I wondered how we appeared in his eyes, but what I saw was blank curiosity, the kind you would give a stranger at your doorstep. A silent inquiry: *What could you possibly want from me?*

When Ann and I moved back home days later, to that second-floor apartment on the coast, he never seemed to look at us again.

Chapter 29

Ann

When I think of inheritances, my mind travels to Bà Ngoại's jewelry safe. I haven't opened it. Though I've been through every corner of the Banyan House, I avoid the safe. Mom nudges me with a tolerant bemusement. To her, this is more evidence of my stubbornness.

"She was a jeweler; you know it'll be quite the stash," she says.

"I'll open it," I promise. But then I find something else to occupy myself.

Perhaps I can't face the safe, because it is Bà Ngoại's final gift, and like the last bite of ice cream, I draw out the anticipation, prolonging the pleasure. Except in this case, I know the discovery will be a mix of joy and grief. As everything is these days.

Yet I memorized the code: *07011965*. The numbers a mystery. I type them into the metal plate, and I open the door. Inside, riches heaped in a pile.

There's that pretty golden bracelet she loved to hold up to the light, inscribed with Chinese characters for prosperity and fortune; her diamond earrings; her wedding band, so thin yet resilient. I sift through the precious metal, the gleam of rubies and deep, woodsy emeralds. Pearls that seem almost indecent in their luster, their perfect roundness. It's Aladdin's cave in there.

My fingers catch on something underneath all the glittering jewelry, a bit of paper pushing through the sparkle. I dig like an old dog who's forgotten where she placed her best bone. Finally, my hand pulls out a tiny piece of graph paper, folded into an origami envelope. When I empty the envelope into my palm, I find a tiny key, rounded at the head, with jagged little teeth running from it.

"Bà Ngoại," I say. "I don't think I can take another surprise."

A bubble of hilarity rises in me. Hoarding her secrets to the last, and doling them out in ways that feel, after all, anticlimactic. An old piece of paper in a safe. What else could she possibly say? Then I see: there are two words inscribed on the folded paper, in her tight little hand. *Gác xép*. Attic. When I see those words, my mind jogs backward.

The attic.

I haven't been up there since I was eight. When we cleaned, we did not think—or want—to go up there, to that forgotten place. Like a corner of the mind you shut away, hoping it'll be someone else's problem someday.

It was in the attic where the critters made themselves welcome, the wildest of all the untamed corners of the Banyan House. Lizards crawled up and down the walls, sometimes leaving their desiccated carcasses behind, graying in the heat. Mouse droppings fell in tidy piles. And yet there were dark, unexplored corners that could entice anyone, especially a lonely child whose imagination felt like her only companion.

The summer before fifth grade, Mom got her dental hygienist certification, and began working long hours at a dentist's office—not the one she later joined with Duke, but one that was forty minutes away from home, near the large city with the huge performing arts hall and fancy Italian restaurants where men took her out to dinner. She brought back Styrofoam containers of mushed tiramisu for me, but I never enjoyed it, spitting the spongy cake and mousse out into the trash can. Thinking how I'd rather have her company than all the desserts in the world.

She'd also begun dating Gary around that time. He owned an upscale tanning salon and, from the rare glimpses I saw, took ample opportunity to sample his own services. His teeth were so white, they reminded me of bleached whalebones. I hardly saw her. Bà Ngoại was helping a friend open up a new restaurant in town, and was often gone, too, delighting in the opportunity to keep herself active. Each, I think, imagined the other was taking care of me. I was often alone, but I wound my loneliness around myself like a mink coat, luxuriating in freedom.

One afternoon, after I'd made my way up and down all the stairs, craning into the nooks of every room, even the overcrowded parlor, the attic began to call to me. That was where random things that Bà Ngoại didn't know what to do with went.

I passed my grandfather Xuân's portrait on the altar and called up, "Don't tell anyone, Ông Ngoại."

I thought I could see him winking down at me. I always liked his face, though it wasn't princely or handsome at all. I couldn't see a trace of my mother in it, though he could have been my uncle's twin.

When I told her that once, she laughed and said, "Oh, but don't you know, I was a stray. Bà Ngoại fished me out of the water like a snapper."

Bà Ngoại said, "Don't be ridiculous, you two. Of course you look like him. See the eyebrows there? Identical."

They weren't, but Mom and I dropped it. When I saw my grandfather, I compared our features. Nothing at all. But that wink, maybe that phantom wink was mine.

In the attic, I tripped across piles of magazines to get to the interior of the room, ducking my head to avoid the steeply pointed ceiling. The dust felt thick, like a dry rice cake I had to choke down. It was so hot I wanted to throw up.

Absently, I paged through a stack of old English gardening magazines. I saw a naked dress form, ivory and water-stained. I half expected a spindle holding a silver needle, glinting for my finger.

I could see the drive from the tiny window, which was dusted and empty, except for a mound of swamp cicada shells resting on it like a sacrifice.

A moth fluttered past my head. Its wings against my skin made me back up and knock my leg against something low-lying on the floor. I saw the trunk then. It shone brightly even in the dim attic, a tinny color that to my eyes looked cheap. I traced over the dents, the sharp latches. There was a place for a key, but no key, of course. I didn't know who it belonged to, but I wanted to rest my head on it, to wrap my arms around it. I sat there next to the trunk for a long while, listening to the birds and chittering squirrels breaking up the silence with their squabbling voices.

Soon, I heard Bà Ngoại calling from downstairs, cranky from having to talk to people in town. I brushed my hand over the top of the trunk once more, then wiped the dust off, hurried downstairs. It wasn't long before Mom and I moved away from the Banyan House, to a new build that Gary owned, and life sped quickly ahead. I never thought of the attic or the trunk again; to me, it was one of those odd curiosities of the house, a mystery never meant to be solved. Until now.

Looking at Bà Ngoại's scrawled note, I instinctively know the key belongs to that silver trunk I found so many years ago, its steadfast mate waiting all these decades. I walk to the attic, hot and sweltering, still full of years of dust, someone else's memories. I find the trunk, right beside the stained dress form I remember. The lock opens easily.

Inside, I find a folded red dress threaded with gold peonies, the outline of a pheasant cawing into the void. I want to touch the silk, but my hands feel too dirty. Or maybe I feel I'm too dirty, laden down with all my newly hatched resentments toward Bà Ngoại. But I do anyway; I lift the cloth, and underneath I see a child's wooden boat, crudely carved and gnashed on the side, as if it has encountered an accident. I keep turning the boat over and over in my hands. The sails are painted a sky blue. A part of me wants to save it for Kumquat, but it's not mine to keep. But who does any of this belong to, now? The living must trespass on the dead; everything left behind a gift, an inheritance, no matter how unintentional.

Underneath the boat, there's a photo of a man I don't recognize. The photograph is black-and-white, edged with a neat frame of white. He has that look of a person who couldn't possibly exist anymore, distant as a constellation. He's young, eighteen or nineteen, and movie-star handsome, with thick, pointed eyebrows that make him seem like he's frowning at you, though playfully, and dark eyes with striking bottom lashes. The lashes arrest me. You sometimes see men with thick lashes, but the abundant bottom lashes are uncommon.

But then I catch it. His eyebrows. That faintly sullen expression. If I squint, I see my own face. My mother's face.

For one suspended moment, my heart stops beating and all I can see are tiny dust mites falling like stars. Like a universe has exploded.

I turn the photo around and read the inscription, written in Vietnamese.

To Minh, my Little Mouse. All my love, Bình.

There's a loud thudding in my brain. I wrap the photo and the boat in the fabric of the dress, a red shroud. I bury it all back in the trunk and hurry to return the key to my grandmother's safe, feeling as if I've transgressed, even as I know she meant for me to find the photo.

Did she want me to know that my mother's father, my true grandfather, was this movie-star man with the crawling lashes? What else could it be? One does not keep a photograph for fifty years without a reason.

In front of the altar, I curl my hands into fists, facing my grandmother. "Is it true?"

I wonder if she intended for me to tell my mother. To bear the burden of the aftermath. I can see how it'll happen. Mom, her eyes wide and weeping, separated again from the memory of beloved Xuân, perhaps the only man to have ever loved her unequivocally. The last safe space for her. How could she not kill the messenger for taking away her father yet again? And then what does it change? There would be a wedge between us, and Mom will have lost yet another parent.

"You coward," I say to Bà Ngoại's portrait. "You could have done it yourself."

She doesn't reply, though distantly, I hear something beating against a window upstairs. Or maybe it's against my heart, trying to battle its way out of my chest, where things have become too hot and spiky.

I want to destroy the altar. To throw the oranges until it all comes down. This shrine, this woman, who has always monopolized my adoration. I think of Crystal and their car ride down a dark road. I think of Mom, her bristly resentment curled tight like a porcupine. How many more moments of cruelty lie under the surface of my memories?

But I don't destroy anything after all. Calmly, I go to the altar and I place Bà Ngoại's portrait facedown. This is her punishment. She does not deserve to watch us.

Later, the secret tugs at my chest, threatening to billow out of my mouth. *Bình*. At dinner, I watch my mother pushing gingery bits of chicken around a bowl with chopsticks, biting her lip absently.

I think I'll tell her. "Mom."

She blinks toward me. "Con?"

What can I say? My intuition, my hunch, is nothing more than a sickly moment in the attic. I'm tired, and I'm pregnant. Hormones, they say. Hormones are madness, and I won't ruin everything, not now.

"Let's work on the nursery tomorrow," I tell her finally.

"Really?"

I watch her brows shoot up with pleasure. Her smile is bright and uncomplicated, and for once, I accept this moment of joy between us. In my mind, I say, *Do your own dirty work*, Bà Ngoại.

I'll stay with my mother. Not because I can't go, but because I want desperately to know her—for Kumquat to know her—without the wedge of my grandmother between us. The RV and those Western sunsets will have to wait. Right now, the Banyan House is the only home for us.

I don't return to the trunk. Somewhere in my mind, I bargain with myself. If I never open the trunk again, I will never have to know for sure. I can just wash the knowledge off myself like a patch of stubborn dirt. The gown, the boat, and the photograph can remain a vivid nap-time fantasy that rises in a mirage-like shimmer in an attic of an old house that I happen to own, though not, as I've discovered, without strings attached.

Chapter 30

Hương

The children are back in school now, and the beach is tranquil again. Restaurants have shortened their hours, eliminating the lunch specials they used to lure in the vacationing families during the summer months. This time of the morning, there are no lifeguards. The cool breeze comes back like an old friend, and when it touches my skin, I close my eyes and lean into it.

On the radio, there's talk about tropical storms that begin on the Caribbean islands and sweep up into the States, but it's distant to me now. Today, the waters have a kind of languorous rhythm. Like slow sex. Waves green as jade, with white curls on top, baby hairs ruffled by the wind. They move in scalloped ripples that gently touch the sand, then recede with a dancer's grace.

The day feels fresh, new. I decide to swim out today, toward the horizon this time. I'll go with the tide.

When my feet touch the water, there's a chill in it, making my toes curl in on themselves. But I go in anyway. My morning swims have centered me and calmed the storm inside my mind. In the water, my memories lose their sharp edges, like river stones forced smooth. While not a friend, exactly, the sea has given something to me, and with that sort of gift comes a kind of trust, no matter how flinching. My fear has not completely gone away. Now, it lures me in.

The salt of the ocean makes me feel more buoyant than I did at the pool, and my arms now pass through the water with purpose. More easily than they ever have. Behind me, my legs kick the water back into place.

I think of Ann's first bath, how after the sweat of that makeshift sauna room at the Banyan House, we were both starved for water on our itchy skin. She'd been frightened at first, her red little face screwing up like a rosette, but then, in time, she relaxed, allowing me to slip a washcloth under her neck folds, between her toes. I took as much care as I could, thinking how like a baptism it felt. How, if I could, I would have squished my body in that little plastic tub with the nylon hammock, right along with my baby. Afterward, I smelled her skin—springlike, verdant, with a whiff of sweet milk—and vowed to cherish her all her days. Mothers and their promises. Unspoken covenants. Without them, we might let ourselves slip into darkness.

Did I always cherish her, though, as I was meant to? No, not by a mile. But do I now? My heart has grown larger, inconceivably, since my mother's death. Now it's large enough to hold all of us, including Kumquat. Including myself.

Pride crests in me as I move farther out, carried by the strength of my own body. I want to tell Ann all about it. Swimming is the first thing I have done, perhaps ever, solely for myself. This keeps me moving.

Soon, my feet touch a smooth mound of sand bar and I can stand upright, like in one of those cartoons where the character is marooned on an island with a single palm tree. I'm tickled by it. My toes squish in the sand and the sun warms the top of my head. Around me are the miniature shadows of fish dipping in V-shaped schools. The wonder of it all. Though I'm not far from the shore, it feels miles away.

I get on my knees and dig through the sand until I find what I'm looking for: the tiniest, most perfect sand dollar. It's a couple of inches in diameter and, from a distance, looks like any other shell. But close up, you can see the petaled heart, the faintly furred exterior. There are no jags in the circumference, and it's a bright, silvery-white color, which is what tells me it's dead. A baby-size creature. I hold it tight and dive back in the water, elated by my bounty.

I can't wait to show Ann. She'll turn it in her hands, running those charcoal-stained fingertips over the smooth surface. Maybe I'll get a smile for it. I've looked my whole life for my daughter's smile.

Clutching the sand dollar, I swim again to shore. But now the water feels more rebellious. It pushes against me. The color of the sea has deepened to a forest green, and there's an odd funneling shape in the foam. It feels like the sea is parting, like an aisle being cleared for a new bride.

Though I struggle, I still sigh, "*Oh.*" Because this new revelation of the ocean is beautiful, even as it terrifies me.

A tangle of seaweed hurtles toward me. I begin to kick away to avoid it, but when I do, I shoot backward like a rubber band.

It's then that I realize: I'm in a rip current. It's pulling me out to sea.

I shout for help, though there is no one in the ocean to hear me. Then I am kicking, kicking. My arms are lifting so high, it's like I'm reaching for the rungs of a ladder. But water is liquid, and there's nothing to grasp on to. I feel my body twisting against my will, and then it's there again, that old terror. The knowledge that the ocean is bigger, greater than I can ever understand, and who am I but a woman alone, struggling against the forces of the world?

I'm under. My energy leeches from me, into the water around me, like a drop of paint in a large bucket. It would be easy to give up.

When I glance up toward the surface, I see a small orb of sunshine and all I want is to get back there. To land. But the ocean is strong and I am weak. I sink lower and lower, and the seawater begins to fill my lungs. First my nose, tearing my sinuses open, then my chest, weighing it down. I tell myself, *This is what you deserve.* There is divine justice in this drowning.

And yet.

Inside me, there rises a greater desire. The steely rebellion that made me brave once. Brave enough to refuse to die. I have lived a shadow life, and a part of me knows that this is not enough, has never been enough. I want more. I will not drown without a fight.

Then I'm kicking again. My arms take on a new strength, and I bargain with the world—*Let me have more time. I will not waste any of it.* The light grows closer.

When my head breaks the surface, I take deep, gasping breaths. The current is still pulling, but now my swimming has taken on a new rhythm. I'm no longer desperate.

Beth's voice in my head: *Don't fight; swim left or right.*

I'd laughed at the singsongy rhyme then, meant to stick like taffy in the heads of young children, but now it is a saving chant for me. I angle my body and swim to the right. It takes every last gasp of strength in me, but I keep my eyes forward. I keep moving.

Just a few strokes between me and death. A few breaths.

A minute later, I'm free of the current. As soon as the water's pull ceases, I rest, letting my feet touch the floor of the sea. The sea closes up. Everything is normal again; no foam, no seaweed. Sweet air bathing my lungs. As if it had never happened.

Miraculously, the sand dollar is still in my hand. A lucky charm. I swim back to shore, then pick my way on the sand. The swimmer man, Cliff, is there again near the edge of the water. He whistles when he sees me, running in my direction.

"That was some current," he says. "You okay?"

I puff out my cheeks and nod, adjusting my swimsuit, which has twisted revealingly around me. "I think so."

"I was about to hop in and, well, save you."

"Gentlemanly of you."

"Not sure it would have done any good in a rip current, but you figured it out."

"Hardly," I say, hearing how winded I sound.

"Well, I'm impressed for someone who could hardly swim a few months ago. Something like that would have gotten to any swimmer, even a strong one."

I flip my head so that the water pours out of my ear, then flip to the other side to do the same. The ocean water is hot as it slips down my neck. "Are you stalking me, Cliff?"

He smiles and there are sweet little dimples in his cheeks. "No. But I never got your name."

"And why do you need my name?"

"So I can ask you out."

I laugh gently as he frowns. "I'm too old for you, Cliff. You should be bopping around with some beach bunny."

"See, that's why I need to ask you out. You swim and you alliterate. The whole package. Besides, you know what they say about age."

"It's just a wrinkle in time?"

"Sure, why not."

I study him. He's wearing board shorts with red hibiscus on them, shirtless, so I can see the thin line of hair trailing down to his navel. He looks handsome and uncomplicated and fun. Maybe in another life.

I wonder what he sees in me: a woman with too much baggage, too many wasted years. Then I think: *Maybe that's the root of all my problems*. With men, with life. I'm always asking what they see in me, and never considering what I see in myself. Which matters most of all. If I can survive a riptide, I can certainly survive some time without a man.

"I'm not really in a dating frame of mind," I tell him.

His face drops and he runs a hand through his hair. "Okay then. That's fair. Thanks for the honesty. But if you ever change your mind—"

"I have your number," I say, trying to smile back. "My name is Hương. Not for dating, but for friendship. We swimmers need to look out for each other."

Embarrassed, he gives me a short wave and jogs off. But before he dives into the water, he turns and calls, "Stay safe, Hương."

When the sun brushes his back, he looks like a smooth, earth-toned dolphin. Though my limbs ache and I still feel shaky from the rip current, there's a song in my heart as I drive home to the Banyan House, the hard-won sand dollar rattling around in the cup holder beside me. I think my mother would have been proud. Her fighting spirit rearing inside me, at a time when I needed it most. But it's not really hers; it's mine. My fight. My own brand of grit and kick and survival. All I think about these days are legacies, but there is something to be said for finding something that's all your own, like a secret power never meant to be shared.

Chapter 31

Minh, 1990

The Banyan House seemed to reject the trunk from the beginning. Wildly, I thought the house had feelings, and sometimes I'd see things moved around, as if by the invisible hand of a disapproving house-keeper. I tried not to take it personally. The trunk, a shoddy thing that had been beaten down from wear, was useless, except to store my few mementos, carefully laid. I would sometimes find the trunk moved—from my closet to the library. Sometimes in the ballroom. It gave me a prickly feeling, reigniting all the old superstitions I had tried to bury when I arrived in America. I wondered if I was becoming senile, so aching for companionship that I formed my own ghostly universe inside the house.

While Hương and Vinh were on their honeymoon, I went to their new apartment. Hương had given me a key to look after the place. There was no reason for me to go, maybe, but I wanted to see it, the home Vinh had found them. The one that would contain my daughter and her children. I brought the trunk with me. Bình's photo was in there, and I had a notion that the trunk should live with my daughter, my reticent girl. His daughter, too. It was romantic foolishness, but I couldn't shake the thought.

Their apartment was nicer than anything I started my marriage with. It had two little rooms, and a back patio bordered by palms.

Someone had hung a dolphin plaque on the front of the building, painted it a glaring turquoise. The neighborhood wasn't the best, but I saw plastic tricycles in front yards, a little blow-up pool. It reassured me to know other children had left their mark.

Inside, their apartment was bare—I had offered some of the Banyan House's linens and china, but Hương refused. "That old stuff would creep me out," she said. I knew what she meant.

Once, she took me to Macy's, where she allowed me to buy her a toaster oven, a chrome monstrosity that would take up most of her counter.

"Do you even eat toast?" I asked, but she gave me such a smoldering look that I only counted out the bills, slid them across the counter to a bored-looking salesclerk.

Her dish towels said things like "Home Sweet Home" and "Home Is Where the Heart Is." These cheap little décor touches were getting popular in the suburban neighborhoods near us, but I never understood it. If home was really so sweet, why do you need to advertise it? Hương spent the entirety of a paycheck in Macy's. I tried to push my money on her, but she refused.

"We're starting brand-new," she declared, pride lacing her words. Her arms hung heavy with bags. I ignored the spasm of hurt I felt—I understood that "new" meant separate from me.

"Isn't there *anything* I can give you?" I asked.

"No, Mẹ, not a thing."

Brand-new, evidently, also meant empty. Their apartment had a burgundy recliner and a sofa printed with pastel flowers. The wall-to-wall carpeting was beige and stained rust brown in the corners. I wanted to get on my hands and knees and scrub. Years later, I still remembered all my tricks from cleaning houses, though the Banyan House never took to any of my ministrations, becoming even filthier, as if in protest. I thought, belatedly, that I never really taught Hương how to clean or cook or do laundry, any of the little things I just did for her and Phước, thinking not of their independence, but of how I wanted them to enjoy what little was left of their childhoods. I didn't clean now. Somehow, I knew Hương would take it as a sort of criticism, though I meant it as another offering.

The fridge and freezer in the apartment were empty. Past the kitchen, their bedroom had one queen-size bed and two mismatched nightstands. The dresser was filled with Hương's clothes. I took out a shirt and held it to my chest for a second. The years she was young were my working years. I was away often. I didn't always remember to listen. No doubt she held it against me. But I made a vow that I'd do better by her now, even if that only meant loving her children harder than I'd ever loved anyone before. I let myself think briefly about a little brood of children rambling through the Banyan House, filling those empty rooms at last. Maybe I had been waiting all my life for a second chance, reclaiming all I had missed from Hương's childhood in her progeny.

Now I know that to be an unfair wish. To steal from another to heal oneself—the sign of true selfishness. But back then, I was ignorant and impulsive.

I sat on their bed. It was hard, unlike our worn-in mattresses at the Banyan House, but there was a good spring to it. I guess there was something lovely about new things after all.

The guest room closet was crowded with Vinh's things: black trash bags full of clothes, books, some video games. He was a bit of a hoarder, which I could relate to. He wouldn't notice another thing. I slid the metal trunk in, then set some folded towels on top of it, placed a cardboard box in front. Hiding the trunk felt sad, like a burial. I almost wanted to say a few words, for Bình or for Hương, for us all. Our lives were stretched apart, the three of us who could have once been one family. And now my daughter at the beginning of her own family. I wished her greater success than Bình and I had managed.

What was my plan with the trunk? I suppose if she had asked me about it, I might have told her the truth about her father, even if it meant hurting her, possibly severing what weak bond we still had.

Maybe I even wanted to provoke disclosure, using the trunk as a sort of bread crumb back to the past. But when I did see it again, over a year later when Hương returned to the Banyan House, exhausted and heartbroken and towing her wide-eyed baby, I told the movers to place it in the attic, where neither of us would have to deal with it. She never mentioned it, and neither did I. It was never the right time. Or perhaps, I was never the right person to tell her.

That day, though, I turned away from the trunk in my daughter's closet. I locked the door of her apartment and drove home.

Later that night, Hương called from her honeymoon as I was getting ready for bed, layering lotion on my arms in thick swaths. I knew I wasn't old, but I felt a heaviness beginning to settle around me. My skin was looser. Gravity had become surly toward me. Lacking the purpose of work and raising children, I struggled, sometimes, to meet the day.

Maybe it was the house, the loneliness of it. It was just me there in those days—and occasionally Phước, when he showed up to dinner, his hair mussed, eyes bright with ambition. Never really looking at me, just past me, into the future I was blocking. What mother doesn't occasionally wish to rewind time and relive the past, like a music box played in reverse, eerie yet comforting all the same, in its tilted familiarity?

Hương's voice sounded small when she spoke. "Mẹ? How're you doing?"

She never asked how I was doing. I think she was often afraid of the answer, not wanting my problems to burden her own overcrowded life.

"What's wrong?" I asked immediately.

"Nothing." She was annoyed. "Can't I call to say hello?"

I thought about how as a kid she'd duck her head into my thigh, avoiding the glances of other kids. She hated school, would try to follow me home after I dropped her off at the front of the building, until a teacher had to hold her back, her wails echoing as I walked home without her. She was tight-lipped when I asked how it went. Like she was punishing me for leaving. It was hard to pry anything from her then, too.

I said, "You can, con, of course. How's your honeymoon?"

A slight pause, so imperceptible. I glanced away from my reflection.

"It's great," she breathed at last. "The lake house is beautiful. Sunsets, Mẹ, they're so bright. Like some kid scribbled a crayon in the sky."

"Tell me more," I said, settling into my chair.

"The water is calm here, nothing like the ocean. It feels like paradise."

"And how's Vinh?" That handsome boy with the boatload of charm; the inky demons over his shoulder. I saw the whole of him right away—he could be swayed toward dark or light, as easily as a cattail bowing in the wind. He might be her greatest curse, I felt, but how could I tell her that?

"We ate fish last night that he caught. Took him most of the morning. I wanted to make cá kho, but there wasn't enough of it. The neighbors are nice." I thought about how she had avoided my question. Not exactly refusing to speak about her new husband, yet sidestepping him all the same.

Her voice drifted, and I thought of the way sand flutters down the beach after a strong wind. The way it forms a cloud before shaking itself over the water.

"That's wonderful, con. I never had a honeymoon."

"Oh."

"I mean, I'm glad you are having one now. That time alone is important; it shows you the truth of the person you married."

She cleared her throat.

"How are things at home?" she asked.

"Exactly the same here," I said. "I went to check on your apartment. It looks good."

She laughed, self-consciously. "No, no, I know it's nothing much now. But it's safe and there's some room to grow. We're just starting out. Vinh is going to do great things after college, I know it. A professor in the family! And then I'll quit the restaurant and stay home with our kids."

"I can always help," I said. "If you need money."

"No, Mẹ, you save for your retirement," she said. "You deserve to rest, too."

"I'm okay," I insisted.

There was a thump and her voice lowered. "Mẹ, I'm going to go now. I'll see you at home later."

"Happy honeymoon," I said to the dial tone. I lay in bed and tried to calm the flutter of fear. *Helpless,* I thought. Even through our early years in America, I had not felt such a way since Xuân died. My last thought was of the trunk, and its accompanying key, which I had hidden in my safe, patiently awaiting its mate.

And then, in the attic of the Banyan House, the trunk breathed in decades' worth of dust and yellowed dreams, until Ann, my other girl, lifted the lid after all those years, releasing the shadows that I had tried to hide.

She's angry at me in death in a way she never was in life, and though it hurts that old ancient part of me that remains tied to her, I wonder if her anger will also release her. And to me, there is freedom in imperfection. To know and love another's flaws—now, I know that to be a gift.

What I would not have given to tell Ann the whole story, from beginning to end, from that hot day on the side of the road when handsome Bình saw me, really saw me, for the first time, all the way to my final hours, when my last thoughts were of her and Hương and Phước, my three lost children. Maybe then she would understand how love cannot possibly be simple, or easy, despite all the adages to the contrary. When we choose to chisel pieces of our heart away to offer to another person, we must always make decisions. What flaws will we lift to the light? And which will we bury, in the hopes of protecting ourselves and others?

We all make mistakes. I say this not as a way to absolve, but as a way to connect myself to the generations of women who came before, and those that will follow. But I won't seek forgiveness.

Instead, I would tell Ann, "Con, secrets are a menace. They will spill from your mouth like angry, writhing eels, or they will fill you up until you combust. There is no escaping them. I've done us a favor."

And she might look at me in that old, trusting way, too. Or she might turn from me, a final indictment. For a moment, I sink with the weight of what I have lost, and I'm desperate for the heavy numbness of true death, the way I could feel, at last, empty and free of the world and its terrible, twisted consequences.

Chapter 32

A n n

It turns out Kumquat and I very much like being in Wes's boat. When we are on the lake, Kumquat kicks extra hard, which makes my stomach burble. I laugh, self-consciously, my hand on my rounding belly, but Wes doesn't seem to care about any of the unglamorous parts of pregnancy. In fact, he is sort of charmed by it, my bloating silhouette, my frequent need to rest. Sometimes I catch something in his expression. Worship. But I don't fool myself that it's for me; I think that Wes, like all of us, reveres the capacity of life—and hope—to emerge in unlikely places.

Where we are on the coast, the leaves don't change, but the seasons pass all the same, some elongated, others stubbed off before they begin. Fall, a mere divot between summer and winter. Now the smells in the air are more pert; they carry with them a whiff of change. I almost hear bells in the air, a tinkling herald for the holidays to come. The stores are beginning to fill with orange plastic pumpkins and huge sacks of candy that stack in the aisles of big box stores.

Last week, I caught Mom stringing some lights along the front railing of the Banyan House. She placed a doormat on the front of our house that said "Home Sweet Haunted Home" with black bats flying around. When I raised my eyebrows, she gave a sheepish shrug. "Why not? It's the season," she said. I remembered how much she loved those kitschy little touches. In the house we lived in with Gary, she had beautiful tea towels all over the place and rustic signs for every room in the house. "Bless This Mess." "This Is Us." As if she could manifest familial affection through some well-placed objects.

But still, my heart seizes when I see her making the Banyan House a home. My feet plant a little firmer in the dirt; the resolution to stay gets stronger. Kumquat would not be able to trick-or-treat from an RV.

In the boat, Wes hands me a back pillow and a Snapple iced tea.

"You like lemon, right?"

"My favorite. You are so good at this. At taking care of people," I say.

"Trying, Annie."

"I think about Elijah sometimes."

"You do?" He sounds cautious.

"I think he's lucky to have a dad like you."

"May I touch it?" he asks, setting an oar down to gesture at my stomach. "Him, I mean."

"Yes," I say, surprised.

His hand strokes the outside of my shirt, above my stomach. The sun is beginning to set a little sooner, splashing the sky with Kool-Aid colors. The horizon stretches in front of us and I can see the lake houses with their long decks, sprinkles of light coming from tea candles on their patios. Kumquat shifts against Wes's hand.

"Wow," he says, leaning back. "I felt him. It's wild. I had forgotten."

"I can't stop looking at those houses. What would it be like to live there?" I ask.

"I like the Banyan House better. It's got character. Not like these lifeless buildings."

"But lifeless means unwritten, you know?" I insist. "You can make your own history."

"The Banyan House has plenty of history you can borrow. Remember all those times we played footsie under the table while your grandma brought us oranges every ten minutes? She thought we didn't know she was checking up on us."

I smile. "Even outside of her gaze, we never got that far."

"Third base," he says, mock offended. "My basement, remember? But we were just kids. Unthinkable that it was so long ago. And now you're going to be a mom."

"I'm the most surprised of everyone."

"You wait. You will be amazed at yourself," Wes says. "I really didn't believe in that kind of love before Elijah. It's *desperate*. You become an animal. I took him in my arms and his eyes were like mirrors. I saw everything I wanted to be. Even if I never did get there."

There's that old darkness in his voice, getting harder to ignore, even as I welcome him into my life and my bed. I like Wes so very much. And yet when I try to imagine him in my future, reaching for Kumquat's hand as he trips among the fake hay bales and past mailboxes strung with cotton webbing, the image splutters. It's early yet, and there are no commitments between us. Sometimes, I think that's a blessing to love without expectation, though "love" is not exactly the right word to describe what is between Wes and me. "Saudade," perhaps, a Portuguese word for longing. Homesickness.

My body is growing, and I'm carrying on in the Banyan House with a staggering sense of contentment. Kumquat's room is starting to resemble a nursery. Mom hung eyelet curtains that sweep the floor. We added a bookshelf, and I bought a copy of *Pat the Bunny*, which I propped up on the shelf, open like a fan.

I set up one of the spare rooms for a studio and I work in a corner, secretly painting and writing, and dreaming. Sometimes, when I can't sleep, I switch on the little table lamp and paint. Often, Kumquat is awake with me, kicking to let me know he approves. Those nighttime sessions have become a time just for us, a creative spark we don't share with anyone. Mom asks me what I'm working on.

"A fairy tale," I say.

"For the baby?" she asks.

"For all of us."

I like to sit with Kumquat on the swing under the banyan, barefoot and sketching. Mom calls me in for dinner, or sometimes I'll cook, something simple like poached fish or shrimp tacos from a box. Afterward, Mom and I read until it's time to sleep. She's given me a book of Vietnamese fairy tales and I flip through it, reading about the legend of the Jade Rabbit, the Kitchen Gods, the origin of the salty sea.

I try to put the knowledge of Bình out of my head, but when I see Mom kneeling by the altar, her palms pressed together against her forehead, I have to clamp my lips. There is a cosmic injustice to knowing something she doesn't. I have tried to forgive Bà Ngoại, but I can't bear to look at her face, though Mom has righted the portrait so her keen eyes stare back out at us, betraying none of what they know. I avoid the altar. I let the fruit rot, until Mom changes it out herself. If she notices, she doesn't say anything. After all, how foolish would one have to be, to hold a grudge against the dead?

And I have my own little secrets, harmless as they are. Wes sometimes sneaks into the Banyan House after Mom goes to bed. He doesn't really need to. I don't think she would care, but I still resist revealing too much to her, even now when things are calm between us. Old habits die hard.

One time, he texted to let me know he was waiting outside with bare feet so he wouldn't wake my mother. I giggled as I ushered him up the stairs, each of us cringing every time the floors creaked. We fell into my twin bed and held our hands against each other's mouths to silence the sounds of lovemaking. Afterward, he cradled me and his breath was warm on my neck, his fingers laced in mine. I slept soundly then, without a single dream.

When I woke in the morning, I found Wes in Kumquat's nursery. He was crouched low, sanding the floors, the toolbox next to him like a faithful dog. The boards where he knelt, formerly rough and stained, were now a fresh light color, covered in a thin layer of sawdust.

I watched him for a few minutes before he noticed me. The way his whole body moved when he worked, the furrow of his brow.

"I'm sorry. Is this weird?" he asked, standing up.

"No. You're a really bad sneak, though." I grinned. "Could wake the dead with all this noise."

"And then your grandmother would really haunt me," he said. When he saw my face fall, he blinked in confusion, but then hurried on. "I just noticed that the boards were in bad shape. And I thought of Kumquat crawling on the ground, his little hands and feet. Splinters."

I sat next to him while he worked. I read through all Kumquat's little books that morning, until I got hungry and fixed us oatmeal. Mom didn't say a word when she saw Wes in Kumquat's nursery, but something darkened in her brow. I wondered if it was jealousy. That my life had broadened a little, outside of her. I knew what she was thinking—that I had moved quickly, recklessly, from Noah to Wes. Not that she was one to talk, with the string of men she'd always brought around. Up until lately. Though she's beautiful and still young, she's been monkish since Duke. The only signs of her private life are the piles of wet towels heaped in the laundry room, and an occasional scatter of sand on the steps leading up to the porch. More secrets. This house is lousy with them.

In the boat, I rest my hands on my belly, thinking of Noah and all he's missing. He and Alice would have bought the shiniest Montessori toys for the baby, but they likely would never have set foot in the nursery. Noah, changing a diaper. Unthinkable.

"Wes," I say. "You would have been a good dad. You are."

He hikes up a part of his shirtsleeve so I can see his arm, right up near the shoulder. There's a tattoo of a bird there, a heron whizzing in the sky. Underneath, a small notch of skin, maroon colored and lightly speckled, with a thin ring of white scar tissue.

He says, "My dad used to get really mad sometimes at us, me and my brother. It'd be for nothing. Like maybe we were too loud or I had forgotten to turn in my homework or something. Dad would chase me and whip his belt around his head like a lasso. Just roaring. One time he cornered me in the basement and something snapped—I threw an empty paint can at him. He got so pissed. He held me down and stubbed his cigarette into my skin. It hurt like hell."

"Fuck," I say.

"I just couldn't understand what makes you want to burn your own kid."

I reach to touch his arm. "I didn't know that about him. About you."

"I didn't have the words for it. I felt like I had to bottle it up to protect people like you from my ugliness. And obviously, it's embarrassing. You were so good and pure. It didn't seem like something you should know about me."

"You were a child. It wasn't your fault."

"Sometimes when I think of being a dad myself, and Elijah getting hurt like that, I get so sick. I wanted to kill my dad. When he died, I just felt grateful that I'd never have to bring Elijah around to see him. He would have whupped any of us boys for wearing tutus. If he ever touched my son—well. I wonder if you can inherit evil."

"Maybe," I say. "Or maybe it's not something you inherit, but something that runs through you, another person's trauma, their violence. It sits below the skin until you name it. And you root it out like a cancer."

"Curing the evil."

"Not curing, exactly. Just letting it run its course."

When I tell him about the trunk and Bình, a small part of me whispers that it's not my secret to tell. But I think I'll burst open if I don't. Once, I watched Mom take the wet sheets outside, spreading them over the porch railing so they fluttered like brides' trains in the wind. She turned to me and there was a rare, free smile in her face, and I saw the man in the photo looking out at me. I had to walk away, lips clamped.

"So what do I do?" I ask Wes. Even though I know.

He runs a hand through his hair. "You tell her, of course. What's the good in hiding it? Let me be the first to tell you: Secrets never stay hidden. Someone always has to deal with the fallout."

"But what if it changes everything?"

"You can handle it," he says. "You've always been stronger than you think."

Later, after he takes me back to his apartment, after he lays me gently on the bed and runs his fingers over and across and in my body, I try again to imagine it: Wes moving into the Banyan House, helping Mom with the lawn, building bookshelves for the nursery. Bouncing the baby to sleep, then crawling silently next to me, cupping my body with his. The vision is so enticing I almost gulp. It doesn't splutter this time. As we melt into each other, I see the moon, I reach for it.

Afterward, he leans on one arm. With the other, he winds one of my hairs around and around his finger, so tightly that it looks like a sausage in its casing, red and swollen. "You make me want to try again. You and Kumquat."

Hearing his name, Kumquat turns slightly, which makes my back uncomfortable. I think Wes and I haven't achieved a level of intimacy that would have allowed me to ask for a back rub, but when I shift, he seems to know. His hand caresses my tailbone.

"He knows your voice now. What does trying again look like for you?" I ask.

His dark hair is slicked like wind-thrashed waves. He's not looking at me anymore, but he's tense and hopeful. There's a feeling with wings that perches right on both our souls.

"You'll be the first to know when I figure it out, Annie."

Then I tip myself forward and we are touching foreheads, and there is nothing left to say, only all the things to remember, to feel. I feel the thoughts race between us. Things we can't bear to pull outside ourselves yet.

Chapter 33

Hương, 1991

There was a time when Ann and I nearly drowned. Not in the sea, or in a pool, but in the despair that hung around us, thick as webbing. I ignored the pull of hopelessness, but when it dragged me under, I could not find the surface. It was my mother who saved us.

Ann's birth softened nothing between Vinh and me. When she was a newborn, I held her close to me, whispering in her ear, "Help, help, help," but I should have known that burden was too much for a baby. She turned away from me, already independent, aching for her own space. After the two weeks of confinement at the Banyan House, we moved back to the apartment with Vinh. He seemed indifferent to us, though sometimes he'd kick the fancy stroller Mẹ gifted us, perturbed by the changes in his life. Like he couldn't believe a baby needed baby contraptions. Fatherhood was not living up to his expectations, though he never shared what those were. Between us, a silence so loud and vacuous that I thought my voice might echo if I spoke into it. I almost felt sorry for him, so lumbering and awkward in his own house.

For a time, the nursery was a small corner of our bedroom, partitioned off by a screen so I could keep the baby close, especially for night feedings, when her cries were earth-shattering to me and irritating to Vinh. I kept Ann's diapers and clothing folded in a little bin decorated with elephants. I loved the way they looked there, shell colors so pastel-light and beautiful and neat.

At night, I sang soft Vietnamese songs I recalled Mẹ singing for Phước and me. I wondered if Ann would remember any of them later. Ann, with the English name and American upbringing. Ann, with her dissatisfied father who increasingly seemed to want nothing more than to be away from us. We could go days without seeing him, and it was like living with a tramp dog, never sure when he'd return in a gust of dissatisfaction. Sometimes I'd find his clothes strewn on the couch, like he'd vanished in them, the ultimate disappearing act. They smelled like alcohol, the stench strong and repellant, a stark contrast to the new-born Dreft I used for Ann's laundry. Once I saw his wallet sitting on the couch and wondered how far he could go without it, but it turns out, tramp dogs find their way without currency.

Vinh and I had not been intimate since I'd returned from the Banyan House. The doctor recommended waiting six weeks, but Vinh didn't seem to care one way or another. Late one night, shortly after Ann and I returned to the apartment, I put my hand on his waist, near the bone on his hip, my usual signal for intimacy. Even in our worst times, through the violence and despair, he'd wanted me. I wanted him too. I thought that if we could connect again, even through our bodies, that might ease something in our marriage. But he took my hand and coldly, precisely, moved it onto the cold sheets between us, like a traffic bump. *Slow down,* he seemed to be saying. That desire he once had for me was replaced with something more confusing. He still wanted to possess me—but in a way that felt divorced from tenderness.

So it perhaps should not have been a surprise when, the first week Ann and I were home, he hit me. It was almost a relief when he did, like I had been waiting all this time. I'd made macaroni and cheese from one of those blue boxes I used to devour as a kid. I thought it would make dinner easier for us all, and I was tired, so very tired, after nursing all night. It didn't seem so offensive. I told myself macaroni and cheese was wholesome. We could be like the Cleavers. Vinh didn't agree.

"This shit doesn't even look like food," he said.

I sighed. "Why don't you cook for once, then?"

"Because I work. For our family."

"Is that what you call it?"

After he slapped me, I held a frozen bag of peas to my cheek in front of him, no longer hiding my hatred.

"I didn't marry one of those lazy white women," he said, his voice a bit preachy, like he was standing at a lectern for hapless wives. "You know what I like. What all men like. Hot dinner, beautiful wife. It's easy, even for a stupid whore."

"But anh," I said, my voice saccharine, holding the ridiculous frozen vegetables to my face. I'd grown teeth, though they were still nubby, unable to cut flesh. "You are never even home. How am I to know how to be beautiful for a ghost?"

He dumped the bowl of orange-bright macaroni on the table, and if he weren't a grown man, bigger than me and full of anger, I would have found him laughable. He reminded me of a toddler, upsetting food when it didn't appeal to him. I wondered how, exactly, I had once found him so appealing. My desire for him fizzled more with every moment.

"Clean it up," he said, walking out of the house again.

It was his punishment, and to my credit, I guess, I didn't clean it up for days, just left it congealing there for him in an orange mound until the smell and the flies made me give in, and I brought it to the black trash can out back. That night, I saw a racoon rifling through the can, drawn to the rot. Vinh never gave the mess more than a smirk. We could both see the blooming purple rose on my cheek, and understood the extent of his power, and mine.

In early fall, as Ann and I were settling after a midnight feeding, her small fist curling around my thumb, her sweet sweaty weight pressing on my arm, the phone rang. It was shrill and insistent, and it woke Ann up, wailing. I picked up. The first thing I thought of was an accident, Vinh's body wrapped around a telephone pole, those intelligent eyes frozen wide-open, streaked with death. Or perhaps he'd finally decided to leave us. My mind flitted through the possibilities.

"Hello," I said, voice heavy with sleep and dread.

There was breathing, but no words.

"Hello," I repeated again. To my own ears, I sounded squeaky and frantic.

The breathing increased in speed, a shadow away from a pant. It creeped me out, made me think of those true crime reports I'd watch on Channel 9 News, the way burglars would call first to see who was home. I laid Ann in her crib, which made her wail even more.

"Please," I said finally, the plea so cloying in my voice that it enraged me. Then, "My husband is here. I'm not alone, you know."

The woman's voice on the other end of the phone—finally more than a breath—laughed softly. It wasn't a cruel laugh, but it also wasn't kind. A spectator's chuckle. She hung up. The call unnerved me. That night, I couldn't sleep. Thinking and wondering and knowing.

For some reason, I thought of my father, though my memories of him are scarce. Maybe in a time of vulnerability, a girl wants her father. I imagined that Ba came in a boat to whisk Ann and me away, his hair flapping in the wind like a jaunty captain. He raised a hand to us. "Come on, girls." I remembered my father to be a gentle man. I once disdained gentleness, confusing it with weakness. But now I wanted the sweet wind of a favorable day. I would do anything to waft away with my daughter on a wooden boat.

When I woke and saw Vinh's shoes at the foot of the bed, his body sprawled next to mine, I felt as if something vital had been taken from me. I leaned over him and placed the pads of my fingertips on his closed eyelids. They were warm and thin—I could almost feel the bulge of his eyeballs under my fingers. What would happen if I pressed harder? He sighed lightly, and I removed my hand from his face. When he slept, I saw the boy at the bookstore again, flirtatious and gentle even in his audacity. It was when he opened his eyes that I began to know fear.

Still, the three of us held together, a fragile family connected like a paper string of people, until we didn't. The night before Halloween, Vinh came home. He usually stayed away after drinking, for which I was grateful, so I didn't expect him. I'd been ignoring Mẹ's calls and Vinh's dirty laundry. I wasn't happy, but I was pantomiming an approximation of joy.

I was singing "Monster Mash" to Ann: "*I was working in the lab, late one night . . .*"

I'd bought pumpkin window clings from the dollar store, and cut out a paper wreath in fall colors, dangling it in front of Ann. She kicked at it with her feet, dimples deepening when she laughed. She was perfectly beautiful, with shell-shaped ears and downy hair that fell gently across her forehead. Her eyes were big and intelligent; they reminded me of Vinh's, though she shared my cupid's-bow lips and curving brows.

In my imaginary single-parent life, Ann and I lived in a sitcom, beloved by our hometown, showered with attention from elderly aunts and uncles. We owned a quirky bungalow with blue shutters. When she grew older, she'd lie next to me in bed and share her secret crushes. I thought we could have gotten on well in this imaginary life, with only each other.

"*The ghouls all came from their humble abodes,*" I sang softly.

I put her to sleep and dried the dishes. The apartment, for once, felt festive. It made me want to shimmy around the room. But then Vinh came home, just after Ann's bedtime, and jammed his foot on the shoe rack by the door.

"Motherfucker."

Ann was in her crib, in a proper nursery now, gently breathing in her swaddle.

"Shh," I said. That made him angrier.

"Why do you keep spending my money on all this *goddamn stuff?*" he roared.

"Please be quiet," I said.

I held my robe close to me. It was chilly for Florida, and I had been sewing a costume for Ann. Little Red Riding Hood, with a pair of socks embroidered to look like boots with buckles. The hem of the cape was trimmed in gray-brown fur from the quilting store that had cost way too much, but I liked the symbolism of it. A relic of the wolf, claimed by Little Red as her trophy.

He shrugged off his army-green coat. His eyes were bloodshot, and he reeked of beer, like he'd bathed in it. "This is my house, isn't it?"

"I don't know about that," I said.

I was tired, annoyed, and bold. After all this time, I had become less timid, ready for the slaps when they came. Ann had made me courageous. I knew it was time to leave Vinh. I'd planned it out. I'd save enough money, once I went back to work, and I'd buy us a place far away, where he couldn't find us. Not that he would try; he had no interest in us as people, only objects cluttering his space. And to me, that was fine. Who cares about the feelings of a person you are about to forget?

"What the hell does that mean?" he asked.

Vinh wasn't a terribly tall man, but he could draw himself up, making himself look menacing when he wanted to. Sometimes, I wondered what it would be like to hit back, to see his eyes roll into his skull, like one of those creepy wooden puppets. I thought about his soft eyelids under my fingertips. Not a monster after all, but just another man. Vulnerable, like us all. Maybe I wanted to kill him, just a little. It was an insane thought, driven by sleeplessness, by being preyed upon, but I thought it most clearly in that moment, like a plan just hatching.

"You're barely here," I said.

"Do I have to get permission from you to go out now? Are you my mother? Fuck that. A grown man asking his wife if he can play with his friends. Do you know how stupid you sound?"

"I know more than you think," I said. I stood behind the couch, as if it would shield me. "Your whores who call in the middle of the night, testing me? What's stupid is a man who doesn't even bother to hide his tracks."

"Jealous, em?" He grinned, but it was a hateful grin, one that made me want to groove his face with my fingernails.

I continued, "The nasty smell of alcohol on you. Your wrinkled clothes and that job you keep saying you'll leave but never do. You know what I realized, anh? What I should have known all along? You are a loser. You've always dreamed well. But in reality, you're shit I wipe off my shoe."

Improbably, Vinh's eyes sparkled. For an insane moment, I thought he was amused, that maybe we'd laugh this all off, this strange blip in our marriage when we forgot to love one another, but the sparkle was something else.

"I'm shit to you, huh?" he said. "So shitty that you gossip about me to all your friends, your mother and brother who think they're too good for me?"

"They are. Ann and I are, too," I returned. My mouth, my testing mouth. "You're not fit to be her father. You are not worthy of having a family."

At first, he looked hurt. It shocked me, that hurt. Perhaps that's why I took a step toward him. But he evaded me, and sprang toward the nursery, faster than I could have imagined from someone who was nearly slurring his words. He went to Ann's crib, and I was on his tail, but he had the element of surprise on his side. He easily grabbed Ann with one arm, jostling her awake. Her cry scraped against my chest, a razor shredding my bravado until all that was left was raw fear. She stared at me with wide, helpless eyes.

"Let her go," I yelled. "Please, anh. I'm sorry. Please."

"Oh, don't worry," he said, cruelly. "I'm just going to have fun with my daughter. Be a good dad, like you want."

He began to throw Ann up in the air with one hand, not even looking to make sure he was catching her. By then I was bawling, trying to get close to her. But I was afraid of disrupting his focus, of creating a distraction so that she'd fall. Wildly, I thought she looked like a sheet of pizza dough, tossed up and down, formed from a soft mass into something glutinous, even more pliable. She was crying so hard, her breath came out in ragged hiccups.

"She can't breathe. Can't you see," I begged.

"She's fine. Just having fun with her ba."

"You're a good dad, I'm sorry, I will never say that again," I pleaded.

I had no shame, not anymore. I would have groveled if it would have helped, I would have kissed his feet, washed the soiled underwear of all his mistresses. I just wanted my daughter back in my arms. Her little face was terrified. She was still wrapped in the swaddle, but it was coming loose around her, and when she was airborne, she seemed like a phantom, like a white cloud hung from the ceiling.

"What do you know about fathers?" he said finally. "You barely had one. Your mother was probably a whore, just like you."

He caught Ann in the end, unraveling the swaddle a little. She kicked against him. Sobbing. Then he seemed to sober, looking down at her as if he didn't know her. For a brief second, his eyes met mine, and they were wide and seeking. Alarmed, even. He seemed to be asking for something from me. So I went forward and held my arms out for Ann, and he gave her over. Then those eyes I once loved shuttered again.

"Get out of here," he said. He sat on the bed, eyes closed.

I packed Ann and me up—we didn't need more than what could fit inside a duffel bag—and showed up at the Banyan House. I didn't want to, but we had nowhere else to go. Mẹ appeared in her pajamas, the blue forget-me-not print starting to fade, and her hair was scraggly around her face. I could tell she'd lost weight since we were last there. She didn't tut or reprimand, as I was afraid she'd do. She opened her arms.

"Come inside. Come home," she said.

A part of me wanted to protest that it wasn't my home, that I had made a mistake. It has always been difficult to admit my failures. But the thought of returning to Vinh, to that apartment, felt like a trap. Instead, I handed Ann to her and let her make me a cup of tea. I didn't speak and she didn't prod. Between us, steam from the tea, a sleeping Ann in her arms. We sat up until the clock chimed eleven, then went upstairs.

That night, Ann and I stayed in my old bedroom. The mattress was lumpy, and we slept fitfully. Every few hours, she'd wake up and wail, as if remembering her trauma. I was anxious about her head, wondering if you could actually addle a child's brain by tossing her. I shushed her as best I could. It seemed the house folded in on us, protectively or maybe with a sense of worry that we would disrupt the peace. Let in the wolves.

We stayed there until Vinh came for us, a week later.

Mẹ was grocery shopping, and Ann and I were sitting on the couch watching an old movie. I was imitating the pinched, fast-talking trans-atlantic repartee for Ann, which made her giggle—her first laughs came out in that week at the Banyan House, released in sweet, airy puffs that captivated us. She loved the house. I caught her staring at the walls, delight on her face, her coos loud and direct, as if she were speaking to someone. I wanted to see it as she did, but where she found wonder, I saw peeling wallpaper and a sense of my own failure.

Mẹ gave us space, but always seemed to show up when I was tired, taking Ann from me without any fanfare. They walked around outside a lot, bundled up in sweaters. I saw Mẹ pointing out the banyan tree to Ann, giving her a leaf to hold up and consider. Sometimes, I saw them looking at each other contentedly, their faces gentle and glowing, and I felt oddly separate from them. I was grateful, yet mixed into the grat-itude was loss. Ann seemed less *mine* in the Banyan House. But I shut my mouth, knowing if I said anything, it would be too much.

The day Vinh came, I saw his old Honda coming up the drive through the window before I heard him. I put Ann on a blanket and bolted the doors, drew the curtains. Something in me felt the rush of danger.

"Shh," I whispered to Ann, and she turned contentedly to me, trusting.

He knocked, quietly at first, almost politely, then louder, until he was banging on the door. I thought, *Not by the hair of my chinny-chin-chin.*

"Open the *fuck* up, Hương," he slurred. "What are you hiding in there? Who have you snuck in now?"

His obscenities were so nasty, so pointed, that I was glad for a second that there were no neighbors who could hear. Then I realized there was no one who could hear. I went for the phone, but before I could dial anything, there was a giant crash, and the glass began to rain. I ran back toward Ann.

Vinh was standing in the living room, having crawled through the front window frame like a villain in a horror movie. He looked around mockingly. Palmed the edge of a lace antimacassar, then flicked it away from him.

"Still a dump," he said. "This, you prefer this to our home?"

"You told us to leave." I stood between him and Ann.

"Well, now I'm ready for you to come back. Come on, Hương. What will people say?"

I thought about the women whose numbers he kept, the ones I knew he spent nights with. His buddies who had poured all the hating into him. Susceptible Vinh. He came toward us, his steps soft and sure as a panther's.

"You broke the window," I said, dumbly. "You broke a *window.*"

"So what. Your mother can replace it. She's loaded, isn't she? Not that you'd know, looking around here. Em, we really should talk about your crazy family's priorities."

His tone was conversational, if wavery from alcohol, and it unnerved me.

"You have to go," I said. "I called the police."

"You didn't," he said with a knowing smile. "Besides, what the hell would they do to me? I'm your husband. I'm her father. We're a *family.*"

I considered how none of us knew the meaning of that word, not really. We were all trying at the shape of one, hoping for the transformative power of love and the perseverance of will, but really, we were operating in the fog of our own assumptions, our tired stereotypes. And they hadn't worked, not one bit. This nightmare was bound to play out eventually, killing one or both of us.

Vinh reached for me, and my first instinct was to glance at Ann, looking up at us with her big eyes, her tiny broken heart. I thought of this being what Ann remembered when she thought about marriage in the future, this pattern of hate and hitting, of unbridled violence, and I couldn't bear it.

"No."

I pushed back at Vinh for the first time, more forcefully than I thought I was capable of. He toppled over a footstool. He looked incredibly foolish there, sprawled about, and I knew it was a small man who needed to hurt his wife and child. I would leave him, I decided. I would never look back.

"Don't ever touch me again," I said. "You are nothing to me."

He blinked. Ridiculously, I saw a shadow of hurt cross his face.

Then he was up on his feet, more energized than ever, looking like he had just gotten a second wind at a sports match. He pushed me up against the wall and held his hand to my throat. His laugh made its way to my ears across a great distance. The pain soared up my shoulders, through my skull. The impact of my body against the wall made it shudder. A photograph fell somewhere close by. I saw the shattered glass within reach of Ann and when she rolled onto her stomach, straining toward me, I gasped, kicking my feet against the wall.

"No, wife, stay," Vinh said imperiously. "We have things to talk about. How you think this is going to go. How it's actually going to go."

"Anh," I gasped.

He continued as if I hadn't spoken. "Your attitude, all that defiance. I forgave you at first, because you'd never seen a real marriage. You didn't know how it was supposed to work. Then all the accusations about women and ghosts breathing on the phone. So self-righteous.

You are no angel, no matter what your pathetic mother says. Your family, living like white rich people, but still trash like the rest of us. Well, em, I've had enough of it. Of you."

Ann began to wail, and as the spots took over my vision, ink blots growing in front of me, I said her name, faintly, like a kind of prayer. If this was it, I wanted my last glimpse of the world to be her face. My Ann. The only person I would have fought back for.

I heard a door open in the far, far distance.

Vinh's eyes cleared and it was like he saw me at last. Something crystallized in his expression. He mouthed my name, but what fell from his mouth was a grunt, deep and settled, like a clod of dirt hitting the earth. Another strangled sound.

Then air, blessed air, rushed into my lungs. I slumped to the ground. Without thinking, I kicked away from Vinh and scooped Ann up, away from the glass.

"It's okay, baby. It's okay, you're safe," I said.

She quieted, and I looked back then. Vinh was against the wall, his eyes rolled back in his head. Warm blood spilled from his neck, onto his shirt. I remember thinking it looked like an inlet, long and narrow, surrounded on all sides by blue. Mẹ stood next to him, her hand pressed to her mouth. She still had her purse slung over one shoulder. Her keys were in the door.

"Mẹ?" I asked. I tiptoed to her. Pulled her away.

"The knife, Xuân's knife. I carry it in my purse," she said, horrified and pointing.

I saw it then, lodged in the back of Vinh's throat, the handle pointed out, toward the ceiling now. I wondered how hard she had to press. Whether she gave him warning or shoved it right in. She was a slight woman, but stronger than she looked. My mother, who had only ever done everything properly, so decorous that a sugar cube couldn't melt in her mouth. My mother, the murderer.

"Is he—" she asked.

"He's very dead," I said, a little hysterically.

"Hương," she said. Her breath was short and panting. "I couldn't let him hurt you."

"Listen to me," I said, suddenly protective toward her, my shivering little mother. "He was a bad man. A very bad man. If you didn't kill him, he would have killed me eventually. We will take care of this, Mẹ."

We went back to the parlor, Ann on my hip. I reached for Mẹ's hand. My eyes latched onto a glimpse of the serpent wallpaper in the dining room. The faded spot on the banister where everyone rested their hands before ascending the stairs. That stupid, out-of-tune piano we never learned to play, with its yellow keys and a piece of sheet music dappled with mold. I tried to focus on everything inconsequential to clear my own mind.

"I'm sorry, Hương," Mẹ said. "I've never killed anyone before."

"Of course you haven't. Sit down, Mẹ, you're in shock."

Ann nestled in my shoulder. She was quiet then. I know a good mother would have taken her away from her father's corpse, locked her safely in her room where she couldn't be moved by the evil, but I couldn't leave her, and I couldn't leave my mother. And perhaps, on some level, I wanted us to bear witness to what had happened together. Ann was fatherless, and I was husbandless, and yet we were still here.

There was glass and blood and, a few feet away, the drained body of my husband. The floorboards soaked up his rage, and then he slumped, dead and empty. I remembered how he had looked that first day at the lake house, staring out so doggedly at the water, waiting for it to gift him something that would make him feel worthy, manly, like the rest of them. In that moment in the Banyan House, I didn't feel sympathy or understanding for him—I would never feel like that again toward him—but something softer settled in me, a wish for peace, ours and his.

For a long time, we didn't move from the couch. Mẹ's hand threaded in mine, warm and trembling, Ann yawning into my shoulder.

Eventually, I put Ann, now sleeping, down in a pack and play in the kitchen, where we could hear her if she cried. But she didn't. She slept through that dreadful night, long and restfully, not even a sigh.

We wrapped Vinh's body up in a quilt, the one with an Americana print of crowing roosters and steepled fences, rolling him tight until he looked like a giant cigar.

There was no talk about the police now. We knew they would not help us, two Vietnamese women and a baby (the start of a morbid sitcom), and that there would be no future in which iron bars did not await us. Ann, given up to the foster system. My mother, implicated in a crime of unspeakable grisliness, shamed forever. Would they have believed that we did it in self-defense? We did not want to rely on the judgment of the law. Out here, in this overrun swampland, we made our own justice.

We moved the body into the trunk of Mẹ's Oldsmobile. The night was cloudy and dark, and we were grateful that it hid our sins. When I stared dumbly at the body, Mẹ shut the trunk.

"It's over," she said.

"What have we done?" Now we'd traded places. The panic began running up and down my body, settling in my throat in hot waves, while she was suddenly calm. Strategic. Her old self again.

She ignored me. Her focus was bright and beaming, the surge of genius or determination lighting up her face. "He left you. There was a note. It said, 'I wasn't made for this life. Don't try to find me.' And you'll be heartbroken, but no one will be surprised. We won't even file a missing persons report. How many men disappear from their families each day?"

"And the body?"

She faced me. "The swamp. Bodies always turn up there. With luck, he won't be recognizable when they find him."

It was impossible. And it wasn't. It was common news now when some fisherman found the wreckage of a boating accident, or a plane crash, or a run-of-the-mill homicide. Decades blurring the bodies, miring those old crimes in a morass of red tape that no cop cared to untangle. There'd be a whiff of sensationalism, but then the laziness would take over, a sense of dullness at those everyday horrors.

"I'll do it," she said. "You stay here with Ann. Clean the parlor up; try vinegar and a rough cloth. If that doesn't work, baking soda."

I laughed, wildly. "Is this a house-cleaning trick you learned? Will you become the Martha Stewart of murderesses?"

She didn't reply, only placed her hands on either side of me, cementing me into place. At the last second, she pulled me close and dropped her lips onto the side of my head. Not so much a kiss, but a benediction for courage.

"Okay?" she asked finally.

"Okay." Whatever happened next, I would not leave my mother to bear the consequences alone.

As she drove away, I began sprinkling baking soda on the bloodstains. There was no stench yet, but I smelled a faint saline odor. For the rest of my days, I would scent a *wrongness* in the parlor. Mẹ later filled it up with junk—magazines and appliances and weird garage sale finds and overlapping rugs to cover the pale splotches where blood could not be scrubbed out—just so no one could set foot in there. I wished I could have burned down that whole room.

When I heard the Oldsmobile moving back up the drive, hours later, I washed my hands with hot water and ran outside. The sky had a stubborn yellow tint to it, perhaps some leftover pollution, or the rot of red tide meeting the horizon. Shadowed cypress trees rose and bent, branches waving as if they were flagging down taxis. I could hear the croak of frogs and the birds burring gently in their nests. The clouds had dissipated, and now the moon rose like a button against a navy coat of a sky.

Mẹ got out of the car, limping a little. Tired, sweating, even through the chill. There was a stain near the collar of her shirt.

"It's done," she said.

But it was never done. That night, as I watched Ann sleep, I thought of what we had taken from her. A father. A family. Yet what might have happened if he had lived? Even if he did not kill me, there would always be the shadow of violence. A life for a life. But it wasn't just my life that my mother had bargained for. It was Ann's, too. He died so the two of us could live.

That knowledge did not take away the evil of what we had done, but it was enough for me to live with the secret forever. I would never tell Ann. She would know no complicity in my sins.

Yet the wedge would always be there between us; that choking guilt of knowing my mother and I had killed my daughter's chance at a family. In exchange for our safety, I would have to live with the gaping distance between me and my daughter, and harbor a secret that threatened to crush us all. What kind of bargain was that?

Chapter 34

Minh

There's something different about Ann and Hương both. Where Hương seems to have grown more solid, Ann is wispy. She's floating through her days, caught in a private dreaminess that makes her mother wary. I can tell Hương is suspicious of Ann's flowering love. She sees in it the reflection of her own tortured marriage.

Wes leaves his toolbox in all corners, waiting for Hương to change her mind about letting him help fix up the house. It irks her. Even in my incorporeal state, the house starts to feel different. It's been full of women for so long, it doesn't know what to do with a new presence. There's uncertainty in the air, a shimmering excitement, and it's partly Ann's new affair, and partly Hương's old fear at being discovered for our crimes. My crime.

I watch her tiptoe into the parlor, staring at the floorboards. Does she smell the old rust of blood? Feel the phantom grit of baking soda on her fingertips? She lifts the rug and presses her face to the bare floor. Sniffing. But he is long gone, disappeared in the swamplands with no trace, no questions. That the world forgot him so quickly is, perhaps, more an indictment of its capacity to care for the lost ones among us than of Vinh himself. She shuts the parlor door gently behind her.

Nevertheless, Hương watches Ann with an intensity that bodes ill for them both. I know that something is churning inside the Banyan

House. Even if I were there, flesh and blood, brimming with my old vigor, I could not have stopped it.

That girl from high school, Crystal Something, she starts coming over again, and when she arrives, she grabs Ann by the hand and they laugh and race up the stairs. Sometimes she brings her daughter, a small strawberry blond girl with knobby knees and an iPad attached to her hands like another limb. Ann is tender toward the girl, leaning forward to offer her a cup of juice or one of the many porcelain dolls no one wants. Crystal's daughter plays on the floor between them as they talk.

Once, they discuss Wes. Crystal's girl is curled on the window seat, her hands tightly fisted around the waists of a pair of Barbie dolls that she inches up the glass planes like rock climbers.

Crystal asks, "But you know what happened between him and Fiona, right?"

"I know she's gone now. And their son. California, right?"

A son. What kind of man lets his wife and child go? I remember Wes from the old days. There was a fragility to him even then, and he looked to Ann as a kind of hope, the way one might seek a buoy in a dark ocean. I did not like that he seemed to need her. A fine line between need and desperation.

Crystal leans forward. "Fiona and me would sometimes go for a drink back in the day. BK: Before Kids. That girl could spin an entire room around her finger. Irritated me so much. Even Peej got all schoolboy around her, the ingrate."

"She was beautiful?" A note of jealousy creeps into Ann's voice.

"Well, yeah. But honey, so are you. That's not the point."

"You're right. Go on."

"After we had babies, we got really boring, so then we all started a book club to keep us social, you know, except no one read at all. We just gossiped. A few months in, she started looking miserable, would leave in the middle, saying there was an emergency at home, though no one had called. And then she didn't show up for book club at all. Her best friend Lacey went by their house and said all she could hear was

Fiona sobbing and sobbing through the open windows of the house. Wes slamming the door and brushing past Lacey to get on his motorcycle. Their marriage didn't last long."

"So no one ever found out what was wrong with her?"

There's a pause. "Well, I mean, some people say it was Wes. He seems all right now, but he was never the most dependable. There were rumors."

"But Wes wouldn't hurt anyone."

"You know there are many ways to hurt someone, girl. Men can be inventive."

"Oh, I know." Ann's voice is weary.

"I'm not saying he did or didn't do anything wrong. What the hell do I know—" Here, Crystal gives her daughter an apologetic look. "Oh, sorry, pumpkin, don't tell your daddy I said that—I'm just saying: protect yourself. It's not just you anymore. And me, I'd want to know if it were my man."

"Wes is all right."

"If you say so," Crystal tells her doubtfully.

Ann looks up to see Hương standing by the door, and when she gets up to close it, her eyes turn stormy. Hương opens her mouth, but then shuts it when she faces the wood of the door. They are destined to relive this circle of chaos. Moving together, then snapping apart, like one of those hard golden bracelets that I'd unlatch from my wrist every night before bed.

That night, still angry from the invasion of privacy, Ann looks at her mother as if she wants to say something, but instead they eat in silence. Between them, the old irreconcilability.

The next afternoon, Ann's mooning over one of those cheesy jewelry commercials on TV, the ones promising diamonds and everlasting love. Black-and-white images of kissing couples—always a blond woman and a James Bond–like man with perfect hair—against a flowery meadow you can almost smell through the television set. Ann sighs. She's looking particularly radiant in nothing but an old chambray dress, her feet settled on a paisley cushion on the couch, hand resting on the swell of her belly.

"The brightest love of them all," a cashmere voice murmurs from the television. The woman in the commercial holds up a solitaire ring on her left hand and twists it to catch the sunlight, which reflects to overtake the screen in a brilliant whitewash.

"How beautiful," Ann says, stroking a strand of hair between her fingertips.

Hương frowns. "Pig shit."

Ann startles out of her reverie, the dream slipping from her eyes. "Love is pig shit?"

Hương is silent. Ann drops the lock of her hair and goes to the window. Her bare feet on the floorboards. Her hands pressed against the panes.

She says, "Just because you haven't experienced it doesn't mean it doesn't exist."

Finally, cruelly, Hương says, "Well, look at the evidence. My father. Your father. He's gone, isn't he? And . . ."

She gestures toward Ann's stomach, the air around her, the absence of a man next to her. And the second she does, she sees that it's a mistake. This implication of Ann's weakness. Ann's eyes suddenly turn dark. I see a flash of Vinh's scowl. Hương does, too. It startles her so much she shrinks back.

"Why are you like this?" Ann asks in a low voice.

"Let's not do this."

"Every goddamn moment I get a shot at happiness. You're like a black cloud. Are you *utterly* incapable of joy?"

"Forget it, Ann. It was a stupid joke."

"It wasn't. I know you."

In Hương's pause, long and bated, I know she's thinking of Vinh holding her against the wall by her neck, baby Ann reaching toward broken glass. That wretched nightmare. Because she loves Ann so much, and yet in such a twisted way, she sometimes cannot see the difference between the two of them. She only sees another mistake, on the verge of happening.

"It's just," Hương says finally, "you seem to be moving so fast with Wes. He's here all the time."

"So you don't like him?"

"I like Wes fine, con," Hương says. "I wonder how much you should invest in another man. After all, you're carrying Noah's child. You may change your mind."

"I won't."

"You never know. And we had a plan. You and me and Kumquat." She sounds pleading now, and I want to say, *See? That's what being a grandmother is.* Coveting something that isn't yours. Hương continues, "We were going to live here, the three of us. I can protect you both."

Ann's laugh barks into the air, crueler than I have ever heard her. I want to hold my hand to her mouth to make her stop talking. To stall the rift forming fast between them.

"When have you *ever* done that?" Ann asks, venom in each syllable. "Chosen me over yourself or your shitty boyfriends, or Gary. Did you know how often he told me I was stupid, ugly, worthless? He'd say it while your back was turned, whenever he wanted to take me down a peg. Sneer it in a pig whisper. You pretended not to hear any of it, so you could have your picture-perfect little marriage. Well done on that."

"That's unkind."

Ann's voice is squeaky and angry at once. "He told me I was the reason you never had another child with him. Said it was because you were so sick of dealing with me."

"That's not true."

I know it's not. Hương told me she never wanted any more children after Ann, because she couldn't imagine loving anyone in nearly the same way. To her, it felt immoral to have another child, when she'd given all she had to Ann already.

Ann continues, "The only person who ever protected me was Bà Ngoại."

Hương clenches her hands and looks around the room, at my towering books, all the cane furniture that came with the house, the faux sunflowers in their vases. I know what she's thinking: my protection came at a cost.

"My mother," she says, "*stole* you from me. You were supposed to be my child. Mine. And ever since you were born, she saw you as her second chance. Because you know what, Ann? Your bà ngoại was a shit mother. She may have been an angel on earth as your grandmother, but she left me and my brother every chance she could. She was a shit mother."

The edges of my vision darken. If I weren't already dead, I would want to die now.

Ann looks like she's been slapped. "That's not true."

"You don't want to believe it. You have no idea. But you will never see that because it's always been the two of you in your fantasy world. All the secret giggling, things you hid from me, your own mother. Your real mother. There was never room for anyone else between you and your grandmother. At least now there are no more secrets for the two of you to keep from me."

The tears are running down Hương's face now, and they're both shocked, like they can't believe they're finally speaking so clearly.

Ann's expression flickers. Then, when she speaks, it's with a slowness, almost as if she's in a trance, stretching each word out like taffy. "You'd be surprised. The things I could tell you, Mom."

No, Ann. Not like this.

Hương is furious. "Don't bother. I don't have the heart space for more secrets. You know what? Maybe she *should* have been your mother. Maybe I was never cut out for it. Not everyone is meant to have a child."

Too late, she realizes she's uttered the fear Ann feels about her own baby, the thing every single woman feels on the precipice of motherhood. It's too cruel.

"It's such a shame, then," Ann says, "that Bà Ngoại died."

"Instead of me?"

Ann is aloof as she stands and silently walks out of the house. I can't follow her where she is going, but still, I feel torn. One side of me bending to run after Ann. The other part crouched near Hương. My hurt daughter.

Hương presses her nails into her palm so hard that she draws blood. For once, I don't want to rush to Ann's side, defending her against her mother. I see the crack in Hương's armor now. She falls to her knees.

"Mẹ?" she says, in a small, beseeching voice. Asking forgiveness for her words. If I could, I would give it. She wasn't wrong.

I want to rewind time so that I can hold her tighter. Love her longer. I remember how whenever my children used to hurt themselves, I'd kneel to look into their tear-streaked faces. Blowing on their cuts with my breath. They hiccupped so bravely, my little soldiers. And always, I asked the same question, the one I would ask all their lives, with varying degrees of seriousness.

"Will you live, darling?" I'd ask, brushing their tears away with my fingertips. "Can you find a way to survive, for Mẹ?"

Chapter 35

Ann

I cannot live like this.

After Mom leaves for work, I go on a tear. I'm rifling through the cavernous closets, messing up all that we organized just months—can it only have been months?—ago. Through the air fly the dirt-streaked rags, the fuzzy washcloths, linen that sighs of mildew. Inside the ottoman: Victorian novels, hair curlers, blank printer paper so thin I can see the gnats move through it. Every corner of the house, inscrutable.

"Where are they?" I demand to Bà Ngoại's portrait on the altar. "I know you have more secrets."

I take a stick of incense and I wave it in front of her like a sword. "I'm not taking the fall for any of this." What do I mean, exactly? My crumbling relationship with my mother? The secret festering in me? All I know is that I want to turn everything inside out, like slitting the stomach of a beached whale, allowing the dark contents to spill out into the light.

There's silence, though I'm seized by a deep cold in my veins, a sudden ice around my limbs. I scream like a crazy person. I feel like I'm actually going crazy.

"I'll tell her everything," I whisper.

There's nothing but a key, a photograph, and this pressure inside me: To tell, or not to tell? I go to the attic, key in my pocket, and take the photograph out of the trunk. Those eyes, so unknowable, mock me. I'm furious at Mom, but inside my fury, I want to protect her still. She, who believes so little in love. What would happen if I took away one of the very last shreds of faith inside her?

I pocket the photograph.

Downstairs, I enter Mom's room. Neat, as always, with a novel on the nightstand, and her pajamas, folded at the foot of the bed. "Wear your clothes twice, and you'll do less laundry," she once told me. I rifle through her things, as she once did mine, when I was a teenager. If I can't have privacy, neither will she.

There are the scrubs, still soaked in her Estée Lauder perfume, and her silk slips, heaped in a pile near her underwear. An old CD player, some photo albums. I open one and flip through it. And I stop short.

Inside are pages and pages of my drawings, printed from the old blog I've stopped posting on. Years' worth, from when I was just starting out, and my lines were so unfamiliar and amateur. She kept every single one. In her careful script, she labeled each with the date. Never once has she mentioned having seen my blog. It was a secret resentment of mine, perhaps, how little she cared. But now, this. Another discovery.

My breath catches.

I take Bình's photograph out of my pocket and study it. My grandfather, though not the man I have been worshipping, the wink from the altar. This man is a stranger to me, and to my mother. I could upend her world. It would be so easy to be cruel.

Yet even in my anger, I can't. The fury sizzles away, a drop of sweat on hot concrete. My mother, with her enigmatic gestures, her doormats and that binder, the gestures of a love I could never hold in my hands. Never an object, an offering, but the very air around me. The breath inside me. Her love is not flawless, a solitaire sparkling from a smooth hand. Rather, it reminds me of a geode—rough and worn by time yet cracked, occasionally, to reveal a vibrant cluster of crystals. A fine and constant heart. She has always reached for me, in her own inscrutable way.

I decide that I will not take her father away from her.

In the kitchen, I light the gas stove. The flame springs up, blue as headlights down a dark path. The edges of the photo crisp, then the smoke tendrils into my nose. When the last bits burn, my fingertips catch the fire, they get hot and swollen. I stick them into my mouth, where the wet heat soothes the pain.

"You take your secrets back," I say aloud. "We're starting fresh."

There's a brush of breath near my face and I turn in surprise, expecting to see Bà Ngoại. But nothing. That nothingness is what makes me shudder.

My destruction complete, I curl up in bed and I sleep.

Then I'm dreaming about the banyan tree out back. In my dream, it's sprouted giant wings, it's a bird with vines for a plume that whips around and around, gnashing the clouds. A great indigo-blue storm breaks and the tree is swirled up in it, a rising phoenix. I chase after it, holding a newborn Kumquat in muslin cloth.

"Not yet, don't leave, not now," I cry.

The tree seems to pause and turn toward me, as if considering. I can't catch up, I'm out of breath. I wonder where it's going, and why I can't follow. Lightning cracks suddenly, splitting the tree in half, felling it to the ground. It drops into the earth, making gaping canyons that separate me from the rest of my world.

I stand on one side, opposite the house, watching as it moves farther and farther away from me. My mother and Bà Ngoại stand in the yard, mouths open. They are wearing old robes, arms raised toward me and Kumquat.

"Just jump!" Bà Ngoại yells.

But I can't leave Kumquat, and I'm afraid, so I stay fixed, desperate.

"Jump," she says again.

When I wake, I'm at the foot of the stairs. There's a terrible pain that rips a scream from me. Mom runs down to me and the last thing I see is her toenails, painted a gorgeous mauve color, the color of a fading bruise.

Chapter 36

Hương

Eight months later, I'm back at the hospital where my mother stayed after her fall. But it's my daughter this time, and the circularity makes my throat clench. Cosmic injustice, again. But I'm different now. I will not be left helpless; I will be Ann's strength. Whatever words we exchanged are quashed out of my consciousness. It's just me and her, and the baby, now. Nothing will get between us this time.

There's something about the smell of a hospital: cotton balls and scalpels, which remind me of bleeding wounds, which remind me of Vinh.

I think of him now, more than I have in two decades. I remember the way he slid that receipt across the table at the bookstore that first day. The heat of his eyes. How when we were together, the world fell still for once, docile—until it wasn't, until the danger reared like a dragon, all teeth and bright whorls of fire.

"Mẹ," Ann says, her voice softer than a falling leaf. She never calls me that. Soon, her hand is in mine, but it feels thin, not fully there. "I'm cold."

This hurricane-threatened October is chilly and humid. The air is heavy with a promise unfulfilled. We're huddled up in cardigans, mine the color of an olive leaf, Ann wearing a rust-red one with big gold buttons, loose over her hospital gown. She drowns in it, even with her swell of a belly.

"You're going to be okay," I tell her.

It's really the only thing I've said, more or less, since I've been here. And I'm not lying, at least not when it comes to her physical well-being. The baby is fine, miraculously, and Ann is, too, though she's shaken and her mind wanders sometimes. They're keeping her for observation; then she can come home.

That boy Wes visits, bearing every kind of cuisine in the world for us, until I have to tell him to stop, no one needs a tour of international cooking at a time like this. But faint dimples appear in his cheeks and I know he's pleased. He was never the problem, I know this now.

Sometimes, that strange Crystal girl comes, though now she looks more substantial, having put on weight and shed most of her clown makeup. I tell her I'm glad she's here and she looks up at me in heartbreaking surprise, as if no one has ever said a nice thing to her in her life.

"Where else would I be?" she says.

Then she just goes on reading aloud to Ann from the latest celebrity magazine, twisting her mouth into impressions of movie stars that make Ann double over laughing, shouting, "Stop! Ow." Once, Crystal brings a speaker and turns on songs from when they were in high school, some of which tug at my ear, those old familiar chords. *I buy my own diamonds and I buy my own rings.* They holler the lyrics, mangling some of them, using a remote control as a microphone, pumping their pale limbs in the air like they're at a rock concert.

"Come on, Miss Hương!" Crystal shouts. "Dance with us."

When I shimmy a little in my chair, reddening, Ann beams.

The nurses come to frown at the noise, but I frown back at them, their audacity in interrupting the girls' joy, and they scuttle away again, shutting the door with a hard thwack.

Sometimes, it's just me and Ann. Her joy simmers to nothing, and what's left is something raw and glowing, a coal dying in on itself.

"Too much excitement?" I ask.

"Sometimes I get this brief glimpse of what life could be, you know? Without all the grief. Without the history."

"So let it go, con. Your grandmother would have wanted you to be happy."

She plays with the strings of her gown, now looped up toward her front. I think I see Kumquat moving, but it could have been a shift of the sunlight.

"I've been dreaming about so many things," she says. "A hot little house on stilts. It was surrounded by sewage. Bats rustled in the eaves. And then sometimes I think about Bà Ngoại. The man in the moon."

When she talks, I can almost hear my mother, her breath firm next to me in the trailer. I can't remember the last time we were all together. My heart seems to beat faster.

Ann continues, "Bà Ngoại and her gloomy house, and us in it, rattling around."

"Like ghosts."

"Yes, exactly. What are we doing there? What are we all doing? Doesn't it feel like we're trapped sometimes?"

"We don't have to stay, con."

"Where would we go? It's the only place we've known. But I'm so sick of it, sometimes, Mom."

She cries softly, and I have nothing to say, no answers to give. Her fall has left her feeling betrayed. The bottle has spilled, and everything comes out, a flood of feeling. But I'm not scared anymore. I can hold her now, and I can hold her pain. I will keep us from drowning.

A doctor comes in, a man with stone-gray hair and frameless glasses. He looks like an actor playing a doctor, so firm and conciliatory. He says that it's normal to feel traumatized. "Give it time," he says in that patronizing, drawn-out way I hate. I want to pummel him, and he's aware of this, so he backs away. When he leaves, his cologne trails him. I think that I'm making a reputation for myself at this hospital. A tiger mom, is that what they say? I don't mind it.

"Mom." Ann sighs. "There's something I have to tell you, I think."

Her eyes droop. I tell her, "Shh, con. You'll tell me later."

"It's important." But her voice is so low I'm not sure she knows what she's saying. "I keep forgetting why."

I stroke Ann's hand until she drifts off, fitfully. Out the window, the day has that strange hazy quality, partly smoke pollution, partly the onslaught of something new.

Earlier, Phước and Diane visited. They brought us phở that Diane made—too much cinnamon, though I appreciate her kindness—and Phước tried to talk as little about the house as he could, but I could see it there in the room, his avarice, arching like a cat about to spring.

"We can talk business later, Chị Hương," he said, his voice so cloying it reminded me of homemade banana candy, the black squares wrapped in cellophane that Mẹ used to buy us at the market. "Ann's health is the most important."

Ann gave him a disdainful look as she rearranged her pillows. She was tapping on her phone. When Phước and Diane first saw her, they had stared at her stomach, asked questions about the baby and its father. Ann gave as little information as possible, and when they turned to me, I shrugged, guarding Ann's privacy. Finally, Phước backed away.

"We have no business to speak of," I said. I'd been ladling out soup with a plastic hospital spoon and accidentally spooned some on my hand. "Shit!"

Phước was sanctimonious. "Shh. What will they think of us."

"Thank you for the soup, Cậu Phước," Ann said, "Aunt Diane."

He puffed himself up. "Yes, well. That's what family is for, isn't it, con?"

Diane looked out the window. She hadn't said much—I thought she was having one of her odd moments, the ones where she slipped from the room, leaving behind the husk of her body. It happened often in group settings, as if she thought we wouldn't notice her soul-absence.

Phước never did. I wondered if she made it a habit of slipping out at home, leaving her body behind so her mind could wander.

"I had five miscarriages before the girls," she said dreamily. "The babies sort of float around me now. Not *them,* of course. Maybe just the souls they forgot to take with them. Isn't that something? How the dead never really leave?"

She traced a shape in the window, but I was too far away to see what she was drawing. There was a bit of a witch in her. I could see her kneeling by an open fire, breaking herbs into a pot. The image made me shiver.

"Diane!" I hissed. "We don't need to talk about that now."

Even Phước looked aghast. "Maybe we should be going. Diane?"

She turned to us, a brilliant smile stretched across her plain face. "Oh, your baby is just fine, Ann. I see how eager he is for life—and you along with him, though maybe you don't feel that way now. Soon, he'll be wriggling in your arms, and then you'll put him down, and he'll shoot off for college. It'll happen before you remember to take a breath."

I was oddly reassured, though I went to stand by Ann's side, bristling on her behalf. She seemed mesmerized by her aunt. Phước gathered their things and pulled Diane by the elbow.

"We really should get back," he said.

Diane took one last glance out the window. "The storm is on our doorstep now. Don't let it surprise you."

The day was clear as a newly washed glass, without even a trace of clouds, though the air was cooler than it had been in days past. Ann and I exchanged a glance. In private, we sometimes called Diane "the Weatherwoman," our oracle on all things meteorological. I could see her in a pink suit with wide lapels, her heels pointing toward her map.

Before he left, Phước turned to me and, his voice tremulous with feeling, said, "This isn't over, chị."

Despite myself, I pulled my sweater closer to my body.

When they were gone, Ann and I stared at each other. Then she said, choking in laughter, "This is really awful soup."

Now she is asleep, her hands curled under her chin, the way they did when she was a baby. I think of what Vinh has missed out on, and then, as my mind does, it separates him into two. The man before the anger—or when it was deeply buried, fossilized in his goodness—and the one after. What unleashed it? Once, I might have reproached myself, thinking I had done something wrong. But now I know that rage unmitigated is always bound to overspill.

Though it does no good to imagine an alternate version of our story, I can't help myself.

My husband, the man who could have been, would have perhaps been a doting grandfather. He might have put Kumquat on his shoulders, carried him around and around, laughing as the baby kicked his face. Found odd little things at garage sales that he would repaint. Mixed rice with broth for Kumquat's breakfast, the way I had for Ann. Maybe Kumquat would have been his second chance, if he'd lived. Stranger things have happened.

But then there's the real man, dead for decades, his remains scattered somewhere dark and hot, among the gators and scum. Mẹ never told me where exactly she left him, and I didn't want to know. The tragedy of no one remembering him—not his friends or family, his daughter, not even me, not really. But these years later, I regret nothing.

As I move to sit, Ann's phone buzzes and rings. I look at the screen. Noah. Maybe it's curiosity, or maybe I'm just fed up with men who don't live up to their promises, but I pick up. Ann is sound asleep, so I go into the hallway, gently shutting the door behind me. I can see her through the blinds, her breathing regular, still curled up like a croissant.

"Hello," I say.

"Oh. Is this—that is, I'm looking for Ann Tran," he says. He's rushed but polite. I take in the sound of his voice, which is unremarkable but pleasant.

"This is her mother, Hương."

"I've heard so much about you," he says, committed to the niceties.

When I don't reply, he stumbles a little, which reveals that perhaps those things he's heard haven't been wholly flattering. "I'm just hoping to talk to Ann. I've been—well, I've been begging to come see her for months."

"Months," I say. Ann did not mention this. She does not mention him at all, and I must revise the image in my head of Noah the deadbeat. "What could she possibly have to say to you?"

"Look, this is awkward, Ms. Tran."

"Hương."

"Hương," he says apologetically. "I don't really think we need a mediator. I just want to talk to Ann face-to-face. In person. There's a lot to say."

"Hmm," I muse. "You don't think you've said enough?"

There's a silence as he processes this. Wondering how much I know. Readjusting his strategy.

"Look," he says reasonably, "we've all made mistakes. Haven't you? But I love her. More than love her—I need her—and the baby."

I think, but don't say aloud: *Does she need* you, *though*?

Noah continues, his voice brimming with earnestness, "I didn't handle it the right way at first, but I'm here now, and she's *gone*. I don't think that it's too much to ask for one conversation. I'll come to her. I've always wanted to come to her."

"She's indisposed."

"Indisposed? What does that mean?" He sounds annoyed now.

I can see him shoving a hand through his hair, breathing quickly through his mouth. Trying to control himself. I'm inclined to hang up on him.

But then there's Kumquat, the boy who may grow up without a father. Would I, of all people, want that for my grandson?

I nod to a nurse passing me in the hallway. She indicates the "No Cell Phones" sign with a pointed raise of her eyebrows.

"She's in the hospital," I whisper. "She had a fall last night on the stairs."

"A *fall*?" His voice is ragged, and I know that whatever else went on between them, he cares for her. Who wouldn't? Fierce Ann.

"She and the baby are fine. We'll be home tomorrow, maybe sooner."

There's relief in his voice, then something wooden. "The baby. I don't even know the sex."

"Ann will tell you when she's ready," I say.

I move to hang up, but something stops me. Maybe it's the sight of Ann in the hospital bed, her hand now moved to her stomach, cradling the swell. Months from now, will she be back here, alone except for me, searching and wondering why she didn't let Noah in?

I know so much more about regret than I care to, and I know how stubborn my daughter can be. It's not in my nature to interfere. But just this once, I do. I whisper the address to Noah, like I'm giving him an incantation for good fortune. I feel like a fairy who has given the prince the magic map, though the princess may just vault herself right out of the castle when he arrives. But at least I will have played my role. Without saying goodbye, I hang up. I absolve myself of what comes next.

When Ann wakes, I'm by her side. I have a glass of water for her. Even though she can do it herself, I put the rim of the glass against her lips.

She asks, "What's wrong? You look distracted, Mom."

"Before you went to sleep, you wanted to say something to me. You said it was important."

She cocks her head and blinks. After a pause, she says, "I can't remember."

"Are you sure?"

"I'm just glad you're here. Thank you, Mom. For everything."

Then she smiles, brilliantly and openly, and something in it takes away the sting of the lost years. All at once, I'm the mom who's always been at her bedside. In my mother's absence, I take up the place that was always meant to be mine.

Chapter 37

Ann

Mom fusses over me, but the truth is, I'm hardly there. I've wandered in my mist again, thinking about the fall and the stairs, the terrible danger in this house. The Banyan House was once the only home I could imagine, but now it shape-shifts. It feels unhappy, perilous in its brokenness, its perpetual disorder. Like it's waiting for something terrible to happen.

When we arrive home from the hospital, I walk through Kumquat's nursery, pressing a hand against my aching back. Despite all Wes has tried to do, I see floorboards that are not wholly nailed down, corners from which spiderwebs spring, almost as if they were seeded there. The tiny windows make the house feel darker and gloomier. I feel an itch to crawl through them, even in my highly pregnant state.

I've taken to drawing things for Kumquat's nursery: mostly hyper-realistic foliage and landscapes, not something that comes naturally for me. I think about how I once wanted to draw a book about the creatures of the swamp. Aliveness is a difficult thing to capture. It takes more time and detail than I'm accustomed to.

"You should draw the banyan tree," Mom says once, looking over my shoulder. We're sitting at the kitchen table, staring outside. The tree is bigger than ever and seems to sway like a weary, overburdened woman on her way to the kitchen. It fills me with new dread.

"I have. I can't get it right, though."

"Think of how long it's been here," Mom says. "It weathered all the storms. Banyans don't get washed away, they just dig deeper. They're stubborn like us."

She's standing by the stovetop putting the jasmine tea on. I'm not drinking coffee anymore, as it upsets my stomach, so she brews weak tea, sweetened with just a little sugar and, sometimes, evaporated milk. I think of how Bà Ngoại and I would drink coffee in the afternoons, swirling our spoons around as we talked.

Mom never talks about her, but sometimes I catch her wearing one of Bà Ngoại's sweaters—the Big Bird yellow one with the huge buttons she got at a church rummage sale. Sometimes, I slip on Bà Ngoại's padded house shoes. Once, I see Mom wearing one of my old tortoiseshell hair clips, angled to catch the loose strands from her bun. We molt in and out of one another's clothes, trading identities. Mom will be a grandmother soon, and I'll be a mother, and we'll still be in this house breathing in the last wisps of Bà Ngoại, as if her scent is a substitute for her warmth, her flesh-and-blood aliveness.

I haven't forgiven her entirely, but I have found my way back to the love. Perhaps it was the fall, and my mother, who will not leave my side. I see how far mothers will go to protect their children. Bà Ngoại was no different. And who has not lived a life of regrets?

After I burned the photograph, I felt the secret bury itself inside me, like one of those coquina shells that uses its hard edges to wriggle into the sand, protecting itself from the onslaught of the tides. I understand that the last gift Bà Ngoại gave me was anger, something sharp to whittle away the worst of the grief. My missing her has become a matter of course, a dull ache, a fading bruise. But my rediscovered love for her is the balm I needed.

"What do you want Kumquat to call you when he's born?" I ask.

"Oh." Mom is pleased. Her eyes dew a bit, which I didn't expect. "I think he can call me whatever he wants. Bà Ngoại? Grandmother? Hương?"

"No, he won't call you by your name. No child of mine will disrespect an elder that way."

"You sound just like your bà ngoại when you say that."

But the sting isn't in her words. It feels ever so slightly like a compliment. I shade in one last bit of the mushroom stalk.

She continues, "You know that when you woke up every morning, as soon as you could walk, she was always the first person you went to. I could hear your feet padding across the hall, the creak of her door opening, then you two talking in her bed. It sounded like babble to me, your secret language. I'd dress and do my hair, and then you'd be ready. There was nothing for me to do. I should have been grateful that you were being taken care of so well."

"You weren't?"

"Gratitude and resentment are the two things I feel most when I think of your grandmother," she says.

"What about love?"

She's surprised. "Of course love. Always love."

I tell her about my project for Kumquat. Not the foliage, but the fairy tale I'm beginning to write and draw. Thinking of the binder, which I don't mention, I show her the sketches, laying them before her. She hums as she pages through them.

"Oh, Ann," she says, pleased.

Then she gets to the last image, the one of Chú Cuội, clinging to the banyan tree as it unroots and escapes the earth. The story doesn't have a happy ending. I tell her that I worry that it's too depressing for a children's book.

She says, "When I was young, I used to hate the ending of that story. But now I think: What could be happier than freedom?"

"I'm not a writer," I admit. "This may be horrible."

"Or it could be the best thing you've ever done."

"Second best," I say, tapping the side of my belly.

We're just finishing up our tea when the doorbell rings its strange, jangly tune. I don't know how I know, but it's not a package on the porch, and it's not Phước trying to weasel his way in again, or Wes with his half smile, or Crystal with her funny little gifts, like the stuffed succulent she got for Kumquat as a joke, the one that mirrored the baby's movements and squeaked when the baby did.

"That thing is uncanny," I'd said.

"I think it's cute," Mom said. Crystal had beamed at her.

Now Mom gets the door and her voice is hushed. I stand and I wait.

When Noah enters the kitchen behind my mother, he looks so handsome and familiar, I almost catch my breath. His fair hair is tinted with gold, like he's been at the beach, and that jaw with its uncertain mouth begins to work up some words. I want to reach up and brush the strands from his face. The affection hasn't quite died, I suppose.

I notice the flowers in his hand—expensive pink roses tied with a silver ribbon—and his wrinkled slacks, the biggest anomaly of all. He leans back, in uncharacteristic hesitation. I wonder how I look to him, wearing a flowing dress, my hair unkempt, barefoot in front of a sketch pad. A past version of me might have been a little unnerved at being caught in such disarray, but now I just lift my chin higher. I put my hand on Kumquat, who's kicking mightily, quieting him. We talk through the embryonic walls, the baby and me, and I tell him not to worry, Mama is here.

"Wow, Ann. You look gorgeous," Noah says, falling back on the old compliments. But it pleases me anyway. "How are you feeling?"

He comes forward. Mom takes the flowers from him and busies herself in another room with a vase. For a second, I think he's going to reach for my belly, but I don't think I could bear to be touched by him yet, though the sneaking memory of our intimacy still moves me, just a little, a jumping needle on a broken odometer. Sensing my retreat, he heaves a gesture resembling a shrug.

"Let's go in the parlor," I say, and he follows.

"The parlor, Ann. You have a parlor."

"I know. This house is wild, isn't it?"

"You've never told me anything about it."

"That can't be true," I say, but then I know it is. I wonder why I never let Noah into this world. Would it have changed anything if I'd let him see more of myself?

He picks a wingback chair that creaks dramatically when it's sat upon, and I rest on the piano bench. It's not comfortable, but it's the seat farthest from him, and I think I need my distance. I'm not even mad at Mom, who I suspect has orchestrated this whole thing, because I know that this moment has been coming for a while, and Noah has traveled all this way.

His arms hang. "I've missed you so damn much, Ann. I called every day—at least for a while. I texted. I emailed. Would have shot up a thousand flare guns if I thought you'd notice. It's all so simple: I just can't be without you. And I can't be without the baby, either."

"Wait," I say, but of course he doesn't, he just plows on like he could talk over my objections, a lawyer in the court of love.

"It took me time to get there, I know," he continues. "But I'm here now with you. I'm so sorry about Alexis, my parents, all of it. You are right. They didn't see you as my wife. You didn't make that up, and I'm sorriest of all that I pretended not to see it for so long."

It's almost a relief to know that what I'd sensed for so long was true. But it pains me to know that their opinion mattered so much more to Noah than the reality of our relationship.

Kumquat, no longer the size of a kumquat at all, kicks his feet against me. It's as if he's telling me to be strong, that forgiveness is for chumps. But still, I find myself thawing under Noah's gaze. I've heard these words before, via phone and text and email, but something about the way they fall from his lips now changes their shape so they can really reach me, penetrate that deep crevice in my heart.

"Thank you for that," I say. "For acknowledging me."

"And I just hate that I wasn't there when you fell. It wrecked me to think of you in the hospital alone."

"But I wasn't alone. I'm not now," I say, though not out of spite. "I've had everything I need here. Without you."

"But I'm here now. Don't you want to be together? For the baby? For us?"

"I don't know."

He deflates. "I don't think we can stop loving each other that quickly, Ann. It's simply not possible. I imagine the three of us together all the time. You and me and the baby, in our house, working in the garden while he plays in a wheelbarrow. Making dinner, sleeping in on the weekends. We're a family, and we always have been."

You don't put a baby in a wheelbarrow, I want to tell him, *just for photo shoots and other absurd occasions,* but I can tell he's put some thought into this.

"I've been seeing someone else," I tell him. I don't mean this to be a reason, or an excuse, but I also have no desire to hide Wes from Noah, or vice versa.

"Okay." He takes a moment. "I haven't."

His eyes are hurt, and he's right to be hurt, perhaps. It is awfully quick; even I know that. Wes offers me something, but it's not what Noah has given me. All the versions of me, all the kinds of love I've offered to men, rise in me, clamoring against each other. A small, sad part of me wants to take Noah into my arms, feel him breathing in my hair. Like nothing has changed at all. Maybe if we can rewind time, Bà Ngoại would be back, too, and things wouldn't be so heavy. I'm tempted, but I sit on my hands so I won't reach out to him.

"That's okay. I understand," he says finally. "I drove you away. But we have to be together. We just have to, Ann."

The desperation in his voice summons pity, because to me, Kumquat and I are past him on a long road, looking back over our shoulders.

"What about your parents?" I ask.

The hope lights up his eyes again. He sees the opening in my question and seizes at it. "They have nothing to do with you and me, and the baby. They'll get over it. But even if they don't—"

There it is again, that sweet denial, the forceful optimism that has made him so successful, so adored. I wonder why I never saw it before, how he has always managed to delude himself and others. How it works. It's a kind of magic-making.

"It's a boy," I say. "I call him Kumquat, because, well, he was the size of one."

"He's definitely not anymore."

"You've missed a lot," I say, but not with malice, just factually. Then, "Do you want to feel him?"

Noah rushes to the piano bench, and he's too big to fit, so he kneels in front of me. His hands rest on my belly, and when I look down at him, he looks so grateful and worshipful.

"Yes, there he is," Noah breathes. The wonder is genuine. It softens me.

"You know that our lives don't fit together," I say. "They never really did, and we tried, but now I'm ready to admit it. Aren't you?"

I'm not trying to be contradictory, and I'm not trying to hurt his feelings. It's the most evident thing in the world to me. His hands don't leave my belly, and his eyes are pleading.

"Do you love him?" Noah asks.

At first I think he's asking about the baby, but then I understand. The dichotomy of his mind—this man or that. As if my emotions were so tangled in men that those could be the only options.

"You'll always be a part of Kumquat's life," I say, unwilling to give an answer to a question I haven't figured out for myself yet.

Mom invites Noah to stay the night, and though he is frustrated, his quest thwarted, he regains some hopefulness as we eat dinner together. He praises Mom's meal—sautéed watercress and tiny shrimp in a caramel sauce, nothing like the food he normally eats—with such extreme gratitude and desperate insincerity that Mom raises her eyebrows at me, as if to say: *Is he for real?* Noah, the pleaser. Yet he hardly eats anything at all, like that time I cooked thịt kho for him for hours, and it wound up mounded under his napkin, nearly untouched.

After dinner, I give him the tour and begin to see Banyan House through his eyes. To him, it's a curiosity more than an affront. Odd and creaky and a little dirty, but interesting. Charming, even. We tell him stories about the house. His mind, ever quick, tallies up what it would take to restore it. I can tell he wants to offer help, even as he knows that's not possible.

"You could refinish these floors. They would gleam," he says. So many men hoping to fix the house. Fix us.

"Yes, we could," Mom says serenely.

She likes Noah, but cautiously, waiting for me to give her permission. Under the table I squeeze her hand. She doesn't know my heart, not entirely, but she tries, and for now, that is enough. She goes on a walk after dinner to give us space, and I show Noah the nursery. I point out the little books I've gathered, and the crookedly sewn blanket we made. The eyelet drapes, the little blue pegs for Kumquat's towels. Even still, the room feels a little dark and depressing, and I think maybe this is a temporary nursery after all. I crave the sunshine, the ocean for my son.

Noah is flipping through *Goodnight Moon*. "I remember this. My mom used to read it to me, and she'd get to the part about the mouse, and it was my favorite. All the tiny things in that room."

"I liked when they got to the red balloon." I smile.

I tell him about the fairy tale I'm writing and his eyes light up in wonder.

"That is genius, Ann," he says. "I'm more excited about your book than mine."

"Liar," I tease.

He's looking at me with such tenderness, such want, that I let him come closer, wrap his arms around my middle. He's a breath away from me.

"I'm huge, just tremendous," I say. "A beached whale."

"You are perfect," he says.

He's kissing me in a familiar way, his arms wrapped around me with such ferocity that I almost step back. His hand moves up to my neck, stroking so tenderly that I want to cry. I forgot what it was like to be loved in Noah's specific way. But when I do back away, he looks so hurt, so lost.

"It'll be okay, Noah," I say. I mean it.

That night, though Mom makes up the guest room with moth-eaten sheets, Noah finds his way to my room and lies in the bed next to me, chastely, with air between us.

"I wish I could tell you how much I've changed," Noah says. His hands are fisted beside his body.

I turn to see his profile and it's so handsome I want to cry. I hope Kumquat inherits the best of both of us. At least he'll know who his father is.

I say to Noah, "You aren't the only one who has changed."

The moon is so bright and big, and Kumquat is between us, and the bed is much too small. But our scents mix and something about it feels like an ending, one so sweet that I cry a little. Maybe Noah knows it, too, though he is slow to see things that are right in front of him. He brushes the tear away.

"Don't worry, Ann," he reassures me. "We'll figure this out."

Kumquat kicks and it's hard enough that I almost see the outline of his foot through my nightgown. Noah puts his hand on my abdomen.

"Baby boy," he murmurs. "How your parents are gonna love you."

I smile as we drift off to sleep, the three of us peaceful and happy, arms wrapped like down jackets around each other. The window is cracked open, and through it, a whoosh of wind soars, hitting me on the side of the face. I almost rise to shut the window, but I'm just so tired and comfortable. Sleep finds me easily.

I don't dream at all, so when I hear a voice, far away but insistent, like the chiming of an alarm, I pay attention.

Run. Ann, run!

The first thing I see when I open my eyes is mighty flames licking around us, prancing like wild hyenas before a hunt.

Chapter 38

Minh

When Phước was young, he was often beaten by other boys. He never ran fast enough, so he would stumble home with bruises and cuts. Once, an ugly scrape running down the side of his shin, though he wouldn't tell me what had happened, only shoved me off when I tried to look. I went to the school to talk to the teachers, but my English wasn't up to the task back then. I rambled angrily until they drew me to the door, vapid smiles on their faces, no closer to assuaging my worries.

"Don't ever do that again," he'd hissed at me when we got home, and I didn't, because I knew I was making things worse for him. But what could I do? Where could we go?

My sweet, tortured son. I wanted to teach him to fight back, but I didn't know how, either. He needed his father. Xuân was gentle, but his protectiveness was fierce. Even the bullies respected him, cowed by his decency. I wished I had some of that bottled up for Phước. My love wasn't enough. So the days went on and Phước withdrew more and more, until he finally left, his pain crackling between us, a live wire set to destroy.

At the Banyan House, when the gash of jagged lightning comes, I feel the house physically heave, as if it's been struck itself. The floorboards tense, their groaning a sound I remember from my past, the turn of a sick man in a bed. The glass strains against the window frames. The house has always known what was coming, long before the humans did. I don't question how I can feel it—after all these years, the house and I finally are one—but there is a phantom pain in my ribs, an odd shattering feeling that makes me want to fold inward. I can only watch.

The storm is sudden, but strong enough for the lightning to find the spark of fire already glowing at the foot of the banyan, its dry core catching faster than I think possible. The fire burns first from inside the tree, as if its branches are an artful birdcage wrapped around the dancing flames. I can almost smell the smoke. A shadow darts from the tree, each panicked footstep a punch to my soul.

I could have loved him better.

The fire creeps along a vine that drips so delicately onto the ground, lights the leaves, travels with an evil mischief, until it gets to the rotting siding of the house, where it skims upward, to my Ann's room, where she sleeps next to Kumquat's father. Suddenly, I'm traveling with the fire, as if it courses between my legs, a steed that races fast into our crumbling castle.

I see the wallpaper falling, I hear the branches crackling. I can't feel the heat, I'm far from some of my senses, but it is so bright, I want to look away from it. Yet ghosts are powerless; we can only watch.

In her sleep, Ann has a small frown on her face, and I bellow her name.

I call it over and over again, shouting against the wind. I can almost reach her, if only I could just tear through this dreadful mist, this veil between us. I pray to the gods. *Let me save them. I will give it up, this corporeal world, and all the last threads tying me here,* I bargain. *My memories for their lives.*

I would die again and again for my girls.

"*Ann, run!*" I scream, one final, desperate command.

Ann shifts in her sleep next to Noah, and then her eyes open. She sees the flames. Her instinct is to reach for her stomach, the sweet precious baby who lives there. She shakes Noah awake, and to his credit, he's quick about it and decisive. He shields them from the flames, my beloved babies, ushers them out the door. Everything had gotten hot, I can see, and Ann's forehead threads with sweat, the way it used to after a long bike ride in the summer, when the hair would stick to her neck, crisscrossing down her back.

Run, I think again.

Hương stands in the hallway in her pajamas, cradling herself. She looks small and lost, and I remember the way she stood on the doorstep to the Banyan House the day she finally decided to leave Vinh. She'd been stubborn, too, under all that sorrow. The will to live coursing strong within her.

I want to scoop her and Ann up with me, take them straight to the moon where the milky glow could cool them, keep them protected. But the flames are loud now, insistent and angry.

Hương shakes herself when she sees Ann and Noah. "The house," she says helplessly.

"Forget about the house. Come with us, Mom," Ann pleads, her voice cracking.

Noah says, "We have to go now."

Hương glances behind her, as if there is something she needs to keep, but there's nothing valuable there. Clothes and knickknacks, old magazines I never threw away. I'm furious at myself for hoarding so many things. The fire eats it all like kindling, hungrily, insatiable. It's made its way to her bedroom and it begins to crawl up her dresser, a quick lizard lashing its tail.

The three of them are moving fast now, skirting the flames that warm the floorboards and fill the house with all the light and brilliance it never had. Ann and Hương grab photos in frames, a book here or there, whatever they can carry in their arms.

I want to tell them to travel light, the way is dark.

The Banyan House feels like a beaten thing, shriveled in on itself. It only takes them minutes to leave the house and my heart along with them, though every once in a while, Hương trips, if not on purpose, then by some instinct to stay. She clings to the banister, then the old sideboard. The house, against all odds, has sunk its grip into her. But Ann's hand on her mother's arm is firm, and in her eyes I see the instincts of a mother, too. To protect, even when it seems impossible.

"Now, Mom," she says, tugging Hương along.

One last backward glimpse and they are gone.

Noah leads them out into the yard, and they back away from the house, watching as flames pour out of the windows. There's loud cracking, the sound of violence. His arms are limp at his sides. Ann is calling the police, the fire department, but it's too late. The house is fire and heat, a burning furnace, flames so eerie-bright and tall, like rushes of neon hair that stand straight up. The oddest part is the windows—lit squares that remind me of recriminating eyes. They burst and glass rains down, a beautiful storm.

I see Banyan House for what it is: a home for women, a shaggy, worn, and vicious protector of the bruised, the tender. We grew up in that house, and in turn, it grew inward on us. It could tolerate no less than our full devotion, even in death. And when we began not to need it, it crumbled. A mirage that could not sustain itself without pain.

"The house. Mẹ is in the Banyan House," Hương cries.

I'm not, con, I want to yell. But I'm weak, untethered again from her world.

She's kneeling on the ground and rocking herself back and forth like a baby. I think of all she's lost, all she continues to long for. I want to float myself next to her, inside her, just so she is one shade less alone. But then Ann is there in my stead, holding her mother's hand, her other hand resting on Kumquat's familiar swell.

"Bà Ngoại isn't there," Ann says. "Listen to me, Mom. We released her. She's nowhere, she's everywhere. But she's not trapped in there."

Hương whispers, "It feels like she's burning, too."

"No, Mom. I promise you. She's free. Like Chú Cuội. I promise."

Noah looks on at them helplessly, clinging to one another, both mesmerized by the growing fire. He seems relieved when they begin to hear sirens. Now he knows what to do, who to talk to. How to resolve this problem. Ann, he cannot resolve, he can't even understand. When she turns and sees him, she gives him a sad smile, laced with gratitude and something else, a quiet finality.

"Don't be afraid. We'll start again," Ann says. I don't know if she's talking to her mother or her former lover. Her words sound like a prophecy, but she's absolutely matter-of-fact when she says it. Her resolution steels her.

Noah opens his mouth to answer, but then the firefighters are there with their long hoses, their shiny yellow hats. Noah screams to them, pointing to the house. He's trying to save what he can, but what we know is that nothing can be fully saved.

The flames become smoke, great gray puffs that rush upward and outward, and Ann's mouth is agape, taking it in. When the water from the hoses touches the fire, there's a gigantic hissing. Like a sigh from the universe. There will be nothing left but scorched earth. The smell will linger for days.

She gathers her mother and they walk away from the house together. The banyan tree continues to glow, even as the stream from the hoses rains down on it, smothering the flames.

The edges of my seeing are growing black. It all feels abrupt and sudden, this departure, the second death. I think of so many things in the span of one second, the last flicker of light. I think of Ann's downy head on my arm, the way her lips curled in her sleep, mouthing undecipherable things. I think of her son with light brown hair and big seeking eyes, years later, running toward his grandmother Hương, his sweet cry of "Bà Ngoại!" beckoning her arms open. I think of my own son, quietly miserable, as unsavable as the rest of us. Wanting me, perhaps, more than I ever understood.

Then, with one final gasp, I see a shadow turn toward me in the distance. Xuân. There's that steady nod of his head, a curl of his fingertips, an invitation for my own hand.

He mouths the words: *Come home, em.*

In his love-lit eyes, there is a question. He's waiting for one last touch, the moment when we can rest together. My hand slides into his, and inexplicably, I can feel the warmth of his grasp. How love, for all its treachery, finds me in the last, unexpected moments of light.

Chapter 39

Ann

The house was decimated. Days later, after the firemen were long gone and the birds settled back in their perches, Mom and I picked through the sooty remains. Noah came with us, but stayed at a distance, giving us space. We spent longer than we should have in that graveyard of a home, but there was nothing to take with us in the end. Even the banyan tree had been felled, crisped up until it was nothing more than a pile of firewood. Greatness reduced to so little. I was sorry to see the tree go, despite how much I hated it toward the end. The swing, too.

As we turned to leave, I saw something gleaming on the ground and picked it up. It looked like a band, silver and fine.

"I think it's part of a watch," Noah said, turning it over and over again. Tracing the faint outlines of an R. "Looks like a Rolex, maybe."

Something caught in my brain, but before I could examine it, Mom took the watch from Noah. She studied it for a few seconds.

Then she said, "It's not a Rolex. It's the gardener's. Some knockoff, probably. Nothing he'll miss."

She slipped the metal band into her pocket and we walked on. The storm had done its work. The burned-up bits of our home looked like they'd come from a nightmare province, gaping holes where ornamentation should be. I picked through it all gingerly, but I felt calm inside. Businesslike. I'd already said my goodbyes the night of the fire.

"So what should we do with this dump?" I asked.

"We could rebuild it," she suggested. The small, cowering woman I saw the night of the fire was gone. There was a quiet peace to her, and I was glad to see it.

"We could sell it," I said.

"Furniture included," Mom quipped.

"As is. No returns."

The stress of it all made us erupt into hysterics, until we were clutching each other, wiping tears of laughter onto the broken earth, Noah looking at us with a mixture of concern and faint contempt. I felt badly for him, in a way, stuck in this warped little fairy tale when all he wanted was the perfect wife, an orderly life. I could see now that we were all too messy for him, but he'd never admit it, so I would have to be the one to leave.

"Poor Noah," I said to him.

"What a waste," he said, almost peevishly.

He kicked at some dirt, and I didn't tell him that none of it had been wasted at all, because I knew he would not see it that way. Mom and I shared a small smile.

Days after, when we were at the rental house provided by the insurance company, we tried to pretend we were a family. He made us scrambled eggs with fruit and toast, and ate Mom's dinners with theatrical gratitude, praising the meals to the skies. The kettle was always filled with water for my afternoon tea. Solicitous Noah, with his easy manner, his full arms. Generous to a fault. Who in their right mind would leave such a man?

But I've never been of sound mind. I come from a tribe of women who are ravaged and joyous, loud, raging, tied to our own convoluted histories. We are a knot of branches, mud-speckled and ever-searching, and the man to make his way inside is someone who must grow from the same earth, the same brokenness. Or maybe, the men who come to us will only ever be visitors. We claim squatters' rights in our tangled histories.

While Mom was out handling insurance interviews, shaking her head no-no-no when they asked about arson and enemies, I sat down next to Noah on the stiff sofa. Nothing like the worn-in furniture in the Banyan House, stained but shaped for human bodies, cradling each curve and groove. Now we'd get new furniture. My heart thrilled at the thought.

"Isn't it time to go home, Noah?" I asked him.

"I could stay. You and Kumquat could be my home."

I traced the curve of his ear, and he leaned into my hand. He closed his eyes, but even when he did, I could imagine their sea-blue depths.

"Your tenure. The book. Us—it'd never work," I told him gently.

I felt it was a line, but he nodded anyway.

"I'll still love you," he said.

I smiled. "I give you permission to keep loving me, but it'll be different, right?"

"You'll always be the mother of my child."

"That's a fact."

"I should probably go soon," he said.

"Of course you should. And I'll stay here. You can visit anytime. We will always welcome you. And Noah. I forgive you, if you forgive me."

"For what?"

"For hiding so much of myself for so long. For considering a future where you might not know our son."

He looked fond as he touched my belly. "Baby Kumquat."

He was gone within the day and no one was particularly surprised, though the rental did seem quiet without him. He promised to come back when the baby was born. We thanked him for being steady, feet-on-the-ground Noah. At the airport, I blew him a kiss through the window of the Oldsmobile, perfectly intact after the storm, watching as he walked away from us.

I told Kumquat, "He'll be back, baby. Not to stay. But he won't forget you."

Mom and I went through the motions of deciding what to do with the Banyan property. It was funny to call it that without a banyan tree. It burned to the ground, defeated after the centuries by a common thunderstorm. Phước and Diane went to the Bahamas for a long vacation after the fire. Mom told me he was looking for real estate in Denver. It was time for a change. Her voice hardened as she spoke.

"Will you miss him?" I asked.

Briefly, she said, "No. The brother I knew is long gone."

"Well, he won't want the Banyan House now, anyway. Would Bà Ngoại be disappointed if we sold the land?" I asked. I almost slipped and said "will," as if she were still here with us.

"She'd never be disappointed in you," Mom said. The bitterness that was usually in her voice when she talked about Bà Ngoại was gone.

So we did sell the land, and it fetched more than we expected from a couple from South Dakota hoping to build a winter house, though neither of us was concerned with haggling at that point. I bought us a lovely new three-bedroom cottage a few blocks from the beach, using some of the profits and the insurance money from the fire. The cottage was clean and quiet, without a speck of grandeur. If anything, it felt so classically Florida, with its leaning palmettos, the teal blue accents, the brick pavers out front. We stocked up on sunscreen and bathing suits. Mom came home with a gaudy, melon-shaped kiddie pool for Kumquat, and I had to smile at the image of her dragging the green-and-pink plastic pool across the lawn, defiance sketched across her face.

"He's gotta learn how to swim," she said.

"He won't even be able to hold his head up."

"Don't you worry about it. I'm looking out for my boy."

We're determined to live out this tropical dream. On weekends when we aren't working, we haul ourselves to the beach with a cooler. We drink grapefruit-scented seltzer and eat bánh mì sandwiches. Sometimes, I even take myself into the water, introducing Kumquat to the warmth of the Gulf, as tender as a mother's caress. Mom swims and swims, her tan arms conquering every wave.

"You learned," I called once, marveling at how purposeful her body had become.

She didn't answer, only kicked her legs, splashing the water up toward the sun.

We don't talk much about the Banyan House after the fire, though sometimes Mom wonders about some object she left behind. I don't remind her that nearly everything is burned, and anything salvaged belongs to the land now, and its new owners. Probably, we'll never quite let go.

Mom and I find new ground with each other, tentative at first, but with increasing familiarity, until we're bickering about where the plates go and what color to paint the nursery. Eventually, she shrugs and says, "Okay, you win. You're the mother." Noah checks in often, sometimes sending extravagant bouquets—not to woo me, but to reassure me. *We're good,* he seems to be saying. *We'll always be good.*

I feel a rush of warmth when I think of him, hardly romantic in nature, but nostalgic all the same, filled with the conviction of his goodness and utter lack of suitability for me. It's the happy ending that's always been meant for us. Later, when his book comes out, the inscription reads: *To Kumquat and his mother. Always.*

Wes comes by the cottage a few times, and he watches me as I sketch, now taken by a new madness. It's as if the fire has burned the walls inside me, too. I draw Chú Cuội's mountains, large and foreboding. Tiger cubs flailing through the air. I draw the lovely Hằng Nga in her sumptuous bed, her mass of hair waved around her pillow. Again and again, I draw the moon.

Late one night, the last words come to me, and I pencil them at the bottom of the sketch. Finally, I bind the pages together at the office supply store in town, smoothing each down. I place the book in Kumquat's room, across the hall from my own. In this cottage, there's just enough space for the three of us, no more and no less.

"You should publish this," Wes says, flipping through the book. "It's goddamn gorgeous."

I smile, and it's a secret one. "Maybe."

After Noah, things are cooler between Wes and me. We don't sleep together, perhaps because I'm huge, and perhaps because the space between us has grown too wide. He still brings food and gifts—seashells he picked up on an evening walk, a wooden truck he thinks Kumquat would like—but he doesn't stay overnight. I watch him go. These days, he takes his motorcycle everywhere, and it suits him, that gunning, the quick wind down the road.

"He can stay, you know," Mom says. Her voice is contrite. "I liked him fine."

"You didn't."

"Maybe not at first," she protests. "But I do now."

"I like him, too," I say.

But I don't go to call him back. I settle down in the rocker we bought for the nursery and I read Kumquat the tale of the man in the moon. The book I wrote. Mom stands leaning against the doorjamb, listening. Once, I would have found it intrusive. Now I like thinking of her there, with us but a little separate. As it always should be with the ones you love.

I say, "And sometimes, during nights with the fullest moon, Chú Cuội comes home again, riding a silver chariot drawn by clouds in the shape of steeds. His wife and children are long gone, but he watches over the generations after them, still clustered at the foot of the great mountain. When they wake, they can sometimes see a shadow passing above, something warm and gracious and full of otherworldly love."

Mom smiles. "That is not how it ends."

I set the book down and rock a bit. "I added a new ending."

"Good. About damn time we all got a new ending."

The day is new when Kumquat presses against me, so hard that my water breaks in a quiet little stream down my legs, onto the tile in the bathroom. Two weeks before his due date.

"Little one," I admonish. "It's too early."

But the boy has it his way, as I suspect he always will in this household of women, Bà Ngoại's rescued portrait on our altar, another pair of eyes to watch him. I put on a comfortable dress that billows out, a muumuu. I'm not going to the hospital to impress anyone. I make one last cup of tea and sip it until Mom sees me, yells at me to grab my shoes.

"We're not going to *brunch*, Ann. Get your ass up."

She drives me to the hospital, white-knuckled the whole way. I laugh at her.

"It's okay," I say. "First births take forever. He'll be here when he's here."

She answers by cursing at a driver who's cut her off. The sun creeps up above the clouds, shining in thick ribbons on the Gulf. Winter is almost here, and there's a bristling stiffness in the air. A held-breath kind of feeling. For a second, the Oldsmobile feels like it's floating on the water, like it could glide right to the horizon.

We call Noah, and his excitement travels down the line, out through the speakerphone for Mom to hear. "I'm coming. Tell Kumquat his dad is on his way."

Even with all the first-class plane tickets money can buy, Noah doesn't quite make it on time. Kumquat is small when he arrives, but his shriek fills the ward. I'm still laughing when they place him in my arms, this baby boy with the screwed-up face, the pounding fists. He's soft and red all over, and nearly weightless.

"Hey, little man. You can stop fighting now. Mama's got you," I say.

"We have to take him to the NICU," a nurse tells me.

I wave her off. I know they must do their job, but my boy is in my arms, and I feel like I've waited lifetimes for this. Soon, he finds my breast and latches on. I pull the blanket over his little shoulders. It shifts when he eats.

"Go on, greedy," I tell him. "You've got a lot of growing to do."

"Will you call him Kumquat forever?" Mom asks.

She's in the corner dabbing her eyes. Her arms reach for Kumquat and though I don't hand him over quite yet, I lean toward her so she can see him. The nurse takes him, finally, and Mom and I are sitting there in the room gazing at each other, two mothers.

"I'll call him Bình," I say.

"Bình," she repeats, a little surprised.

"It means 'peaceful.' Noah's parents will probably call him Ben."

She tests it again on her tongue. "Bình, okay. I like it. That's who he'll be."

In the hospital room, I can almost feel Bà Ngoại with us, her sharp glance and capable hands. She'd be here tucking me into bed, telling my mother to grab something or other. She'd boss us into oblivion and then we'd sleep blissfully, like babies, knowing that everything is under control. But here, in real life, it's just us, as much children as we are mothers.

I turn over to catch a smidge of sleep, waiting for the moment that they bring Bình back to me.

When Noah arrives, he's breathless. I help nestle Bình into his arms.

He gasps. "Oh, you perfect child. I have never seen a prettier baby."

"He looks just like me," I say, winking, and Noah laughs.

"Your mama has gotten funny," he says to Bình. "All this time. She was in her little turtle shell, until you freed her. Look at her now. Warrior woman."

I smile, but what I don't say aloud is that I freed myself. In a few days, Noah has to leave for a conference, but he promises he'll be back soon. He's bought preemie diapers, onesies with woodland animals hopping across soft-as-air cotton, and thick cylinders of formula, though I tell him we don't need it. The house becomes full with all the toys Noah lavishes on Bình.

"I can help out, financially," he says awkwardly. "With a bigger place. You know I have the money. Or Brandon and Alice do."

"No," I say. "We're just fine."

"At least let me start a college fund."

"Just keep visiting him. Be here with him as much as you can. We have time to figure out the rest."

Noah kisses the baby once, twice, on his plump fisted hands, and he's gone, but the sting isn't there, because I feel sure that he will be back again.

After almost a week of milk-feeding, of weight gain and sleepless nights walking up and down the hall to the NICU, we're approved for release, like jailbirds who've proven good behavior. Mom and I breathe a sigh of relief, but then I think of packing Bình up in the car and starting it all up again, and I feel the twinge of nerves. As Mom is zipping the bags, the door opens.

I see the balloons before I see him, a pastel collection of shiny Mylar hearts in every color imaginable. "BABY" one of the balloons spells out, each letter bleeding into the next in puffy marshmallow script.

Wes pokes his head from behind the balloons. His smile is rich and slow, like the drip of honey.

"You've cleaned out the whole gift shop," I say. I inch up on my elbows and give him my best smile.

"You deserve it all," he says, coming to the side of the bed. "More. I'll clean up the whole Gulf Coast of balloons if you want them."

"We don't have room for all Ann's admirers," Mom grumbles.

She leaves, her presence unruffled and so gentle that we barely notice her going. Today Wes is in khakis and a polo with small white buttons. He doesn't look quite like himself, but like the Sunday church version.

"You have a baby. You are a mother," he says.

"Are you always so obvious?" I tease.

When Wes sits next to me and sidles his hand closer to mine, I take it. I'm wearing an old sundress and white sneakers—I forgot the socks—and when I catch a glimpse of my reflection in the window, I think I look young. Like I did in high school, when Wes and I would sneak to the backyard to kiss and dream. I see him fiddling with his keys. He's nervous. Outside, the sky is a pretty cornflower blue, such a safe, dependable shade.

"You look happy," Wes says.

"Thanks. My feet are very swollen," I say, swinging them a little from the bed.

"They are beautiful, like the rest of you. Where's the little man?"

"He's getting checked out one last time. Finally making weight, like a miniature wrestler. You won't believe how cute he is, Wes."

"I would believe it." He smiles. "How are you feeling about everything now? Selling the house? Starting over?"

"We're feeling okay. The house was a nuisance," I say, though I don't fully believe it. "Without Bà Ngoại, it became a crumbling old thing, not worth anyone's time."

"Still, we had good memories there."

"The best."

The nurse comes back with Bình in a blue-and-white swaddle. He looks like one of those hors d'oeuvres, a pig in a blanket, with his head poking out, tufts of black hair fuzzy and stick-straight in the air. His skin is pale, closer to Noah's complexion than mine. He squawks and Wes laughs, such a deep rich sound of joy, a cello on a spotlighted stage.

I say, "This is Bình, my son."

"Perfect, like I expected him to be. Hi, little mannie."

Bình fits beautifully in Wes's arms. They are both sizing each other up. Wes reaches over with one finger and Bình punches at it, all bravado and puffing.

Wes sighs deeply. "Annie, I have something to say, but I really don't want to say it."

I take the baby back and jounce him in my arms, listening.

Wes continues, "I think I need to go to California for a while. Fiona decided, well, I helped her come to the conclusion, that Elijah needs his dad. Maybe it's watching you become a mom through these months. It's primal, that bond. And I ignored it for too long, because of pride, maybe, or feeling like I'd do more harm than good. But that's bullshit. I want to know my son. And I just don't know how long it'll take, so I mean—geez."

"So you're saying goodbye," I say.

He bites his lip. "Not forever?"

I like thinking of him in California. Now, tucked in the gauze of newborn love, I can't imagine a life without it. I want him and Elijah to reclaim that for themselves.

I say, "It's okay, Wes. I always said you were a good father, and I don't know much about fathers, but I know what it means to love someone. Your ions are full of love."

He goes to me, and he's cupping my face. He looks like he wants to thank me or kiss me, or both, and there's that familiar melting in me at the sight of his sad eyes, but it's more distant now, like a dream half remembered. Then Bình shifts and lets out a sound of protest, not a cry, but something closer to a burp, earthy and unromantic.

We are laughing in relief as we pull apart.

"Well, that's that," I say.

"I'll walk you out at least," Wes offers.

Mom comes back in the room. She takes one look at us and the side of her mouth quirks like she's going to say something, but instead, she quietly stuffs some hospital diapers into the bag.

Wes helps buckle Bình into his car seat and I sit next to my baby in the back. Mom gives me a raise of the eyebrows, and when I nod, she pulls away from the hospital. On the sidewalk near our car, Wes lifts his hand, his grin so wide that the dimples come out.

"See you later, Annie," he says.

I want to tell him to take his time. It's the one thing we can't replenish.

Mom drives us home, weaving painfully through traffic. Bình falls asleep on the way and I watch him with satisfaction, the way his breath moves in his chest, how his mouth compresses in his sleep, as if he has something he needs to say, but just can't get out. Like he's chewing on a question of his own.

Ten minutes from our cottage, while stopped on the bridge home, I see the beach out the window. The sun glances brightly off the white sand. I put my hand up to my forehead like a visor. The water is bluer than the sky, overshadowing the heavens with its deep vibrance, its sparkling surface. Bình twists in his sleep.

"Mom, pull over. Stop by the beach."

She parks near some charcoal grills heaped with burnt-out black coals. Someone's green plastic pail lies upended in the shade of the trees, spilling out a host of shells: striped yellow cockles, mud snails that remind me of a complicated Regency hairdo, the round and indecent curve of a broken nautilus. I take my son in my arms and walk to the sand, carefully picking my way past the burls. Mom walks behind me. We breathe in the salt and the lightly floral scent of the ocean, mixed with a sweet powdery smell coming from Bình, who remains sleeping, trusting.

I go to the shore, where the cool water meets the warm sand. Above us, the cumulonimbus clouds look almost volcanic, rising in pyramids, squat at the bottom near the horizon and pointed where they touch the heavens. Lit from within by the radiance of the day.

"Look at that," I say to Mom, pointing.

In the sky, there's the faint sphere of the moon, like a scar that hasn't fully healed. Shadows stain the surface, blue gray, gathering into a familiar shape.

"Mặt trăng," she says, wondering.

"Isn't it amazing," I whisper to Bình. "Even in full daylight, Chú Cuội is up there."

He smacks his lips in his sleep.

But then I think, the shadow on the moon doesn't look like a man at all. With the whorls of blue, I see a woman in profile, her hair spilling over her shoulders. Eyes downcast, looking always toward the earth. Looking like she's praying.

I wet my fingertips with salt water and spread it on the baby's lips. Bình opens his mouth, then makes a sound of protest, eyes glued shut. His first taste of the ocean. The first of so many.

"Let's go, con," says Mom, glancing at the baby with the anxiety of a new parent herself, as if he'll melt in the sun.

The three of us make our way back across the sand.

I hum to Bình the rest of the way home. His mouth moves in questing circles, as if trying to locate the source of the salt on his lips, or perhaps trying to find me in his hunger. He makes sounds that remind me of small animals, rustling in their nests. When his eyes open finally, in the carport of the cottage, I see in them the depths of my own longing, realized. I see myself and my mother, as well as his own namesake. Bà Ngoại, too, grooved in every step we'll continue to take, even the ones that lead us away from her.

"Coming?" Mom asks, next to the door of the cottage, keys jangling in her hand.

In our new home, there is no banyan tree, no spacious rooms that wind up three stories, no objects crowding every space or locked trunks with hidden keys. It's going to be a smaller kind of life. I take one final look upward through the car window, toward the cold blue of the sky, with its bobbing ball of a moon. I tap the moon's outline on the glass, like Morse code, like a promise between me and Bà Ngoại, me and Chú Cuội, and all those tired old secrets we have managed to contain.

To my mother, I say, "We're right behind you."

Acknowledgments

A debut novel feels like a really long first date: You're swept up in all the excitement and anxiety, hoping against hope that you don't blow your shot at a forever-story. Luckily for me, I had my unparalleled agent, Abby Walters at CAA, who was the very best guide I could have hoped for. Thank you, Abby, for that life-changing email. I'll always think of Stauf's in Grandview with such joy. And thank you for every day thereafter, acting as the book's champion—and my own personal writing fairy godmother. Additional heartfelt gratitude to Jiah Shin and the rest of the team at CAA, who look out for me in so many ways.

Thank you to Molly Gendell, my editor, for falling in love with the Tran women as much as I did. For asking the right questions and pushing me to see their stories more clearly. I knew from the first time we spoke that your vision would transform the book—and it has! I'm more passionate about the story than ever, thanks to your thoughtful and generous eye. And a huge thank-you to the Mariner team, especially Eliza Rosenberry, Rachel Berquist, Stephanie Vallejo, Renata DiBiase, Ploy Siripant, and Ivy McFadden.

Thank you to my dear friends. To Jo Anna Gaona Albiar, whose texts about everything from our daughters to the joys of Olive Garden make me feel seen. To Rebecca Fox-Gieg and Ronni Glaser, both of whom shower our family with bountiful love and books. To Ojus Patel, my life partner in writing and motherhood. To Lizzie Duszynski for the faultless reading recommendations and Animal Crossing updates. To the sweet Davises, the best neighbors in the world. To Kathleen Blackburn, Michael Palmer, and Julian Palmer, for keeping us in your hearts.

I'm grateful to all the editors who continue help fulfill an impossible dream for me—making a living from my writing. To Joanna Goddard, Katy Elliott, Faith Durand, and most especially, Leslie Stephens, who was the first to let me write in the way that felt truest to me. Thank you for all those book-related nudges, Leslie, including the copy of *Before and After the Book Deal*. Thank you to the wonderful readers who wrote in, sharing your own stories in response to mine, and urging me to write a book. This is for you!

I wrote this novel as a nomad wandering around Ohio and I'm grateful to all the libraries who hosted me. (Libraries are magic!) I will always be an unabashed teacher's pet. Thank you to Mrs. Callahan for letting a lonely second grader eat lunch in your classroom, to Mr. and Mrs. Crump for never making me feel like my dreams were too big. To Dan Raeburn for leading my very favorite workshop in the world and Lee Martin for your gentle guidance. I've learned so much from you all. I remain incredibly grateful to all the supportive colleagues and teachers in my MA and MFA programs.

Thank you to my family, whose sacrifices are never taken for granted. My bà ngoại and ông ngoại who raised me as their own and never held back a bit of love. My ma tư, my second mother, and my other aunts and uncles who helped give me a childhood full of memories. My stepfather, Greg Crawford, for dropping me off at school in the mornings and taking me fishing. And the whole extended family and my in-laws for the support and well-wishes. Most especially, thanks to my mother, Hanh Nguyen-Crawford, for bravely giving me new life in a new land. I would not be anywhere I am without you.

Lastly and most of all: Thank you to my daughter and my husband, who continue to be my loudest cheerleaders and truest soulmates. Dan McGuckin, you are the best father and husband, my shining example for equal partnership. Your generosity and unfailing belief in me stuns me every day. And to my girl, Ellie; I owe you the whole world. You have been my light from the moment you opened your eyes. It's such an honor and delight to be your mama.